"I know" he said. A prick of howling sorrow touched him. "God, Elena, I wasn't criticizing. I read about the accident when I called up your name on Google."

An icy mask stiffened her pale face. Violet shadows showed beneath her eyes. "I don't want to talk about that."

"I'm not asking you to." He skimmed a spray of bread crumbs from the bare wood of the table. "My mother died violently. I think I know a little about prurient interest."

She gazed at him impassively, mask still glittering and cold. "I'm sorry," she said without emotion.

Around her there was a disturbance, a bending of the air like the fine bands of heat waves that rise from a fire. For a moment, Julian thought it seemed there was fire flickering out from her very skin, like in the pictures of saints, but there was no mistaking the cold on her face.

Abruptly she leaned forward, pushing her plate away so she could put her forearms over the table. Her eyes, fierce and sapphire, burned in her face. "Do you know how many times men have wanted to sleep with me because I survived such a gruesome accident?"

"Elena—"

"Do you know how often some reporter has come in to do a story on a restaurant and heard the rumors of my past and tried to get it out of me? I'm like a priest who gave up the calling—everyone wants to know the story." Her eyes narrowed. "I will not give you a story, Mr. Director."

The Lost Recipe for Happiness

BARBARA O'NEAL

A Bantam Discovery

THE LOST RECIPE FOR HAPPINESS
A Bantam Discovery Book / January 2009

Published by Bantam Dell
A Division of Random House, Inc.
New York, New York

Book design by Helene Berinsky

Library of Congress Cataloging-in-Publication data

O'Neal, Barbara, 1959–
The lost recipe for happiness / Barbara O'Neal.
p. cm.
ISBN 978-0-553-38551-9 (trade pbk.)—ISBN 978-0-553-59168-2 (mass market)
1. Women cooks—Fiction. I. Title.
PS3573.I485L67 2009
813'.54—dc22
2008026619

Printed in the United States of America
Published simultaneously in Canada

www.bantamdell.com

BVG 10 9 8 7

For Christopher Robin (aka Neal Barlow), with love.

You know why.

ACKNOWLEDGMENTS

Gigantic thanks to my wise and wonderful agent, Meg Ruley, and the whole gang at Rotrosen—Andrea, Annalise, Christina, and Kelly—for multiple readings and suggestions and meetings. I am *eternally* in your debt. Thanks to my editor, Shauna Summers, for knowing how to nudge me into my best work, and to Christie for endless, endless conversations about the book (and other things). Thanks to Camron Welch, executive chef at Sonterra Grill, who helped illuminate the battlefield of restaurant kitchens and the daily life of a chef; to all my compatriots in the restaurant life at Michelle's and Papa Felipe's; Cocos and the Blue Fish Cove, and all the others along the way.

PROLOGUE

Along Elena's smooth white back is an ancient scar that cuts downward in grotesque beauty like a long, graceful snake. It begins at the joint of her right shoulder and sails south across her shoulder blade, then her spine, swoops around the lower edge of her left ribs and across the unguarded softness where vital organs once lived, and finally ends deep in her left buttock. In places, it looks like a rope, dark pink and angry; in others, it submerges beneath the flesh, showing only a slight white scratch above the skin.

Men love it, thinking themselves so original, so generous in their tracings of it, so accepting. In fact, it is the lover's version of slowing to look at an accident on the freeway, equal parts horror, fascination, and, if there is any wisdom, gratitude. Some ask her what happened. Some do not. All of them wonder.

But only Elena's ghosts know her story. The ghosts who travel with her. The ghosts she protects. The ghosts who will never leave her.

Summer

Red onions are especially divine. I hold a slice up to the sunlight pouring in through the kitchen window, and it glows like a fine piece of antique glass. Cool watery-white with layers delicately edged with imperial purple . . . strong, humble, peaceful . . . with that fiery nub of spring green in the center . . ."

—MARY HAYES GRIECO, from *The Kitchen Mystic*

ONE

Elena had been expecting Dmitri for more than an hour when he finally stormed through the back door of the Blue Turtle, the Vancouver restaurant where they both worked.

She'd come in early, as was her habit, to cook in the agreeable quiet of the Sunday morning kitchen, when the young apprentices and line cooks and dishwashers were all still abed after their Saturday night revelries. Her only companion was Luis, the forty-something El Salvadorian *commis,* who stirred his stockpots with a hand so brown and squat it looked like a hand balloon. He sang cheerfully under his breath, a bloody old Spanish folk song about a conquistador taking revenge on his enemy. It made Elena think of nights at the VFW when she was eleven or twelve, drinking Cokes while everyone danced the two-step. No doubt it made Luis think of bodegas back home.

Humming tunelessly along with him, Elena stood at the stove, stirring pale pink shallots and yellow onions with a long wooden spoon, thinking of the things she needed to check for service today. She thought of conquistadores and the plate armor they'd worn to protect themselves from arrows.

Mainly, she thought of Dmitri, who had betrayed her.

Her whole body ached this morning, back and hips from the old injuries, shoulders and neck from trying to erect the armor she had to assemble afresh each and every day, finely honed plates of sharp arrogance and bad language beneath which she—the secret and guarded Elena— could hide. She rolled her shoulder blades down her back, reminded herself to stand tall.

Shake it off.

When the onions were nearly done, she crushed garlic with the flat of her knife, and was about to scrape it into the mix when Dmitri burst through the back door. Hearing his fury in the slam of the door, she pulled the pan off the fire and turned to meet his anger.

Long and lean, with severe planes in his beautiful Russian face, he strode through the kitchen and flung a newspaper down on the counter. She turned off the burner and wiped her hands.

The paper was turned to the front page of the Lifestyle section, and featured a photo taken two weeks before. Of Elena, dressed in chef's whites at the end of a shift, long blonde hair pulled back from her face beneath the bright scarves she had adopted as her trademark. She lifted a glass of wine to the camera with a crooked smile and a saucy cock of a brow. It was a good photo, she thought again. It made her look younger than her thirty-eight years, sexier, charming. The headline read:

STANDING UP TO THE HEAT
BLUE TURTLE CHEF SAYS LIFE AS A FEMALE IN THE KITCHEN IS NOT EASY, BUT WORTH IT

"I saw it," she said mildly.

"You are fired."

"What?" Her head jerked up. "Come on, Dmitri. It's not my fault she liked me better than you. And you're right there in the first paragraph anyway!"

"It is my kitchen. Your focus should have been on the restaurant, on the menu. Not on yourself."

"It is not *your* kitchen!" she said, slamming her knife down on the counter. "You have the *title* of chef, but you know as well as I do that we built this menu and this kitchen together. It's as much mine as it is yours."

"Is it?" He raised his index finger. "One question, hmm?" When he got angry or excited or passionate, his speech slipped into the Russian accent he'd labored over many years to lose. "Whose name is on that door?"

She wiped her hands, heat in her throat. "Yours."

He grabbed the paper, slapped it with the fingers of his other hand. It sounded like a gunshot. "And where is the *chef* of the Blue Turtle in the article?" His eyes, the color of cognac, burned with a yellow heat. "Hmm?"

"Isn't it supposed to be about the restaurant?"

He gave her a withering look. The *restaurant* did not belong to him. The kitchen did.

"You told me to talk to her." Elena shrugged. "I talked."

A long, simmering silence hung between them, filled with the scent of onions and bruised garlic and the New

Mexican chiles she'd asked to have imported. Feigning disdain for his tantrum, she turned the burner back on, pulled the pan back to the fire, and scraped the garlic into it. The back of her neck burned with satisfaction, with worry and loss, with desire. She could smell him over the food, a heady mix of sweat and spices, cigarettes and sex, which he'd not had with her. Beneath her armor, her flesh wept.

"It was revenge, Elena."

Methodically, she swirled the garlic into the butter, and put the spoon down. Met his eyes.

The minute the reporter had come through the doors with her old-school feminist hair—steely, frizzled salt and pepper—Elena had known she had a chance to get back at Dmitri.

And more, she'd earned it. Not only had he seized the glory from their joint effort to create the menu and the environment of the Blue Turtle, but two months ago, he'd moved out of their shared apartment to live with a girl with breasts like fried eggs and the guileless hero worship only a twenty-three-year-old CIA graduate could afford.

That would be the Culinary Institute of America, not the Central Intelligence Agency.

The garlic could not be neglected. Elena stirred in fire-roasted Anaheim chiles, letting them warm slowly. The scent had zest, dampness, appetite to it. Even Dmitri could not resist bending toward it, inhaling it. She looked at the top of his head, the thick hair.

Looked away.

The interview might have started as revenge, but it had become something more as Elena let herself open up to the reporter, her sharp eyes, her sympathy. "She was a feminist,

Dmitri," she said in the calm voice she had cultivated, "a woman who wanted to do a story about a woman in a man's world." She adjusted the flame the tiniest bit. "I gave it to her. And it worked—the restaurant is on the front page of the Lifestyle section."

"You're fired," he said, punching the air with a finger.

She rolled her eyes. "Don't be ridiculous."

"Oh, I assure you, I am not. When I come back here in an hour, I want you gone, not a trace."

"Dmitri!"

He turned, crisp as a Cossack, and marched out of the kitchen.

Automatically, Elena pulled the skillet from the burner and stared after him, pursing her lips. He'd fired her in the past, when they'd had one of their spectacular fights, only to call an hour or a day later to beg forgiveness. He needed her, Elena knew. More than he had sense to realize.

And he would likely calm down this time, too. Call later and beg her to come back.

Luis, who had pretended not to watch the scene unfolding, tsked.

Elena, embarrassed, shook her head. "He'll get over it."

"*Sí.*"

But there was, suddenly, weariness in her. Too many fights, too many late nights spent trying to fix whatever it was that had gone wrong. She felt the exhaustion at the base of her neck, along the backs of her eyes. She lacked the energy to go another round with him. As much as she hated to start over—again!—this was broken. It was time to admit it.

She should never have begun. From the moment of

their first meeting, she'd known that he was dangerous to her, a woman in a man's world. For well over a year, she had resisted him, sticking to her unbroken rule to never sleep with a man who had power over her, and Dmitri was even more dangerous than most, a chef with a Russian accent and the mouth of a rock star, a man with that intelligent, amoral twinkle in his eye.

But he pursued her, relentlessly, and Elena had fallen. Fallen to his genius as much as his beauty, fallen to his supposedly undying adoration of her, the mark of a man who lived on his charm.

Now she would pay the price. This silent Sunday morning, she folded her apron and put it on the pass-out bar, then went to the staff room, changed from her chef's whites and clogs into jeans and a long-sleeved shirt tie-dyed in soft pink and orange, with tiny dancing skeletons on it. A gift from one of her sisters last Christmas, to remind her of home. Packed everything from her locker into the duffel she carried to and fro, and finally went out to the dining room for one last look.

The Blue Turtle had been her home for three years, the menu a loving union of Dmitri's old-school French methods and Elena's Santa Fe roots. Vancouverites, adventurous eaters that they were, adored the exotic fusion. The restaurant was a success in a very crowded market, and was attracting international press attention.

This was her home, not some faraway town. A blister of fury zapped from the base of her spine through the top of her head. *Bastard.* How *dare* he banish her like this?

Luis raised his chin. "*Vaya con Dios.*"

Elena nodded. Hiking the duffel over her shoulder, she swallowed the hollow sense of loss and headed out to the softness of an early Vancouver morning. For a long moment, she stood there on the sidewalk with a hole in her chest, trying to think what to do.

How depressing to lose yet another home. Another and another and another. She had grown fond of this one, had thought perhaps it might be the *one* place. Her place.

Now what?

Across the street, English Bay lay like a mirror in the fresh opalescence of morning. A storm gathered in the distant west, sending a gust of rain-scented wind over her face. She shook loose the hair on her shoulders, and tried to bring her mind to something practical. What could she have for breakfast? There was some fresh spinach, perhaps a hunk of cheese, some pear salad left from the night before.

A man suddenly stepped out of the doorway, and, startled, Elena took a step backward to let him pass. There was an air of confidence about him, something both severe and sensual. Very dark glasses hid his eyes. A thin, hip goatee circled his mouth. She admired the spotlessness of his black jacket, the jeans he wore casually beneath it. Strong thighs, she noticed, relieved to discover Dmitri had not entirely killed her pleasure in the opposite sex.

The man gave her a nod. "Good morning."

She inclined her head. A silk scarf, ribboned with faint orange and pink stripes, looped around his neck. Elegant. Smart. Maybe he was French. *"Bonjour,"* she said with a faint smile.

To her surprise, he paused. "Are you Elena Alvarez?"

"Who wants to know?"

"Sorry," he said, tugging off his hat and sunglasses in a single fluid gesture. He had the uncanny grace and coloring of something supernatural—a vampire, perhaps. Tumbles of black hair fell down on a pale, finely boned face. "I'm Julian Liswood."

"Ah." The owner of the restaurant. He carried a newspaper under his arm—he must have seen the article. Elena brushed her hands together—finished. "Dmitri already fired me, so don't bother."

His lips, the only pool of color in his face, quirked. "On the contrary. I came to Vancouver to speak with you. The commis in there told me you had just left. Do you have a few minutes?"

"Sure."

He studied her face. "You're quite blonde," he commented. "For someone named Alvarez."

"Does that figure into the discussion?"

A flash of a smile crossed his mouth. "No."

Elena waited. He wasn't what she'd always imagined, either. The face was not beautiful—that high-bridged nose and sharp cheekbones—but the hair was good. His eyes were steady and very dark and intelligent. It was hard to tell how old he was, but she knew he'd made his first movie when she was in high school. A decade older than she? He didn't look it. Behind them a wind swept closer, bringing with it the sound of rain.

"Will you let me buy you breakfast?" he asked. "We'll talk."

"I'm a chef, as it happens, and my apartment is not far

away." She hoped he would offer her a job. "Why don't I cook instead?"

"Sadly, I do not have enough time. I have to fly to LA this morning to pick up my daughter."

"Then by all means, let's go to the Sylvia." It was an agreeable and famous old hotel.

They walked there beneath a sky that grew darker by the moment, heavy with rain. He moved with such effortless, long strides that Elena looked at his feet to see if he was actually touching the sidewalk. She felt a little dizzy, overwhelmed, and tried to think of something to say. "Don't you have a movie out right now?"

"It's just gone to DVD." He looked sideways at her. "Are you a horror fan?"

"Not really. I like ghost stories, but the slasher flicks are too violent for me, honestly."

"I prefer ghost stories," he said, pulling open the door.

She looked at him. "Why don't you make more of them, then?"

"The others are in fashion." He tucked his hat in his pocket. "They finance my smaller projects."

A man in a white shirt and white tie came hustling forward and seated them at a table by the windows. Elena ordered tea and milk; Mr. Liswood, coffee. In the corner, she saw a cluster of uniformed staff whispering, looking their way. She nodded toward them. "You've caused a stir."

He skimmed the jacket from his shoulders. "I don't think it's me."

A woman held up the newspaper and pointed to the picture. She waved, smiling. "Oh," Elena said, pleased. She waved back.

"Your first taste of fame?"

She thought of long ago, the New Mexico newspapers. But that had been more notoriety than fame, so dark and heavy she'd had to flee to escape it. "In a way," she said, then shifted her attention back to him. "But you're no stranger to it, are you?"

"I am not usually recognized for myself," he said, "but for the wives I have unwisely collected."

His rueful straightforwardness disarmed her, and Elena laughed, the sound shaking loose from some rusty place in her chest. His wives were tabloid fodder, starlets who began their careers in the teen slasher flicks that had made him his fortune. Restaurants were a sideline. Celebrity owners were not always the most adept, but Julian Liswood had earned the respect of the press and—harder to capture—his workforce. The Blue Turtle was the third he'd opened to spectacular success.

Elena said, "They have been rather beautiful wives, as I recall."

"Well, you know what they say: never marry a girl prettier than you."

She thought, with a pang, of Dmitri. "Been there."

"Hard to imagine."

"Oh, believe me—" She almost said, *there have been so many men,* but that would have been too frank. Outside, rain began to splat against the window. She shivered slightly. Pulling her cup toward her, she said, "Now, tell me, Mr. Liswood, what do you have in mind?"

"Please call me Julian."

"I'll try. Julian."

He took his time, stirring a lump of rough brown sugar

into his coffee with a tiny spoon. His oval nails were mani-
cured, and she wondered what kind of man had time for
something like that. But of course, in his world, the veneer
of such details would be required. She envisioned a cocktail
party sparkling with beautiful people, manned by obse-
quious servers. It made her nervous.

Finally, he put down the spoon and tapped the newspaper on the table beside him. "You have strong views of the
restaurant business."

"Are you waiting for me to apologize for it?" she asked.
"I've been in kitchens for nearly twenty years. I'm tired of
holding my tongue."

Amusement flickered over his mouth. "Not at all. I'm
intrigued."

She took a breath. "Sorry. I might be a little testy just
this minute. It's never fun to be fired."

"No." He leaned back as the server, a young woman in a
tan oxford shirt and black pants, approached. She was dewy
and lean, with a smile that could bring in a lot in tips. She
was also slightly messy and Elena wanted to brush her off,
tell her to tuck her shirt in and iron her blouse next time.

Instead, she listened as the girl explained the buffet, and
exchanged a slight smile with Julian. No one in the restaurant business ate at a buffet if it could be avoided. "I'd like
the asparagus omelet," Elena said. "Fruit instead of potatoes, please, and a glass of grapefruit juice."

"I'll have the mushroom omelet," he said, handing her
the menu. "Potatoes with mine, and a glass of milk instead
of grapefruit juice."

As she departed, Julian said, "You may know that the
Blue Turtle is not my only restaurant."

"Of course." There were three in a line down the west coast. Vancouver, San Francisco, and San Diego. "I worked as a line cook, then was promoted to sous chef at the Yellow Dolphin."

"Yes. I know."

There was a soft fall, a short pause. "Expensive hobby, restaurants," Elena said into it.

"It's more than a hobby, actually." The words were mild, but Elena reminded herself that he was a man with considerable power and influence. Who was probably going to offer her a job if she could keep the chip off her shoulder. Or at least hidden.

"Sorry. That was rude."

One side of his mouth lifted in a half-smile. "Don't apologize. It's true that I don't have the background you do, but I didn't choose restaurants by accident. I love the business—bringing together a chef and a location and a direction and a staff and seeing what happens."

"You've been very successful."

"By trial and error. The Purple Tuna—are you familiar with it? In San Diego?"

"Somewhat."

"It failed twice." He grinned. "Luckily, enough cash will hide a multitude of sins."

Elena was surprised into a laugh. "Is it successful now?"

"Yes. I kept changing the dynamic until it worked."

"Which dynamics?"

"Staff. Menu." He met her eyes. "Chef. The location is brilliant, and the building is beautiful. It took three years to get the rest of it right."

Letting go of a long whistle, she said, "That's a long time to keep a restaurant afloat. Why bother?"

"It's a puzzle. I don't like to give up until it fits together."

She thought of the many, many elements that went into the success of a restaurant—menu, food, ordering, cash flow, décor and presentation, and most important, staff, front and back, all those personalities, often very high strung. "Very complicated puzzle."

"Exactly."

Leaning forward, he shook his hair off his brow and said, "Tell me, Elena, what are your five favorite foods?"

She tamped down a sense of anxiety. Was this a test? "Hmm. Favorite everyday dishes? Or favorite restaurant dishes? Or what?"

"Five best things you've ever eaten, anywhere."

She considered. In the service area, someone loaded hot glasses into a rack. Outside, a breeze coaxed ripples into the satiny surface of the ripening bay. She narrowed her eyes and chose honesty. "My grandmother's homemade tamales, fresh out of the steamer. A cup of hot chocolate I drank in a restaurant by the Louvre in Paris. A plate of blue-corn cheese enchiladas with green chile in Santa Fe." That was three. She paused, letting others bubble up. "A bowl of buttered squashes at a museum restaurant. And—" she sucked in a breath and snatched one of the hundreds swirling up, "a roasted garlic soup, in New Orleans." She brought her focus back to Julian's face. "I've been trying for years to reproduce that soup and still don't know why it was so spectacular."

He nodded.

She sipped her tea. "Now you."

"Of course." His eyes, she noticed, were not just brown, they were blackest black. It made him seem wise. "A plate of roasted lamb in New Zealand, made by a housewife who put us up when our car broke down."

"Oh, I forgot lamb! I love lamb."

"That was one. Two was a strudel our next-door neighbor used to make, back when I was a kid." He held up a third finger. "A bowl of green chile in a greasy spoon in New Mexico. Espanola, as it happens."

She raised her eyebrows—she'd mentioned Espanola in the article. "My uncle probably made it."

Julian chuckled. "A steak pie in Aspen, and"—he gestured toward her—"a zucchini blossom with blue cornbread and piñon stuffing."

She pressed her hands into *namaste* position. "Thank you, kind sir."

"The last three are why we're here."

A ripple of nerves shot through her gut. "Okay."

"The steak pie was in a failing restaurant. The chef is a drunk, the owner was a ski bum who had no business sense, and the building is challenged, though in a very good location."

Elena hazarded a guess. "And you bought it."

He smiled. "Yes."

The food came, steaming hot, served on heavy white porcelain plates the server set down with no attention whatsoever to presentation. The parsley on Elena's was at the top—as it should have been—Julian's at the bottom. She couldn't be silent. It would have been like letting someone leave the restroom with toilet paper stuck to her shoe. "Miss?"

The girl turned. "Did I forget something?"

"No, it looks beautiful—but can I ask you a question?"

"Yeah, I guess."

"Are you new to this job?"

"Yeah. Only three weeks." She winced. "Does it show? They're pretty shorthanded and I didn't get trained that good."

Elena gently touched the girl's wrist. In her smoothest, least threatening voice, she said, "The food here is beautiful. The setting is spectacular. You can make a lot of money if you pay attention to little details."

She blinked, fearful as a rabbit. "Yeah? Like what?"

"Tuck your shirt in better. Stand up straight. Serve the food as if the diner is in for a giant treat."

She bit her lip, confused. "Okay."

"Parsley at the top, right?"

"Oh!" She smiled. "Right. I forgot. Anything else?"

"Grapefruit juice and milk."

"Be right back."

Julian picked up his fork. "You say exactly what's on your mind, don't you?"

"Did I embarrass you?"

"Not at all. It was compassionate."

"Good." She picked up her fork, admired the omelet, and took a bite. "Mmm. Very nice. You were saying?"

He took a moment to turn his plate slightly, chose a spot, cut a small triangle and sampled it, then a cube of potato, then another small bite of omelet. Paying attention. "I was about to say, those three things came together. The Aspen restaurant. The bowl of green chile in Espanola, and your zucchini blossom appetizer."

"And?"

He lifted a brow. "I would like you to come to Aspen and be my executive chef."

TWO

STANDING UP TO THE HEAT

*Blue Turtle Chef Says Life as a Female in the Kitchen
Is Not Easy, but Worth It*

BY JACQUELINE GREER

Wade into the kitchen at local favorite the Blue Turtle, overlooking English Bay, and the air is as laden with testosterone as it is spices.

Men—of all ages and races and nationalities—fill the narrow aisles between stoves and ovens. There are boys who've yet to grow a beard cutting chickens and peeling onions on the prep line; a sturdy man of sixty with a potbelly and the uneven gait of bad feet who shouts out orders in Spanish. The executive chef himself, Dmitri Nadirov, is a smolderingly handsome Russian of the Mick Jagger school of beauty. Men everywhere.

And then there is sous chef Elena Alvarez, a study in contrasts. A woman in a man's world. A blue-eyed blonde who shouts orders to the saucier in an archaic Spanish, her slight frame and faint limp belying the power in her arms that can haul heavy iron skillets. She orders the line cooks to get more potatoes under way, answers a question from a waiter, fields a challenge from another line cook, all the while shaking a pan filled with aromatic meat and thoughtfully answering this reporter's questions.

Alvarez is cagey about her background, though she admits to growing up in El Paso and Espanola, which is not far from Santa Fe, where she began to cook after a car accident that broke her back when she was seventeen. Also not a subject she wished to discuss.

Trained in the emerging Santa Fe style as a young woman, Alvarez was chosen from a field of thousands to study in Paris under star chef Alexander Moreau. She spent four years in Europe, three in Paris and one in London, before coming back to the U.S. to work in top-end kitchens in New York City and San Francisco. . . .

THREE

Despite her hope that Julian was going to offer her a job, Elena felt a splash of surprise. "Executive."

"Yes." He ate. Waited patiently. Took a sip of coffee.

"I'd kill to have my own kitchen. Of course." It was Elena's turn to measure him. "What are you looking for?"

"I want you to create a menu, get the restaurant moving, see if you can turn it around."

"How long would I have?"

"One year."

"Fair enough." She cut a bite of egg. "What kind of menu?"

"Elena's menu. It's Aspen. It's a moneyed crowd. They're choosy but willing to be adventurous. Use all that moxie and give me a menu that's western or southwestern, but also definitely upscale and gourmet."

"What, like the Coyote Cafe?"

"Your call." He lifted his coffee cup. "I am more fond of Cafe Pasqual's, though it's not as high end. Both are very good."

"I haven't been to Cafe Pasqual's." She rarely visited New Mexico. It seemed shameful suddenly. She tried to take a bite of omelet, but it sat on her fork, taunting her. "And if it doesn't work in a year?"

He shrugged. "I'll let you go, and try something else."

Airlessness moved through her lungs. He said it so easily, the challenge, the promise and consequences. For him, it was a business gamble. For Elena, it was her career. Her life.

And yet, hadn't she been working toward this for nearly two decades? "When would you need me?"

A slight lift of one shoulder. "As soon as possible. I'm moving my daughter to Aspen to get her out of LA for a while, and we're planning to be there by August 1. I'd like to get started shortly after that, get the new menu in place and work out the bugs before the ski slopes open."

"Is there a firm date for the slopes, or does it depend on snow?"

"It's December 9 in Aspen. So"—he narrowed his eyes, gazed in the distance—"we'll aim for a soft opening by late October, early November, aim for a grand opening mid-December."

Dismayed, she said, "So, you'll be on-site?"

"Yes. Does that bother you?"

Yes, she wanted to say. His presence would be distracting, in so many ways. That urbane intelligence. The still gaze. Those sensual curls. Aloud, she said, "Not if you don't get in my way. If you tell me it's my kitchen, I'll take that pretty literally."

"Understood." He'd neatly finished his breakfast while they spoke, invisibly eating while Elena thought and talked.

The server whisked away his empty plate. Elena noticed the girl had tucked in her blouse. She smiled. The girl smiled back.

Julian said, "There are a couple of conditions."

"I'm listening."

"I get final approval of the menu, and I want to hire someone to professionally write the descriptions."

"No problem."

"You'll have control of the kitchen staff, naturally, but the current manager stays, and—uh—I'm pretty sure we need to keep the chef."

"The drunk?"

"Yeah."

"Interesting choice," she said, inclining her head. "Why do you want to keep him?"

"The steak pie. The fact that the place has made some money in spite of the fact that there are so many problems. He's a James Beard award winner. Obviously a lot of talent there." He pursed his lips, peered at something in the distance, a vision of what might be, perhaps. "But, basically, it's a gut feeling. Could be right, could be wrong."

Elena speared a vivid red strawberry, a fruit at its prime, and fell into admiring it. The smooth red flesh, quilted with the tiniest seeds. It tasted slightly grainy, imbued with the sunlight of a summer morning. "Mmm." She stabbed another and held it out to Julian. "Have a taste."

He bent in without hesitation and took it from her fork. She glimpsed his tongue. "Excellent."

She handed him another one, which he took with his fingers. "The chef in Aspen—he's executive now, right?"

Julian nodded. He knew exactly what she was asking.

The chef would be demoted—he'd hate her the minute she showed up.

"That might be a little volatile," she said.

"A challenge, I'm sure," he said, but there was no apology in it.

"What's his name?"

"Ivan Santino."

She wrote it down and stuck it in her pocket. If she had to deal with him, she'd want to go in armed. Someone in the community would know something about him, surely.

Then for a moment, she said nothing, trying not to let anticipation or fear rush her into anything. Without hurry, she ate some more of her omelet, savoring the sharpness of Swiss cheese, the smoothness of asparagus. She broke a corner of her toast and ate it.

Across the table, Julian was a column of still energy. She liked his face, his black eyes, that tumble of curls, but more than anything, she liked that he could sit there with his hands clasped unmoving around a coffee cup and wait for her to think.

She also liked that he would make a big move for the sake of a child. "May I ask about your daughter?"

He lifted a shoulder. "She's fourteen—running with a crowd I think is too fast."

"And Aspen is slower than LA?"

"No. It's a lot smaller, however, and I can keep an eye on her more easily."

"Good for you," Elena said, and meant it. Finished with her meal, she put her napkin aside and picked up her tea. "What will you pay me?"

He named a figure that was a third more than she currently earned. "And because accommodation is so difficult in Aspen, we'll see to it that you have living space. A condo, probably."

"I have a dog," Elena said. "I have to have some space for him. Yard space."

"Bring him. Everyone in Aspen has a dog."

She thought of her two-year-old rescue mutt, a fluffy chow-Lab mix with a head like a Saint Bernard. "Probably not like Alvin."

Julian grinned, showing teeth for the first time. The eye-teeth were a little crooked, and she liked him for not fixing them, even with all of his millions. "Alvin?"

"From Alvin and the Chipmunks, remember them?"

He laughed. "I'll have to see this dog."

The sound of his laughter was weirdly familiar, a song she remembered from long ago. Scowling, Elena took a breath. "I'm very excited and flattered by your offer, Mr. Liswood. But my policy is to never say yes to anything without thinking about it on my own. I need to take a walk."

"Of course." He stood with her. "I do need an answer fairly quickly. We need to get moving, and if you are not interested, I'll need to move on to my next choice."

Elena pushed away her nervousness. Told herself to take her time anyway. He wouldn't run out and get another chef before the end of the day. "I understand," she said with as much cool professionalism as she could muster.

"This is my cell phone number." He gave her a business card and held out his hand. "Thank you for coming."

"My pleasure." As his long fingers clasped her hand, she caught the scent of his skin. Not the food preferences she sometimes picked up, but simply his skin, himself. It smelled of rain hitting the earth on a summer evening. "I'll let you know by the end of the day."

"I'll look forward to that."

Their hands were still linked. Palm to palm. Eye to eye. She liked him. She thought she could trust him.

And yet, there was some darkness about him, sad and lonely, lingering in the air around him. Now she caught another scent, still not food, but a waft of old-fashioned perfume. She didn't move for a moment.

He didn't move away. The air seemed to buzz.

Damn it.

Elena pulled away. "Thank you, Mr. Liswood. I'll let you know as soon as I can."

"A pleasure meeting you, Ms. Alvarez." His eyes twinkled. "I look forward to hearing from you."

The rain had slowed to a soft drizzle, and Elena fetched her dog Alvin from the neighbor who kept him while she worked. They headed for the seawall. If she didn't walk, all the broken bits of her—the shattered hip, the pinned left leg, her spine—stopped working.

So, every day, rain or shine, blizzards or gales, Elena headed out. Here in Vancouver, it was mainly to the seawall that looped around Stanley Park, always next to the water, a six-mile trek that kept her joints lubricated and head clear.

What a morning! The article and the Blue Turtle and getting fired and Julian Liswood and the possibility of a kitchen of her own. It was so much to think about.

And there at the center of it all was the fact that her

home was gone. Again. Dmitri and the Blue Turtle. Her heart burned with sorrow and anger, like those flaming hearts on saints.

Not that it was a surprise. It had taken three months, three months of breaking up and getting back together in wet and heated make-up sessions; and more recently, three weeks of late night phone calls—both his and hers.

The usual. Civilized breakups probably happened, but not between a Russian man and a Latin woman.

But she also felt the end was solid now. This time, they would not get back together.

A slap of wind gusted over the water, and Elena winced against it. This was not how she had imagined her life would turn out, that she would be nearly forty and still husbandless, childless, rootless. As a girl, curled up in the corner of the kitchen in the roadhouse where her grandmother had tended bar, Elena had read every fairy tale known to man. All the pretty American Disney ones, with princesses who had flowing blonde locks and long white gloves. Cinderella, notably, with her lost shoe and the determined prince who knew he would find her, who would not give up until he did. She had liked Snow White, with her black eyes and black hair, and it seemed her world of seven dwarves was a comforting depth of family. There was Sleeping Beauty, locked away in her briar, and enchanted cats who turned into princes, and cursed orphans, and fairies who brought blessings spiderwebbed with curses.

There was simply no doubt in her mind that she would one day find her own prince. He would kiss her, and Elena would Know, and they would Live Happily Ever After.

Depressing that none of that had materialized. She

loved her work, but honestly—how much longer could she do it? It was a challenging occupation for those with good health. Her pinned, patched body was not in that category.

Alvin, sensing Elena's mood, nudged her hand with a wet, cold nose. The king of empaths, Alvin was high-strung and utterly devoted to Elena. He couldn't bear it if she was shouting or weeping or distressed in any way. "It's all right, baby," she told him, rubbing a hand on his silky red head.

Now fate had delivered a chance. It rose through her like a harp note. *Executive chef.*

It would be a make-or-break opportunity. Visible. Public. There would be reviewers from high places, and some of them would still judge her more harshly because she was a woman, and American, and trained in Santa Fe. Her long education had taken her many places after that, San Francisco and Paris and London and New York, but that was what the bios all said, "a woman chef trained in Santa Fe."

Colorado was awfully close to New Mexico. Her family was there still, and she sometimes visited, but only for brief stints. Watching the seabirds whirl and spin in the air above the rocks, she saw a map in her head, with one star each on Aspen and Santa Fe, and a red dot showing Espanola in the northern New Mexico mountains.

Alvin licked her hand, bumped her knee. "I'm okay, honey. Promise." Reassured, he pranced along, tail swinging, head upright and eagerly alert. Elena had found him in an alley when she first arrived in Vancouver, an abandoned puppy of five weeks, a fluffy ball of red fur. He loved snow—Aspen would be his idea of heaven.

But—a binge-drinking chef who'd be pissed that Elena

was taking his kitchen? That should be lots of fun. It was also cold in Aspen. How would all the arthritic points in her body react to that?

"Get real, Elena," she said aloud, fiercely enough that Alvin licked her hand. There were no real objections. The opportunity was heaven-sent.

Well, except for Julian himself. Cloaked in that vampire stillness, so clean and tall and searingly intelligent. There was something real and solid about him, and yet—talk about trouble! A famous director with piles of money and a long stream of beautiful girlfriends and wives, who were a Who's Who of one-bean-for-lunch actresses who kept the tabloids in business. But it was that flavor of sadness surrounding him that tempted her. He was hungry. Starving.

Luckily, he was so rich and so accomplished and so out of her league they might as well have been different species. His appetites would run to an entirely different sort of flavor than a chef from New Mexico.

When she finished the six-mile circle, Elena sat on a park bench in the sunshine, Alvin at her ankle lifting his nose to the air. A breeze rippled over his red-gold mane. She waited to see if her ghosts would have anything to say, but the air stayed still.

From her pocket, she took her cell phone, checked the world clock function to make sure it wasn't the middle of the night in London, and pressed 5 to autodial her friend Mia.

"Hello, baby," Mia answered in a voice as smooth and melodic as the Lady of the Lake. "I'm on my way to meet a juicy man. Can it wait?"

"No." Elena smiled, imagining Mia's choppy black hair

blowing around on a London wind. "You're going to move to Aspen anyway, so forget about him."

"Aspen? Why am I moving there?"

"Because I have been offered a position as executive chef in a new Julian Liswood restaurant and I will only take it if you agree to be my pastry chef."

"Oh, my God! Liswood the director?"

"The same."

"This is fantastic." She paused. "Oooh, the timing is horrible! I might have to think about this, though, you know? The man is really good. I've been meaning to talk to you about him."

Elena heard something in her friend's voice. "Who is it? You haven't mentioned anyone."

"I just didn't think it was going to be anything. He's . . ." She laughed breathlessly. "I'm still afraid to talk about it very much."

"Oh, but I need you, Mia. This is what we've been planning for a million years."

"Is Dmitri coming?"

"No. He fired me this morning." She sighed. "It's a long story. I'll explain it all in person."

"So the breakup is on?"

"The breakup is finished, finally."

Mia took a breath. "Good. He was bad for you."

"Why didn't you say that before?" Elena frowned. "Never mind. Not important today. Will you come?"

A beat of hesitation. "I have to think, sweetness. I'll call you in a week or so, okay? I really have to go now. Call you soon."

"Okay, I—"

But there was the sound of a man's laughter on the other end of the line and Mia was gone. Elena frowned and clapped the phone closed.

When she hung up, she called Patrick, the third member of their team, but only got voice mail. "Hello, this is Patrick," he said precisely, and she thought of his coxcomb of blond hair, his excruciatingly neat appearance. "Leave a message."

Elena smiled. *"Allo!* I have a wonderful opportunity for you, *h'ito.* Call me."

As a hired car transported Julian to the airport—he disliked navigating streets in unfamiliar cities—he drew the newspaper from his bag and unfolded it to show the article about Elena.

The likeness was a good one, making her look saucy. She was no longer young. Not quite forty. He suspected by the way she moved—a little unevenness in her gait, a certain stiffness of the lower spine—that there were physical challenges. The camera loved her face, that thin straight nose and high cheekbones. Blue eyes in a Mayan face. Blonde hair around that olive skin.

And Jesus, that mouth.

Careful, man.

After his fourth divorce, seven years ago, Julian—weary and embattled—had given up alcohol and taken a vow of celibacy. Surrounded as he was by the banquet of temptations that was Hollywood, it seemed the only way he could get his head on straight. His last wife, Mallory, had been a yoga teacher who ran the highly successful studio he'd called when he found his body resisted running more and more each year. Yoga had been a boon, centering him, allowing him to see his life for what it was.

Which, ironically, nudged him into realizing that he and Mallory had absolutely nothing in common. She was a spiritual being, ethereal and without high appetites of any kind—for food or sex or even music—and while she'd been a lovely teacher, not such a great life match.

Feeling profligate over women and wine and too much of everything, he gave up sex and alcohol after the divorce. To be a good father, to be a decent human being, he had to figure out how to live with too much money and too much power and try to be whole and human.

His celibacy had lasted twenty-eight months. He ran, practiced yoga, poured his thwarted sexual energies into his films, his restaurants, and the practice of being a father to his daughter.

One rainy San Francisco day, he'd ducked into the kitchen of the Yellow Dolphin, and there had been a woman taking tomatoes out of a basket. She was new to the place, her skin faintly sallow, her hair fine and ordinary beneath a bright scarf, her body hidden beneath her stained smock. Ordinary, really.

And yet, he stood rooted, his ears hot, the back of his neck swamped with blood, staring at her plush mouth. As he stood there, airless and stunned, she sliced a thick wheel from a tomato and tasted it with an expression of distance and internal focus, obviously gauging the depth of flavor. Those lips moved in the most ordinary of ways, pressing together, pursing.

Julian left the restaurant and went for a run, thinking

maybe extremes were a bad idea. Balance in all things. That evening, he found a willing partner and ended his celibacy.

But this morning, when he saw that mouth again, on Elena, who stood on the sidewalk in front of the Blue Turtle, looking both angry and crushed, he had been dismayed to realize her mouth still had the power to stun him.

He had nearly turned around without saying a word. And yet, he'd flown to Vancouver to meet her.

He'd done a great deal of research on the sous chefs in his existing restaurants, looking for one who might have the skills to move up that last step. Elena had won in every category—she was known for sharpness and good humor and intelligence. Every chef he spoke to admired her clever and sensual food. He liked that she had her roots in the West, that she'd worked in all the major food markets.

She was such a shoe-in that he'd really only come to Vancouver to meet her in person.

As the car looped through the streets of Vancouver, he tapped the paper on his knee. The women who tempted him most were never the great beauties, though God knew he'd had his share of those as well. It was stories that snared him, and Elena Alvarez was a composite of opposites and mysteries he found deeply intriguing. He read the article again.

His cell phone rang. The display showed Elena's name. He answered warmly. "Elena, I hope the news is good."

"I have questions," she said in the faintly and uniquely accented voice—a hint of a drawl, the softening influence of Spanish, a musical dash, perhaps from the time in France. Entirely unique. "Can I bring two people with me?"

"Absolutely. Anyone I know?"

"No one from the Blue Turtle. Patrick is a sommelier with genius for the front of the house, and Mia is a pastry chef. Very talented, both of them."

"Aside from the two I mentioned, everyone else is your call."

Julian heard her take a breath, as if to steady herself. "All right, then, Mr. Liswood. I'm all yours. The sooner I get out of here, the better."

"Excellent. I'll fax the contract and get on the condo right away."

"Don't forget I need to bring my dog."

"I won't forget." He paused. "Welcome aboard, Elena."

"I'm honored to have the chance. If I haven't said so, thank you. Very much."

"My pleasure." He hung up and held the phone tenderly in the cup of his hand for a long moment until the car stopped at the airport.

He tugged his hat lower on his head, hiding his hair. Dark glasses hid his face, and the combination made him anonymous. Until the recent security crackdowns, he'd traveled as Jonathan Craven, the antihero in his block-buster horror series, but 9/11 had put an end to that. Now he was simply Julian Liswood. Not many security guards recognized the name by itself. Directing was not like acting.

Settled into his first-class accommodations on the plane, he remembered to be grateful for the extra space for his long legs, and flipped open his cell phone, dialed the number of his business manager. "I found my chef. We're a go for the Aspen restaurant," he said, watching two burly men load bags into the hold. "Let's meet this evening."

FOUR

ELENA'S BEST FOODS
Paris Hot Chocolate

Very nearby the Louvre is a strip of tourist shops and eateries.
One is a two-story restaurant with beautiful young waitresses
and a counter in front to sell chocolates. It's called Angelina's,
and I think it was famous at one time. The walls are baroque and
a little grimy, with mirrors and gilt. There, three expats in Paris
retreated on a miserable, rainy November day in 1993 and huddled together, wishing for home. Until the chocolate came, a big,
boiling hot pot of it, served with a pitcher of thick cream. Patrick,
who had been there as a child, smiled and poured.

"Now taste," he said.

Mia and I, mourning our language and our homes and our
boyfriends, who lived ten thousand miles away across an ocean,
picked up our cups. I took one swallow, and a chocolate river
opened into my throat, down through my chest. I *swam* in it.

Patrick laughed.

FIVE

Elena had met Patrick and Mia in Paris. The trio were eager students at Le Cordon Bleu, giddy with possibility and miserable in their Americanness and clumsiness with the language.

Mia was a soft, round Italian-American girl with clouds of hair and breasts and lusciousness, who could prepare pastry so seductive that she never lacked for lovers, though she could not master the art of keeping them. She made Elena think of her lost siblings, and that led her to sit down next to Mia the first day of class. They bonded immediately.

Patrick was a Boston blue blood with a flair for service, who fussed over details and beauty. He joined Elena and Mia a week into the program, rejected by a pair of French youths who disdained Patrick's slight and boyish plumpness, his nearly albino paleness.

On long rainy afternoons, the trio huddled in the tiny apartment they shared, and nursed hangovers from drinking too late in tucked-away spots with black-clad human commas who made Elena think of beatniks. As they warmed themselves with coffee, shivering beneath shawls and blankets, they spun a dream of opening their own restaurant—Elena as chef, Patrick in the front of the house, Mia as pastry chef.

Now, fourteen years later, they would have the chance. Within three days, Elena had promises from both of them to join her in Aspen, and three days after that, she was on the road in her Subaru that had plenty of room for Alvin, her possessions, most of which belonged in the kitchen— she didn't even have many clothes, since she spent most of her time in chef's whites—and herself. She nestled a gera- nium, a bright magenta bloomer, in a secure spot. It was the one thing she'd carried from place to place to place all these years, grown from a cutting she'd taken from a plant in her grandmother's restaurant.

Place to place, she thought. Place to place to place to place. God, she was getting weary of always moving on! And yet, what choice was there? She was a chef. She went where the work carried her.

She arrived in Aspen on a Tuesday afternoon. "Look at this!" she said aloud, just in case Isobel was listening. Her sister never showed up in a car, which Elena could under- stand, but she talked to her sometimes anyway. "It's like a scene from a View-Master!"

Mountains towered into the air on three sides, around a town that was scattered down the valley like spilled Tinkertoys. The landscape was painted in seven shades of green—aspens and grasses and junipers—and twelve shades of blue, from sky to mountain and back again, with splashes of gold here and there, like jewelry. On the ground was ocher and red, a little pink granite.

Dazzling.

Between the craggy peaks, a thunderstorm gathered, and she remembered suddenly how violent those late afternoon storms could be. She pressed on the gas, realizing she'd slowed down to drink it all in.

"Man!" Elena said to Alvin, who was hanging his nose out the window she had rolled down for him, his long fur blowing back from his face in red-gold streams. "Can you *believe* this place?"

There were spiderlike cyclists in vivid spandex, and runners with muscular thighs and skinny torsos; backpackers with dreadlocks and ponytails; golfers in pale pastels dotting a green settled against an astonishing view of a big, big mountain carved with ski runs.

"What *am* I doing here, Alvin, huh?" she asked. The smell of millions wafted through the fine, thin air on currents of privilege. Houses the size of her high school were tucked away all over the valley, only visible when the sunlight caught their windows and made her turn her head to see what flashed. "I'm so out of my league."

Alvin grinned at her, his purple chow tongue dripping. His long fur glistened red and gold in the sunlight, his big black face agreeably blunted and broadened by what his vet theorized was probably Newfoundland. Or Saint Bernard. Or something. When he walked, he pranced, and his tail swept up in a perfect curl.

"Yeah, of course *you're* happy," she said. "You'll probably be discovered here and become a big movie star and then you'll never want to take walks with me again."

Place to place, she thought, following the directions Julian had emailed to her. *Don't get too attached to this one.*

She found a complex of townhouses scattered along a creek, and her apartment was on the end, close to the road. A pair of ancient cottonwoods stood sentry, and a fenced area butted up to the river, providing a safe place for Alvin to get outside.

Beneath a pot of bright pink petunias, she found an envelope with a key, and let herself in. Alvin raced ahead, relieved to be out of the car at last. Elena dropped the keys on the table, opened the back door for Alvin, and happily walked around.

It came furnished, with a southwestern mountain flavor—heavy wooden furniture and pottery-patterned fabrics. A few expensive-looking prints of local landscapes and portraits of Native Americans hung on the walls. The kitchen was small but high-end, with granite countertops and two sinks and lots of storage. She pulled open the fridge and was touched to discover it stocked with milk and eggs and cheese, and a couple of bottles of wine. Nice.

Upstairs was a loft bedroom, tucked beneath the eaves and overlooking the slopes. On the bathroom sink—also granite—was a bowl of beautiful fruit and chocolate, a very expensive bottle of French bath oil, and a heavy linen card with a note scrawled on it in a thin, somehow aristocratic hand:

Welcome, Elena! I hope you'll be happy here. Rest tonight and call me tomorrow. Julian.

Bemused, she raised her head, tapping the note against her hand as she admired the glass bricks making a swirl around the shower, the giant raised tub, the elegance of detailing. Alvin padded into the room, snuffling things along the route. She patted his head. "We're not in Kansas anymore, Toto."

Toto flopped down on the thick aqua carpet and licked his balls.

She had planned to head for the restaurant almost immediately, just to take a look around, but a thunderstorm stomped into the valley, violent and flashy. Alvin was not pleased, and Elena curled up with him in the bed, putting her arms around his shivering body. Rain pounded down on the skylights, and the bed was deep and soft, cozy with a thick duvet. She fell asleep.

When she woke up, the rain was gone, birds singing. She leashed Alvin and headed out to visit the restaurant.

The newly washed sky was a brilliant, rubbery blue, and leaves on the famed aspen trees glistened with beaded rain. Even in August, there was a bite to the air, and Elena inhaled with pleasure, half dizzy with altitude. She would get used to it again, but in the meantime, it made her feel slightly giddy.

There were lots of other people about—dogs and runners and tourists. A skinny mother with her healthy brown hair in a ponytail jogged by with a stroller. "Great dog," she called out as she passed, and Elena smiled in return. Perhaps Aspen would be like Paris, where a dog could provide entrée.

As if he'd heard the woman, Alvin pranced more prettily, lifting fringed legs like a Clydesdale horse. He stopped periodically to snuffle deliriously at the blog notes left by who-knew-what animals on the bases of trees and lamp-posts and the springy ground. He'd never lived anywhere but the city. The wild animal scents were making him drunk.

The restaurant stood on a side street in an older neighborhood, a Victorian-era house that had been refitted as a restaurant in what appeared to be the late seventies, that ever so elegant decade. *Ugh!*

Elena paused on the sidewalk to get a feel for it. And suddenly, there was Isobel, a slim teenager with curly hair tumbling down her back and pale constellations of sexy freckles over her golden skin. A tattoo of a sun adorned her left breast. "Huh," she said, tucking her hands in the pockets of her jeans. "Not very welcoming, is it?"

"Not very."

Alvin leaned hard on Elena's knee, shivering slightly. She reached down and threaded his floppy ear through her fingers in a soothing gesture. Very softly, he growled.

There was a lot of work to be done, but there was a lot of potential here, too. Elena nodded to herself, pulling her fingers through the down-soft hair beneath Alvin's ears. The old sign, reading *The Steak and Ale,* hung in weathered neglect over the wide wooden porch, where tables and chairs were scattered in clusters. Good. Since Colorado had no indoor smoking, an outdoor smoking area was a boon. She climbed the steps. "Let's check out the inside."

A sign in the window said the restaurant had been closed for remodeling and would be open under new management on November 2. A ripple of nervousness went through her. A little more than two months. Not much time.

Tying Alvin to a post on the porch where he could

watch the passersby, she took the key out of her pocket and fitted it into the front door. It groaned open into a small foyer with a set of stairs leading up immediately.

"Bad *feng shui*," Isobel commented. "All the *chi* will flow right outside."

"Mmm." It would also be a headache for wait staff, who'd have to navigate the tiny area and compete with guests waiting to be seated. She pulled a notebook out of her pocket and wrote, *front door/stairs.*

Moving through the rooms, she eyed the window treatments and art on the walls and the table settings laid out for diners who would never see them. The whole place was faintly bedraggled, dated. Dark. The rooms were too small. In her notebook, she scribbled, *upgrade fireplace, paint, Diego Rivera or Oaxaca art. Milagros? Day of the Dead?*

Upstairs was the bar area. A tiny secondary kitchen was tucked toward the back, and everything that was wrong with the rest of the place was magnified here. One positive was a bank of windows high on one wall that let in a lot of natural light. Elena pursed her lips. A good granite countertop and more workspace and it might be a good pastry kitchen.

Near the freezer were the service stairs. Not great stairs, either—narrow wood, with a landing—but someone had installed high-quality rubber gripping on the treads. She'd seen worse.

The downstairs kitchen area was, thankfully, much larger, with several workstations, a large walk-in fridge, and a bank of high-end dishwashers. Good. Nothing like falling behind in dishes to throw the rhythm of a night's service out of whack.

There were upgrades needed here, too, and she wrote them down—stoves, new rubber matting, fresh paint, if only to give it a feeling of being modernized. The old paint was grimy, a pale industrial green.

All in all, it wasn't terrible. Elena hummed under her breath as she opened drawers, checking the inventory of pots and pans, then she headed down a short hall. In the back was what seemed to be a staff room. Elena peeked in, flipped on the light, and jumped a foot when a body sat up on the cot. She gave an involuntary cry.

"Jesus," said a grouchy voice.

The man was as lean as a sword, with springy hair pulled into a ponytail. He swung his feet to the floor and glared at her with very bloodshot, very vivid blue eyes. His long face was overly sensual, the mouth wide and full, the nose aggressive, his chin sporting the grizzling of a black beard.

"What the fuck are you doing?" he growled. Despite the foul words, his voice was stunning—dark and rich. He held a hand up against the light.

"I could ask you the same thing."

"Sleeping. Or I was."

"Maybe your house would be a better place to do that."

He glared at her. "Don't tell me—you're the princess come to save the restaurant."

"Princess? Hardly." She crossed her arms, leaning against the threshold. "I am the chef Mr. Liswood hired."

"Mr. Liswood?" he echoed. "You mean the big dick director?"

"You must be Ivan," she said, and thought, *Shit.*

"Bingo."

He looked at her, challenge in his eyes. She wondered what he expected her to do right now. "Why are you sleeping here, Ivan? Do you have housing issues?"

He snorted. " 'Housing issues.' That's rich. Is that how they teach you to talk out there in the big city?"

"Don't be a dick. It's an honest question."

For a moment, he peered at her. Alcohol fumes came off him in waves, and the odor—human male sweat mixed with the specific bite of tequila—made Elena think of Espanola, of the men who would play poker in a garage set aside for the purpose. They all smelled like this the next morning, and if you were smart, you steered clear of them.

"Everybody has housing issues in Aspen, sweetheart," he said, and even with all the sarcasm and nastiness, his voice was unruined—the velvety darkness of an orator. He pulled himself to his feet and paused, staring down at her, his shirt in his hands. He made her think of Rasputin with that long face, the intense blue eyes. She swung backward to let him pass, but only just enough.

He shot a look sideways as he went. "I'm the best cook that's ever lived," he said, and sauntered away, his back too thin, a tattoo of vines curling around his spine. A sense of brokenness, something lost, came to her, and she let it waft around in the air between them, the smoky purple of bruises. She smelled lemons. Lemon bars? Lemon meringue? No, not so sweet.

It would come to her.

"That would be impossible," Elena replied, "because that title belongs to me."

He turned, his mouth lifting on one side.

She said, "I'll see you Friday."

It startled him, but he covered with a nod, tossing his shirt over his shoulder as he headed out.

Elena stayed where she was. *Trouble, trouble, trouble.* Something cold walked down her spine, and she looked for her ghosts, but none were there, or at least, they did not show themselves. Shaking it off, she took a breath and turned off the light. "I need to cook," she said in case they were listening. "Let's go see the grocery stores."

And then Isobel was there, wandering in from another room. "I wanted to see where he went from here," she said. Her teenager hair was as glossy as fingernail polish. "That one is broken, I think. Be careful."

Elena nodded.

"You need to call Mama," Isobel said, putting a hand on the counter, admiring the space. "Dolores is sick."

The usual thread of resistance spun itself around her spine. "I will. Later. Come on. Let's go check out the stores."

Kitchens were often the only safe place in Elena's world, and when she needed to think or rest or feel centered, she headed right for the stove. This afternoon, she wanted to find out what kind of ingredients she could buy off the shelves here, what would have to be ordered.

As she headed toward the grocery store she'd found on MapQuest before leaving the apartment, she heard her sister's nudge again, "Call Mama," and knew she needed to do it. Mama, who was Maria Elena, was technically Elena's grandmother. Technically, because her real mother had abandoned her, so Mama took the role.

Elena's father, Roberto Alvarez, had gone into the Army

during Vietnam. The second son of the family, all proud, poor farmers in New Mexico, descended from the Spanish conquistadores who settled the area in the 1700s, Roberto had been born with wanderlust. When a recruiter showed up at his high school one day, Roberto joined the Army on the spot. He did his basic training in El Paso, where he met Donna DeWalle at a 7-Eleven store. Donna was fifteen, ripe as a peach. Roberto, lonely so far from home, fell in love with her in three seconds flat.

Donna, fast and busty and blonde, was the daughter of a bartender at a roadhouse that did a brisk business serving soldiers. She, predictably, got pregnant—and this being before legal abortions, they got married at a justice of the peace just before Roberto shipped out and got himself killed six months later. Before he left, he made Donna promise to name his child either after him if it was a boy, or after his mother, Maria Elena, if it was a girl.

Elena, the little girl born on a windy moonless night, was left a lot to her own devices. Donna was a party girl who left Elena with her own mother, Iris. All three lived in a little apartment nearby the roadhouse where Iris worked, and Elena had her own bedroom overlooking the river. Mexico was there on the other side, looking much the same as America. But it was different. Everyone said so.

She went to school with migrant workers and played jacks with the children of soldiers and learned that she was very smart. Every year, she was the smartest girl in the class, and there was one reason why—they lived right around the corner from a library.

Elena's grandmother Iris loved reading, especially big sagas by the likes of Sidney Sheldon, and historicals and gothics by the thousands—Victoria Holt and Mary Stewart and Norah Lofts. It was her escape. She didn't drink and she didn't like people very much and thought television was idiotic, so she would sit on the porch and smoke cigarettes and read novels. To this day, when Elena heard someone cough in that rattly, heavy-smoker way, she had a flash of Iris reading, her breasts spilling over her ribs and down her sides beneath a housedress, a light shining over her shoulder, smoke rising in a blue cloud around her.

The pair of them went to the library every week to check out books. By the time she was seven, Elena could read chapter books, and she read them by the zillions.

Nobody cooked in *that* world, not at home. Breakfast was Cheerios or Life cereal. For lunch on weekends, she had grilled cheese sandwiches and bowls of chili. Supper was whatever the roadhouse was serving as the special of the day—open-faced turkey sandwiches with gravy on squishy slices of white bread; refried bean burritos; tacos fried crisp; beef stew; or posole. Sometimes, the old cook, a man with a grizzling of white on his chin, would let Elena help with something—tearing lettuce, or peeling ears of corn, or putting sliced pickles in a dish for the counter.

While her grandmother served beer and rum and Cokes, Elena curled up in a warm corner of the kitchen, like Cinderella, and read her books. It was safe and cozy and there was always a friendly adult around to get her a drink of water, or soda if she begged. She felt protected there.

When Elena was eight, Iris got cancer and died. For a while, Donna tried to do the right thing, but she was mixed up with a man who didn't want anything to do with children. He wanted to move to Dallas and Donna wasn't about to miss her chance, so she put Elena in the car and drove to Espanola and the Alvarez family home.

Donna pretended that she'd just brought Elena to visit, counting on their grief and love of their lost son to get them to let the little girl into their world a little bit, even if she did have the bad luck to be born as white-looking as her mother, all blue eyes and pale hair.

But Roberto's mother, Maria Elena, for whom Elena was named, insisted they make her welcome. She was tucked into the couch with blankets and pillows, in a place that smelled strange and felt strange, and she cried, missing her grandmother.

In the morning, Donna was gone. Gone like a wisp of smoke. The Alvarezes adjusted, shifting a little to make room—there were already twelve children in that house, including two cousins, what was one more? Elena was right between Isobel and Margaret, technically her aunties, one six months younger, one a year older. They all shared a room with a sister two years older, Dorothy, who hated Elena and never did warm up.

All she had with her were the clothes she'd worn, a pair of extra underwear, and a Victoria Holt book her grandmother had been reading when she died, *The Mistress of Mellyn*, which Elena was ashamed to have stolen from the library. She had never lived anywhere but the little apartment near the restaurant.

That was the beginning of Elena's betweenness. Between the world of white and Spanish, as they said in those days, not Mexican, which meant something else. Spanish, to differentiate from Indian, which is what some white people wanted to be elsewhere, but not in New Mexico, where Spanish ruled. Spanish the language. Spanish the colors. Spanish the food. Spanish the music and the dances at the VFW. Spanish the customs. Spanish the everything.

Every night, Elena curled around the book and buried her face in a blanket and cried silently. It was like she had a hole in her heart, or maybe even worse, like there was a hole in her chest where everything she loved had been cut out. She couldn't breathe with it.

There were two points of light. One was Isobel, so close to Elena in age that they were nearly twins, their birthdays exactly six months to the day apart. Isobel, the youngest girl, made room for Elena, pushing her socks and underwear to one side in a drawer so Elena could put in her meager belongings, shoving chairs around at the dinner table so Elena could sit beside her.

Elena was smitten with Isobel and her shiny hair and her curvy mouth and her big teeth, coming in with their little ragged edges. She had a big, loud belly laugh and she liked blue fingernails and she was always getting in trouble for something. They slept in the same bed, were in the same class at school, wore each other's clothes. At night, when Elena wept in homesickness, Isobel just curled up next to her and smoothed her hair, murmuring Spanish words of comfort: *Sleep, little child. You're safe now.* Words Elena didn't understand at the time.

The other joy was Mama, Maria Elena, who wrapped her namesake in worn thin cotton aprons and stood the little girl on a chair next to her while she cooked for the multitudes. She told Elena to call her Mama. She showed her how to measure flour and pat out tortillas and stir a pot of stew. And there, again, Elena was safe.

What else could she have done with her life but cook?

At the supermarket in Aspen, Elena simply walked the perimeter at first, to check out the layout. It was predictably big and bright and clean, with all the accoutrements of a high-end grocery—a stunning bakery, acres of deli offerings, and a produce aisle with piles of the very freshest arugula and purple fingerling potatoes and grapes the size of her palm.

But to her surprise, she also found an aisle bursting with a plentiful display of Mexican ingredients—dried red chiles of many varieties, big and small; canned and pickled green chiles; masa and corn husks and spices and almost any other staple a person would need. It seemed bizarre that such a wealth enclave should have such good Mexican supplies, until she spied a short dark man in a plaid shirt and jeans weighing a plump package of chicken.

Of course. Such a heavy tourist market would require huge crews of construction workers, cleaners, cooks, gardeners, labor that would be supplied by Latin American immigrants in all their forms—legal, green-card, and not.

Standing there in that shiny aisle, with rock classics playing over the speakers, she realized she was going to live closer to home than she had in almost twenty years. The snake of history on her back burned for one long minute, as if it were uncoiling into a live being, a whip of white and orange light. Standing there in the brightly lit grocery store with a vastness of homey foods to choose from, Elena felt suddenly hollow, terrified, and she wondered if this was a mistake, to come too close to home.

"Just cook, Elena," said Isobel, standing by the chiles, her arms slim and young. "Just make the soup."

"I have to cook for Julian tomorrow night." Elena looked over her shoulder. There was no one in the aisle. "I don't know what to make."

"He wants your favorites." Isobel ran her hands over the bags of posole, the yellow cartons of Mexican hot chocolate. "Be yourself."

Elena plucked a bag of dried posole from the rack and settled it next to the bag of masa. Cook. Just cook. Forget about the critics who, like ravens with black shiny eyes, would be secretly hoping for her to fail. Forget Dmitri and failure and the fact that Julian Liswood was maybe one of the most—

Never mind.

There was no other choice. The Aspen restaurant was the chance she'd been working toward for two decades. For that, she would cook. For that, she would start again in a new place, building a new home.

And she would begin by cooking.

SIX

ABUELA MARIA ELENA'S POSOLE

2 cups dried posole (dried whole hominy)
2–3 lbs. boneless pork shoulder
3 cloves garlic, sliced thin
1 onion, chopped
*½ cup mild fresh green chiles, reserving a handful of thin strips for
    garnish*
1–2 peeled, seeded, chopped tomatoes (about 1 cup)
¼ cup chopped fresh cilantro
Salt to taste

Rinse posole in cold water until water runs clear. Soak overnight.

To cook pork, put it in a heavy pan on the stove with a little water, salt and pepper, and let it cook real slow until it's falling to pieces, about 2–3 hours. Remove the pork, leaving the fat in the pan, and brown the onions and garlic, then put the meat back in the pan, add the posole and enough water to cover it all, and bring to a boil. Reduce heat and simmer, covered, till posole pops, about

1 hour. Meanwhile roast the chile peppers (if fresh) in a paper bag in a 400-degree oven for about 10 minutes, remove, cool, peel (skin slips off easily), and chop. Add the chiles to the pot after the posole has popped. Simmer, covered, 4 more hours. Taste for seasoning, add salt to taste. Simmer, covered, 1 more hour. Garnish with cilantro and thin coils of pepper and finely chopped tomatoes.

SEVEN

Julian sat in a big chair, his legs crossed, a lamp shining over his shoulder. In the background played Billie Holiday, singing "Good Morning Heartache," the old jazz sounds a ghostly memory of a time long gone, the best music he knew to write horror. Or anything really.

On a tablet in his lap, he was trying to block out a new screenplay, and had been all summer. It shouldn't have taken so long. He'd done sixteen films in the twenty-two years of his career, and he understood what audiences and the studio wanted of him. This one should have been a piece of cake, the third in a trilogy that had been vastly popular, but it wasn't coming. He loved horror, everything about the genre, but he'd had enough of the type that was selling just now—buckets of blood and nubile girls screaming in terror as they tried to outwit yet another crazed serial killer. It was fun, in its place. It had made him piles of money, his studio piles of money. More money than he could spend, honestly.

He wasn't in the mood for it right now. Not that he

knew what he *was* in the mood for. He'd done a lot of kinds of horror flicks, from ghosts to slashers to an upmarket historical vampire flick that was still one of the top DVD rentals on every list a decade after it had been made.

The past few weeks, there was a taste in his mouth, a hint of something that he couldn't quite catch, a whisper or promise. Thus the pad of paper, no electronics between himself and his imagination, just an open legal pad with crisp white paper and a fountain pen with strong black ink. It made him feel like a bard to write with a fountain pen.

On the paper, he doodled. Music rose in a cloud to the exposed rafters of the cathedral ceiling. What *was* it that kept sweeping through him? On the page he wrote, *yearning, redemption, sorrow, catharsis, hunger.*

He drew a circle around each word and sketched bubbles going out from each one. Horror was always about catharsis, about letting go of pent-up emotions, recognizing that life as it *is* was not so bad.

It was also about redemption—monsters and ghosts and zombies put in their place. He had a flash of a graveyard, an open grave, and a sense of cold loss. With quick, sure strokes, he captured the wisp in a sketch.

Each kind of horror had a particular function, fulfilled a particular longing or fantasy on the part of the audience—and the filmmaker, of course. What fantasy was he yearning to fulfill?

For a long moment he sat still, his pen unmoving, then he pulled a sheaf of papers from the back of the notebook. Photocopies of old newspaper clippings, from the autumn of 1988, most of them reiterating the same information.

The top story was taken from the *Albuquerque Journal*, November 1988. A photo showed the marks on a tree trunk and a hill with crosses standing against a twilight sky.

LOCAL TRAGEDY
Four Teens Dead, One Critical in Car Crash

AP Espanola—Four teens were killed instantly and another critically injured in a high-speed crash on State Highway 76 Thursday night when the driver lost control and slammed into a tree. The teens were all students at Espanola Valley High School. Three were from one family—the driver, Isobel Alvarez, 18, a senior; her younger brother Albert, 14, and the lone survivor, Elena Alvarez, 17, who sustained catastrophic injuries and has not regained consciousness. She was airlifted to an Albuquerque hospital and is listed in critical condition. The other victims were Edwin Valdez, 18, the survivor's boyfriend, and Penelope Madrid, also 17, a cousin to the Alvarez family. Alcohol was not a factor in the incident.

Julian flipped the edge of the paper with his thumb. An ordinary story in ways, both utterly banal and absolutely devastating. It happened every day—cars trying to beat an oncoming train, drag-racing up lonely farm highways, navigating bad roads in the dark; drinking and driving in any fashion at all.

It still left a pit in his belly, a hollowness. Three children ripped from a family in a single swath, two siblings and a cousin dead, and a fourth so badly mangled that it appeared it had taken more than a year for her to leave the hospital.

He fingered the silky goatee beneath his lip. An ordinary horror. Like a murder, a woman being snatched out of a grocery store parking lot and murdered, her body dumped in a field. How many times each year did it happen? Once a week? Once a day?

How did those families survive the loss? He couldn't even bear to *think* of the loss of his daughter, for fear that it would bring it closer. Even he, who thought of dark things for a living, skittered away, whispered preventive prayers to angels he didn't believe in—*never, never, please, not ever that*. The darkness on the other side of such a thought was unbearable.

He'd found the article when he ran a Google search on his new chef. He ran checks on anyone he planned to hire in a leadership position, just to make sure nothing untoward showed up. The Vancouver newspaper article had hinted that Elena Alvarez had experienced a loss in her youth, but had not elaborated.

Catastrophic injuries. What did that mean? How long, he wondered, had she lain in a coma, unaware that her siblings and friend and cousin were dead?

In the quiet room, Ella Fitzgerald started to sing in her haunting way, "Summertime," a song that always sent a knife through his heart. When he'd found the article, he'd wanted to throw it away, forget it, let it go.

And he'd known, equally clearly, that he would not. It was a story he had not explored, another angle on the endless question of his movies—how did people grapple with darkness? His creative curiosity had been snared, even as he was a little shamed by it. Was it prurient or the natural curiosity of a storyteller?

Once the door was flung open, there was no closing it. His muses, skinny and pockmarked, stalked the alleyways of dark events, taking notes on events that made others look away. What, he wondered, were the statistics on people who survived such catastrophic events? Did they tend to thrive or self-destruct? What issues did they face?

From the black granite and cherry table at his elbow, he lifted his notebook computer, rubbed the mouse square with the edge of his thumb and brought up Google. He tucked his pen between his teeth to free his hands and typed, *survivors catastrophic car accidents.*

A slim figure emerged from the shadows of the hallway. "Whatcha doing?"

Julian shut down the search, feeling weirdly guilty. "Nothing, kiddo. What's up?"

His daughter Portia flung herself into an easy chair. "I'm bored."

"School starts in a few days, and it will get better."

"Oh, like I love school so much." She twisted a strand of extra-shiny blonde hair around a finger. Her outstretched foot wiggled. "I miss home."

"I know. You'll make new friends here."

"I liked my old friends."

Julian nodded. "But they were not particularly good for you."

"How do you know people here will be better for me? Maybe I'll find even *worse* friends."

He inclined his head, mentally flipping through the

parental handbook to see if there was a proper answer to a veiled threat. She had been in serious trouble in LA, running with a crowd of kids whose parents had too much money and not enough time. Left to their own devices, with far too many resources, they drugged and drank in great quantities.

"I'm sure you can if you try," he said after a minute. "There must be some stoner snowboarders around. Probably some speed freaks, too, and hey—if you try, I bet you can find some abusive alcoholic boyfriend to punish me with."

She pursed her sullen lips, unpainted and sweet as a Kewpie doll's. Just now, she was still slightly blurry, a soft-edged version of the woman she would be in a few years, but one day she would be a tremendous beauty—a gift that would be more burden than blessing if he didn't figure out how to help her develop the right tools to manage it. If the movies had taught him anything, it was that Beauty often self-destructed.

"I hate my life." Portia blinked back tears. "How'm I supposed to know what to do?"

"Maybe you could listen to your dad, huh? You're only fourteen. You're not supposed to have all the answers."

She shrugged.

"What I'd like to see you do here is make a fresh start. Make friends with kids who have goals and dreams, who want to do something with their lives."

"Oh, like jocks and cheerleaders?"

"Since you're a natural athlete, I would like to see you mix it up with some jocks, actually. But maybe spend time figuring out what you love and find other people who love those things, too. Just find friends who want to believe in life instead of making fun of it."

A little of the tension eased away from her body. "I guess."

Julian mentally wiped sweat from his parental brow. Whew. Right answer. For once.

Flinging herself forward to perch elbows on her knees, she said, "I have an interview with somebody for community service tomorrow. What do you think it will be? My friend Aida is working at a museum. That would be so boring I'd want to kill myself."

Aida was one of the friends Portia had gotten in trouble with, the anorexic daughter of a pop star. "It's hard to imagine her in a museum. What is she doing?"

"She says she's giving tours, but I think she's cleaning bathrooms." Portia made a face. "Gross. Will I have to do something like that?"

He knew a lot of people who'd had to spend time in community service, mostly for drinking-and-driving offenses. Portia had a lot of hours to work off. "It seems like there are a lot of jobs out there, kiddo. My suggestion is to think of something you wouldn't mind doing as a volunteer, then see if they have anything like that."

"Like what? They probably don't have anything to do with fashion."

"Probably not." He thought a minute. "Something with animals? Maybe skiing? God knows there's plenty of skiing here."

"Get off the skiing, Dad. I'm not going to ski. It makes your thighs fat."

"Muscular," he corrected, but raised a hand to stop the

argument before it continued. He'd chosen Aspen in particular because he believed she could not live here when the slopes were open and continue to resist the lure. "Okay. Animals, then."

"I'll think about it. Can I get on the Internet?"

He grinned and passed the laptop over to her. She was only allowed access to the Internet through this laptop, and only in his company. She probably did go to Internet cafés, but that was limited access, too, so he looked the other way. "All you had to do was ask."

"This is stupid, too, you know," she said, flipping open the laptop.

"Probably." He doodled circles on his page. In one, he wrote, *sorrow*.

"You don't have time for this, to monitor my every move. You have movies to make. People to see."

He grinned without looking up from the page, and drew a line between two circles. *Descent,* he wrote into the second circle.

"Are you working on a new movie now?"

"Sort of. It's not going that well."

She tapped something into the keyboard and waited, her poreless skin bathed with blue-white light. "You want my opinion, slasher pics are overdone."

"That would be my opinion, too, kid, but that's what they want."

"Life is short, Dad. Maybe you should make the movie you want to make."

He grunted, thinking of the mountains of responsibilities that surrounded him, not the least of which was this child. Slasher flicks seemed to satisfy something in the public right now. Maybe a reaction to the war, and he couldn't completely ignore that.

As he gazed at his daughter, however, he realized where his resistance lay. He didn't want to make a movie about fresh young women being preyed upon by twisted bad guys.

Huh.

"What?" she asked him.

He shook his head. "Maybe you're right. I'll think about it."

"Werewolves," she said without looking away from the screen. "I like werewolves."

He chuckled. "Of course you do."

On Thursday, Elena set out her *mise en place* for the meal she would prepare for her new boss. She had to move a stack of cookbooks off the counter to the floor—big, heavy books she'd checked out of the library for brainstorming purposes—and set out the pork and onions, the cutting board and her exquisitely sharp and expensive knives, carrots and celery and herbs for a vegetable stock.

Light fell through the window, a round pale spill like a moon on the counter. Elena tied back her hair. Into the CD player went Norah Jones, soft and smoky and easy to sing along with, and she rolled up her sleeves to start cooking. There was something about this kitchen that made her think of home ec classes in junior high.

Chopping carrots into perfect rounds, she let her mind drift there. Back to school, which had bored her to death for the most part. The chalky sameness, the too-easy sums and the dense questions asked by students over and over again. Whenever the priests spoke of original sin and all the evil that had come into the world because of Eve, Elena thought of school.

But junior high threw a beautiful curve—she walked into home economics the first day and *swooned* over the tiny kitchens with their individual stoves and fridges and sinks. Isobel took shop, metals and wood, scorning the traditional female pastime of cooking, but Elena was in heaven. She loved the cabinets stocked with cookie sheets and casserole dishes, the drawers full of matching flatware, the cupboards with matched sets of Corning Ware that didn't break. Every tool imaginable was there, too—whisks and wooden spoons; spatulas and graters; measuring cups in metal *and* glass. The knives and thermometers were checked out of a big locked cabinet, and more than once they had to wait while the knives were counted at the end of a period.

In that tidy world, she learned the alchemy of a white sauce, browning the flour just so in clear butter—"Very slowly, girls!" shouted Mrs. Mascarenas. "You don't want it to burn!"—to make a roux. Then adding milk for a sauce, more milk for a gravy. Elena played with it, delighted by the way it could hold so many different flavors so easily, an envelope filled with cheese or onions or beef stock. Magic! She discovered that changing the butter to lard or bacon fat could make it heartier, that too much flour defeated the flavors and made anything taste dusty, that she could use the same ideas and make a satiny broth.

Twenty years later, her kitchen in the condo reminded her of that long-ago home ec room, the well-stocked smallness, the clean and orderly elegance of it. No poverty had ever wafted through these rooms, that was for sure.

Alvin strolled out to the backyard and lay down in the sun, his red-gold coat glittering, his big black nose lifting to the sky, perhaps scenting the change that blew in from the north, the possibility of autumn lurking up the pass.

Humming along with Norah, Elena poured olive oil into a heavy pot, and when it warmed, she dropped in three cloves of garlic sliced lengthwise into three or four pieces each. When the garlic was slightly tender, the flavor steeped into the oil, she dropped a thick chunk of pork shoulder into the pot and seared the meat on both sides, then scattered the chopped vegetables over it, covered it with water, and left it to stew.

The familiar, homey smell filled the air, coaxed knots of tension from her shoulders, lending enough comfort that she could carry her cell phone outside to the patio that looked south. The potted marigolds she'd picked up at the grocery store, and the geranium she had carried all over the world, were perking up in the warm sunshine. She poked a finger into the soil, taking cheer from the yellow and orange and magenta faces.

Hmm. Maybe marigolds would be a pretty garnish for the plates at the restaurant. The idea carried enough frisson that she found her notebook and wrote it down.

Marigolds. Mary's gold. The flowers of the dead.

Holding her phone in her hand, she looked south, toward the hard, high blue ridges of mountains. Over those peaks, a few hundred miles as the crow flew, was Espanola, a sullen and sun-bled town just north of Santa Fe where what remained of her family still lived.

Settling at the picnic table, Elena looked at the lush green slopes around her, slopes that would be covered in snow and humans this winter, and dialed the number for her adopted mother's house. Maria Elena lived alone these days, sometimes caring for one grandchild or another, wearing her stretch pants and the crisp striped shirts that hid her round little bowling ball of a tummy. She answered on the fourth ring, sounding rushed. "*Hola!*"

"Hey, Mama. Are you busy?"

"Elena!" she said. The surprised joy made Elena run a thumbnail down her thigh. "Never too busy for you, *m'ija*. What are you up to?"

"I don't have long to talk, Ma, but I just wanted you to know that I moved and I'm in Colorado." She said the last with a happy rise at the end of her words.

"You moved. What about your man there in Canada?"

"We broke up. I told you that already."

"You give up too easy, Elena." She tsked. "That's why you're not married still."

"He gave up on me, and I don't want to talk about it." She peered at the split ends on a lock of hair. "How're my sisters?"

"Margaret keeps on getting fatter and fatter, you know. Julia's got her grandkids with her this week, and Rose is just working away. She's started teaching. We're so proud of her!"

Rose, three years younger than Elena, had gone to college to study nursing, and married another nurse. They lived outside Santa Fe in a nice house with three nice kids. "Tell her I said hi."

"You could call her yourself."

"I will," Elena said, though she wouldn't. There were always such vast silences in their conversations, the vast quiet of two dead siblings between them.

"Where in Colorado are you?"

"Aspen."

"Ooooh." The word was layered with meaning. "You working there?"

"Yeah." Mama never seemed to grasp the layers of kitchens, the line cooks and prep cooks and sous chefs. They were all just cooks to her, but Elena said it anyway, "I'm the executive chef of a new restaurant. The boss of everybody." She plucked some lint from the knee of her jeans. "And you know, it takes a lot to get a restaurant going, of course, so it might be a while before I could come see you."

"Sure, sure."

The familiar silence fell between them. Elena hadn't been home in three years, and that visit had been for one day at Thanksgiving. Like conversations with her sisters, visits home were laden with unspoken losses. But she loved Maria Elena and didn't want to neglect her. This was the way they'd worked it out, over time. "I'll call you, Mama."

"Okay. Be good, *m'ija*."

After she hung up, Elena sat on the table, feet on the bench seat like a teenager, the phone in her left hand. Restlessness crawled down her crooked spine, burned in her shattered hip.

Isobel settled next to her on the bench, her long hair shiny in the sunlight. Tipping her face up to the sun, she closed her eyes. "She doesn't mean anything with the man stuff. It's just what she knows."

"I know." Elena wiggled her shoulders to loosen the tension there, thinking of the town, surly and squinting on the edge of the desert. "I should visit her, I know I should. I just can't breathe when I think of it."

"She's seventy-six."

"I know."

On the lawn, Alvin growled softly, hair on the back of his neck lifting a little. "Shh," Elena said, and rubbed her foot over his back to soothe him.

"Careful of Ivan," Isobel said.

"Duh." In her imagination, his face rose, the thin back with its vining tattoo. Defensively dangerous, like a dog who had been starved and beaten in a backyard.

Rubbing the sole of her foot over the fur of her own beautiful dog, she resolutely did not acknowledge the burn in her hip, and thought instead that she needed to get some walking routes mapped out, or the broken places in her body were going to freeze solid. Stiffness and dull pain radiated from the hip joint, upward and through her belly. The drive had been too long.

Just a little longer, she said, to the fates who had overlooked her that long-ago night. *Just let me make my mark and then the body can fall apart.*

EIGHT

Mayan Hot Chocolate

6 cups milk
1 mild green chile, roasted, skinned, and chopped
½ vanilla bean, cut in half lengthwise
½ cup granulated raw sugar
3 oz. Mexican-style chocolate, coarsely chopped
1 tsp cinnamon
pinch salt
2 eggs
Stick cinnamon

Measure fresh cold milk into a heavy saucepan, and stir in the chile. Scrape the vanilla bean into the milk and break up the pod. Add sugar, chocolate, cinnamon, and salt. Heat over medium heat until the chocolate melts and the milk is steaming hot, but not boiling. Remove from the heat and strain, then pour it back into the saucepan.

Beat the eggs in a mixing bowl. Stir one cup of the hot milk mixture into the eggs and stir vigorously, then pour the milk-egg mixture back into the saucepan and beat with a whip or *molinillo* until it's as foamy as a bubble bath. Pour into hefty mugs and garnish with cinnamon sticks. An excellent seduction drink.

NINE

Julian arrived at five minutes after seven. Although they had spoken several times via email and by phone, Elena hadn't seen him since the morning in Vancouver when he'd offered her the job.

Before he showed up, Alvin paced the apartment with his mistress, psychic as always as she changed clothes three times, trying to decide whether she should be crisply businesslike, or friendly and female, or relaxed and earthy. She wished the apartment were more settled, that she had a sense of who Julian Liswood was, apart from being a really rich guy who was also her boss. That would make anyone nervous.

First she tried a white blouse and black slacks, and her favorite cheery chile pepper apron, her hair drawn out of sight into a braid. It looked so . . . severe.

She traded the girl-cook look for a yellow sundress with a thin white scarf, thinking to be a little arty, but that just looked like she was trying too hard to be French and cosmopolitan. And flirty. Finally, she ditched the dress and donned a turquoise T-shirt with a thin white sweater over it, and jeans. Earrings of silver, hair loose on her shoulders.

Voilà! Elena.

She and Alvin paced some more. She was too early. Picking up the phone, she punched in Mia's number and got her voice mail—but of course it was quite late in London. "I'm totally nervous," she said. "Julian is coming for dinner and I want to be brilliant." She paused, imagining what Mia would say. "You're right, I should just be myself, be friendly, use good manners. I can do that. Thanks." Grinning, she hung up the phone, then impulsively dialed it again. "I really can't wait for you to get here."

Alvin suddenly jumped up and barked an alert. Elena took a breath, brushed a hand over her shirt. Alvin rushed to the door with her, one floppy black ear cocked, his eyes on her face, then the door: *Is this what we've been waiting for?*

She opened the door. There stood Julian, so elegantly hip in black jeans and a very thin linen shirt woven in tiny turquoise and lavender and green stripes that hung with casual artistry from his shoulders. They were wearing the same colors.

For a single frozen moment, she felt so nervous she couldn't think of what to do next. He was so much more beautiful than she had allowed herself to remember, with a big armful of flowers in pink and orange, his eyes black and bottomless as he stood there against a peach sky—the prince arriving at the peasant daughter's house.

And in that moment, as his eyes burned into her, touching her mouth as he bowed only slightly ironically, she saw that he'd thought about her, had spun visions of her in idle moments. "Hello, Elena. You look well."

"Um. So do you. Come in." She kept her eye on Alvin to see how he would react, and at first, it wasn't very clear. Putting a hand on Julian's arm, she said, "Alvin, this is my friend."

Julian, obviously a dog person, held his hand out, palm down. "Hey, Alvin," he said in a low, easy voice. Alvin snuffled his hand, his wrist, the outside seam of his pants, then gave a whuffling sniff and slowly wagged his tail. Julian raised his hand to brush it over Alvin's silky, fluffy head. "Yeah, there you go," he murmured. "You're a good dog, aren't you?"

"Okay, Alvin, that's enough. Thank you. Go lie down."

With a final snort, her dog pranced over to the kitchen and waited for them. Elena let go of a breath. "I never know who he'll love and who he'll hate. Looks like you're on the approved list."

Julian laughed. "He's gorgeous. I can see why you're so fond of him."

"Thanks."

"He looks like an orange bear."

"Yes. The vet told me that he'd seen a lot of dogs named Bear, but Alvin was the first one he thought should really be called that."

"Ah, these are for you," he said, offering the flowers— tiger lilies and cannas and roses, all shades of peach and pink and orange.

"The colors of El Día de los Muertos."

"Are they?"

She nodded, smiling. "Thank you."

"I brought wine, but I didn't know what you'd need for tonight, so don't feel that you have to open this one."

Waving him into the kitchen, Elena said, "I hope you don't mind if we eat at the kitchen table. It's the most comfortable spot."

"That's fine. Smells good."

She inhaled the chile and pork aroma, the hint of chocolate hanging like a whisper in the air. The round table was nestled under the window, covered with a red woven cloth from Ecuador. She'd set it with simple things, shallow white bowls and white napkins and fat white candles on a red and orange saucer she'd found years ago at a thrift store. "Do you want a beer?"

"Please."

Settling the flowers on the counter for a moment, she opened the fridge to fish out two bottles of Dos Equis. "I like wine, too," she said, "but beer is better with a meal like this." Opening both bottles, she handed him one, and toasted, "To our venture, Mr. Liswood."

"To our venture," he echoed, and drank a modest sip. "But you've got to stop calling me Mr. Liswood. It's Julian."

"I'll try." Gesturing for him to sit on a stool, Elena settled on the other side of the granite countertop. It was cold on her elbows. "Thanks for arranging for the condo. It's perfect."

"You might change your mind when the whole complex fills with skiers every weekend. But I thought you'd like the kitchen."

"Absolutely." In the background played Matt Skellenger,

jazz bassist, invigorating but not too intrusive. On the stove, the soup simmered, a sound Elena sometimes dreamed about. "Did your daughter arrive safely?"

"She's here under duress," he said. "But she's here." He sipped the beer. "Let's talk about you, Elena. Tell me what you thought of the building."

"I made some notes." She grabbed her notebook and ran through her initial impressions, touched on some of the ideas she had for remodeling, and listed the most urgent expenditures. "Also, I met Ivan."

His body loosened. "Ah."

"He'd crashed in the staff room and smelled of three weeks' hard drinking, but he did assure me that he was the best chef that ever lived."

Julian grinned. "And?"

"I said that would be impossible because I am the best."

His laughter was as bright as poppies. "That's why I hired you. Chutzpah." He sipped the beer, and rubbed his belly. "Let's eat, shall we? That smells so good my stomach is growling."

Elena jumped up, suddenly embarrassed. "Sorry. Of course. We can talk and eat. I don't know what I was thinking."

His hand closed around her wrist. "Don't," he said.

"Don't what?"

"Flutter. Worry, start the servant-master thing. I hate it."

Trouble bloomed right there, the two of them standing too close with the smell of Elena's posole heating the air. She saw the faded scars of childhood acne on his lean cheeks, faint now, but once not so. She saw the weary thinness of the skin beneath his eyes and the creases along his mouth. He was older than she by more than a decade. He'd been through three wives, one of them twice. She caught a sharp taste of sour cream and potatoes—latkes, was that what they were?—Jewish food. Of course.

In his turn, his eyes showed nothing, only that liquid blackness, focused on her face.

"Where did you grow up?" Elena asked him, moving away.

"New Jersey."

"Really? You don't have that accent."

"We moved to Pasadena when I was twelve."

She flashed a smile over her shoulder. "And you fell in love with movies."

"I bet you read that in a magazine."

"Maybe." She ladled the stew into the bowls, and garnished them very simply with tiny rings of fresh scallion and bright red minced tomatoes and just one strip of chile, roasted and spun into a ring. She carried them to the table.

Julian bent into the bowl. "Beautiful," he said, inhaling.

"One more thing." She fetched a tortilla warmer and carried it with an oven mitt to the table, then settled across from him.

He rested his wrists against the edge of the table. "Tell me about this soup, Chef."

She sipped her beer without hurry. "Pork posole, a New Mexico stew, served with fresh corn tortillas."

"And this is your favorite meal?"

"Well, comfort food, yes. Made from my grandmother's recipe."

"Very pretty." He bent over his bowl and inhaled the steam, evaluating it. Then he picked up his spoon and dipped it into the stew and took a bite, his eyes on the bowl. Elena noticed the high bridge of his nose, the way the hair at his crown shone against the light. "Oh yeah," he said, and bent into it again, taking a more generous bite this time, looking at the ingredients in his spoon for a moment. Nodding, he pronounced it *"Very* good."

She nudged the dish of corn tortillas toward him. "Try one. Homemade."

"Also Grandmother's recipe?"

"Well, not exactly." She pointed to the masa on the counter. "Add water and cook. The hard part is getting the shape. Took me years to master it." She took one out and examined it, smooth and supple, then tore out a hunk to make a cup, and dipped it into the stew. It was her first real bite, not counting the samples tasted while cooking.

—tender explosion of salty broth, subtle sharpness of sweet chiles, pungency of onions and plenty of garlic, and the smooth texture of hominy and the grainy pleasure of fresh corn tortilla—

She closed her eyes. "Perfect."

It was a recipe that never failed. Julian tucked it away with gusto, proving the rule, and Elena relaxed a little. She ate without speaking, enjoying the moment—the fat candles burning, the light fading over the mountains outside the windows, music playing quietly.

His hands were long and graceful as he imitated Elena's method of tearing strips of tortilla, then dropping them into the soup, as if they were crackers. "This," he said distinctly at the bottom of the bowl, "is delicious, Elena."

"Would you like some more?"

He held up a hand. "In a moment, perhaps."

Perhaps. Who said "perhaps"? She smiled. "Take your time. There's plenty."

He took a long, healthy swallow of beer. "Did your grandmother teach you to cook?"

"She did." It was complicated, her story of cooking, so she said, "But we have to talk about you until I finish eating."

"I don't know how to cook," he said, settling comfortably. "No one bothered to teach me. It was assumed a wife would do it for me."

"Shocking."

He inclined his head. "Traditional. After my mother died, my father and I subsisted on Hamburger Helper and Swanson's."

"You could teach yourself to cook."

He gave Elena the smallest, most appealing little twist of his lips. "I buy restaurants instead."

She laughed. "Interesting choice."

"Money allows a lot of interesting choices."

"It does," she agreed, thinking of her own salary, which, even before she'd taken this position, had been quite good for a woman on her own. One of her early bosses had been a financial consultant in his real life, and had shown Elena how to draw up a budget and stick to it, how to invest in retirement accounts, how to build a credit rating—all things no one in her working-class world had thought to tell a child, especially a girl. The security was no small thing for a woman whose body might give out at any time. "Not that I'm in your league, of course."

"Well, not to be arrogant, but not many are. I got lucky."

"Talent might have had something to do with it."

A shrug, not diffident, just sure. "A lot of talented people don't make money. I was in the right place at the right time."

Elena inclined her head. "It's more than luck."

His black eyes, so hard to read without the marker of a pupil, were direct as he said, "My dad drove a truck."

"Mine worked at the post office. My adopted father, anyway." She paused to drink some beer, let the food settle. She could sometimes be a pig, eating more than she needed, but over time, she'd learned to take breaks. The soup spread its good cheer through her body. "This really is my comfort food," she said, and sighed. "It's grounding, after a big change."

"Maybe it should be one of the menu options."

"You read my mind. But let's not talk about that yet. Tell me more about yourself, Julian. What was your comfort food when you were a child? If I'd asked you the same question—and given an ability to cook—what would you have made for me?"

"Potato latkes," he said without a moment's hesitation. "With sour cream and applesauce, hot off the stove."

Elena was careful not to smile in satisfaction. "Is your mother Jewish?"

"My father was. My mother was Italian. She's been gone a long time."

"I'm sorry."

"Her death was the reason we moved to LA. My father couldn't bear it. And you know, he never did marry again."

"That's sad."

"Or touching. She was his soul mate, and despite everything, they had to be with each other. It wasn't easy, the Italian and the Jew, in our old Jersey neighborhood."

A hollowness moved in her chest. "Do you believe in that? Soul mates?"

"I don't know. It's hard, in the modern world." His mouth turned wry. "And, well, I've been divorced four times."

"Ah. *Serial* soul mates."

He laughed. "Is that the voice of experience?"

"Oh, I've had lots of soul mates. Souls mating for an hour or two." The words sounded bitter, and she gave him a glance under her lashes to soften it. From nowhere rose a memory of Dmitri, curling around her, his lips pressing into her spine, his sex nudging her flesh. She turned the beer bottle in a precise little circle. "Once or twice," she said more quietly, "I believed in it."

"And your parents?" He picked up a tortilla, rolled it into a tube between long fingers. "Was their marriage happy?"

"No. My father died in Vietnam before I was born, and my mother was a party girl. My father's family adopted me when I was eight, but they were Catholic, and married for life." She lifted a shoulder, thinking of Maria Elena and Porfino, of his sullen silences, the red sharpness of the ignoring, the bristling heat of their union. "Not quite the same thing as a soul mate."

"Cynical."

"Maybe." Elena wanted to sigh. Roll her eyes. She wanted to say, *I'm thirty-eight years old and have had six major relationships, and at some point, I believed each time that* this *time we would bond forever.* Instead she gave him a practiced, easy smile to lighten the mood. "Restaurants are not the place to be if you want to focus on relationships, you know? Sometimes, you make a trade for work you love."

"I'm in a business like that myself." His face was sober. For a quiet moment, there were ghosts crowding the room, his and hers, possibilities that had once shimmered and had then tarnished. Elena felt the prickling of his hunger, as deep as her own, and tried to brush it from her knowledge.

"I'd like this to be the house soup," Elena said to chase the ghosts away.

"One of them. Yes. What else have you come up with? Any ideas?"

"Yes," she said. "Let me serve the chocolate and I'll show you my notes."

Julian bent over his cup of chocolate and inhaled. It smelled of cinnamon and chile. As he sipped it—slowly, as if it were a powerful alcohol that would make him lose his head—he felt as if he unzipped the outside layers of artifice and masks and walked out of them, unencumbered in his own skin. Elena's face captured him, plain and exotic at once, her long eyes and a mouth like some creature from a fairy tale, a mouth to seduce, red and soft and lush; her skin which could be sallow, he guessed, and the shadows below her eyes that would show exhaustion too easily.

They talked about the menu, about parameters and ingredients and philosophy. "Food should be beautiful, fresh, and wholesome." She held out a hand, palm cupping something luscious and invisible. "Sensual."

He nodded, listening.

"I want to go with my roots, with southwestern cuisine. Authentic, but high-end." She leaned on the table earnestly. "I think we can go bright and smart and sexy and authentic."

"I think so."

She inclined her head. "I also want to go with as much organic food as possible. It makes it more expensive, and it's not always possible, but making the attempt is worth it."

"I have no problem with that."

"Good."

"Have you come up with ideas for menu items?"

"A few, but I'd like to bring Ivan into the process, so he feels included. Patrick and Mia will be here this weekend, and we can all brainstorm a menu together."

He felt he could sit here for a year, never moving, letting her spiced hot chocolate, cinnamon and chile laced through it like a love spell, fill his belly. Finally he gave a nod. "Good." He roused himself, thought of his daughter who should not be left unsupervised for long stretches. "I've got to get back to my daughter, but I'll be at the meeting tomorrow. Is it two p.m.?"

"Right," she said, standing up. "I'm meeting the kitchen staff then, but I'd like you to come a little later if you don't mind. Give me an hour alone with them first."

"Absolutely." He shook down his sleeves, pleased. "How about three-thirty?"

"Perfect."

"When will your people be here?"

"Patrick is supposed to be here in the morning. He called from Denver this afternoon. Mia should be here by Sunday." She sighed a little.

"Trouble?"

"Not really. I wanted to have my allies with me tomorrow, but Mia's coming from the UK and couldn't get here that fast. Patrick is—" She paused. "He's generally reliable, but he's been in an on-again, off-again relationship with someone and it was on again all week. His lover can't decide whether he wants to come to Aspen or not."

"Is the lover a restaurant person?"

She frowned slightly. "He is, but I hope he doesn't come. He's brilliant, and I'd offer him work if he shows up, but he's difficult and demanding and maybe more of a headache than I'd care for just now."

"And tell me about Mia."

"Pastry chef. Seriously talented." She gave him a grin. "Sometimes a little unpredictable—not once she gets here, but knowing when she'll actually arrive. She could be here tonight, or three weeks from now."

"I trust you. Email me a copy of your notes, will you?"

"Yes." Elena walked him to the door. Alvin jumped up and trotted over, his tail wagging.

Julian bent and scrubbed Alvin's ears, reached lower and scratched his chest. "God, he's just gorgeous." He straightened, gave Elena a crooked smile. "What if we call the restaurant the Orange Bear?"

Pleasure blazed over her face, making it beautiful for a moment. "Oh, yes! I love that. You hear that, baby? You're going to be famous!"

Alvin sat down abruptly and leaned on Julian's leg. He chuckled. "Suck-up," he said. Then, "Excellent work, Elena. I look forward to seeing you tomorrow."

"Thanks. Me too."

For a moment, he lingered, reluctant to leave the ease of the room. She eyed his torso. "You must be a runner."

His mouth quirked. "Skinny, I know."

"Are you fast?"

"Some days. Some days not. My daughter is the athlete."

"She runs?"

"Skis." He pulled out a wallet photo and showed her a photo of a very pretty blonde teenager in pink ski clothes. "She's been a natural on the slopes since she was four."

"Gorgeous. She really looks like her mother."

Who was Ricki Alsatian, the actress who won the Academy Award for her role in *Power*. She got her start in Julian's early films, usually playing the nubile babe who survived the horror. "She does," Julian said. "That's actually causing some trouble between them. I don't think Ricki likes it much. She loves Portia but it's hard enough to be an actress past forty, and that much harder to see your youth reflected back to you."

Elena's face stilled, and Julian sensed her holding her tongue. Barely. She handed the photo back to him.

He held the picture in his fingers for a moment. "She's only fourteen. I've gotta figure out something to keep her from—" he lifted a shoulder, "going in the wrong direction. She's lost."

"So has she been skiing in recent years?"

"Yeah. Until a year or two ago, she was very focused on

the goal of becoming an Olympian." Tucking the photo back into his wallet, he gave her a wry smile. "Here's the trouble—skiers have very muscular thighs."

"Oh, God."

"I know. It's crazy, but she's also been living in a pretty crazy world where a size six is kind of getting up there. I'm hoping if she's here in the skiing world, it'll counteract some of the LA bullshit."

"Good for you."

"We'll see how it goes." He tipped his fingers to his brow. "See you tomorrow."

TEN

FROM ELENA'S NOTEBOOK

INGREDIENTS LIST
Organic pork and chicken
Organic beef
Game meats: duck, venison, elk, pheasant
Chiles, lots of different kinds; green and red. Chimayos and
    Anaheims, anchos, etc.
Cornmeal, blue and yellow, but not corn
Goat and sheep cheeses
Nuts—piñon and pistachios (maybe cashews? almonds?)
Tree fruits—apples, peaches, plums, pears
Citrus—orange, lemon, lime, grapefruit
Squashes, of course, pumpkins, zucchinis, yellow, calabacitas
Onions, tomatoes, garlic, avocados, mangoes, tomatillos
Chocolate, bitter and sweet
Tamales as a cornerstone? What can we do with tamales?
    (everything!)
Garnishes: whole pinto beans, marigolds, spinach leaves?

ELEVEN

Elena lay on her bed an hour later, amid a pile of Post-it notes and cookbooks, pages open to glossy photos of food. There was a glass of Italian red wine at her elbow, a rerun of *The Sopranos* on cable, a notebook on her lap.

She thought of Julian and the restaurant and her menu. Mostly about Julian, who had more heat and salt coming from him than she had anticipated. Her skin prickled as she imagined his black eyes, his long-fingered white hands, his liquid grace.

Men, she thought with a sigh. She was such a weak and flawed woman. She knew that. She was fond of sugar and wine and too much coffee, which made her heart rush. She liked sex and the malty smell of it lingering on her thighs. She liked men, nearly all of them, for all kinds of reasons. She liked Tony Soprano's big belly and big nose because he was such a mix of dichotomies—a murdering gangster who could pat a cheek and shred her heart. Men like him made her want to cook, to feed them, to lie down with them and put their heads on her breasts.

Not only the big, lost boys, of course. She liked Lance Armstrong's hard muscles and Morgan Freeman's freckled nose and Lorenzo Lamas's bad-boy grin and Naveen Andrews and—

Well. *Men.*

Alvin snored loudly at her feet, curled up like a kitten, his feathery gold tail protecting his stuffed crocodile. In the notebook on her lap, she lazily drew connections between notes, letting the shape, the colors, the textures of the menu rise in her mind. Blue tortillas and yellow cornmeal, red tomatoes and sweet orange peppers. Purplish duck and white pork and the thick reddish brown of chocolate and cinnamon. Chiles, of course, and roasted vegetables for those cold winter nights. It should be hearty food to nourish skiers, with a handful of lighter offerings for the skinny crowd. For spring, they would shift the menu somewhat, but for now, she would focus on winter food.

Julian had asked her what her *philosophy* of food was. She'd always imagined it would be a delight to uncover and express that, but instead, she was finding it terrifying to take a stand, develop a particular and notable vision—it could go either way. Soar or sink. Fly or flop.

And yet, if she sat on the fence, offering lukewarm retreads of other people's ideas, she would fail without question.

Food. *Her* food.

The fingerprint of a chef was born in childhood. She remembered drinking red Nehi soda and eating potato chips on the concrete back step of her Uncle George's store on a hot day, the sky as cloudless and plain as a piece of turquoise plastic. She thought of women cooking tamales in somebody's kitchen, the ripe smell of simmering pork and red Chimayo chile filling the air. Her Aunt Viola's tender, pale yellow cake with sprinkles of shredded coconut stuck to the frosting. Watermelon straight out of somebody's field, hot and sweet and thirst-quenching like nothing else in the world. Hot dogs roasted on a barbecue with little black lines of crackly skin.

She narrowed her eyes, sketching chiles and tomatoes and pigs along the edge of the page. Tamales were hearty, and the structure made it possible to put almost anything inside. Duck? Venison? Peaches? A swirl of flavors rose against the roof of her mouth, a depth of dark sour cherry, the smoky gaminess of fowl, tender roasted onions.

Rubbing her foot over Alvin's silky back, she felt excitement in her throat, her sinuses. *What if, what if, what if?* There would be challenges, of course, in working with the new staff, but those could be surmounted, surely. Even Ivan, with his Rasputin face, didn't scare her. If Julian believed in him, then Elena would give him the benefit of the doubt. Perhaps they would create some magic.

The sudden trilling of her cell phone was startling, even more so when she realized it was the European double ring she'd assigned to Dmitri. Dismaying how the sound rushed through the cupboards of memory and threw moments out onto the floor. Some good. Some bad.

She debated over whether to answer. She had not really had time to build up her defenses against him. No good could come of it.

Except, perhaps, revenge. She was no longer sous chef to the dashing Dmitri Nadirov, but an executive chef in her own right, with a menu in motion and a restaurant to command. Flinging her hair back out of her face, she punched the button. "Hello, Dmitri."

"Elena!" His thickly accented Russian voice poured through the line.

She waited. It was a good trick with men who expected women to carry the conversation, one she'd learned from a cook early in her career. *Let them talk,* she said. *You'll learn a lot more.*

"How are you?" he asked.

"I'm well, thanks."

A string of featureless seconds built between them. He cleared his throat. "I am calling to apologize, Elena. I was rash when I fired you."

Aha. "It was time, Dmitri. We knew we shouldn't get involved, that it would mean one or the other of us would have to leave the restaurant when we split. It's fine."

"We are professionals, surely. The Blue Turtle belongs to you as much as to me."

"Which is something you only say when you've been an asshole."

"Perhaps that is true. I am an asshole. It is the nature of the job." He paused. The sweet, sweet flavor of triumph filled her mouth as she anticipated the next words. "I need you here."

"I found another position, Dmitri."

"What? Where? I have not heard that! Are you working for that pig Gaston Mitter?"

Gaston was a giant of a chef, known for tantrums and spectacular food. "No," Elena answered with a snort, and let their breath fill the line. "I'm working for Julian Liswood. In Aspen."

A three-second pause. "Aspen. He has a restaurant in Aspen?"

She smiled. "Not yet."

"Who is the chef?"

"Dmitri," she said quietly. Chiding. "Who do you *suppose* it is?"

"You?" His shock was insulting. Surprisingly stinging.

"Yes," she said. "Me. He offered me the job five minutes after you fired me. I'm sitting here in my new apartment in *Aspen,* and I'll be meeting with my staff tomorrow."

He cursed bloodily, filthily.

"You fired me," she said.

"But you knew I would come back to you."

Her anger billowed into a fire. "You are not God, Dmitri, and I am not one of your subjects, to come crawling back every time you decide to forgive me for whatever imagined sin I've committed."

"Elena, you are the only one who understands me. You've always been the only one."

"No," she said wearily, closing her eyes. That was how he seduced her, every time, making her feel as if there were not another woman in the world who understood him. Only Elena. A *soul mate.* The lining at the top of her stomach burned. "I'm done, Dmitri. Please don't call me again." She hung up.

And yet, in the silence, she felt stung and lost. For a moment, her head was filled with the memory of his mouth, of his thick, skilled tongue and elegant fingers, splaying her like a succulent fish. The man was a lover, lusty, focused, sensual. He could make sex last two hours. Three. For a time, he had been her home.

She took a long breath. Let it go.

He had been her home. And now, he was not.

At two o'clock the following afternoon, Elena met with her staff for the first time. Patrick, newly arrived and smelling of aromatic soap, walked in with her, his hand at the small of her back.

Her pinned and riddled and broken-down back.

It had been a grim morning. Maybe, she thought, it was hunching too much from turning her back on Dmitri. Maybe it was the hard work and the long drive and the stress of the past week. Maybe it was Dmitri's call and her own expectations. Or maybe it was all of it.

Whatever. Before she awakened, she'd been dreaming of Chimayo chiles, ground to a sweet and powerful powder the color of the red earth of New Mexico, dreaming that she held a small mountain of it in the palm of her hand, and pressed one finger into it, and tasted it, and there was gold like sunlight, in her throat—

And the alarm went off. She slammed into her body, a crab-self, curled and cracked, feet and hands like claws, frozen hips, stiff spine, body heavy and misshapen. Agony to move.

Lying on her side, with her eyes closed, she said aloud, "Fuck."

Over the years, she ordinarily hid at such times, crawling into a tub of hot water, or to a bottle of tequila. Shame burned her when anyone else saw her drawn up like this, like a very old woman, stooped and stiff.

This morning, she was at least alone to struggle with all

the batteredness. Spine, hips, shoulders—all protested every slight movement, as if rust had settled into each tiny bone of her back, clogged the hips and rotator cuffs and shoulder blades. The muscles were like old rubber bands.

"Alvin," she cried out, and he knew by the tone of her voice what she needed. He pranced over to the side of the bed and leaned against it. Very slowly, Elena put a hand out and used his strong body to brace herself so she could ease out of the envelope of covers, one inch at a time. He was patient, happy to have a job to do to serve his beloved.

It nearly always brought tears to her eyes. How had she lived so long without a dog? *This* dog.

Easing into a squatting position, she stretched the lower spine, not a pain-free process. She used yoga breathing to get through it, to the point where she could actually stand. From there, she hobbled into the bathroom and ran very hot water in the Jacuzzi bathtub. Alvin trotted along beside her, looking up worriedly.

"It's all right, honey," she said, gratefully.

The tub proved to be too tall to climb into. She tried. Up two steps, brace herself on the side, lift the leg—

No way. Feeling ninety, she pulled a big purple towel off the rack, wrapped herself in it, and sat down on the step. Alvin stuck with her, leaning on her shin.

No tears, she told herself, gritting her teeth.

Gathering resources, she ran her fingers through Alvin's long fur, tugged on the velvety black ears, and tried to figure out what to do next. She had the meeting this afternoon, the first with her new staff, and she had to be able to put a good foot forward.

A shower. It wasn't as therapeutic as the hot water in a

bathtub, but the warmth would help a little, and this was a high-end shower with a bench and jets that came out of the wall every which way. Half bent over, unable to completely straighten, she turned it on.

There was a little plaque of instructions on the wall. *To Operate Mr. Steam*, it began, *turn the nozzle below to the right and wait.*

Steam?

Elena followed directions. From behind the walls came the gurgling sound of water boiling. After a minute, jets of steam came from the nozzles, filling the glassed-in space perfectly. A light above the stall gave it a cheery aspect, and she hobbled in, pulled the glass door closed behind her, and settled on the bench.

Nirvana.

By the time she emerged, her joints were still a bit stiff, but functional. She wanted to send Julian Liswood a love poem.

Patrick arrived just before lunch, driving a black BMW convertible he'd rented in Denver. "It suits you," Elena said, capturing her hair in her fist so it wouldn't end up with a thousand tiny knots.

He tipped his head without an ounce of deference. "I know."

She laughed softly. The wayward child of American Irish Catholic royalty, Patrick's breeding showed in his meticulous grooming. His blond hair was mussed and gelled exactly, his skin as clean and poreless as a child's, his nose always just a little in the air. He made Elena think of the prized cocks she used to see at the county fair, spoiled and beautifully feathered. Boston raised, Paris trained, New

York tested—he was the best of the best when it came to creating the atmosphere and a dining *experience* for a customer. Elena trusted him implicitly.

He didn't much care for her exuberant displays of physical affection, so instead of a big hug, she gave his arm a squeeze. "I'm so glad you're here. Mia will arrive this weekend—it'll be like old times."

"I found an apartment, a two-bedroom place over the carriage house at the back of some estate. She can rent with me if she likes."

In the blazing blue and yellow summer day, they drove the short distance to the restaurant. A knot of tourists were examining the menu. "Sorry, folks," Elena said, getting out of the car. "It's closed for now. Come back in November."

Patrick paused on the sidewalk, surveying the property. She stood beside him, giving the computer in his brain time to gather elements, get a reading on the place. His face showed no reaction as they climbed the steps to the front doors. Wordlessly, he pointed out a loose board on the step, a dead pine tree branch hanging over the porch.

On the step, she paused to put on her game face. She remembered she was a tough girl from a tough town with too many brothers and mean cousins, that she'd been trained by some of the best in the business. She'd worked her way up through the ranks, from private in the scullery to captain of the line. Now general. *Jefa*.

Patrick pulled open the door, gestured her to lead, and came behind her. Two fingers lightly fell on her spine—*I've got your back.*

And there they were, her troops. All men, which she'd expected. Ivan, the sous chef, with his Rasputin face and burning blue eyes, leaned insolently against the wall, one foot braced behind him, his arms folded over his lean belly.

"Hey, Chef," he said. Next to Elena, Patrick vibrated, tuning into the sound of that bearish voice, the voice of an orator, a serial killer. "Who's your pretty sidekick?"

Elena took off her sunglasses, not speaking as she took the case out of her purse and put the glasses away.

Ivan was dressed in a more elegant way than she would have expected, in a long-sleeved silk T-shirt and low-slung jeans.

Next to him was a dashingly handsome Mexican in his late twenties, with soft dark eyes. *"Cómo está?"* he said, dipping his head politely. North Mexico, his accent said.

"Bueno, gracias." Northern New Mexico, said Elena's. *"Cómo se llama?"*

He stepped forward politely, his dark hand splaying over his chest. *"Me llamo Juan Diego Vialpando Garcia."*

Elena smiled. A good omen that a man should have the name of the Indian peasant to whom the Virgin Mary had appeared in Mexico, where she was known as the Virgin of Guadalupe. *"Me gusto mucho."*

He gave a charming little half-bow. "It is an honor to meet you, Chef."

"Thank you."

A stocky, balding man with shrewd eyes and very expensively cut trousers stepped forward. "Chef, I'm Alan Cody, the house manager."

"Good to meet you. I've already met Rasputin there," she said, gesturing to Ivan. "Tell me about the rest of our staff."

"I'm happy to do that."

Patrick took a step closer, an elegant bodyguard.

"Everyone," Alan said, "this is Elena Alvarez. She's most recently been sous chef at the Blue Turtle in Vancouver, which is where we found her and seduced her away." He gave Elena a grin.

"I heard she was fired," Rasputin said in his dark voice.

"I was," Elena said. "A reporter did a story on my food style and Chef didn't like being upstaged. I suggest you remember that."

He raised an eyebrow but said no more.

Alan wrung his hands, but when war didn't break out, he said, "Well, of course, this is Ivan Santino. You may not know that he studied at Le Cuisine in New York, and won a James Beard award for best new chef six years ago."

"I did not know. Well done."

He inclined his head.

"Next to Ivan is Juan, whom you've just met. He's been with us for three years, and he's a master saucier."

"Among other things," Ivan said.

Alan introduced a trio of others, all young men with the look of restlessness that told her they'd not yet found their kitchens. Maybe they were ski bums, here for the access to the slopes. It was standard to offer season passes to employees, and Julian also preferred to help find housing.

These boys were exploring and gaining experience, and Aspen wasn't a bad place to do it. The youngest of the group was a pale blond with dark brown eyes who said his name, Peter, in a cheery voice. He couldn't yet be twenty-one.

"Thank you, Alan," Elena said. "I'm looking forward to working with all of you." The twinges in her lower spine started up again, and she wanted to lean or sit, but straightened the tiniest bit instead, remembering to pull her shoulder blades down her back.

Show no weakness.

Lifting her chin, she met the eyes of each man in turn. "As Alan just said, I am Elena Alvarez. I originally studied in Santa Fe, then moved to San Francisco, then spent three years in Paris, at Le Cordon Bleu. I did stints in London and New York before I returned to San Francisco, where I eventually worked my way up to a sous chef position at the Yellow Dolphin, which is one of Julian Liswood's most successful restaurants. I believe it was his first?" Elena looked to Patrick for confirmation, and caught him glaring at Ivan. He felt her gaze, recovered, and nodded.

"His first," she confirmed. "Three years ago, Chef Dmitri Nadirov and I were hired to develop the menu and open the kitchen of the Blue Turtle in Vancouver."

"What's ours going to be called?" the young Peter asked.

Elena grinned. "The Orange Bear."

"Cool," said one of the boys.

"I like it, too." She let a puddle of silence build. Establishing command. "You must have questions."

"Are we creating an entirely new menu?" Ivan asked.

"We are."

"Are you going to fire all of us?" one of the young ones asked.

"No. I'm actually only bringing in two of my own people. One is Mia Grange, a pastry chef from London, and this is Patrick Nolan, sommelier and maître d'. We studied together in Paris and worked together at the Yellow Dolphin."

"Hel-*lo*, Patrick," Ivan said, and managed to make it into a slur. Something sharp arced between them. If Patrick was a prized cock, what animal was Ivan? Slouched there against the wall, too thin and hungry, he made her think of a blue-eyed coyote.

God, he was going to be so much trouble! She hoped he would be worth it. "We have a lot of work to do before we reopen. Let's get started, shall we? You boys pull some tables together. Patrick, will you get the supplies out of the car?"

Juan stepped forward. "I will make coffee, *Jefa*."

An ally. She nodded. "Thank you."

They moved. "Ivan, will you go down the street and get some snack food? I'm sure you know the best place to get something."

"Did you really call me Rasputin?"

It bugged him and pleased him. Elena smiled. "Have you ever seen a picture of him?"

"No. History wasn't my thing in school." He stood too close, deliberately crowding her, an intimidation move that often worried women in a busy kitchen. He smelled of soap, not tequila. An improvement.

Elena took several twenties from her wallet without moving away. She leveled a gaze at him. "Get a selection of sandwiches and sweets and chips, just whatever."

"The grocery store will be cheaper and faster than any of the sandwich joints."

She glanced around the room, noted the studiously not-listening minions. "Whatever you think is best."

"Ah, hell, let's just go with something decent." He took the money. "Back in twenty."

◆ ◆ ◆

Out in the blue day, Ivan lit a cigarette as he headed for the sandwich shop. A woman with her hair swinging in a ponytail glared at him and he blew the smoke skyward. Ordinarily, he might have goaded her. He was the native here, after all, and he'd bet she wasn't. Natives were as scarce as hen's teeth, and there was a huge gulf between them and the obscenely wealthy Others, who thought it all belonged to them.

But today, his mind was on the new guy.

Chef had come in, bringing with her that air of a snow queen from some old fairy tale, with her pale hair and exotic face and the air of the tragic about her that took the heat from Ivan's anger. Behind her, taking the position of a bodyguard, protective and fierce, was a young man. The sun from the door was on him at first, blotting out details, so Ivan couldn't really see him until he moved out of the light into the room.

Something stirred, hot and orange, at the base of Ivan's spine. The queen had brought a prince with her, a prince who carried with him a fragrance of wealth and privilege, an aura of the way things should be done. Ivan, cynic of the highest measure, knew a long moment of airless surprise, stunned by his reaction. Patrick was not his type.

And yet.

Fuck, he thought, exhaling. He bent and stubbed out the cigarette in a pot filled with sand. *Fuck, fuck, fuck.* Life was hard enough these days. He didn't need another challenge. Another fall. It was a miracle he wasn't dead already. One more would probably kill him.

He would have to be careful with that one. Careful, careful, careful. He went inside the shop.

When they were all assembled around two tables shoved together, with sandwiches and coffee and soft drinks in big glasses from the bar, Elena outlined her vision of the structure of the restaurant. Alan and Patrick in charge of the front of the house, Alan as general liaison between front and back, Patrick manager of the floor staff and service questions. "I would like consultation in final decisions," Alan said.

"Consultation," she agreed, "but Patrick has final decision."

He shot a sullen look toward Ivan. "Fine."

"Ivan," she said, "tell me about the two kitchens. How does that work? What would you change?"

"I'd have to give it some thought," he said, layering tomatoes and cucumbers, goat cheese and olives on a croissant. His fingers were deft, his arrangements unstudied and beautiful, a fact she tucked away. "We've used the lower level as a restaurant, the upper as a pub, so the food choices were a little different."

Elena made notes. She wanted to have cohesiveness through both floors. The upstairs would be the pastry kitchen; downstairs, the main. Upstairs could be a warming and assembly kitchen. "How well does the dumbwaiter work?"

"Fine."

"We need a list of anything that's not working or inefficient in the kitchen as it is." She waved the pen at the trio of boys, too. "Everybody. Anything you can think of that's a pain. Obviously, we're not moving the major equipment, but what else could be better?"

They looked at each other for a while, then tentatively offered suggestions. She wrote them down. "By next week, I want everything you've thought of, all right?"

Nods.

"What's the menu?" Peter asked.

"That's what we're going to do here, brainstorm." She patted a folder filled with copies of the list of possible ingredients that she'd assembled, and a paragraph about her philosophy. "First, I'd like to get a feeling for where you all are with your own flavors. Take a second and think about the best food you've ever eaten. Alan, you want to go first?"

He narrowed his small eyes even more. "That's hard."

Elena speared a forkful of fresh spinach and tomato. "Take your time."

"Can we narrow it down? Best meat dish, maybe?"

"Sure." She wanted a feeling for what each one felt toward food. Was it a job or a passion? "But not everybody has to pick the same category."

He stared into middle space. "One thing was a trout cooked over a campfire."

Rasputin groaned, and Alan looked abashed, like a dog reprimanded by a beloved master. His eyes even looked a little moist.

Elena held up a hand. "Best is best. Go ahead, Alan."

"The other was a lobster bisque in a San Francisco diner. So creamy and rich you had to eat it in tiny, tiny bites."

Around the table they went. Barbecued pork, a chicken

masala eaten late on a foggy London night, a piece of pecan pie at a diner in Georgia.

When his turn came up, Rasputin put his sandwich down and delicately wiped his fingers. "There are three," he said. Immediately the air in the room shifted subtly, his voice filling the space like a strummed cello, priming them all for his revelation. The young cooks leaned forward. Alan took a bite of his sandwich as if he were watching a movie. Next to Elena, Patrick sat utterly still, a ripe plum in his hand, washed but not eaten.

"The first," said Rasputin, "was a duck breast roasted with wine and cherries. Those plump, hot cherries with shreds of slow-roasted, tender meat and just a hint of nutmeg . . ." He swallowed in memory, and everyone swallowed with him, mouths watering. ". . . spectacular.

"The second was a lemon cake from a bakery in Paris."

Elena allowed herself a very small smile—she'd smelled the lemon on him at their first meeting. She would get Mia on it.

"It was a very fine crumb," he continued in his rumbling voice, his hands feathery in the air. "Three weightless layers, bright pale yellow, like fresh egg yolks, and a very, very light zesty lemon icing between layers." He closed his eyes in memory. "It was like sunlight."

The table was rapt as he opened his eyes and looked at each person in turn, lingering on Patrick and Elena, telling them his story. Perhaps reeling them in. "The third was a mango, when I was twenty-two, fresh from a market on the street in Mexico. I'd never eaten one. It was big, red and yellow, and just that exact firmness, you know, like a young breast, like a boy's lower lip."

Juan ducked his head, embarrassed, muttered a curse in Spanish.

Rasputin only lifted his mouth in a bare half-smile. "I took it to the beach and sat there in the sand, peeling the skin away with my teeth, and ate it whole, the juice running down my face and hands, and I didn't even care because it tasted like that first minute you meet somebody you're going to fall in love with, that first minute when you *know*."

Even Elena was leaning forward, seduced by that sexual voice, the sensual pictures he drew, and his magnetic eyes, which were focused on her mouth, then on Patrick. Boldly.

Patrick sat without moving, his aristocratic nose cocked upward, as if trying not to smell something a little impure. His cheeks were quite red.

"Thanks, Ivan," she said, raising an eyebrow.

He blinked, lazily. "Anytime."

Flipping open the folder, she passed around her notes. "Let's get a menu together, shall we?"

TWELVE

JUAN'S CARNE EN SU JUGO

1 lb. thinly sliced bacon
1 lb. round steak or other lean cut of beef, cut into 1–2 inch strips
2 medium onions—1 chopped, 1 sliced and grilled
3–4 fresh jalapeños, washed and sliced into wheels (leave the
  seeds in)
4 cups fresh beef broth
2 cups pinto beans, cooked and drained
1 small head of cabbage, shredded
½ cup cilantro
½ cup scallions, thinly sliced
Juice of 1 large lemon
Lemons, quartered

In a heavy pot, brown the bacon and then drain it on paper towels. Put the steak and chopped onions into the pot, cooking them in the hot bacon fat and stirring for about 2–3 minutes. Put the chopped bacon back into the pot, add the jalapeños, beef broth, and beans, and let simmer for 1 hour. Taste for seasoning and add salt and pepper if needed. Add the cabbage and let the soup simmer again just until the cabbage is tender. Add cilantro, scallions, and lemon juice. Serve with grilled onions and lemon wedges on the side.

THIRTEEN

Elena dreamed of a stag, running in a field. The light was the silver gray that could signal dawn or dusk. It was a powerful creature with points she could not count and it was in danger. As it leapt over a ravine and hung—far too long—in midair, she held her breath, wanting to cry out, and she could not.

With a gasp, she startled awake into her brightly lit bedroom, her body nestled between piles of open cookbooks and scattered notes, both her own and those of her cooks. For a moment, she could not decide what had awakened her. The television played some shopping program narrated by a man with a nasally Texas twang. Rustling through the notes and cookbooks, she found the remote control and clicked the television off. The clock on the nightstand read 2:48 a.m.

Wiping the weariness from her face, she sat up and scraped the scattered notes into a pile, closed the cookbooks, and stripped her clothes off. Alvin snored in the corner, oblivious. Elena plumped up the pillows and turned off the light, taking a long breath to settle herself.

But sleep slithered away. She lay in the dark going over the lists and tasks still to be accomplished in the next four weeks. The soft opening was slated for November 2, with a grand opening to follow on the first day of ski season. They'd been working their asses off for five weeks and had four left.

Four weeks.

She turned over, dislodging with a toe a cookbook she'd left on the bed. It fell on the floor with a bang. Alvin woke up and barked a warning. "It's okay, honey. It was me."

He woofed softly, but licked his lips and fell back asleep.

Elena stared up at the skylights. Stars twinkled, and a wash of pale light came through the rectangles. The middle-of-the-night quiet made her feel absolutely alone. Banished.

She hated to sleep alone. As a little girl, she slept with her grandmother Iris, and felt utterly bereft in the big bed alone after she died. That period happily only lasted a few weeks, and Elena was plopped down in New Mexico, sleeping with Isobel and Margaret in a double bed where they fought over the covers and tangled up together on cold nights. She had slept alone in the hospital, with the sound of machines and beeps and cold loudspeakers, and wept nearly every night with loneliness for almost a year.

Get over it. Think of the restaurant. Focus on the positives.

It was coming along very well. Patrick and Alan and Julian tucked their heads together over selections of chairs and tables, tablecloths and settings. Elena insisted that the plates be plain white porcelain, the better to show off the food. Patrick pushed for glass chargers with a slight greenish cast that knocked Elena out. Alan liked bare tables for lunch, and at first wanted snowy white tablecloths for dinner, but was overruled by both Patrick and Julian, who ordered linens from Ecuador—gorgeous wovens in clear, unpolluted shades—turquoise and green and pink.

Elena, Ivan, and Juan, together with the three line cooks already in place, worked on the back of the house. A good menu had to meet several standards. The first was the demands of the customer: who would be eating this food? Sitting over endless cups of coffee, white and pink and blue sugar packets scattered over the table, they hammered out their ideal customer with Julian—an upscale skier or vacationer, mostly sophisticated and well educated about food, who spent a lot of time outdoors and a lot of time traveling.

In addition, Elena wanted the local market. She wanted the Orange Bear to be a place people came to relax after a long day, to have a date with a new lover, to create traditions for their families. If they had visitors, they would bring them to the local icon, but not just because it was famous.

Julian had grinned at her over that. "Big plans."

She shrugged. "Why dream small?"

Another standard they had to decide was cost. There were plenty of restaurants in Aspen in the high-end range, but Julian was known for creating restaurants for the creative classes—pricey but not stratospheric, which suited Elena perfectly. It gave her a lot of room to work with a variety of fresh ingredients without having to satisfy the upper echelons of the gourmet crowd. Not that Elena couldn't do it—she could. She didn't *want* to. Food should never be that serious.

Of course, cost also referred to food costs, which needed to stay below 30 percent to hit the profit margins Julian expected. As executive chef, this would be entirely Elena's realm. She had to create a menu that was flexible enough to embrace seasonal ingredients as much as possible, with dishes that would economize by drawing from the same pool of ingredients.

She was stuck with certain realities—just as it was impossible to run a bar without margaritas and martinis, she couldn't have a Mexican menu without avocados and chiles, in season or not. But they were also lucky in that much of the stock they'd require was very inexpensive. With Ivan's help, she tracked down the best suppliers in the area, and she started working with the regular drivers and staff to develop relationships. It turned out that Ivan was a native of the area and knew just about everyone. A help.

Next, the food had to be possible to prepare in a restaurant kitchen, and the menu itself cohesive. Nobody wanted just another upscale Mexican, and that was where the work came in—they had to create a menu that was Mexican in spirit, but also delivered something zesty and exciting. Elena gave copies of her ingredients list to the entire kitchen staff, stocked the kitchens, and encouraged everyone to experiment. She had one quirk: no whole corn kernels.

"No corn?" Ivan had asked. "What's more traditional than corn?"

"I don't care. I don't like the way it takes over. The texture is too much."

He raised a laconic brow. "But we can use corn*meal*. Corn *bread*."

"Yes."

"Whatever."

Some days, several dishes passed muster—taste and presentation and consistency of preparation; other days, none did. But slowly, slowly, a menu began to emerge.

The days began early, when she arrived at six, giant Starbucks latte in hand, to unlock the doors. Alvin came with her and settled on the porch outside the kitchen door, where he stayed more or less happily until lunchtime, when Elena took him for a walk, both for him and to stretch out her stiffness. The whole staff loved him. Peter rigged up a baby gate to keep him on the porch, not wandering around the kitchen itself, as he was inclined to do. Juan brought him bones. Ivan saved him slivered bits of fat.

Elena liked to arrive before anyone else, to go over her plans—recipes for soups and small plates one day, experiments with main dishes another. When she had organized the tasks for the day, she'd pour another cup of coffee and wander into the dining room to see what work had been finished the day before. Construction crews were covering the walls with texture, and refinishing the floors with Saltillo tiles, replacing the crumbling bar.

Next to arrive was Juan, with whom Elena got along very well. He liked the fact that she was fluent in Spanish, even if he teased her that the version she spoke was archaic and funny to listen to. Juan would begin the tasks of opening the kitchen, getting things ready for the boys who would come in an hour later, two of them bleary-eyed from partying late into the night, the third alert and cheery. When the restaurant opened, prep cooks would do much of this work, but for now, they were all cooking everything so they could learn what worked and what didn't.

Juan was turning out to be a cornerstone of her kitchen. Elena suspected it was Juan's steadiness that had kept the original restaurant in business. A young husband and father from Mexico, Juan had a soul that was much older than his thirty-year-old face, and he had a knack for corralling the kitchen like a wise old sheepdog, nudging the young cooks along, smoothing tensions, making puns in Spanish to Elena to make her laugh, making filthy jokes to appeal to Ivan's sick humor.

Last to arrive each day was always Ivan, who swaggered in around ten, drinking hot water with lemon and bringing with him a collection of CDs for the day. His taste ran to baroque classical and old Led Zeppelin.

Thus began the music wars. Juan liked ranchero music. Elena's tastes ran to girl singers—Norah Jones, k.d. lang, some Lucinda Williams. The ski boys groaned over all of it, but she simply couldn't stand the hip hop and hard-line rock they liked. Ivan took over the music realm, and Elena allowed it, mainly because they agreed that Bruce Springsteen and Mellencamp were gods.

Each day, Elena or Juan gave a lesson in some finer point of the staples they'd utilize—how to make beautiful tortillas, corn and white, and tie corn husks for tamales, and skin chiles without being blistered, and make a mole.

Finally, then, they would start cooking. Trying dishes, scribbling recipes, tasting them, serving them, making notes, trying them again. Over and over.

At lunch she took Alvin out for a walk, reveling in the

light, thin air, the color of the sky. Afternoons she spent on administrative tasks—creating schedules, creating ordering lists, setting up the computer models that would streamline her life later.

In the evenings, exhausted and stiff, she sometimes had supper with Patrick, but mostly they were both so tired they went home—he to pore over restaurant supply catalogues and Internet sources, she to comb through cookbooks and food theory.

Rasputin was not thrilled about being demoted to sous chef, and Elena suspected he'd never been a joy for a woman in his kitchen—he was old-school, battle-minded and arrogant. In the small kitchen, she found herself sometimes deliberately crowded and bumped, but after a few days, when she didn't respond to any of his intimidations, even he mellowed out—by all accounts he was lucky to have a job at all.

By the end of five weeks, they had most of a menu and most of a dining room. Patrick had assembled a staff for the front of the house, and Elena had been doing interviews for three days to round out the back—prep cooks and dishwashers and runners.

In the darkness of her condo, with faraway stars winking overhead, Elena's body began to relax.

They were ready, at least for a series of tastings. They would prepare and serve the menu for three different groups. The first would be for the restaurant staff, the second for some of Julian's business associates, and the third and final would be for a local group they would hustle up by any means necessary—relatives of the staff, local businesspeople, neighbors—to come and eat for free and help them test not only the food itself, but the training of the staff, front and back.

And that was a lot, Elena thought, drifting off. A lot.

In a rattletrap trailer without any heat, Ivan Santino cranked open the panels of the window and lit a joint. His hands shook slightly, the legacy of a heavy night of drinking and a nightmare. The nightmare was old, as faded in places as a movie that had run too many times, but there was still enough red evil in it to blister him into wakefulness. Some people took tranks and antidepressants and god knew what else, all neatly prescribed by doctors so everybody could get rich. He figured a little weed was better all around. Fast and efficient—even as he held the smoke in his lungs, the edge of terror bled away. Another hit, deep and thick into his lungs, and the slight trembling of his hands eased. It was good shit, from his buddy Billy Kite, a native like himself, who supplied half of Pitkin County with whatever it wanted—meth, pot, crack, pills— a luxurious business in a town with too much money and plenty of time to play. Billy drove a Lexus SUV.

Ivan took one last toke, very short, and pinched the end of the joint between his calloused forefinger and thumb to save for another time. Thoughtfully, he blew it out and sat admiring the meadow beyond the trailer, an open stretch of long, pale green grasses and tiny mountain daisies. On the horizon was a line of dark clouds edged by dawn. A weathery day. Good. He liked weathery days. Liked being in the steamy kitchen with music playing and food shaping up in pans and pots and trays, the smell of frying meat and bleach from the dishboys mopping the floors and the waft of rain blowing in through a door. The best, man.

Every now and then, Ivan liked to have a joint before work, especially if it was the kind of day when he was going to be making things up, trying new flavors and colors. Weed exaggerated things, brought out new notes he might not think of otherwise. There was plenty of time to play with ideas for the new menu, and he'd discovered something energizing in Chef's ingredients list. New brightness, new angles, possibilities that had his brain popping in ways it hadn't for a long time.

From his shirt pocket, he took a pack of Newports and lit one. The sharp menthol cooled his throat and he exhaled with a sense of deep well-being. This whole business with the new chef was taking him by surprise. It was hard to needle her. Hard to want to get rid of her, though that had been his original plan when he heard he was being replaced.

That first image he had of her, of a snow queen from some old fairy tale, had not gone away. There was some air of the tragic around her, some long-ago secret she didn't tell, like a queen who had lost her kingdom. He saw it in the way she moved so stiffly sometimes when she thought no one was looking, the way she almost dragged her left foot when she was tired, how she had to brace herself to lift a heavy bowl of masa.

Meditatively, he smoked. For now, he'd let her alone, because it was thanks to her that Patrick had come to Aspen, to this restaurant. Every day, he was happy to go to work; every day, he thought of little tidbits to offer the sommelier, who liked sweets and savories and being right. Patrick was fastidious and highborn and out of Ivan's league by six classes, but it didn't seem to matter. He couldn't stop thinking of him, and in his company, he was captured every day by some new detail. His water-green eyes. A pursed mouth, like a Kewpie doll. Those elegantly clean hands with the precisely cut nails.

Ivan took a drag off his cigarette and looked at his own nails. His hands were scrupulously clean, of course. A chef was careful with things like that, but his nails were butt-ugly. He should take better care of them.

Vaguely, he was aware of a creeping sense of quiet in himself, a thing that hadn't been there in a long time. Cooking gave it to him. Love gave it to him, not that he'd been real lucky in that sense. If he was honest with himself, he also knew not drinking gave it to him. No nightmares when he left the booze alone. But also a little too much reality.

Smoking peacefully on a still mountain morning, just slightly high, Ivan Santino, who had been kicked down every time he tried to climb out of the shithole he'd been born to, wondered if this might be one more chance to make good.

A beat-up old Chevy pulled into the gravel drive. Ivan stood up, recognizing a buddy from the White Horse, a dive the next town over. He felt vaguely embarrassed to be caught high and dreaming of Patrick, as if the movie played on his forehead. "Hey, brother," Ivan said as he opened the door. "What's up?"

Damon came forward, his hair grimy beneath a blue stocking cap he never removed. "I killed an elk this morning," he said, gesturing to a dent in his grille. "Dressed it right there, and wondered if you might be able to use some elk meat for your restaurant."

Ivan turned down the corners of his mouth. "I don't know, brother. Maybe. Why don't you bring some on over in about an hour? I'll be there then."

"Will do."

"How much you looking to get?"

Damon named a figure that would keep him in JB for a few weeks. Ivan nodded. "Come talk to me at the restaurant. Bring some bones. There's a chow mix hanging around who'll go apeshit over them."

On a Thursday afternoon in late September, Elena peered at the green card presented to her by a dark-eyed young man from Mexico. A man she hoped would be her last hire—a dishwasher. It looked to be in order, along with everything else, but good forgeries always did, didn't they?

What a headache.

A bubble of irritation at the absurdity of the whole game burst between her eyebrows. Without Mexican workers, the service and agricultural businesses in Colorado— maybe all of America—would collapse. Unfortunately, there were so few Mexican workers allowed in on legal green cards that millions flooded over the border to claim the jobs illegally, forcing them to present forged documents that were only uncovered if the INS staged a raid, at which point thousands of workers were deported, only to flood back in again as soon as they could raise the money.

It was fruitless, demoralizing, and hugely expensive. Better to create a system of allowing more temporary workers to enter legally—and voilà! Crime down in every quadrant.

Unfortunately, she was stuck with the system as it was. Without a doubt, there were illegals in her kitchen, alongside those who had secured proper documents by some miracle. She had to be careful—the laws were tight in Colorado, despite the tourist- and agriculture-based economy—and while fines would be annoying, the bigger worry would be losing a chunk of employees in case of a raid.

The green card and Mexican driver's license looked to be in order. Elena stood up and held out her hand. In Spanish, she said, "You're hired. See you at eight a.m. Monday."

He smiled and gave her the charming little bow that always made her think of medieval manners. Old world and courtly. *"Gracias."*

As he left, Julian came in through the back door. "How's it going?"

The day was crisp, not yet full autumn, but no longer summer, and Elena could smell the sunlight on his jacket, a tweedy silk in oranges and browns. She wanted to pet it.

She straightened, tapping the stack of applications together. "Good. Finally." She shook her head. "Staffing issues were more difficult than I anticipated."

"Yeah, that's always the trouble with a tourist economy . . ." He plucked a pitted black olive from a bowl. ". . . getting enough bodies to do the work."

Elena waved the papers. "And the state has really cracked down on undocumented workers. I could have had twenty dishwashers and prep cooks by now, but their papers were not particularly believable." As it was, half her kitchen spoke either Spanish or Vietnamese. The rest were ski bums, as were a lot of the front-of-the-house crew. "How is your end going?"

"Patrick is a gem," he said.

"Absolutely. And you haven't even seen him in action with customers."

Ivan came in from smoking a cigarette. "Hey, Boss Man," he said in his rumbling voice. "*Cómo está?*" Pulling a lid from the steamer, he reached in and nimbly snatched a tamale wrapped in a corn husk. "I got something for both of you to try. Check this out."

He grabbed a plate and dropped the bundle on it, smoothly snipped the tie around the corn husk and let the tamale roll out of its covering. A heavenly scent wafted into the air.

"What *is* that?" Elena breathed, drawn to his magic.

He cut the tamale into slices. They held in elegant rounds, the masa firm but not dry, the color a faint pale red. A secret little smile played over his lips as he held out the plate. "Taste it."

Elena took a fork from the basket on the pass-out bar and captured a small bite. The flavors exploded, spice and meat, filling her throat and sinuses, then sliding away to a lingering complexity that urged her to take another bite, start again.

"Oh, my God," she murmured, obeying the urge for a second taste. She closed her eyes. Pressed her fingers over her lips as if the food might run away if she let it. A silken combination of subtle layers—earthy and gamey and dark, a thread of cinnamon and languid chiles and something she couldn't quite capture. She looked at Julian. He was reaching for a second bite, too.

"This is fantastic," he said. "What is it?"

Ivan shrugged, his eyes glowing turquoise with barely concealed pleasure. In his typical way, he crossed his arms, watched Elena's mouth move, rubbed one finger on his chin. "Mole—I've been experimenting."

"Yeah, but what's the meat?"

"Elk." He looked up as Patrick came into the kitchen, neat as a pin in a crisp blue shirt and jeans. "Some buddies of mine hit one on the highway out west and they dressed it and brought it home."

"Is that legal?" Patrick asked.

"It is." Ivan grinned. "The state patrol issues a limited license at the scene. It's good for like a day."

"I see."

"Try it," Ivan said. "I'd be interested in your wine pairings for something like this."

Fastidiously, Patrick came forward and accepted the fork Ivan held out, and sampled the tamale with a studied expression of boredom. Grinning over his head at Julian, Elena waited for the flavors to ambush her sommelier.

Ivan waited, too, his body taut and tuned, those intense and hooded eyes trained on Patrick's mouth as he chewed, watching as the taste expanded, and as if against his will, he darted a glance up at Ivan's face, his eyes widening. "Oh!" he said. "That's *marvelous*!"

Though he raised his chin in an attempt to control his expression, a slow, pleased smile spread over Ivan's lips. "What kind of wine would you put with it?"

Patrick frowned, moving his lips, and reached for another bite. "It would have to be a very bold wine. Maybe something stronger. Tequila? An ale?"

"Yeah?" Ivan reached behind himself and took out another neatly tied tamale. "Take this one and try some pairings, let me know."

Julian watched Patrick leave, as did Elena. The thin white skin at the back of his neck was flushed red. She looked back to Rasputin with his ragged jeans and big hands, who was also watching Patrick depart. His nostrils were slightly flared.

Elena pursed her lips. Who would do the other more damage? For all that Rasputin had his rough edges, there was something broken in him somewhere. That lostness of wounded child came from him in waves, the same eternal appeal of every bad boy. He glanced at her, smirking, and tossed a tamale from hand to hand.

"Elena, do you have a moment?" Julian asked.

"Sure." She put the fork down. Wiped her fingers. "Ivan, that *is* the best tamale I've ever tasted. Write it up and we'll put it on the menu. If you can come up with some other combinations that are that fantastic, we might do a whole tamale list."

He saluted her without irony. "Thank you."

"And . . ." She waited until Julian went ahead, and took a step closer to Ivan, narrowing her eyes in warning. ". . . leave my sommelier alone."

His eyes were mocking. "He's not my type," he drawled, and looked down Elena's shirt.

"You heard me." She shucked her apron as she headed to her office.

Julian stood in the center of the tiny room, admiring a red glass chile paperweight. He put it down as she came in.

She had not seen much of him these past few weeks, and it was hard not to notice too many things at once—his elegant hands and the sunlight and apple scent of him and his cheekbones. A shimmer moved over her inner wrists, into her palms. "Shall I close the door?"

"Not at all. I was just wondering if you have some time to get out and do some sampling at the other restaurants in town. Time's getting short. I'm particularly interested in getting a feel for prices in this market."

"Good idea." She crossed her arms, trying not to imagine how pleasant it would be to have him to herself for a couple of hours. "This is probably the last night we've got before the insanity begins."

His black eyes were direct. Businesslike. "Yeah, we should have done it sooner, but I could see you were swamped."

"Okay." She yawned, and covered her mouth. "Sorry. I guess I'll go home and get a nap. What are you going to wear?"

"A disguise."

She gave him a quizzical chuckle. "Really?"

He lifted one shoulder. "Actually, yeah. Not much of one, but enough to make people overlook me."

Elena doubted anyone would overlook him, even in a disguise, but that was just her hormones talking. The trouble with not having sex was that she wasn't having sex. "What kind of disguise?"

He winked. "You'll see."

"But I'm still not sure what I should be wearing. Dressed up or dressed down?"

"Dressed up, but not too up."

"Done."

"Good." He clasped those long hands. "One more thing. How would you feel about serving my business associates at my home instead of here?"

"The tasting menu?"

"Yes."

She hesitated. "A home kitchen is not usually the most ideal."

"This is . . . uh . . ." He touched his eyebrow, almost an apology. ". . . a little higher end than most home kitchens. I'd be happy to show it to you."

"Is there a particular reason you want to do it that way?"

Julian inclined his head. Light skated over the high brow. "It's more intimate. We're working on a movie deal and I want it to go my way."

"I keep forgetting you're a big-time movie guy."

"Yeah, that's me. Big-time movie guy."

"You're the boss," she said. "If you want to do it at your place, let's do it there. I'll take a look at the kitchen and figure out what we need. If the prep is done beforehand, Ivan and I should be able to handle the cooking."

"And we need Patrick to serve. This crowd will appreciate him."

Elena smiled. "All right. Let's figure out a time to check out your kitchen, then."

"How about now?"

She glanced up at the clock. "I've got my dog."

"Bring him. My daughter will adore him."

✦ ✦ ✦

Elena had lived in other places where money was visible, or at least you knew it lurked close by. She'd worked in restaurants where a meal for two easily cost hundreds, even thousands with a few good bottles of wine. But in Aspen, luxury leaked from every detail of every shop and home, in the detailing of her condo and the mansions discreetly peeking from stands of trees or towering into the heavens from a hilltop. Aspen wasn't just wealthy, it was stratospheric—royals and movie stars and Saudis had homes there.

Even after just a few weeks, Elena had grown somewhat accustomed to it, and she didn't even blink when she discovered that Julian drove a Range Rover, black, which probably cost close to her annual salary. In a city, it would have been ostentatious. In the high country, the four-wheel drive and navigability would be a boon through the heavy winters. Julian let Alvin jump into the rubberized back hold, and they drove off into the hills, finally turning into a long, graveled drive that climbed through a grove of mixed aspens and lodgepole pines.

Elena commented, "The first yellow leaves I've seen."

"Hard to believe winter is just around the corner." His window was down, allowing a fresh piney breeze to blow through. He held his free hand out in the air, as if to capture the sunny day.

"Do you like the winter?" she asked.

"I do, actually. Cold invigorates me. You?"

"It's been a very long time since I've lived in a place with a real winter. We'll see."

"You grew up with it, though, right? Did you like it when you were a kid?"

Elena said slowly, "I guess. We never had enough warm clothes, honestly. I'm not saying that in a pitiful way, but there were a lot of us and only so many dollars to go around."

"I get that completely. New Jersey is brutal in the wintertime. I remember some relative sent me a down coat—you know the big puffy ones?—for Christmas one year and it was so warm I just wanted to cry."

Elena laughed. "Exactly. I found some insulated gloves once, and it was the same thing. I wanted to wear them twenty-four hours a day."

He glanced at her. "You have a great laugh."

She paused. "Thanks."

The house appeared, not as drastically huge as some were in the area, rambling for tens of thousands of square feet. This was big, with a round turret and several outbuildings, but it was in the human realm. Built of fieldstone and timbers, the colors blended agreeably into the landscape, with balconies and secret patios appearing here and there.

Elena liked it tremendously. "It looks like something out of a fairy tale."

"That's what my daughter thought. I let her make the final choice." He opened the back gate and let Alvin out. "Does he need to be leashed?"

"No, he should be fine. Are you sure you want to let him into your house? He sheds like crazy."

His grin was slight and charming. "I have an army of cleaners. Dog hair wouldn't stand a chance." He waved her ahead on the sidewalk. "Oh, and by the way, my daughter hates it when people tell her she looks like her mother."

"Thanks for the alert."

A trim, well-coiffed woman in jeans opened the door. "Good morning, Mr. Liswood." She nodded at Elena. "We're about to finish up. Will we be in the way?"

"Not at all, Georgia. This is Elena Alvarez, the executive chef at my new restaurant. We've come to look at the kitchen. Maybe you want to show us around?" He smiled slightly. "Georgia is crew leader. I'm sure she knows my kitchen better than I do."

For a long second, between standing on the stoop and stepping over the threshold, Elena tried to decide how to play her dazzlement. As her foot landed inside, and the sweep of light and design drew her eyes upward, she knew. "Wow."

The entryway was three stories tall and bright, with a window at the top. Galleries ran around the opening, and a waterfall fell in tiny ribbons from the roof to a floor below.

"Like it?"

"Very cool," Elena commented, pointing at the neat strings of water.

"The guy who designed it has a great sense of play." He tossed his keys into a dish on a table. "He's won awards."

"This way," Georgia said, leading them along a hallway made of stones. They passed the staircase, which curved behind the waterfall and up to the floor with the galleries. On the other side of it was an office area to the left, with a two-sided fireplace that also heated an outdoor patio, and to the right, a great room.

Which fronted a gigantic gourmet kitchen furnished with gleaming stainless steel appliances—a six-burner gas stove, two ovens, a microwave, and two fridges. Elena opened a silver hooded appliance. "Aha! A steamer. Wow."

Julian said nothing. Elena made her rounds, checking the area for workability. The counters were black granite speckled with gold. Problematic for serving, since granite cooled things so fast, but they could cover the stone. One sink was nestled in an island; the other—by a dual set of dishwashers—looked out to a dazzling view of craggy mountaintops and vivid blue sky. There was a wine cooler, a butler's pantry filled with glassware, china, chargers, and table linens of several matching varieties. "Patrick will be pleased," Elena remarked.

"And the chef?"

"The chef could happily die in this kitchen."

The woman chuckled.

"And do you think the service will work all right from here?" Julian gestured toward the great room, with its shoulder-high hearth against one wall, and glass doors on either side, one set opening to an enclosed patio, the other to vast, multilayered wooden decks. The dining area was huge, with an enormous oak table. The passages were clean and wide. Alvin wandered the edges of the room, curiously sniffing at corners, at vases, pausing to look into the distance.

"How many people?"

"Between fifteen and twenty, depending on who brings a partner."

"We can accommodate that easily from here. You could probably manage a hundred, honestly." She pressed her hands against the cold, cold counter, admiring the wide decks, the views, the *serenity* of so much available, uncluttered space.

"Good."

"It's great, Julian. Excellent design." Elena turned in a slow circle, lust rising in her. "It will be a delight to work here."

"Oh. My. Gosh!" came a high girly voice. "Dad! This is the most beautiful dog I've ever *seen!*" A blonde teenager collapsed on her knees in front of Alvin. He puffed up his chest and licked his lips, waiting to be adored.

She obliged, raising both hands to his head, to his back, moving with the firm strokes of a genuine dog lover. "Ooooh," she squealed, "he's so soft!" She kissed his big velvet nose, and he groaned in exaltation.

"Told you," Julian said with a wink. "Portia, this is Elena, and that's her dog, Alvin."

The girl paused momentarily to look at Elena. Her eyes were enormous and startling, the pale, unbroken blue of a delphinium in a face that was a porcelain oval, absolutely flawless, with a rosy plump mouth. Her pale silky hair tumbled around slim shoulders.

She looked exactly like her mother, Ricki Alsatian. Elena said, "Hello, Portia. I hear you're quite a skier."

She shot a look at her dad. "I guess. What kind of dog is he?"

"Chow and nobody knows what."

"I'd say Newfoundland," Portia said, "that big head. But he has some golden retriever aspects, too, doesn't he? Those fronds on his legs? Are his paws webbed?" She lifted one and looked. "Yep. I'd say chow, Newfoundland, and retriever." She kissed his nose again. "You are the most beautiful dog ever—yes, you are."

Alvin shot Elena a sideways look that said, *Are you registering how to do this?* She laughed. "He's your slave for life. Do you have a dog of your own?"

"No. I've moved too much. It's not fair to them. I *am* doing community service at a rescue center here, though. It's great, I love it. And there's a doggie day care here that lets me volunteer sometimes, too."

"Doggie day care?"

Petting Alvin ceaselessly, Portia nodded. "It's right in town. You drop your dog off in the morning and pick him up at the end of the day, and he gets to play all day while you work, just like a kid. They have play groups and nap times and everything."

"I bet skiers love it."

"Probably. I haven't worked there in the winter."

She was a charming girl, and Elena was surprised, though she was ashamed to acknowledge why. Because she was a rich girl. Because she was beautiful and probably at least somewhat spoiled—how could she help it? Because she was the daughter of a famous actress and a famous director.

And partly, because Elena knew she'd been in trouble. But here she was, an absolutely adorable, flat-chested, soon-to-be-devastating, princess of fourteen. Elena wanted to sink down beside her and find out what she thought about, let her walk Alvin. She breathed in and scented bananas, chocolate, yeast. A jumble that didn't quite make sense.

"You'll have to give me the address and I'll visit," Elena

said. "It might be a good place for him when we get the restaurant open."

"Are you the cook?"

"Chef," Julian said. "*Executive* chef."

"Yes," Elena said, directly.

She only nodded. "I can babysit him sometimes if you want."

"I'm going to be here next week to cook. Do you want to start then? He obviously loves you."

"Okay! He can watch movies with me!"

Looking at Portia, Elena realized she was painfully, deeply starved for the company of females. Over the years, she'd grown used to working in such a male-dominated environment, but she had grown up with sisters. She needed other women in her world.

Mia, she thought, *where are you?*

Autumn

APPETIZERS AND SMALL PLATES

CARNE EN SU JUGO
steak and bacon swimming in savory citrus and chile broth

CHILE TASTING PLATE
an assortment of roasted chiles, served with fresh flour tortillas and sliced avocados

ROASTED PORK TAQUITOS
on blue corn with tomatillos and onions

AUTHENTIC POSOLE
stew with pork, chiles, and hominy

MANGO AND AVOCADO SALAD
light, zesty, and beautiful

STUFFED ZUCCHINI BLOSSOMS
delicately fried blossoms stuffed with blue corn bread and piñon nut stuffing

ROASTED ONION TART
mildly spicy dish, thinly layered with mild chiles and manchego cheese

CHILE VERDE
very spicy stew with chiles and pork and cheese, served with white tortillas

When she worked at her first San Francisco restaurant, Elena had lived above a shop owned by an eccentric black woman, who had traveled to America with a lover from one of the islands when she was a young girl. The lover was long gone, the islands only a memory in her faint accent, but her shop was an explosion of jars and pots and potions, a narcotic blend of scents that went straight to Elena's head when she walked in. The woman, perhaps sixty, was called Marie, and she had a statue of the Black Madonna surrounded by red flickering candles on an altar at the back of the store. She put fresh flowers and offerings of food out and lit tall candles with the seven saints on the wrapper to the dark carved beauty. The altar comforted Elena, a symbol she could understand in a city that was very unlike any place she had ever been.

Marie shouted out when Elena first arrived in the store, "Get, get!" She waved her dark bony hands toward the door, and, startled, Elena had turned to go.

The woman caught her arm, gently. "Not you, child.

The ones you brought with you. We don't want them here. You can take a break, huh?"

The old woman made cups of strong, exotic teas, sometimes spiked with rum, and told Elena stories of men she had known and the dishes she had cooked for them. She was a sorceress, a snake charmer, a voodoo priestess, perhaps, and she knew the secrets of seasoning in a way Elena instinctively understood was her true magic. Starved for a daughter of her own, Marie adopted Elena for the two years she lived there, and taught her the secret language of spices, the way saffron sparked a dish to life, the cleverness of nutmeg, the sharpness of ginger. Marie taught her how to pinch and taste and measure spices, how to blend hot and sweet, bitter and bright, savory and salty.

Now, Marie was in her mind as Elena and Julian ate a spicy fusion of Indian and Caribbean at an Aspen café. The ReNew Café had been open for more than three years to great success. An organic vegetarian restaurant with an eclectic menu, green practices, and a hip, youthful setting, it had surprised everyone—especially the owners—by taking off. They'd had to move once to accommodate the influx of customers, but the owner insisted they wouldn't move again. They couldn't handle a hundred covers and still cook the way he wished, with authentic, organic, vegetarian food made to order.

"How you folks doing?" the server asked. He was lanky and dazzlingly young, his upper body twice as long as the lower.

"It's fantastic," Elena said of her stew. "Excellent spices."

"Good," he said. "Let me know if you want more tea."

That was the other thing—no alcohol was served. The owner was Baha'i.

"The music is good, too," Julian said. "What's playing?"

"Some kind of world-beat thing," the boy said. "I'll check for you."

Elena smiled as the boy ambled away. Julian's disguise had turned out to be remarkably simple—and effective. The curls were tucked beneath a Rastafarian-style knitted hat, and he wore black horn-rimmed glasses and a long-sleeved black T-shirt with wooden beads around his neck. He looked like a weird professor of some esoteric thing, like the history of the Congo or Sufi poetry. "You do nerd really well."

"Yes, ma'am—lots of practice."

"You mean, in disguises?"

His grin turned rueful. "*Nyet.* As a real nerdy guy. When I was seventeen, I played Dungeons and Dragons *and* chess."

"Horrors!"

He lifted a finger—wait. "I also had an entire collection of all of Stephen King's novels, and could quote, word for word, Edgar Allan Poe's 'Raven.' "

Elena's nostrils quivered with laughter. "I'm getting this picture of a very skinny, intense boy. Virgin?"

"Oh, yeah." He waved a hand. "To have sex, you'd have to actually talk to a woman. I couldn't seem to connect."

"With that array of interests? Imagine!"

"I know. Go figure."

"So what changed it?"

"I made a movie," he said, lifting a shoulder. "Suddenly, there were a lot of beautiful girls who wanted to talk to *me.*"

Something about that pierced Elena. "Was it hard, try-ing to figure out who wanted you for yourself?"

"At that point, I didn't particularly care."

Elena laughed appreciatively.

"You, on the other hand," he said, "were probably the queen of your high school, weren't you?"

"Hardly. I was odd woman out, too. Not a nerd, though—I was just different. If it hadn't been for—" she paused, but only for a second, "my boyfriend and my sister, I would not have had any friends, I'm sure."

His dark eyes glittered. Focused. *Interested.* "Why?"

"Well, for one thing, I stood out because I was so white looking, you know." Isobel suddenly appeared and settled into the chair to Elena's left. She shot her a glance, but Isobel folded her hands, blinking in total innocence.

"Go on," Isobel said. "We're both listening."

"Um." She rarely showed up when there were other people around, and telling the story felt suddenly self-conscious. "There were other white kids, but I wasn't in their camp, since I was an Alvarez."

"Lucky for you," Isobel said.

"Lucky for me," Elena repeated. "So I was in between. And," she said, spearing a lovely cube of roasted sweet po-tato, "I was *totally* a bookworm and I got straight A's."

"Boring," Isobel said. She reached for a crust of bread, but Elena shot her a look.

" 'Boring' is the word," Elena said.

"Oooh," he said, grinning. "Not quite chess, but nobody likes a smart girl, either. Were you valedictorian?"

A cold, salty wave of memory doused her pleasure. Isobel vanished. "No. Things . . . got in the way."

"Things?"

She shook her head.

He let it go, taking a sip of green tea. "I've been working on a soundtrack for the Orange Bear."

Grateful for the change of subject, she said, "Spoken like a director."

"And for the same reason—music creates a mood."

"I'll buy that. Are there soundtracks for your other restaurants?"

"Every one."

"What's the soundtrack for the Blue Turtle?"

"Let's see—the CDs are about four hours long, and I usually end up mixing about five or six. For the Turtle, there is some French, some Canadian indigenous music, some East Indian influences. Other things, but those are the basics."

"I never noticed."

He shrugged. "You're in the back. You'd never hear it."

"True." She stabbed a chunk of roasted red pepper from the stew and examined it. "This is really very good," she commented. "So what's on the soundtrack for the Orange Bear?"

"It's better to play it for you."

"You're not doing a bunch of old ranchero favorites, are you?"

His smile was secretive and slow, his black eyes suddenly darker, more intriguing. "Not at all."

She inclined her head. "When can I hear it?"

"Whenever you like."

"Tomorrow?"

"In the evening. I've got a lot to do during the daylight

hours." He met her eyes, lifted his glass of water, and paused. "Your place or mine?" Again that slow, playful smile, a glitter dancing on his fathomless irises. A jewel in a ring on his right hand caught the light, a contrast to the Rastafarian hat.

Not this one, she said to herself. *Not this one.* "I have a lot to do, too. Let's make it at the restaurant."

"No problem."

The server returned. "The music is Lhasa de Sela," he said, fingers resting lightly on the tabletop as he leaned in.

"Thank you," Julian said. As the boy departed, he said, "I think we should steal it, don't you?"

"Absolutely."

"Is our pastry chef here yet?"

Elena sighed. "No. Next week. She said."

"That's leaving us pretty short, isn't it?"

"Not really. We've been working through email, so she's in the loop. I have her absolute promise that she'll be here on Thursday. We don't need her for the first tastings."

"You sound pretty confident."

"There is no one like Mia, trust me. Her almond cornmeal cake is like something you remember from another life. Seriously."

He settled back in his chair. "And if she doesn't arrive?"

"She will." Elena touched her lips with the napkin. "I'm going to find the ladies' room and see if I can get a peek at the kitchen."

While Elena was gone, Julian let himself drift into the music, letting it call up images and stories and colors. He saw green jungles and elephant feet on very black springy earth, and men with loose shoulders and women with hips swaying side to side. Mixed with the scents of nutmeg and cardamom in the air, it lent a powerful flavor to the mood. Very smart.

He caught sight of Elena weaving her way toward him through the candlelit room, her hair shining on her shoulders, that astonishing mouth moving slightly, as if she were talking on a BlackBerry. Her gait was more pronouncedly uneven, and he wondered if she ever used a cane. Her hips swayed. Her breasts.

As she sat down, he said, "You talk to yourself a lot."

A flicker of alarm and surprise crossed her face. "Do I?"

"It's nothing to be ashamed of. Lots of creative people talk to themselves."

She nodded, her eyelids dropping to hide her expression. Hide something, anyway. She speared a vegetable from her dish and held it out to him. "You should try this."

He had the strongest sense that she was distracting him, but he leaned in to take it from her fork. As their eyes met, something arced between them. He felt it in the middle of his chest, and in the base of his skull. The vegetable, a square of roasted orange squash, burst in his mouth, and still he let himself drift in Elena's mysteriousness. A room of their own opened suddenly, empty and inviting, a place with white walls and dark, polished wooden floors and a view of some blue vista through the casement windows.

He saw a thousand details of her face, all at once, her surprisingly robust eyebrows and thin, long lashes and a scar the size of a fingernail on her forehead.

She looked down first.

"How much do you hurt on a daily basis?" he asked quietly.

"What makes you think I hurt?"

He raised his eyebrows, waited.

She shrugged. "Some days a lot. Some days not very much." She carefully put her fork down on her plate. "You don't have to worry that I'll be unreliable. I've lived with it a long time."

"I know," he said. A prick of howling sorrow touched him. "God, Elena, I wasn't criticizing. I read about the accident when I called up your name on Google."

An icy mask stiffened her pale face. Violet shadows showed beneath her eyes. "I don't want to talk about that."

"I'm not asking you to." He skimmed a spray of bread crumbs from the bare wood of the table. "My mother died violently. I think I know a little about prurient interest."

She gazed at him impassively, mask still glittering and cold. "I'm sorry," she said without emotion.

Around her there was a disturbance, a bending of the air like the fine bands of heat waves that rose from a fire. For a moment, Julian thought it seemed there was fire flickering out from her very skin, like the pictures of saints, but there was no mistaking the cold on her face.

Abruptly, she leaned forward, pushing her plate away so she could put her forearms over the table. Her eyes, fierce and sapphire, burned in her face. "Do you know how many times men have wanted to sleep with me because I survived such a gruesome accident?"

"Elena—"

"Do you know how often some reporter has come in to do a story on a restaurant and heard the rumors of my past and tried to get it out of me? I'm like a priest who gave up the calling—everyone wants to know the story." Her eyes narrowed. "I will not give you a story, Mr. Director."

Heat touched his cheeks. Shame. Quietly, he said, "Touché."

"The thing is," she said, "it's so ordinary. How many people die in a car accident every day?"

"A lot," he agreed. "I'm more interested in the fact that you lived, Elena."

For a moment, she stared at him, her hands folded in her lap. Again he had that sense of the bending of the air around her, shimmering heat waves rising around her, but her face was like a painting of a Spanish Madonna, composed and blue-eyed and too sensual for the mother of God.

Abruptly, she seemed to come to a softening. "Look, Julian, I just don't like to talk about it."

"Okay."

The strangeness around her broke, and again he was only looking at the woman he'd hired to run his kitchen, beautiful and broken and strange, but just a woman. "Shall we go?"

Julian nodded. The terrible thing was, her warning only ratcheted up his curiosity even more.

Elena tossed and turned after her meal with Julian, restless in so many ways. She lay in the dark thinking of the menu—was it full enough? Was there enough variety? Too much? Was it too ordinary? Too pretentious?

Not now, she told herself. But then flashes of Julian's

face rose in her mind, the knowing light in his eyes. The way he had of holding her gaze, then sweeping his eyelids down, as if pressing a secret into his mind. She thought of the way his hands—

No, not that, either.

Rolling over to her side, she reached for images of food. Recipes, ingredients. She deliberately visualized a farmer's market bursting with fresh produce—calabacitas and big round watermelons and potatoes. A cat sitting in the dust by the striped tent. Ah, she thought, getting sleepy. The county fair. Her Uncle George, who grew the biggest pumpkins in the valley. Well, at least before his son died. Donnie.

Donnie's funeral. Settling in more easily to the fat pillows, Elena felt her tensions slide away. Yes, Donnie's funeral. That had been a good day indeed.

Elena was twelve years old when Donnie killed himself skidding into the Big O Tires sign just south of the highway. He was racing, of course. There wasn't much else to do in Espanola in those days. Or these either, really.

There were aunts and uncles and cousins Elena had never seen, and everybody was dressed up, shaking out clothes they never wore except to weddings and funerals and high school graduations. Some definitely seventies stuff in the mix, she noticed with scorn, polyester and even a pair of platforms. She and Isobel snorted, heads together. *Kill me now.*

Donnie's father was devastated. Elena watched her uncle warily as everyone milled around the tiny, hot house and spilled into the bare dirt backyard, where folding chairs and picnic tables had been set up. A skinny dog wandered around, alternately whining and begging, weaving his way through the legs of the funeral-goers crowded around the keg beneath the tree. George sat down next to it, drank down his beer in a single gulp, and silently held out the plastic cup for more.

Always so easily distracted, Isobel disappeared with some older cousins. They were smoking behind the shed, telling dirty jokes in Spanish, trying to shock Isobel. Elena didn't like the cigarettes or the jokes, and she stayed behind.

It was July. Elena was bored and hot, and her dress stuck to her back. She'd begged and pleaded to be allowed to wear nylons, but then had to peel them off as soon as they got out of mass, leaving them in a taupe-colored ball in the trash of the church ladies' room. As she stood to one side of the backyard, a big black fly kept landing on her knee, coming back to sniff and prickle, and she slapped at him. When he circled back and bit the back of her neck, Elena went into the house.

She had to blink to clear her vision after the white hot sun, and found herself staring at an enormous spread of food in the dun-colored dining room. Acres of food, in all kinds of colors and textures, their scents mingling in the air like wicked perfume—chocolate and chile and browning onions and slow-stewed pork. Beneath a black wooden cross covered with tiny silver *milagros*—tiny hands and eyes and legs and hearts flying across the bottom—the food overflowed Tupperware and glass and thin paper plates stuck together in threes to make them more sturdy.

Elena watched the women swirling around, arranging, putting things out. Most of it was the usual, a cake iced in white and polka-dotted with halved maraschino cherries; a pile of unidentifiable meat, charred and dry; a lumpy stack of flour tortillas; plain white dinner rolls, the kind that came on trays from the supermarket; and chicken, fried and in barbecue sauce.

It was the tomatoes that drew Elena, and the sliced red and green and yellow sweet peppers; the fresh sprays of scallions stuck in a glass bowl with their tails sticking out like fans; zucchinis and yellow squashes in sticks; bowls of hot pickled cherry peppers and fresh, gleaming salsas with tiny wheels of scallions bobbing up through the red sea; and a dark green salad dressed with tiny oranges. Things that were ripe and fresh in everyone's backyard gardens. Maybe not the oranges, which she thought came from a can, but everything else.

"Are you hungry, *m'ija?*" Auntie Gloria was carrying a pile of tamales to the table. "You can make a plate if you want."

When Elena continued to eye her without speaking, giving only a single twitch of her shoulder, Gloria put the dish down and grabbed a paper plate, then put another one under it. She plucked a tamale out of the bowl, and a little stack of tiny chicken drumsticks and some shredded meat she piled quickly and with expertise into a waiting corn tortilla she took from a lidded casserole with a cow painted on the outside. "Try this," she said, and passed it to Elena. "You ever want to grow some *chi chis*"—she patted her own considerable breasts—"you better eat more."

"Some tomatoes, too," Elena said, "please."

"Good year for tomatoes," she said, nodding.

Elena's mouth watered over the scents rising into the

air—spice and some heavy meat she couldn't identify that must have been the dark shreds nestled into the tortilla. She bit into it and closed her eyes at the hefty explosion of flavor. "Oh, what *is* that?"

"Duck. Your uncle shot some last week up at the lake."

For one long moment, Elena paused, wondering if she should mind. "Like those green-neck ducks?"

"I dunno. If you don't like it, don't eat it."

She shook her head, jealously guarding the plate with the shield of her body, and found a skinny bar of shade resting against the side of the house. In the distance were the mountains, a zigzag of dark blue against the heat-pale blue of the sky. In the air was the smell of weeds and smoke from a distant forest fire.

In her mouth was the first taste of duck she'd ever had, duck fat and salty and seasoned with the special sweet fire of local red chile powders. It tasted of the deepest moments of summer, of swimming in a lake at dusk, of things she'd only begun to think about.

Into the corner of her vision came a black-haired boy. He wore a gray shirt with long sleeves that was a little too tight for him, and dark gray slacks that skimmed his ankles. She didn't speak to him, but she was suddenly more aware of her skinny shins sticking out from her dress without the covering of stockings.

He stopped and looked down. "Hi."

Elena didn't look at him directly. Instead of dress shoes, he had on high-topped Converse sneakers, yellow. His cheekbones were angled harshly, making him look dangerous.

"Hi," she said back.

"What's your name?"

She told him.

His name was Edwin. He didn't like his brother, who tortured him with pinching and punches whenever they were alone, and kicked their dog. He wasn't her cousin, and by the end of the day, he taught Elena to kiss with those lips as red as tomatoes and a tongue that tasted of chiles and summertime. Before they were finished, on a night five years later, he would teach her much, much more.

In her apartment in Aspen, Elena fell asleep. And into her dream, Edwin arrived, as he sometimes did. They were dancing a two-step at somebody's wedding. She was seventeen, and also thirty-eight. Her crinkly taffeta skirts and satin bodice slid over his crisply ironed cotton shirt. He smelled faintly of cinnamon, which he loved, in every variety, in chocolate and cinnamon rolls and tea and even in stew. He hummed under his breath to the ranchero song being belted out by Elena's sister Isobel, who had a voice everybody said might take her to LA one of these days. A cousin played the guitar, and there was even an old man on trumpet whose eyes were the teary red of the eternal alcoholic, but his horn was fine.

Edwin smoothed his hand over Elena's hair, slow and easy, and she was captured in a shifting sense of time, filled with a faraway sense of herself as an old woman, and Edwin as an old man, dancing at the wedding of a great-grandchild, to this song.

She saw her babies, new and mewling, and saw their strong sons. She saw the weddings at which she and Edwin would dance, in blue satin and black suits, in square-necked bodices and pressed trousers. It made her feel light and whole and exactly where she was meant to be. He would be her husband and she would be his wife, all of their days.

A lot of girls she knew worried about their boyfriends cheating when they drank too much, or running around behind their backs, or falling under the spell of another woman, or beating them. Elena did not worry. From that first day at Donnie's funeral, he had loved her. They would be married when she graduated from high school, because they wanted to make a better life for themselves, move to Albuquerque, maybe, where she could have a catering shop. He was a modern guy. He wanted her to work, both of them to work, so they could give their children more than they had themselves. Swaying with him, though, she clasped her secret to herself, the new life growing in her. It would be born before they married, but that was all right.

In her dream, he crawled into her bed in Aspen, Colorado. He curled around her and pressed his lips to her hair and whispered, *I missed you.* His body was naked beneath the covers, and he pushed his hands beneath her old, paper-thin T-shirt, curving his strong palms to her ribs. His bare leg moved over her thigh, and Elena turned to him, tears wetting her face.

It's been so long, she whispered, letting him take her into his arms. *I missed you. I missed you.*

It's true, he rumbled into her hair, his hot breath on her neck, *you and I, the truest thing in our lives. I love you.* His hands drifted over her body, lifting her breasts and putting his mouth down to kiss her chest and her neck. His member nudged her thigh, damp and hungry, and his hands drifted down, sliding between her legs, finding the ready wet heat, and he made love to her with hands and mouth and member, and she wept, knowing even in her dream that it was a dream.

A dream, a dream—Edwin's hands and his long-lashed black eyes that made her think of Julian, and the taste of his lips, things she should have forgotten in twenty years, but never seemed to lose. He came to her in dreams when she needed him, needed release or comfort. He made love to her, just as he was, moving, moving, kissing and touching her until she was—

She jerked awake to an empty bed and her own hands squeezing out a massive orgasm between her legs, and tears streaming from her eyes from a fresh, hot, renewed sense of grief. When it was done, she turned her face into the pillow and let the ripples ease.

Alone, alone.

Always alone.

It was a bad morning for more than the dream. She had them every now and then. Edwin explained that he could only visit for the day, just long enough for them to go on a picnic or dance one dance or—

The dreams left her depressed and aching, and this morning, she was very stiff, as well. Limping into the kitchen to make coffee, she fired up the laptop and shook out her shoulders, tried to stretch her arms overhead.

Everything in her lower back exploded, and she bent over with a gasp. Her legs burned, and something fiery hot and purple burned in her left hip.

Jesus.

The days were too long. She needed more straight walking. A good massage therapist. More resting. In a few weeks, the restaurant would be open and she could get back to a regular schedule, but for today, she'd have to get a massage. Find a hot tub. She typed in her search parameters for massage in Aspen, fighting tears as her lower back spasmed.

The email function on her laptop dinged. Hoping to hear from Mia, she clicked the icon.

To: Elena.Alvarez@theorangebear.com
From: dmitrinadirov@theblueturtle.com
Subject: oh i get it
he just wants to fuck you
www.tabloid photo link 950343h1h932/oapher/

Elena clicked the link and groaned. It was a photo of her and Julian at dinner the night before, when she'd offered him a vegetable to taste. He was leaning in, and she was smiling slightly, and the effect was very intimate. *Liswood's Latest Dish?* the headline read. A blurb beneath it continued in the same lurid vein.

The phone rang and she turned, too abruptly. A slashing sword crossed her spine, nape to tailbone, and she froze, letting it ripple through. Taking a breath, she barked into the phone, "Hello!"

"Good morning, Elena," said Julian. "Bad time?"

"Not really. Do you know a good massage therapist?"

"I do, as a matter of fact. I can call her for you as soon as we're done here."

"Is this about the photo?"

"The tabloids? Yes. How did you hear about it?"

"An email from a friend who saw it," she said mildly.

"I'm calling to warn you that you'll probably have to deal with paparazzi over the next few days, but maybe we can use it to the advantage of the restaurant."

"Huh. Okay. Never thought of that angle." A claw hammer slammed itself up her left thighbone, into the depths of her hip, and her leg abruptly gave out. She sank onto a stool, making the smallest possible *oomph*. "How?"

"I had a call for an interview with a Denver paper. We'll just give it."

"I'm game." She tamped down the irritation over Dmitri's email. "The massage therapist—is she therapeutically oriented?"

"She's one of the best, Elena. Get off the phone. I'll call her right now and have her call you."

"That would be great."

The woman, called not reassuringly Candy, called back within minutes and Elena arranged to have a massage at ten. In the meantime, she could get in a walk to see if that would loosen things up, and go into work, get things going at the restaurant. She gathered Alvin's leash, put on her walking shoes, and realized within a few steps that the weather was changing, the colors turning from the canvas of vivid blue and yellow to the subtler shades of coming winter. Over the blue mountains, clouds hung low like pale gray angora. She had to go back in for a coat and made a note to buy a scarf and hat and mittens in the next few days.

Alvin and she headed down to the river path, where she met the odd runner, hands gloved, legs in Lycra, earphones blocking out the world. Piles of heart-shaped leaves rattled underfoot, and the river rushed by, cold rising from it like a portent.

The tabloid photo didn't bother her. A famous director was bound to be stalked by photographers, and what did she care about what they said about them?

But the email from Dmitri rankled. Bastard. Couldn't stand to see her succeed, even though he was doing very well himself. His jealousy irked her—because it was not the jealousy of a man who wanted a woman, but that of one chef trying to take another down. Specifically a man who wanted to bring a woman down.

Walking briskly with Alvin at her side, her cheeks getting cold, she perversely felt again the piercing loss of him—her lover, friend, absolute ally. They had taken such pleasure creating the Blue Turtle together. He was so zesty, so full of life, so sexy and lusty. Cooking, food, women, sex, music, dancing, travel—Dmitri scooped it all up with two hands, gulped it down. He smoked too much and drank too much and could not be faithful to anyone for more than a few months, but the world felt twelve times brighter in his company.

Tears pricked her eyes. Why did she care about him, anyway? Why did it *hurt*? Why couldn't she, like women she'd known, just walk away from relationships that didn't work out? They'd had a good time. They'd created a restaurant and made lots of love and shared a good solid couple of years. That was more love than many people got.

But this wasn't about Dmitri, was it? She was just getting so bloody tired. Tired of starting over and starting over and starting over. Before Dmitri, it was Andrew; before Andrew, a long stretch when she left men alone except for casual things, when she fell in love with her work in a big way, and studied and cooked and moved up through the ranks. Before that, Timothy, an Englishman she met in Paris. Before Timothy—

Oh, it didn't matter. She was depressed over the dream, that was all. A long-ago love. Of course Edwin seemed perfect—he had lived so long ago. She sniffed.

And she wanted Mia to get here, damn it! She needed another woman in this kitchen. Desperately. Patrick was a great ally, but he was not a female. He wasn't around today, anyway. He'd driven into Denver to check some details of decoration.

The walk loosened her up a bit, so by the time she got to the restaurant, she was at least able to function. Alvin happily curled up on the porch on his blanket, but once the storms came, he wouldn't be able to stay out all day, even if he did have a warm coat. She'd look into the doggie day care Julian's daughter had mentioned.

She had the kitchen to herself for the first hour, and made lists and accepted deliveries. The head bartender was in, setting up glassware and the back bar, and Elena talked with her for a while about drink specials. A burly man in a dark blue work shirt came in wheeling a dolly loaded with cases of various Mexican beers—Dos Equis and Tecate and Negros Modelo. "Getting cold out there," he said. "Might snow."

"So soon?"

"Sooner the better," he said.

Elena nodded, and headed back to the kitchen. The upstairs kitchen had been set up as a serving station and a pastry kitchen. Seeing the empty waiting area, Elena grabbed her cell phone and punched in Mia's number. "Hey, honey," Mia answered. "You're mad at me, aren't you? I can tell by the way the phone rang."

"Not mad, Mia, but I need you to get your ass over here."

"Well, here's the good new, baby—I'm leaving now, Heathrow to Denver. We can cook up a storm all weekend if you like."

A wave of relief washed away about a thousand pounds of tension from Elena's shoulders. "Good. Patrick is going to Denver this afternoon. What if he meets you somewhere and you guys drive back together?"

"I would love that. I've got his cell—I'll call him right now."

"Let me know."

"Did you get my recipe list?"

"No. How did you send it?"

"Email. A couple of days ago. I'll check and send again."

Elena carried the phone to her office. "No, let me check my spam folder first." Sometimes it misread emails and filed away things that should have been sent through. Punching in the password for her email account, she waited. "Dmitri's being a bastard."

"Now there's a surprise. God, Elena, he's always been so jealous of you! He wanted to seduce you to—" She broke off. "That's mean. Never mind."

"It's also true. He wanted me to fall in love with him so he could exert some control," Elena said, admitting it aloud. "And it worked. How stupid is that?"

"Not stupid, Elena, never that. You're too good for him. Remember that."

"Thanks. Hurry up and get your ass into Aspen."

"Soon, sister."

She clapped the phone closed and headed down the back stairs. Halfway down, the claw hammer dug into her hip joint without warning. Elena froze, gripping the handrail as the pain burrowed through her muscles and flesh and into the joint, drilling like a steel spiral. For one long moment pain stiffened her, head to toe. A soft voice, her sister's voice—within? without? she never knew—said softly, *Breathe, Elena. Breathe.*

Holding on to the wooden railing with a death grip to stay upright, she forced herself to inhale through her nose, slowly, imagining cool air moving through the fiery spots. She breathed out, just as slowly, a dragon letting the fire out. After a moment, she sank down on the step, the grip easing, and put her head in her hands, thinking, *I can't do this.*

Why had God even bothered to spare her? For this tawdry life where she'd moved from place to place to place, never settling, now just getting older and more crooked and still without the family she wanted?

Next to her, Isobel said, "Stand up. Stop whining."

Elena closed her eyes, put her arms around her head. Visions of Edwin twined around her in the dream, the piercing perfection of his hands on her, the longing of both of them for a long-past time, for a love that should have been, and was ripped away—

"Get up!" A distinct shove between her shoulder blades made Elena jolt up and grab the handrail.

Ivan came to the foot of the stairs just as she stood. "There you are," he said. "I brought you a present." He waved a tabloid newspaper and made kissing noises. "You and big dick, up in a tree, K-I-S-S-I-N-G—"

Elena rolled her eyes, coming down the stairs as if she were not carrying three claw hammers and an anvil in her lower back. "Yeah, yeah, Rasputin. You're just jealous. You want him for yourself."

He didn't move from the doorway, using his tall body to block her way. Elena smelled lemons and almonds and cake. She tilted her head back to look at him, raising one eyebrow.

"Maybe I am jealous," he rumbled, putting his hands on either side of the threshold to block the way. Their bodies were only inches apart, his hooded blue eyes traveling over her face, her shoulders, breasts. "But not because of the job."

She put up one hand against his chest. "Don't," she said harshly, and shoved him.

With a crooked smile, he took a step backward, then another, and waved a hand to gesture her through into her kitchen. She yanked the paper out of his hand. "Start the tamales," she said. "I've got an appointment at ten."

FIFTEEN

To: Elena.Alvarez@theorangebear.com
From: Mia_grange@askthechef.co.uk
Subject: dessert menu possibles
Here they are, sweetie, a roster of possible desserts. Still brainstorming, though I think this is a lot. I had fun playing with different ingredients:

Pears and apples poached in tequila and brown sugar, with piñon nuts
Chocolate layer cake (remember this one—I think you and Patrick just about ate the whole thing in two hours)
Almond cornmeal cake (I know this is one of your favorites, and it seems to go well with the theme)
Triple lemon layer cake (you have not had this one, but oh, my God, it's great!)
Cheese plate with berries, peaches, apples, or cherries according to the season
Black cherry flan (it's basically a clafoutis, but we'll call it flan and everyone will be happy)
Mexican hot chocolate and shortbread cookies

Playing still with pinwheel tortillas, but thus far, they've been low rent. See you soon!!!!!!!!!

Love,

Mia

PS You look hot in the tabloid photo, but the boss looks like a total geek. Is he? Not really your type, is he?????

SIXTEEN

Julian sat on the deck, wrapped in a thick sweater, drinking a mug of coffee and watching the clouds move in over the mountains, silver gray and blue, moody and dramatic. He loved living here, finally, a place of myth when he was a boy—Colorado—the place to which rebels ran, where you could reinvent yourself. The most beautiful place on earth, he thought now, scrolling through the news on his laptop.

A flag popped up on the screen, an email from his assistant. Hillary lived in a Hollywood apartment and wore chunky shoes and chunky black glasses and her hair in chunky layers, maybe to give her tiny frame some weight. A film-studies graduate, she knew every film ever made, loved research, and was more organized than an office supply store. It was hard to remember what he'd done without her.

A second flag popped up before he had a chance to open the first. One was the details of the interview he'd granted the *Denver Post*; the second was the one he'd been waiting for. *RE: accident,* it read. Two paper clip icons showed in the corner. *This is what I've found so far. More to come.*

He lifted his cup, sipped. Thought about Elena sitting across from him last night warning him that she would not give him a story. That fierceness in her eyes, the unsteady gait of pain. He didn't have any right to dig into her life this way.

And yet.

He punched the first paper clip icon. A copy of a police report had been scanned in. He read it quickly, still telling himself he would leave it alone, leave her in peace, that he just wanted the background to better understand her.

The details were horrific. Bodies in pieces. Elena lying undiscovered in a ditch for several hours through the night, the lone survivor. The only thing that saved her was the fact that she landed in an irrigation ditch. Cold water lowered the temperature of her body, and mud kept her from bleeding to death.

An unexpected wave of nausea rippled through him. For a moment, he closed his eyes, seeing another body, left in a field. Naked and battered.

A long time ago.

He closed the file. Opened the next one. A newspaper article about the funerals, with a photo of four caskets lined up in a small, old-fashioned Spanish church with an elaborate painted wooden altar in the background. Old. He wondered where it was.

Another flag popped up. This one from a business partner. *Script?* said the subject line. Julian rubbed his eyebrow, a spot that had a scar right through it from when he was twelve and took a dive from his bike into a rosebush right before his mother was killed. He'd still had the stitches at her funeral.

He opened the email, knowing what he would find.

Julian, my man, it read. David always talked like that, as if he were the moneyman in a bad movie.

Is there a problem? I expected a script last week and it's still not here. I hope you're just temporarily sidetracked by the new restaurant and not flaking out on me. I know you didn't want to do the slasher flick, but the studio is breathing down our neck for another in the series. You know it'll break records. Call me, man.

Behind him in the house, he could hear the cleaning crew vacuuming the already pristine floors, and he stood up abruptly. "Georgia?" he called.

She came around a corner, her bob curling nicely around her crisp scarf. He filed the image away automatically. "Yes, Mr. Liswood?"

"That's enough for today."

"Sorry, is this a bad time? Were we bothering you?"

"No. Yes." A tangle of irritation bloomed in his throat and he had to take a breath to avoid snapping at her. "No, it's not a bad time, but yes, the noise is bothering me today."

"No problem," she said. "See you tomorrow."

He went back to the table. Took a sip of coffee. Looked at the clouds dropping into the valley. Opened a reply and typed:

David,

Come to dinner in Aspen next week. I'll have the new chef make us a tasting menu and we'll talk about the next projects. I'm not opposed to another slasher pic, but I have some other ideas, too. Next Thursday? Bring Jenny. She can see the new house.

Julian

As he sent the email, he thought, *One down, four to go.* He wrote all four—producers, business advisors, their partners and wives—and pressed Send. Done.

Now he just had to have a story to sell them next week.

Candy, a tall, athletic blonde in her forties, proved to have a great space in the attic of a restored Victorian downtown, and great hands to ease the agony in Elena's hip. The music was simple and quiet, flutes with some underlying bells or something that helped ease her, too.

"What is this music?" Elena asked, groaning when Candy hit a tight spot in her neck.

"Alice Gomez." She eased around Elena and pulled the sheet down, revealing her scarred and misshapen back. "Car accident?" she asked, matter-of-factly.

"Yes."

Candy put her hands flat on Elena's spine, side by side, and gently moved downward, strong fingers tracing the shape of bones, ribs, musculature. "Broken back," she said quietly, "maybe three places?"

Elena felt a flicker of that night, so silent. So cold. "Four."

"Lose a kidney? Spleen, maybe?"

"Both."

Down the hands went, so hot Elena wanted to weep with the comfort of them. "Hip. Hmm. Lot of trouble here now. Are there pins? I'm not seeing this very clearly. Oh—" she said quietly, pressing a thumb into the bound muscles. "Lots of pain here, isn't there? It's a wonder you walked in here."

"I've been on my feet a lot."

"You have to rest more," she said. "But I think you know that." The hands moved, gentle and hot, pressure there, probe there, a lingering, circular centering on the spot over the back of her womb, a womb that was saved, but only the shell of it, not the contents. "It was a terrible accident, wasn't it?" she said gently. "You lost a lot. Other people?"

"Yes," Elena said. The weight of tears pressed into her throat, and she swallowed them away. In the corner, Isobel sat on the floor with a little girl, playing with dolls.

Candy worked and worked, moving energy, easing tightness, shifting heat from tangled joints, pressing coolness into overheated spots.

When Elena got up, two hours later, she could move without wanting to double over every third step. She made an appointment for the same time and day every week.

The masseuse wrote Elena's name down in her book, then stood up, tossing her heavy hair over one shoulder. "I can help you, and you can help by taking more days off—maybe every fourth day, if you possibly can."

Elena raised an eyebrow. "I'm a chef."

"Right. I figured you'd say that. But try to rest more when you're out of there. Get in the hot tub, take long walks, do whatever you can to ease those muscles." She turned and opened a file drawer, flipped through folders and drew out a piece of paper. "Try some of the hip exercises on this sheet, twice a day. You might loosen up a little in a hot shower or bath, then very gently try some of the stretches before you go to bed, and again when you wake up."

"Okay."

"Listen to your body. You must do that to some degree, or you wouldn't be able to do the work you do."

She tucked the card into her pocket. "It's been a big push, getting the new place open, but once we're up and running, it should get a bit easier."

Candy nodded, inclined her head. "Even with the best stretches and a massage every day, you are going to need more surgery eventually."

Elena shook her head. "I had a lot of surgery already, as you may have noticed."

"But what was that, maybe fifteen years ago?"

"Twenty."

"Back surgery has come a long way since then. It's possible you'd have much better results now."

With a slight smile, Elena said, "But even the best means I'd have to be off my feet for three or four months, right?"

"I'm not a doctor, but yeah."

"I can't leave the restaurant that long."

Candy's dark eyes were sober. "You know you're going to be forced to, eventually."

"I know." Elena zipped her bag. She took a moment to consider her word choices. "I've been working a long time toward the goal of having my own kitchen. If I can get through a year here, get it going, maybe then I can turn it over to someone else for a few months."

Candy smiled. "Well, I can help. My prescription is, hot tub every day and avoid being on your feet more than six hours a day."

Elena laughed. "Right. I'll get on that."

Back at the restaurant, the crew was working on setting up stations and space. The music was loud, blaring out rap, too loud. Elena scowled at Ivan as she came in. "What's this?"

He winked at her. "Thought you liked everything."

"Turn it down. Are the tamales ready?"

"Going." He reached over and turned the music *up*, not down. "I like rap."

Elena narrowed her eyes. Behind him, the rest of the kitchen, not including Juan, eyed her curiously to see how she'd handle the challenge to her authority. The jocks—the ski bums—and the Mexicans were bright eyed, the scent of their hot testosterone filling the space with an orange glaze. The rapper blasted out a misogynistic rage poem, *Bitch, bitch, suck my dick, you my ho, bitch.*

She couldn't work to this music. She'd be insane by the end of the day. But the way she managed his challenge would set the tone for this kitchen and this crew. A chef had to be a general, commanding absolute authority.

Ivan knew it, too. He smiled, very very faintly, and took a step closer. "Wanna dance, *chica*?" he growled. He pulled his lower lip into his mouth, sucking on it as he raked his eyes over her body, boldly.

He would, she knew, fuck her as a way to get over. She might even like it. He had that air about him, that air of a man who knew his way around nasty, hot, furious sex, "furious" being the operative word. Sex with him would be violent and edgy and angry.

And she would lose all respect in this kitchen. She would also lose if she complained about his objectification.

Without taking her eyes off Ivan's face, Elena said in Spanish to the Mexican dishwasher, "Nando, go to my office and get a deck of cards."

Rasputin grinned. "Oooh, kinky, boys."

While she waited, she poked around the pots on the stove, took samples of the stews and sauces. "The mole is excellent," she said to Peter. "Yours?"

He nodded, his cheeks bright red.

Frowning, she rolled the taste around in her mouth a minute. "Maybe a little something missing." She gestured for him to take a taste, too, and he complied. "A little more cinnamon? Taste it." She pointed and he took a fresh spoon from the tray, dipped, tasted.

He nodded, taking a step back as Nando hurried back into the room. Behind him came Juan, carrying a slab of meat from the freezer. He looked from Elena to Ivan with an impassive expression, and back to Elena. *"Qué pasa?"* he said, tilting his head. *What's going on?*

Elena shook her head.

"Here's the deal," she said to Ivan. "We have work to do this afternoon, but at seven-thirty p.m., I'll meet you back here for a game of poker. If you win, you can have your music. If I win, I pick."

Juan raised a dark brow, shaking his head slightly. Elena met his gaze without fear. She had an ace in the hole. So to speak.

"What game?" Ivan asked.

Elena shrugged. "I don't care. You choose."

Ivan stroked his chin. "Not poker," he said at last. "I challenge you to a cook-off."

"Like what?"

"Whatever," he rumbled.

"You could do, like, *Iron Chef*," said one of the ski boys. "We could come up with a secret ingredient and we'll be the judges."

"Hmm." Elena lifted one brow. "I'd go for that. But get some more judges. Not just you guys, but people from outside."

"Cooks and servers from other restaurants," Ivan said, arms crossed over his chest. His apron was slung low over his hips, and showed splatters of blood, a spray of something yellow, a mark where he'd scorched the cotton. "A lot of them will close by ten or so. We could serve at eleven."

Elena considered. He would likely know many of them, if not most. No way around that, really. "Okay," Elena said, and pursed her lips. "Each of you guys go out and bring back one item, enough for each of us to use in a dish. We'll cook, what?—three courses?"

"I'm game."

"What if we all bring back the same thing?"

Elena thought about it. "Bring back something that starts with the same letter as your name."

"*En español?*" Nando asked.

"Whatever works," Elena said, laughing. "Whoever wants to can come back by eight-thirty. We'll start cooking at nine." She looked at Ivan. "Good with you?"

"Fine."

"All right then." She pointed at the CD player and looked at Peter. "Turn that shit off." He brought her the CD and she gave it to Ivan. "Aren't you a little old for hip hop?"

"You're only as old as you feel," he said, and sauntered away.

"Back to work, everybody." As they shuffled to their stations and a CD of sixties rock came on, Juan approached her.

"Be careful," he said in Spanish. "You don't want him too drunk."

"Oh, I'm counting on it," she said.

"He gets mean. And if he goes on a bender, he won't be back to work for a few days."

Elena thought of the poker games in her New Mexico garage. "I'll be all right, Juan." She touched his arm. "Thanks for worrying, but I'm a lot tougher than I look."

His dark eyes were sober. "I'll be here, if you need me."

"Thank you." She grinned. "I couldn't run this kitchen without you, Juan, you know that."

"No, it's Ivan you need."

Elena shook her head. "Ivan is the spice. You're the meat."

He gave her a sideways grin. "Thanks, *Jefa*."

She headed to the back and found Ivan at his locker, putting the CD away. "If you don't show up for work tomorrow, Rasputin," she said, "I'll fire you."

He looked over his shoulder. "Nice move, *Jefa*. Better win, though."

"I'm not kidding," she said.

"I get that." For one hot second, she saw the resentment, the fury, in his eyes, and then it was gone. "I'll be here." He slammed the locker closed with a bang. "I'm going to kick your pretty ass all the way to China."

"We'll see."

From her office, with the door closed, she called Julian. "Hey," she said when he answered. "I wonder if I could impose on you for the evening."

"Sure. What do you need?"

"I'd like your daughter to babysit my dog for the night."

"I'm betting that will not be a problem, but let me ask her." He covered the phone and murmured something. "She says that would be *so great*." He spoke the words in a falsetto, and laughed, "Ow! Ow. Quit it. She wants to know when you'll bring him."

Elena looked at the clock, calculated what she would have to do to prepare for the evening. "Say, five? I'll bring supper if you like."

"Hey, now that's a great idea. What's up?"

"Power play," she said. "I'll tell you about it later."

Portia flung open the door when Elena rang. "Hi!" she said. She wore a long-sleeved pink T-shirt and jeans, her hair swept into a ponytail. "I'm so happy you called me to babysit! Come in!"

"I'm glad you were available."

Portia only had eyes for Alvin. "Hi, Alvin! Oh, look, how cute—do you have a toy, baby?" She laughed and reached for the grimy, once-yellow crocodile Alvin carried in his mouth. Alvin happily tugged back, his feathery tail swishing.

"He really doesn't like to go anywhere without it."

Portia tugged high, lifting Alvin to his back feet, and she laughed in delight.

"He loves to play chase," Elena said. "If he lets you have it, he wants you to toss it." She eyed the parquet floor. "Maybe not right here, though. Drop it, baby."

Alvin, looking deflated, sat down. Portia squatted in front of him. "It's okay, baby, we'll play in a minute." The dog sat down and let himself be adored, blinking happily, licking his chops every so often. "Can I take him down to my room until we eat?"

"Of course."

"My dad has been making a CD for the restaurant. He's in his office. I'll take you there."

Elena held up the bag of supplies. "I need to drop this off in the kitchen."

"It's on the way." She rubbed Alvin's head. "You're such a good boy, aren't you? I have a special bag of toys for you, and you can even get on my bed if you wipe your feet first."

Elena grinned. "Alvin, don't you start thinking you're the king or anything."

Portia's eyes flew to Elena's face. "Oh, am I spoiling him too much?"

Instinctively, Elena reached for the girl, touched her shoulder. "No, no. I'm terrible, Portia, seriously. He sleeps with me."

"Oh, good."

On the way through the kitchen, Elena dropped the bags of food, then followed Portia through the vast great room and up a set of stairs and over a walkway suspended over the hallway and great room. "Dad?" she called. "Elena's here."

At the end of the walkway was an open door where Julian appeared. His thick black curls were in disarray, as if he'd been pulling his fingers through them, and he wore a pair of wire-frame glasses that made her think of John Lennon. At the sudden, weirdly endearing sight of him, her heart gave a little jump. That nose—her weakness. Those curls.

He smiled, gestured her into his office. "Hi, Elena."

She found herself smiling. "Hi, Julian. What have you been up to?"

"I'll be in my room," Portia said, and trotted back the way they came. Alvin pranced happily along beside her, his red and gold tail high and swishing.

Elena grinned. "She *really* loves dogs!"

"Yeah." He seemed distracted, checking a piece of paper against another. "Have a seat. I'll be done in two seconds."

Elena looked around instead. The room was large, with cedar paneling on two sides, to give it that mountain feeling. A bank of dormers looked toward low black forest and mountains rising up blue behind on one side. French doors opened onto a balcony that presumably looked down on the courtyard. His desk was simple, heavy wood, his computer a sleek little laptop.

He typed some instructions into the computer and straightened. "You ready? I've been working on this all afternoon."

"Absolutely. Go." She sat in a chair by the desk and folded her hands.

"Oh, no," he said, holding out a hand as the music started. "Don't just sit there."

"Do what, then?" The music poured into the room,

Spanish guitar with a lilting and cheerful sound. She swayed happily. "This is great."

"We can go downstairs. It'll play through the house." He came from behind the desk. "How are you feeling after the massage?"

"Much better."

He took off his glasses as if to see her more clearly, and touched her shoulder. Elena noticed that he had not shaved today. Prickles of beard covered his chin, black and silver. Why was that endearing? She looked away.

"And you didn't have any trouble over the tabloid crap?"

"Um, well, actually, yes." She took a breath, letting him direct her toward the door. "Ivan saw it and he whipped up the kitchen pretty good."

"Ah." He paused on the walkway. "I'm sorry."

"I've got it covered." She moved suddenly and the height made her feel a little vertigo. "Wow," she said, grabbing the railing. "This is cool, but it's also pretty high, isn't it?"

"You okay?" He took her arm.

He was so close and she felt the dizziness of being so high, and for one hot long second, what she really wanted was to press her hand to his chest. Touch his tumbling black curls, the fan of lines at the corners of his eyes. The sultry tone of the music didn't help. He bent close, his hand on her shoulder.

"I'm fine," she said, breathlessly.

He kept looking at her face, and lightly pushed a lock of her hair over her shoulder. Elena clung to the railing, feeling a sense of being suspended in the air, as Julian's eyes touched her mouth, her throat. She greedily devoured details of his face, the way hair sprang away from his temple, the skin so delicate that she could see veins carrying blood to his brain and imagination. She admired the arch of his dark brow, and the moment was so strange and high and out of time and space that she didn't even think to move away when he took a step closer, and then bent down, and—

Kissed her.

Her first awareness was a burst of scent, something spicy and dark, and she swayed under the force of it. His mouth was wide, his lips deliciously lush and slow as he angled his head to fit their noses. She clung to the railings on either side, letting him put his hands on her face. He lifted his head for a blue second, their eyes meeting in confusion and permission, before he bent again, those heavy lashes falling, his hands on her jaw making her feel tiny and beloved.

It was too much, the flavor of him. He tasted of blue water, a lazy lap of lips and tongue that made her breath catch and her back arch. Her breasts touched his chest.

It was such a vivid connection that the part of her brain that would have been screaming warnings was just awash in the green narcotic flood of him. And he, too, made a soft noise of surprise, taking a step closer to slide one arm around her waist. He supped of her lower lip, touched it with his thumb.

Suddenly she gathered herself and pulled back. He didn't move away, but lifted his head. "Wow," he said hoarsely.

"Yeah, but no." She swallowed, forcing herself to take a

step backward, an action that made her dizzy. He saw that and stepped toward her, but she held up a hand. "This would be just a terrible, terrible idea," she said.

He frowned, quizzically. "It is." He stepped backward. "I don't know why I did that. I'm sorry."

She couldn't help looking again at his mouth, a sweetness like hay and morning moving through her blood. "I'm not mad. Let's just not, okay?"

"Okay. You're right. Let's—uh—" He closed his mouth. "Let's go downstairs."

SEVENTEEN

ISOBEL'S RULES FOR DRINKING

1. Eat a *lot*. Then eat some more.
2. Pick one kind of alcohol and stick with it the whole night. No exceptions.
3. Every hour on the hour, drink a big glass of water.
4. Eat some more.
5. If you're gonna do shots, never do more than one per hour.
6. When you get home, drink a big glass of water and take an aspirin.

EIGHTEEN

In his kitchen, Elena seemed smaller than she did at the restaurant. As he sat there, sipping a rubied merlot, watching her roll blue corn tortillas around a chicken-and-chile blend for tiny enchiladas, he could see she was no beauty. Her eyes showed signs of age, a little puffy with too much work, and she had little or no makeup on.

Around them swirled the moody music he'd chosen for the restaurant, a soundtrack as layered and rich and subtle as one of Elena's stews or the little taquitos she made that seemed so ordinary until you bit into one and it exploded in your mouth with a dancing parade of surprises—nutmeg or saffron, or some exotic layer that one did not expect.

Into the music mix, he'd salted some Norah Jones because Elena liked her, and a little Ella Fitzgerald, that "Summertime" he loved so much, and some Alicia Keyes. The girls, a nod to the female artists in evidence at the restaurant, not only the chef, but the head bartender, and even the Frieda Kahlo thread to the decorating—Patrick's doing, not his. Julian had also added some of the Lhasa de Sela the vegetarian restaurant had been playing the other night, with some horns and a Caribbean beat and songs in Spanish and French. There was more, some old Santana and things no one but Julian would have thought to include—a moody old cut from the Rolling Stones, and one from an old bluegrass gospel song, and a CCR song he loved. Like Elena's spices, it seemed odd until you experienced it.

Elena worked without speaking, listening to the music, her head swinging, nodding. Sliding a tray of the tiny enchiladas into the oven, she wiped her counter. "This is very moody," she said, finally. "The songs all have a feeling of yearning to them. Hunger."

A splash of embarrassment filled his throat for a minute, and he could only stare at her, running back through the cuts in his mind. "I guess they do."

"I don't think it's bad, necessarily—people won't listen to it that closely, and it gives a pleasant mood—but you might want to lace in some other things, too. Some upbeat instrumentals, not too over the top, but some Segovia, maybe, some flamenco. Matt Skellenger?"

"I don't know who that is."

"I have a CD. I'll loan it to you. I played it the night you came to dinner at my house."

Julian sipped his wine, smiled slightly. She leaned on the counter, wrists facing him so he could see the delicate skin there, the tracing of blood. He raised the glass. "Excellent suggestions," he said. "I'm not sure I've ever agreed with anyone who criticized my soundtracks before."

Her lips quirked. "Music got me in trouble today."

"What's going on?"

She settled on a stool, her arms crossed in front of her. "Ivan challenged me. It started with the photo, but it's been coming for a while. After I got back from the masseuse, he was playing some rap that was just obnoxious, and it was deliberate." She took a breath. "So I challenged him to a poker game."

Julian frowned. "Poker?"

"It's a man's game, and that's a very male kitchen. They all are, really, but because of the nature of the work pool in Aspen, I've got a lot of guys from places where women are not the boss."

He started to express concern, but she seemed to recognize that, and held up a hand. "It's not actually going to be poker. Ivan wanted a cooking contest, which is better anyway." She narrowed her eyes. "Maybe. He's one hell of a cook."

"So are you."

"I know," she said without conceit. "It'll be close." The timer dinged, and Elena took the tray out of the oven, piled four or five small enchiladas onto a plate and smothered it with chile and cheese, and pushed it over to Julian, then made herself a plate, too. "Will your daughter eat?"

He rolled his eyes. "Not this. Maybe a lettuce leaf." When Elena sat down across from him and dug into a truly enormous plate, he said, "You're not eating all that, are you?"

"Oh, yes." She grinned. "I'm preparing for battle."

"Battle?"

"Yes. I have three things on my side with this kitchen." She ticked them off on her fingers. "One, I speak fluent

Spanish, so they can't talk about my ass or my tits right in front of me, laughing at the fact that I don't know that's what they're saying.

"Two, I really am a very good cook, with my own voice and style. And three . . ." She took a bite, and chewed. ". . . I can drink almost anyone under the table with tequila."

She looked so small and pleased with herself that Julian laughed. "Now there's an odd talent. There must be a story to it."

"I was a teenager in a town where there wasn't much to do. We drank. The boys all thought they were so much better than we were that my sister Isobel and I practiced, like a science experiment—what should we eat ahead of time, how fast could we drink shots, was there a better brand?"

"Ah—the scientific method. I assume," he said, gesturing at the food, "that this is part of it."

"Lots of food to start, and plenty as the evening goes by. Fat and fiber—so beans and tortillas and cheese are very good, but I've learned over the years to add a lot of protein, too, because it slows it all down, keeps lots of food in your stomach."

"And the timing?"

"No more than a couple of shots per hour."

"How do you get around that if there's a round in between?"

"I drink water. Tons of it, and if necessary, I pretend to drink the shot, and then spit it out. Once people start getting drunk, they don't really notice if you swallow. And there's no difference between most brands, but some of the cheaper ones will make you feel like you died the next day."

"You don't anyway?" He shuddered at the idea of drinking shots of tequila all night long.

"Oh, it won't be pleasant, particularly, but a girl's gotta do what a girl's gotta do." She dabbed her mouth, and put her hands on her thighs, elbows akimbo, as if giving herself a breather. There was a lot of food left on that plate.

He looked at her mouth. The mouth, pillowy soft and succulent, that he'd kissed.

"How are you getting home?"

"I'll take a cab."

Julian scowled. "Just call me."

"Oh, no. I don't think I need my boss to see me three sheets to the wind."

Her boss. Boss. She kept calling him that. Putting him in his place. "I might like to see this contest. Who's judging?"

"They're bringing in people from the restaurant community. Chefs, servers, bartenders from other restaurants." She picked up her fork, took another bite. "Sorry, but you can't be there."

"Oh, come on. I'll be a mouse."

"No, it has to be me by myself." She gave him a serious look. "This is a key maneuver, Julian. I need to be the general in this kitchen, and I have to establish my authority on their terms. If you show up, I'm just another fuck."

Her language startled him, and at the same time, he felt a deepening respect for her. The unwashed hair in a ponytail, the lack of makeup, the simple gray T-shirt that hid her breasts, the slightly baggy jeans that did nothing to enhance her curvy bottom—all of that was part of the game, too.

She was far brighter than he'd realized. But a woman didn't rise through the ranks of high-end restaurant kitchens without a lot of guts and intelligence. Period.

Maybe *he'd* just been thinking of her as another fuck. Or something. A line of heat worked its way down from his ears to his jaw, prickling. "I get it."

She picked up her fork. "Thanks."

"Well, will you call me when you're home, anyway? I'll worry."

Her luscious, crooked smile reached her eyes. "Yes, boss. That I can do."

And for one long second, he saw her beneath him, both of them naked, her round white shoulder beneath his lips, his hands in her hair, a flash so hot and vivid that he had no idea where it was coming from. *Jesus.*

He picked up his fork, dug with great attention into the food. "Thank you."

Elena pushed into the restaurant at 7. Her hip and leg were starting to ache again, but she couldn't afford to take anything for the pain. She made her rounds through the front of the house, checking to make sure it would look its best that evening, and she was once again pleased by the elegant sense of tropical joy Patrick had brought to the rooms.

Juan and his family sat at a table near the kitchen, and she stopped to say hello to them. His wife was a shy pretty girl, not much more than twenty-five, and she was quite pregnant with her third child. Their two boys, about two and four, ran trucks around their plates, taking bites of plain enchiladas every so often. Their parents conversed quietly. Spying Elena, Juan stood. "Please, *Jefa*, join us."

She nodded at his wife. "*Hola,* Penny, how are you feeling?"

"Good." They all spoke in Spanish. "The boys are learning their numbers. We might even have a new house!"

"Fantastic."

"I told Penny we had to work tonight, so she brought the children to have supper with me."

"I'm glad you'll be here, Juan. Thank you."

His gentle dark eyes rested on her face. "You need a day off. Soon."

"You know better."

"I can take care of things for a day or two. Me and Ivan."

"I know you can, and I appreciate the offer. Once things are up and running, I'll be happier."

He nodded, raised one finger. "I asked my brother to send me something for you," he said, and pulled a small bottle out of his pocket. It was a holy water bottle, with a carved plastic rose on the cap, and a picture on the front of Juan Diego and the Virgin of Guadalupe. "It's water from the church in Mexico City. And a rosary. He had them blessed for you."

Elena stared hard at the bottle and beads, trying to rein in her emotions. "That was very kind of you," she said, and her voice betrayed her. A tear escaped into her lashes and she picked up the gifts. "Thank you." She kissed his cheek.

He nodded. "Cook with the saints tonight, eh?"

Elena laughed, draping the rosary around her neck, where it fell, cool and reassuring, against her breasts. "I will."

◆　◆　◆

A half hour later, a small knot of employees had gathered, Ivan among them. He was dressed in surprisingly elegant street clothes, a silk and wool sweater in vivid turquoise, with a loop of black scarf around his neck. In his ears were silver rings. He looked like a well-to-do pirate. His jaw was freshly shaved, and he smelled faintly of some exotic after-shave.

"Hey, *Jefa*," he drawled, eyes glittering beneath heavy lids as he looked behind her. "Where's Patrick?"

No wonder he was all dressed up. "He's still in Denver. Not sure when he'll be here."

A slight shrug. "Too bad."

In the kitchen, a festive mood reigned. The radio played an oldies station, and bags of groceries sat on the stainless steel worktable. Juan stood guard over the bags, and behind him were the troops—two dishwashers, the three ski boys and three Mexicans who made up the line, and Alan, from the front of the house. Ivan ambled in right behind Elena. They retreated to the locker room to put on their chef's whites and clogs.

"The rules of this competition are simple," Juan said. "You will each make three dishes—an appetizer, an entrée, and a dessert. You need to make enough to serve twenty— all of us and the judges we have coming from other restaurants. We'll vote and decide who is the winner."

Ivan smiled, very slowly, and bowed toward Elena.

"Be ready to serve at eleven sharp, and you can use anything in the kitchen, but you also have to use these ingredients." He smiled, Pancho Villa in his younger years, and gestured to the bags. "Boys, show them what they have to work with."

"I'm 'P' for Peter, and I chose . . ." He paused for effect. ". . . pomegranates."

Ivan laughed, low and happily. Elena nodded.

"Buckwheat honey," said Brent.

"*Huevos,*" said Hector, grinning at the double entendre, a slang word for testicles, as he put two dozen eggs on the table. The others laughed.

"Rose petals," said Roberto, revealing a bouquet of fresh pink roses, just barely opening. The room roared with approval. He blushed deep red, looking pleased.

"Corn," said Cody, smirking.

"My man," Ivan crowed.

Elena groaned. "I should have seen that coming."

"Achiote," said Alan, and Elena nodded, a dozen ideas arriving at once.

Juan went last. He grinned, his liquid black eyes twinkling, and brought out several bottles of tamarind-flavored Mexican soda. "Jarritos," he said.

"That's cheating," Cody said. "That's a brand name, not an ingredient."

"So?" He shrugged.

"I'm cool with it," Elena said. "Rasputin?"

"It's all good."

Juan looked at his watch. "Ready?"

"Ready," Elena said.

"Ready," Ivan agreed.

"Go!" He brought down his hand. Ivan raced for the walk-in. Elena went to the table and looked at the ingredients, letting her left brain go blank while the colors and scents and textures of the food mingled, swirled. She opened the honey and smelled an English summer afternoon. The buzz of bees, heavy and lazy and deep, the delicacy of rose petals and hearty shortbread and Earl Grey tea. She opened a bottle of Mexican soda and took a sip, delicately rolling it through her mouth like wine, picking up traces of mango and lime, which would pair with the pomegranate and—she narrowed her eyes—pork. Pork sausage? Yes, pork sausage grilled with onions and then stewed in the soda and pomegranates. Baked into a rustic crust, English-style. And shortbread cookies with candied rose petals and rose water. A very light appetizer, then. How to work in the corn?

Ugh. She'd think about it while she got the pie going.

At the back of the house in Espanola had been a one-car garage, converted in the late sixties to a poker room. A big round table sat in the middle of it, and cast-off kitchen chairs made of chrome and vinyl lined the sides. The smell of a million cigarettes and ten thousand cigars clung to the unfinished walls.

Serious poker was played in that room. With beer and tequila, Jack Daniels if somebody was feeling flush. Men played, not women. Never a woman, though sometimes there were women sitting on the sidelines, dressed up for the evening, cleavage showing, eyes lined thickly in black.

But as with everything, Isobel had been driven to be as good as a boy, and she wanted to learn to play poker like the men. She badgered Edwin to teach them. On long summer afternoons, they learned to play, finding relief in the thick shade cast by an ancient cottonwood whose leaves clattered softly overhead in the odd breeze. The Rio Grande lazed by, coppery and clear.

Isobel was too impatient to be a good poker player, in the end, but Elena, who had spent so much time observing the behavior of others, keeping track of what a roomful of possibly dangerous strangers might be thinking, proved to be very, very good. Edwin took such pride in her that he let her tag along to his games sometimes, and even play with the guys once in a while.

Of all the things she'd learned, those poker games had been the training that stood by her best as she struggled to survive as a woman in kitchens. Poker had lent her steely nerves and an ability to bluff, and an ability to hold her liquor. Tonight, in the kitchen, she played her ace. She slid her pies in the oven and glanced toward Ivan's side of the kitchen. He was dancing to his own music, chopping and bouncing and humming under his breath. As he felt her gaze, he looked up and winked.

"Juan," she said, "we need some tequila, and two shot glasses."

He narrowed his eyes. "Are you sure that's a good idea?" he asked in Spanish.

She wiped the counter. "I'm sure."

When he brought the bottle into the room, there was a murmur from the guys. One tucked his hands under his armpits. "Go, Chef!"

Ivan sauntered over, drying his clean hands on a fresh white towel from the stack on the counter. His eyes glowed turquoise beneath the hooded lids, and he cocked a brow as he lifted the shot glass. "May the best man win."

"Most *huevos*," she said, and Ivan chuckled.

They knocked back a shot, then one more, and went back to cooking. Ivan had a beer at his elbow the whole evening, but even when goaded, he didn't drink as many shots as Elena would have liked. And it took a while for her to realize why—he eyed the door every now and then. Hoping for Patrick.

As she cooked, she tried to keep her mind on her task, but the busy hands left a wandering mind. Over and over again, she saw a flash of Julian, leaning in to kiss her. His hands on her face, his black lashes floating down to the high angle of his cheekbone, the feel of his tongue against her, sliding in and out of her mouth, dragging across her lip—

Over and over, desire blistered through her, carrying with it a powerful and peculiar heat she kept nudging like a secret. Lips, tongue—tingling in the small of her back, the nape of her neck. His hand on her jaw—her throat flushed red and she could feel her nipples standing at attention beneath her baggy shirt.

Oh, I get it, Dmitri had written, *he just wants to fuck you.*

She breathed in. No, she definitely wanted to fuck *him.* Julian. Her desire had teeth, violence in it. As he'd sat there in front of her in the kitchen, wearing a neat, discreetly striped shirt in white and palest purple and palest blue, she thought of his chest, and wanted to tear at the fabric. She wanted to bite his neck like a cat, mount him, ride him, scream a lot.

Stop.

Focus.

Obviously, she needed to find a friendly buddy for sex.

The stress of working so much was making her horny, and sex would ease some of the aches and pains, too. Nobody in the kitchen, of course, but maybe once Mia arrived, they could go out sometimes, meet some new people.

Ivan stepped out to have a smoke, and Elena ducked into the break room. Her eyes were red and she squeezed some drops into them, blinking the sting away. Settling on the bench, she pulled out her cell phone and punched in Patrick's code. It rang, a lilting piano piece, but went to voice mail. He was still driving, then. Maybe on his way.

She stood up straight. Inhaled long and clear. Gave herself the eye in the mirror. She wished for company, for the comfort of her ghosts, but nobody came. They never did when she wanted them. Only when they felt like it.

"Fuck you then," she said aloud. Easy for them, on the other side. She unbound her hair, combed it, put it back in a ponytail. A depth of regret and resistance pushed through her—weariness. She didn't want to have to keep fighting for her position forever. She was sick of coming out of her lonely corner, fighting, going ten rounds, coming back to the lonely corner again.

And yet, what choice was there? You could sit down on the side of the road and cry, or you could keep fighting.

In the vastness of the great room, Julian balanced his laptop on his legs and tapped quickly, a rush of inspiration moving through him at last. Outside, the night swirled with fat, cottony snow against a soft pink sky. Pines arrowed into the pastel softness like sentinels protecting the property. It was vastly, unbelievably quiet—the thing people either loved or despised about the town. He drank it in like a drug. All of his life, he'd lived in noisy cities. This silence felt like a benediction, a blessing.

A fire flickered in the fireplace, logs burning with yellow and blue, the crackle of exploding sap sending a spray of sparks out every so often.

He wrote of a man isolated and lonely, a writer perhaps. No, that was too clichéd. A—what? What kind of a person lived the life of a recluse? He wrote fast: *writer, scientist, researcher, naturalist, forest ranger.* Hmm. Naturalist. Botanist. Forest ranger. Yeah, one of those. A guy who lived in the mountains, alone. His company was the landscape, the animals. His name was . . . Julian narrowed his eyes, reached for the first thing that came to mind. *Paul, Peter, Matthew, Jake.* Huh. Jake, yeah. Manly name for a guy with a broken heart. Matthew McConaughey–style, that Texas jaw and strong blue eyes.

Yeah, yeah, yeah. Good.

He sipped a cup of hot, strong spice tea, his only beverage when he worked. The wine with supper had lubricated his thinking a little, but he didn't really like drinking much anymore. It slowed his brain down, which was probably why some people liked it.

And if he were honest with himself, he was thinking of checking on Elena and crew later.

Jake in the mountains. Maybe Jake was too clichéd, too. Think about that. *Jack, Mack.* No, Jake for now. Fix it later.

Putting his cup down, he typed: *brokenhearted Jake in a cozy snowfall. A fire. A blanket in front of the fire. He's waiting, but we don't know for what. A woman appears, wearing a diaphanous robe that reveals and hides all at once. A beauty, sexy and strong, and she slides down behind our hero and begins to kiss his neck. A knock comes at the door. Camera zooms in on Jake's face, showing nothing. He glances over his shoulder, gets up to answer the door—*

There was a sudden bump against his leg. Julian, heavily engrossed in his writing, startled. He looked around the laptop screen to see Alvin.

"Oh, it's you, Dog," he said, reaching out to scratch the red-gold head. It was as silky as it looked. "Where's my daughter?"

Alvin leaned back, throat exposed, a most obvious invitation. Julian grinned and kept scratching the side of his face. Alvin reached up and put a paw on his wrist: *lower.* He licked his jowls, looked over his shoulder toward the stairs to the basement, and worriedly looked back to Julian.

"Problem?" Julian asked.

Faintly, he heard Portia yelling. Into the phone, probably. "You don't like yelling, do you? You want me to go check on her?"

Alvin leapt up and pranced toward the stairs, watching to see if Julian was smart enough to actually follow. They went down the stairs, and as Julian always did, he passed his hand through the strings of water falling in perfectly straight lines from the ceiling two stories above.

As they got to the bottom of the steps, Alvin slowed. Portia's voice, slightly hysterical, came to him clearly. "Mom, you can't just keep doing that! I can't go from school to school, back and forth, it makes me crazy. You won't even be there—you're always on some stupid movie."

Julian paused. This was a new angle. He squatted to put a gentling hand on Alvin's back. The dog stopped agreeably, waiting for a cue.

"If you miss me so much, just come visit me. How hard is that?"

Another pause. His heart lifted.

Portia's voice was absolutely solid when she said, "I will not come live there. Plain and simple. I like it here." The sound of something hitting a wall. He suspected it was a phone.

Julian trotted the rest of the way down the stairs, coming around the corner just as Portia let go of a growl of aggravation. Alvin rushed over to lick her fingers. "Your charge doesn't much like shouting," he said mildly.

"Oh, I'm sorry, honey!" She dropped down to her knees and kissed Alvin's face all over, scrubbing his neck, the fluff of thick hair around his neck. On the floor, her phone began to trill. "Don't answer that," she warned her dad. "My mother is a selfish, clueless . . . *child*."

Julian lifted his index finger. "Watch this." He picked up the phone and punched the green button. "Hello, Ricki. How are you tonight?"

"Julian. I'm fine. Do you have a new movie yet?"

"No. Listen, Portia is settled and happy in the school here and I want her to stay put for the whole school year."

"I miss her, Julian. It's not fair that you have her all the time."

"There's plenty of room here. You're welcome to come visit any time you like."

"But I'm living with someone now, you know that."

"There's room for him, too."

Ricki paused. "Really?"

"We're adults. There's seven thousand square feet in this house. Doesn't he ski? We're getting our first snow tonight."

"Well, I suppose that's one answer, isn't it?" She sounded hopeful, if a bit perplexed. "I'd love to, Julian, if you really mean it."

"I really mean it, Ricki. In fact, I'm sure your daughter would love to see you, so why don't both of you come next week? I'm having a little business gathering. You can come for the dinner and stay a day or two after."

"Business?"

He knew she'd not had as many offers these days. "I'm making a new movie."

"I see. Well, let me talk to Jake."

"Jake?" Julian echoed.

"Yes. You've met."

"Right. I forgot." Scratch Jake as the hero's name, he thought. Scott? Alex? James? Maybe he didn't really have a name. No, that would be stupid.

"I'm sorry?" he asked, realizing he'd blanked her out completely.

"May I speak to my daughter now?"

"Of course," he said. "Here you go, kid."

Portia grinned, her eyes as luminescent as morning. The director side of him knew the camera would love that face. The father side of him would do whatever he could to prevent her from going into the business. "Thanks, Dad."

He thought of the treatment for his script. Maybe the hero wasn't a man. An aloof man was one thing, obvious, easy. An aloof woman, more interesting. "I'll be upstairs if you need me," he said.

"He's writing," Portia said to the dog, clasping him close to her. "You see that look on his face? That means he's disappearing into his imagination."

Julian barely heard her, his synapses clicking as he dashed up the stairs and back to his computer. Settling the computer on his knees again, he wrote, *Blue eyes in a Mayan face. Haunted by the ghost of a dead lover, killed in a car accident that left her scarred for life . . .*

At the back of his mind, he heard her say, "I am not going to be a story." But this wasn't about an accident. It was about a ghost. About—

He paused, a sudden shiver on his neck. Did he want to take that chance, of alienating her? He thought of kissing her on the mezzanine, of the way she tasted like possibility. What if this flare between them had the potential to be something real?

The cynical, so-often-disappointed side of him said, *Yeah, right. Real for how long?* He didn't believe in soul mates anymore.

He did, however, believe in stories. What if the reason she was in his world was to give him the kernel of a new ghost story, something he'd been wanting to write for years? And what if he gave up the story for some possibility of—

A flash of a woman, blonde and small, sitting before a fire, came to him. A suggestion of a shape moved behind her, and she turned, hands holding invisible hands, mouth opening to an invisible kiss. She lay back and her blouse, button by button, was undone by invisible hands to reveal—

Julian blinked. Hot.

Commercial.

Ghosts and sex.

Just like that, the weight of Movie was formed. His instincts had never lead him astray. He opened an email and typed in the vision, and addressed it to the group.

And pressed Send.

NINETEEN

POMEGRANATE BAKLAVA

1½ cups buckwheat honey

1 cup sugar

1 cup water

2 T pomegranate juice

1 T rose water

Seeds of one pomegranate, divided in half

2 tsp whole cloves

1 tsp ground cardamom

1 tsp cinnamon

1 tsp grated nutmeg

1 cup slivered almonds

1 cup chopped walnuts

1 cup chopped pistachios

½ vanilla bean, scraped

2 sticks unsalted butter, melted

1 package phyllo dough

SYRUP: Combine the honey, sugar, water, juice, and rose water in a heavy small pot. Stir constantly while bringing to a boil over medium heat. Remove from heat and let cool, then add half of the pomegranate seeds.

Preheat the oven to 425. Mix spices, nuts, and vanilla bean seeds into ½ stick of melted butter. Butter a 13 x 9 inch glass pan.

On a clean work surface, unroll the phyllo and generously butter one layer at a time and lay it in the pan, then repeat until you've used half the dough. Spread most of the nut mixture and most of the remaining pomegranate seeds evenly over the pastry, reserving about one fourth of the mixed nuts and seeds for the topping.

Continue buttering and layering the dough on top of the filling until all the dough has been used. Brush the top with remaining butter and sprinkle the remaining nuts and seeds over the top.

With a small sharp knife, cut the pastry layers into diamonds, then bake for 50–60 minutes until golden, watching carefully to see that it doesn't burn. Pour the syrup over the hot pastry, and serve when cool.

TWENTY

Around ten-thirty, Elena could hear people in the dining room. "Somebody put the music on," she called out, stirring madly. She'd created a pie with pork sausages stewed in tamarind soda, onions, and apples with achiote. It was heady and strange and sweet, and it worked better than she'd hoped. She'd made cold, light pomegranate soup with caramelized corn and onions that turned out beautifully—the red broth and white kernels and the crispness of a sharp base to start the meal. The pie would be served as the main dish, garnished with red potatoes roasted in their oiled and parsleyed skins.

Dessert had given her more headaches than the rest put together. She considered shortbread with rose petals, but discarded that idea in the end—it would be too heavy after such a rich pie for the main dish. She finally settled on tiny bites of butter pastry topped with rose petals candied in nutmeg and honey.

She tried not to pay attention to Ivan, who worked steadfastly and with absolute focus on his projects. He disappeared into his work, a cloak of invisibility.

At ten to eleven, Juan came around. "How are you guys doing? Are you ready?"

"Do we have someone to help us pair the wines?" Ivan asked.

"I've worked as a sommelier," Brent volunteered.

"I'll do my own," Elena said. "For the first course, I want a zin. Then for number two, a heavy ale. And for dessert, coffee."

Juan wrote it all down, and then went with Brent to look at Ivan's meal. Elena started plating her soup in small white bowls, low and wide. Garnished with fresh mint and tiny rings of scallion and a few more sprinkles of pomegranate, it looked beautiful. "I'm ready."

"So am I," Ivan said. He'd made a very pretty salad of corn and rose petals and mixed greens, nice enough, but compared to her soup, it was boring, and he knew it. His face fell when Juan announced her soup to the diners. She licked her finger and made a mark in the air. He inclined his head, mouth smiling, eyes hard as glass.

They served the main dishes next. The diners groaned at the description of Ivan's shredded chicken and garlic enchiladas in a green-chile hollandaise sauce. "Fancy," she said, but felt sure her actual food would taste better. Juan described her English-Mexican pork pie, and the diners almost all went for it with gusto.

Elena felt sure she'd kicked some serious ass, but as they went back into the kitchen to ready the final dish, he said, "Just wait."

"What did you do for dessert?"

He leaned over and against her ear said, "Pure decadence."

"Chocolate?"

"Not. Even. Close."

She prepared her tiny pastries and waited anxiously to see what Ivan had done. When she saw it, before she even tasted it, Elena knew she'd lost the round. By miles. "Oh. My. God," she said, drawn across the room. "What are you calling that?"

He grinned, licking honey from a finger. "Sex on a plate? Sex when you get home?"

It was a baklava, layers of very thin pastry with pistachios and walnuts and the buckwheat honey and pomegranate seeds, drizzled with pomegranate syrup and sprinkled with little chunks of powdered sugar. Individual pomegranate seeds, like tiny rubies, were scattered around the diamond-shaped serving. "It's absolutely gorgeous."

"Thanks, *Jefa*."

"I'm still going to win. My soup was a thousand times better than your salad."

"Do you want to taste it?"

"Yes." She came around the pass-out bar and held out her hand.

"Allow me," he said, and held out a forkful.

Elena would not eat from his hand, not in this kitchen, with her staff watching. With Ivan himself practically afire with his passion. Not pomegranates, which were by legend a dangerous food. She took the fork from his hand and tasted it gingerly.

And even the smallest taste filled her mouth—sharp and sweet, thick and crisp, an absolutely brilliant mingling of textures and flavors and colors. For one second, she closed her eyes.

"God, Ivan," she said, and took another bite. "You're a fucking *genius.*"

He made a soft noise, a chuckle or a protest, she couldn't tell, and she looked up at him. He gave her a plate, a full slice of the baklava, and she took another greedy bite. Licked the fork, absorbed the flavors.

"I can't think of anything that could possibly follow your elk tamale," she said. "But this could."

For one second, he looked almost . . . stricken. Vulnerable. Then it was gone. He rumbled, "Does that mean you concede?"

She snorted. "Not a chance, dude. But we're definitely putting this on the menu." She took another bite. "*Man*, that's good!"

He glanced away, smiled. "You're something else, boss." He shook his head, wiped the edge of the plate. "Something else."

At the end of the meal, Ivan and Elena went into the restaurant with the staff. Elena said, "Hello, everybody! You look happy."

They clapped and whistled. It was a rough-looking group, long hair and earrings and tattoos, T-shirts and hiking boots and hands scarred by years in kitchens. They'd had plenty to drink, as Elena had known they would, and she'd cover that tab even if it pinched.

"Well," she said, "as many of you know, I'm now the executive chef at the Orange Bear, and Rasputin here"—an appreciative laugh—"was the master of the Steak and Ale. And we have just had a cook-off. Juan is going to pass out some voting slips, and all you have to do is check off which of the two choices you liked best. The most votes win. Any comments?"

"That baklava is to die for," said a very heavy woman in jeans. She made a ring with her fingers, kissed them.

Elena nodded.

"My favorite thing was the soup," said a man in his forties, with weary lines around his pouchy eyes. "It's hard to get the mix right on a cold soup, and it was excellent."

There were a handful of other comments as the ballots were passed out. "Take your time," Elena said, and gestured to Ivan. "Let's get a drink, huh?"

"Amen, sister."

She fetched the bottle of high-end gold tequila from the back of the bar and poured two shots. "Salt, lemon?"

He gave her a look. "Not hardly."

She lifted her shot glass. "To our menu, Rasputin."

"*Salud.*"

They knocked the shots back and Elena felt the sharp pleasurable burn of it in her belly. "I want to take Julian some of that baklava. Save some."

"Tonight?"

She narrowed her eyes. "His daughter is babysitting Alvin."

He laughed. "A dog that needs a babysitter?"

She lifted a shoulder. "He's *my* baby."

Juan called out, "Any more votes?" He lifted a hand. "Thank you. I will add up the votes and come right back."

She poured another shot, feeling the giddy relief of a long week, a good evening. "Another?"

"Yeah, one more." He patted his belly. "Shouldn't Patrick be back by now?"

"Yeah. I'm surprised he's not. But who knows. Maybe Mia's flight was late or something."

Juan came back into the room. "We have a winner."

Elena drank the shot of tequila, sucked air in over her teeth.

Juan said, "The baklava got the most votes for a single food, and the soup was second. The main dishes were close, but the pork pie won by six votes. You were asked to choose the best flow of the menu, too, and you chose the soup, pie, and rose petal bites. So, I am happy to tell you that you chose the menu of Elena Alvarez."

Elena grinned and lifted a hand to accept the applause. "Thank you, everybody. Let's give it up for Ivan, too. Wasn't that baklava amazing?"

There was a whoop or two. She added, "Thanks for coming over. I hope you'll all come back for the soft opening, and try the main menu."

The place cleared out pretty fast. Elena dismissed the staff and told them to go home and get some rest, take the day off tomorrow, and be ready to cook tamales on Monday morning. Only Ivan lingered, cleaning and puttering. Elena thought he was half waiting for Patrick.

The music was loud rock and roll in the kitchen, and they were drinking beer as they worked. When it was pristine, everything in its place, Ivan took off his apron. "One for the road?"

She hesitated. Something about him made Elena feel comfortable. They were the same in many ways—both of them walking that fence between worlds. And yet, a headache nagged at the back of her skull, the pressure of work the next day. "I think I've had enough."

"Just one," he said, and gave her a crooked grin, blood-shot eyes a blazing shade of blue that was almost mesmerizing. "For the sake of bonding."

Elena rolled her eyes. Gave him a half-grin. "All right."

He ambled over to the bar. "What flavor?"

"Whatever, it doesn't matter." Her voice was getting raw. "Half tomato juice."

"Where'd you learn to drink tomato and beer?"

"I grew up in New Mexico."

"Yeah, whereabouts?"

"Just south of Taos. Española."

He shot her a surprised look from beneath heavy lids. "No kidding."

"You know it?"

"A little." He brought over bottles of Bud and cans of tomato juice and set them down on the table. "Mind if I smoke?"

"You can't smoke in here!"

"Come outside then, I need a cigarette." He put on his coat and tossed Elena her sweater. Elena got to her feet reluctantly, feeling the freight train coming up her spine. She swore under her breath.

He offered a hand, and Elena waved it away. "Kicks your ass sometimes, doesn't it?" he said.

"I'm all right."

She followed him out, bringing her beer with her. Snow

floated out of the sky. She leaned on the railing while Ivan lit up. "What's your story, Rasputin? Why are you still in Aspen?"

He shrugged, blowing smoke into the night. "I keep trying to get out, and keep falling right back here. It's like there's some anchor on my ass that won't let me go very far." He took a drag. Looked at her beneath long lashes. "How'd you get out of New Mexico?"

A little drunk, Elena leaned on the wooden post. She sipped her beer, made a soft noise as she mulled the possible ways to answer.

Chose.

"I was in a car accident that killed everybody but me. It was a small town, and you know . . . it was just weird there after that. Nobody really wanted me around. It was too hard for them. So, one of the nurses at the hospital helped me find a job in a restaurant in Santa Fe. It kind of just went from there."

He lifted his cigarette and inhaled, blew it out again. "That's why you limp?"

"Do I limp?"

"Yeah."

"Well, that's embarrassing."

"Nah." He shook his head, came over and sat on the railing beside her. "You're one strong bitch, you know it?"

"Why do I think I'm about to get hustled?"

He met her eyes. "Show me yours, I'll show you mine." He took a drag on the cigarette, blew out a small stream of pale blue smoke. "Scars, that is."

"What are yours from?'

He stuck the cigarette in the corner of his mouth and

abruptly pulled up his shirt to show his belly. "Polka dots," he said, and she could see the faint white circles all over his thin belly.

Cigarette burns, very old. Elena couldn't help reaching for the scars and touched the ruched edge of one. He'd hate it if she cried, so she didn't. "How old were you?"

"I don't know. Five. Four. My mom got rid of him eventually. Funny that I smoke now, huh?" He mimed burning himself with the red ember.

To hide her face, she stood up and turned around, pulling her shirt up in the back to show him the worst part of her own worst scar, the thick ugly pink part that still looked gruesome. "I was in a ditch for a few hours before they found me."

"Pretty ugly," he said.

And kissed it.

Elena froze. His tongue was hot, a vivid contrast to the cold night. A bolt of need moved in her body, through her breasts, between her legs, and she desperately, desperately wanted to fuck. It didn't even matter who. It wasn't about love. It wasn't about roses. It was about pure, physical hunger, like an empty stomach, like grainy eyelids, like gasping for breath after being underwater.

But not Ivan. His game was seduction, male or female, it didn't matter. He had the pheromones to get the job done, too, and she was just drunk enough that it was very, very difficult to remember why she should not do it. What would it matter?

She willed herself not to react to the lips moving on her side. Took a swallow of beer. "You like boys, not girls, remember?"

He was standing behind her, his breath on the highly vulnerable back of her neck. "I keep telling you you've got it wrong."

She turned around. "Quit it," she said without heat. "I'm exhausted."

"And horny," he said, grinning with half his mouth.

And just like that, Elena was transported. The mingled scents of smoke and tequila and tomato juice, probably something about his skin, and she was looking at Edwin, not Ivan. It wasn't that she was having a flashback, or she didn't think so, though it sometimes happened. It was as if Edwin stepped over the body of Ivan and somehow became him. She closed her eyes, putting up a hand. "Don't," she said, and didn't know if she was talking to Ivan or Edwin.

Ivan watched her with Edwin's eyes, smoking.

"I've gotta get out of here," she said, and rubbed her forehead. "I'm going to lock up. You can have the day off tomorrow."

He stood and poured his beer over the rail. "For the dead people."

It was something Edwin always said, long ago. Elena stared up at him, feeling cold biting her back and the taste of winter in the air.

"See you Monday," she said at last, and left him in the cold on the porch.

Back inside, she dialed Julian's number. As his cell rang, she assessed her level of inebriation and decided it was all right. She could handle it.

"Julian," she said when he answered, "can you bring my dog to me? I don't want to sleep without him."

"I'm right outside," he said. "Come on out and we'll go get him."

She peered out the window but could see nothing. "What are you doing out there?"

"Just keeping an eye on things. Come out the kitchen door. Ivan just started walking the other way."

She hesitated, thinking of her restless skin and his mouth and the way a simple touch from someone she didn't even want had nearly set her on fire.

And yet, she really did not want to sleep without Alvin. Wiping her hand over her face, she said, "Okay. I'll be out in a sec."

She clipped her phone closed, turned off the lights, and double-checked the front door. It had been a good night. As she walked back through the dark kitchen, she felt a sense of satisfaction, and paused for a moment, looking around. *Her* kitchen.

In the corner, swinging her legs, was Isobel, wearing the same turquoise tank top that showed the freckles on her breasts, showed the sun tattoo on the right side. Elena waved as she picked up the box of baklava she'd put aside for Julian. She couldn't help opening it, admiring the beautiful pastry. She picked out a pomegranate seed and stuck it in her mouth.

"Beautiful," Isobel said.

"What were you doing in the restaurant the other night?"

"Watching." There was something sad about Isobel

tonight, something restless. "There's trouble in the air. I don't know what it is."

Elena narrowed her eyes, but really, she was a little worn out for portents. She picked another piece of baklava from the box and sucked it off her fingers. "This is so amazing." She offered it, but Isobel never took anything while Elena was watching. She left it open and went to wash her hands. When she turned back, Isobel was gone, but so was a corner of the pastry. Smiling, Elena headed outside.

Julian's Range Rover was parked under a tree. She opened the door and got in, suddenly smelling the apple and sunlight scent of him, and thinking *Oh, this wasn't smart.* Not with her nerves humming the way they were, with her hungers loosed by pomegranates and tequila and cooking.

And—be real—Julian himself.

"How did it go?" he asked, starting the engine.

Beneath her, the seat was heated. "Good. I won. But I brought you some of the dessert Ivan made. To. Die. For. I'm not kidding. The man is an amazing cook."

"Yes." He backed out and drove through the quiet streets. "What is it?"

"I'll just let you taste it. You need to see it, too. How is my dog?"

"Fine. He was asleep on Portia's bed when I left."

"That's very sweet."

It didn't take long to get there, or at least Elena's mind was tired enough that she didn't notice if it did. The cab was warm, the music sweetly seductive. "You are a big fan of the blues, aren't you?"

He chuckled. "You noticed."

"How'd that happen?"

"Lived in a lot of mixed neighborhoods." He shrugged. "The blues say things nothing else can."

She nodded, leaning her head back on the seat. White thick snow fell from a sky made pale by clouds. She thought again of Ivan's words, there at the end, sounding exactly like Edwin, and it spooked her. "Do you ever wish you could have a conversation with somebody who died?" she asked.

He glanced at her. "My mother. How about you?"

She remembered, suddenly, that he said his mother had died violently. But if she asked about it, she'd have to share her own story. "I never want to talk to my real mother, though she isn't dead as far as I know. Isn't that funny?"

"Not really. Not if she was a bad mother."

"I can't really remember her."

"I have to work pretty hard to remember mine anymore. It's like I have memories of memories, nothing real anymore."

"Memories of memories," she echoed. "I know that feeling."

"What dead person do you want to talk to?"

She leaned against the window, looking up toward the sky. "All of them. My little brother. My old boyfriend. My grandmother, the one who died when I was eight."

"What would you talk about?"

"I don't know," Elena said, realizing that she was a little drunker than she'd first thought. "I'd ask my grandmother what was in her French toast that made it so amazing."

Julian chuckled.

"How about you?" she said quietly.

He shook his head. "I'd be afraid to ask the things I really want to know." He paused. "If she suffered."

Elena thought of Isobel. Blinked a rush of emotion away. "Yeah." They were pulling into his driveway, a light shining from the tower like a beacon, snowflakes falling through the beam of light. "Fairy tale," she murmured.

"That's how I feel sometimes, too."

"Really?"

"Yeah." He braked before he went into the garage so that he could gesture at the house. "I mean, Jesus, look at it. I'm used to it, mostly, but if I remember to stop and think, it's amazing."

Elena liked him for admitting that. He pulled the Rover into its bay and the garage door went down. The garage was clean, everything organized by unseen minions, no stacks of stereo boxes or discarded toys or athletic equipment, the floor swept, the concrete clean beneath their feet. She picked up the box with the baklava and followed him inside.

They entered a family room area with a pool table and a bar in one corner. A bank of windows with French doors looked out to a patio with a hot tub. Elena felt disoriented. "Are we in the basement or something?"

He nodded. "This is where Portia's room is. Let's get your dog."

Oh, yeah. She took a breath and resolved to pretend to be sober, and followed Julian down the quiet hallway to an open door. The light from the hallway showed a big bed. Portia's blonde hair tumbled down the side of the bed, and her slim white arm was flung over the furry red body of

Alvin, who snored contentedly, his head nestled on the pillow.

Elena couldn't help it—she laughed. Quietly, covering her mouth. Whispering, she said, "Even I don't let him sleep right on the pillows!"

The dog heard her, raised his head. "Come on, honey," she said, and made kissing noises to call him to her.

His tail thumped against the covers, and he licked his lips, but he didn't get up.

"You traitor!" she said quietly, putting a hand on her hip.

Again his tail thumped, but as if he was absolutely too exhausted to hold up his head another second, he fell back to the pillows. In seconds, he was snoring again.

Elena rolled her eyes, but she was laughing. Waving her hand toward Julian, she went back down the hall. "Obviously, he's not suffering from the loss of me."

"Oh, I'm sure he missed you. It's just that Portia has a way with dogs. They all love her like that."

Elena touched the middle of her chest where a certain emptiness bloomed all of a sudden. "Well," she said. "I guess you can just take me home, then. I'll come pick him up in the morning."

"You don't have to go, Elena. It's a giant house. I have seven bedrooms. I'm sure there's one you'd find comfortable."

It seemed perfectly logical. Ordinary, even. "I was going to get in the steam shower," she said, mostly irrelevantly.

"Try the hot tub."

The light was ordinary, falling from overhead lights in an upscale but still rather plain family room. Julian wore a knit blue hat and a blue scarf and a leather bomber jacket that was really quite sexy. She looked at him for a long time, thinking he had the best face, so subtly carved, a little too sharp, showing its age a little bit, but still just so good to look at.

He looked at her mouth.

A whirl of images blazed through her mind—his kiss earlier, the musky purple scent of that moment, heavy in her breasts and thighs and lower belly; Ivan kissing her scar; Edwin speaking through Ivan's mouth. "I think I'm probably crazy," she said suddenly.

"A little drunk, maybe?"

"Is it obvious?"

"No," he said.

"Your eyes are saying yes."

He laughed softly, showing his teeth, and that made her like him even more. "Crazy how?"

"Oh," she sighed, "a lot of ways. But right now, I think you should make me a cup of coffee and you can taste this baklava, and then, yes, I will sleep in one of your bedrooms. But not yours."

His eyes stayed slightly crinkled in a smiling way. "Okay," he said, taking her hand. "Come with me. I'll give you your choice."

Up and up they went, to the first floor, and then the second, curving around the strings of waterfall, lit at night with very soft blue spots that made the water shine beautifully. Elena reached out and cut the water with her fingers. "Sorry," she said when Julian looked around.

"I do it all the time."

"It's kind of fun."

On the landing of the second floor, he flipped on some lights. "Let me give you a few choices. My bedroom and offices are that way"—he pointed down a carpeted hallway—"and down the other direction are some ordinary rooms with good views. But I think you might like a quirky room."

"Okay."

He led around the gallery into a tower with a window seat and stairs going up to a loft. It was furnished with California mission–style furniture, antiques she thought. There was a Frieda Kahlo print on the wall. "This is very good," she said. "I love this room."

"I thought so. Let's have that cup of coffee, and you can get some sleep."

Elena didn't move. The lamps were square stained glass, the linens in colors of wine and pale gold and earth. Julian stood a little too close, or maybe she had moved. She wanted to put her hand on his sleeve. Lean in and breathe his smell. Yearning buzzed in every nerve, not like the lust she'd been feeling earlier, but a tangle of lures that seemed to tug on her cells equally, as if he were a giant magnet and she assembled of iron shavings.

She looked up at him and he was looking down, and then he said, "Maybe it will be better if I just let you get some sleep."

"Okay." She closed her eyes. Swallowed. "That's probably a good idea."

But he didn't move right away. There they stood, Elena with Ivan's sinful pomegranate baklava in her hands, Julian with his hat on, his hands loose at his sides.

He said, "You have the most beautiful mouth I've ever seen."

Some instinct of self-preservation, some being of wisdom made her shake her head, take one half-step backward so she could open the box in her hands. "Here," she said, breaking off a piece of baklava and holding it out to him. "You have to try this."

Instead of taking it with his fingers, he bent and took it with his mouth, as she must have known he would do. His tongue touched her fingertips; his mouth closed around them.

Elena made a sound. Before she could draw away, he captured her wrist and held her there, sucking on her fingertips.

And then the tastes emerged, all that sweetness and texture, and he straightened. He swallowed. "Wow." He blinked. "Wow. More."

Elena laughed, shoved the box into his hands. "I absolutely cannot feed you pomegranates and still go to my bed alone."

"That's what I was hoping, actually."

"Good night, Mr. Liswood," she said, shoving him out the door. "Don't wake me too early. I'm sure I'm going to have a terrible hangover."

He gave her a sideways grin, pointed at a door. "There's a pharmacy in that little bathroom there. Drink plenty of water."

"Thank you."

"Good night, Elena."

She closed the door. Leaned against it, closing her eyes.

After a moment, when the closed eyes made her feel dizzy, she straightened. It was almost as if this room had been created with her tastes in mind. The carpet was thick, dark brown, like chocolate, and the furniture seemed almost to whisper secrets from long-ago Spaniards, priests and conquistadores and passionate women with mantillas over their hair. The walls were washed a terra-cotta color, earthy and rich. It was a room that made her think of Texas, of New Mexico, of the places she'd left behind. Edwin and Isobel and her mother, and the mother who'd left her.

A sharp, unexpected sense of loss, thickened by drink and exhaustion, rose in her throat. Maudlin tears rose in her eyes, and she recognized, just in time, the beginnings of a snuffling, embarrassing crying jag.

Just don't, she said to herself.

In the medicine cabinet in the bathroom, she found a selection of over-the-counter medicines, one of which was ibuprofen, which she downed with a giant glass of water. It was deadly silent in the rooms without Alvin, and she realized she hadn't spent a night without him in years.

Glancing at the clock, she saw it was past two. A hollow feeling emptied her lungs. The silence was deep, deep, deep. Empty. In the morning, she would be hungover, but at least this way, she'd have her dog ASAP upon awakening.

She stripped out of her clothes and padded into the shower. The massage and the tequila had helped—if she had a good steam in the morning, she'd probably be in pretty good shape. Humming under her breath, she turned on the shower and stepped into the spray, closing her eyes as the water scoured away the grease and sweat of cooking.

The day rolled over her in tidbits. The dream last night. Julian's kiss. Ivan's touch on her back.

Edwin's voice. A chill touched her. That was a little too weird.

Just horny, she told herself as she climbed into bed. Naked, since she had nothing else to wear.

Get some sleep.

He was waiting for her by the fire, his coppery back facing her, cloaked in shadows, his shoulders gleaming in the firelight. Elena recognized him—Edwin!—with a sharp catch to her breath. For a moment, she paused, worried that there was some breach in what she was going to do; perhaps she owed another allegiance or—she couldn't remember. Something about it frightened her, something made her want to hesitate, even as she was drawn forward by his black hair, his silken skin. He turned and there was fire in his black eyes, a sharpness that—

"I have been waiting," he said, in a voice that had the thick gold depth of buckwheat honey, almost too strong for pleasure. A woman collected it by the banks of the Rio Grande, and called it Pancho Villa honey because it was so strong.

Elena hesitated.

Beyond the windows, snow fell in thick, cottony flakes. Elena wore a long gown that buttoned up the front. The fire crackled, smelling of sap and pine and smoke. The warmth burned the front of her and left her back chilled. Always the way with a fire.

He held out his hand. "Come sit with me," he said.

"What are you doing here?"

"Sometimes, they let us come when you need us." He began to brush her hair. It sparked static.

"Do I need you?"

"Yes, Elena, I think you do." He bent and kissed the back of her neck. "I'm here to protect you."

"Protect me from who?"

He ran his hands through her hair. "From everything. Within and without."

Elena knew it was a dream, but as she leaned backward, she could feel the warmth and solidity of him. "You don't feel like a ghost."

He laughed. And what a sound that was, the low hoarseness. She'd forgotten the loose depth of his chuckle. It brought tears to her eyes. "A ghost wouldn't do you much good, would it?" he said.

She tumbled into his arms and let him lie her down on the floor.

"You look so beautiful," she whispered, touching his thick black hair, long by today's standards, but not by those old days'. It was cool and heavy against her fingertips, and an odd, sharp pang touched her. Was he real, not a dream?

"I'm not a dream," he said raggedly, bending down to kiss her. His mouth was a shock, remembered and not. Familiar and yet new.

She opened her eyes, suddenly afraid. Afraid she would see his skull or his bones or nothing at all.

But there was his brow, smooth and brown; there was his hair, black and satiny, falling against her cheek. There were his lips. She had forgotten so much! *So* much!

Fear and erotic longing rose in her, a sob. He kissed her throat, tears in his eyes falling on her chin, and lower, kissed her chest and her breasts, her belly, then shifted in the way of a dream and they were joined, joined and rocking. Hard. He touched the places that ached, smoothed his palms over the irritated nerves, his penis filling up the empty place, rubbing her higher and higher. Hard. She came, arching against him, moaning into his mouth, taking both his orgasm and his tongue with a ferocity that seemed it could be heard into Montana.

And then she slept.

Hard.

TWENTY-ONE

BANANA AND CHOCOLATE CHIP PANCAKES

1 cup all-purpose flour
1 T sugar
2 tsp baking powder
¼ tsp salt
1 egg, beaten
1 cup milk
2 T melted butter
2 large bananas, cut into slices
Broken pieces of chocolate or chocolate chips

Combine the dry ingredients in one bowl. In another bowl, mix egg, milk, and butter, then stir wet and dry together quickly until blended, about 10–12 firm strokes. Do not over-mix, or pancakes will be tough. The batter should be slightly lumpy.

To cook pancakes, an electric skillet or large cast-iron pan will yield the best results. Heat the pan until it's hot enough that water will dance on it, then grease it lightly and pour batter by ½–cup measures onto the pan. Cover each pancake with a few slices of banana and chocolate, let bake until dry open holes appear on the pancakes, then flip. Serve with butter and syrup of your choice.

TWENTY-TWO

Before she opened an eye, Elena felt the heaviness of too much drink. Dry mouth. Raw throat from sitting around with Ivan smoking, and from the harsh gold of tequila. Tight band of discomfort over her eyebrows.

What had she been thinking? Tequila shots?

Soft light bumped against her eyelids, and she cautiously opened one, a little disoriented. Her vision fell on a small square of a window, one in a series marching around the curved wall in a little row like square portholes. Through it she could see, perfectly framed, a long-needled pine tree with a fresh dusting of snow. The sun was shining. Snow glittered.

She rolled over, testing her memory of the night before to be sure there was nothing too awful in there. A blur of Julian sucking her fingers. The sensation of having had sex—but surely not!

No, no. She clearly remembered telling him to go, shutting the door against him, taking a shower and climbing the stairs to the loft where she now slept. Naked.

And she'd dreamed of Edwin again. Dreamed of having sex with him.

She started when she shifted and there was Isobel, sitting cross-legged on the bed, her feet bare. "You scared me!" she said, blinking. Her sister didn't look the same, somehow. It took a moment to realize what it was—Isobel's freckles, the beautiful spice on her skin, were faded. When she spoke, her voice was thin, as if it was coming from a faraway place.

"You need to go see Hector's sister," Isobel said. She looked worried. "There's something wrong."

"Hector from the kitchen?"

Isobel nodded. "Soon," she said. And then, "Portia likes banana and chocolate pancakes."

Elena dozed slightly, waking when she felt Isobel lie down beside her, brushing her hair. "*H'ita*," Isobel said, "you have to let go."

"Mmm," Elena said, remembering the dream of Edwin, the feeling of him around her. She kept her eyes closed as Isobel gentled her hair, easing away the headache. There had never been anyone like Isobel in her life, the giggle, the zest, the joy in living. It seemed somehow right that Isobel's light could not be so easily extinguished as by simply dying. The mighty vividness of her couldn't help but go on. "I will," she said, and drifted off again. When she next awoke, Isobel was gone, and for a moment, Elena was terrified. She sat up straight in bed. "Isobel?" she cried.

Her sister spoke from a post by the window, her back to Elena. "Go fix the pancakes," she said.

Elena felt the almost-loss in her throat, tears in her eyes. "Don't go yet, okay?"

Isobel turned, and Elena felt a tear spill out of her eye. "Go cook," Isobel said gently. "I'm here."

Julian was making a pot of coffee, with deep morning sunlight falling liquid over his shoulders, when Alvin trotted into the room. The dog paused to be sure Julian noticed him, then headed for the glass doors. Julian let him out, and waited as Alvin watered the scrub by a tree. Steam rose from the snow.

It was a brilliant day, the sky so blue it provided an absurdly vivid backdrop for the snow. By nightfall this snow would be gone, given that sunshine, but it wouldn't be long before it covered the slopes that were the town's lifeblood.

The dog came back to the door and Julian let him in, patting the silky head. He really was the softest damned dog. "I bet you're hungry."

Alvin waved his tail and accepted a bowl of food, and some water, but after a sip, he was plainly still waiting for something else. He sat politely by the counter, chest up, polite eyes boring into him. "What?" Julian asked.

The tail swept the floor. His mouth opened slightly, showing the purple tongue.

"Oh, I know." Julian said. "You want your girl, don't you?"

He panted.

"Let me just make a cup of coffee and I'll take you up to her."

"Dad," came Portia's voice, "he's a dog. He doesn't speak English."

Curses, Julian thought, aware that he'd had some vaguely shady thoughts about *how* to wake Elena. "Hey, kiddo."

She slumped at the counter on a stool, wearing pink flannel pajama bottoms and a giant T-shirt. Her hair sparkled in the sunny kitchen like silver floss. "Hi. I'm hungry."

"You? Hungry?"

She yawned. "It's Saturday. I'm tired of not eating all the time. Maybe I'll go for a run later or something. You have to have energy to run."

He nodded, wondering what he could fix for breakfast. He didn't want to go into town, but was there anything here worth cooking? "Frozen waffles?"

"*Packed* with transfats and white flour, dude."

"Oh. Sorry. Hmmm." The coffee stopped gurgling and he poured two cups.

"What are you doing?" she asked. "I don't drink coffee."

"One's for Elena," he said without thinking.

A deep pause. "She spent the night here?"

"Not like that." He turned around and looked at her. "She's in the guest room."

She raised her hands, palms open. "None of my business."

"It is your business, actually. You live here, too, you know. I wouldn't want to make you uncomfortable, Portia."

She stared at him for a minute, a thousand small betrayals swimming over the surface of her irises. It shamed him. "Really?"

He nodded. "Really."

"Okay—here's the truth: it's weird when your parents have a boyfriend or girlfriend over."

"She's not my girlfriend. She's my chef."

"I get it," Portia said.

"Hello—I'm warning you that I'm here," Elena said from the doorway.

Alvin wiggled happily toward her, head down, body arched, looking like a comma. He shimmied into her legs and Elena chuckled, a low earthy sound, and she knelt, or kind of crumpled, to kiss him and hug him, rubbing him all over.

"That was awful," she said in a ragged voice. "I missed you so much." She held Alvin's muzzle and kissed the velvety snout, then between his eyes, and Alvin made a low, pleased noise. Licked her nose very politely.

Julian wished to be a dog. Her fine hair was loose on her shoulders, long and pale. For the first time, he noticed a thin, faint scar edging from the top of her shirt, along her collarbone. Inexplicably, the sight made him think of his mother.

After a minute, she stood up, and Julian saw the swollen eyes, the extreme paleness. "You all right?" he asked.

"More or less," she said with a tilted grin that made her look about sixteen. "I'd kill somebody for that coffee in your hand."

"It's all yours," he said. "Cream and sugar, as I recall."

"*Bueno.*" She looked at Portia. "He was sleeping on your pillows when I got here, and he wouldn't come with me. You're a real dog charmer, aren't you?"

"But look how happy he is to see you now!"

"Yeah, yeah," Elena said. Alvin dashed into the great room, grabbed his crocodile, and brought it back to her, his head and tail high and happy. Elena grabbed it and yanked, letting him play tug-of-war for a minute before she took it away and tossed it toward the hallway. He danced toward it, and leapt on it as if it were a live thing.

Julian watched her with a sense of airlessness, feeling stricken, starving, yearning, and for no earthly reason. Her hair, stick straight and too fine to be particularly alluring, was combed, but hardly styled. She looked a little hungover, and she wore the same clothes she had on last night.

And he really would have liked kissing her good morning.

Elena sat across from Portia. "How was he last night? He seems very happy. Did you guys have fun?"

"We did." She grinned. "He is such a good dog!"

"I couldn't stand not waking up to him this morning, so I had your dad come get me from the restaurant and then you guys looked so peaceful, I didn't want to disturb you."

"That was nice. Thanks." She frowned. "There were some fireworks, though, and he totally freaked out. Does he always do that?"

"Oh, yeah. He's absolutely petrified of thunder, fireworks, anything like that. I tried drugs but they don't really help."

"Poor baby." Portia rubbed Alvin's back. "I'll do some research, ask around, see if there's something to do for it."

"I'd be so grateful if you found something to help him." Elena put her cup down. "Now. How about if I make breakfast to thank you both?"

"You don't have to wait on us, Elena," Julian said.

Elena inclined her head. "You don't actually know how to cook anything, do you?"

"Uh—"

"He offered frozen waffles," Portia said.

"Ugh!" Elena rolled her eyes. "Well, I'm *starving*," she said. "And I am—as you may remember—a spectacular cook."

He smiled. So did Portia.

Elena narrowed her eyes, as if she were reading something written on the air. She peered at Portia carefully, and Julian swore he again saw that odd bend of the air around her, a shimmer of heat or light or something. "Let's see—you are a pancake girl, aren't you? Is it . . . nuts . . . no, bananas. Banana and—is it chocolate?"

Portia's mouth dropped. "How did you know that?"

Elena raised her eyebrows ruefully. "Well, here's the deal—it's kind of magic." She grinned, and for the first time, Julian noticed that she had a great dimple deep in her right cheek. "I can smell things sometimes, like an aroma of cooking food. I smelled latkes around your dad, and bananas around you."

Portia looked wary. "Are you making that up?"

"No. I know how it sounds." She took a sip of coffee, raised a hand as if swearing before a jury. "I swear it's true."

"That's weird," Portia said, tucking her hair behind her ear. "But kind of cool."

Elena nodded. "So, banana pancakes?"

"Sounds great." She swirled off the stool. "I'm going to go brush my teeth."

Elena smiled after her, an expression of softness around

her eyes. After a moment, she stood and looked around. "Where is everything? I see bananas. Any chance there are chocolate chips or bittersweet chocolate or something in here?"

Julian wiggled his brows and reached into his stash in the cupboard. "How about Dove chocolate?" he asked, bringing out a bag of small bars.

"That will do very nicely." She put them on the counter next to a bowl she found, and opened drawers, cupboards, familiarizing herself with the kitchen. "Hmmm. I don't see measuring spoons."

Something was different about her this morning, and Julian finally put his finger on it. "You're not limping."

She scowled. "Do I limp a lot? Ivan said that last night, too. I wasn't aware of it."

"Not really. Just a little, when you're tired or something. Still"—he inclined his head frankly—"you're moving a lot more freely than usual."

"That's the tequila. If I wanted to be a drunk, I'd never have any pain at all."

"Speaking of drunks, how was Ivan last night?"

"Fine." She pulled open a drawer and crowed, pulling out a set of measuring spoons and cups. "He wasn't drinking the way I expected. Maybe he's turned over a new leaf."

"Was that a test?"

She met his eyes. "Partly. Mainly, it was just to show the kitchen I'm in charge."

He nodded. "How'd you do?"

"I won. And we cooked for a good portion of the kitchens in town, so the respect ratio will be high."

"Excellent."

"Hand me the flour," she said, pointing, and he passed it over. "And now we have our big week, huh?"

"Yeah. How are you feeling about it?"

"Good, honestly. We're going to have a tamale party to-morrow, making tons of them. And Mia was getting on a plane the last time I spoke to her, so Patrick should be bringing her here any time."

"Good."

"The staff tasting is tomorrow night, your party is Thursday, right?—we need to hammer down that menu, by the way—and the soft opening is Saturday."

"Pretty exciting."

She touched her lower ribs. Smiled up at him. "It is."

Her cell phone rang on the counter and she frowned at it. "Do you mind? It's Patrick. He went to get Mia."

"Go ahead."

Her body angled away, and Julian stood up, walked to the window to give her some privacy. The new snow made the air so bright and clean it was like a glass of fresh cold water. He crossed his arms, thinking of Portia's resistance to skiing, wondering how to get around it. Maybe they could go snowshoeing, get her feeling excited about it all again.

When did the tide turn toward such skinniness, any-way? It seemed to him that there used to be lots of lean, lanky girls, but also girls with lush breasts and lots of gor-geous ass, and still others with the supple squareness of athletes.

Then one day, they all showed up to casting calls look-ing like coat hangers.

Behind him, Elena said, "It's your call, Patrick. I trust your judgment."

He turned. His gaze caught on the white skin over her collarbone, on the line of her throat. Traveled over her delicate wrists and battered hands, and her breasts, too, more evident here than at the restaurant, where she camouflaged her body beneath chef's coats or loose T-shirts. Very nice breasts, full and natural.

Her mouth was tight when she hung up the phone.

"Problem?" he asked.

"Mia's not coming. She's in love and her man doesn't want her to leave. So, I'm without a pastry chef. Patrick is going to see if he can find anyone appropriate in Denver. He has some connections."

Julian shrugged. "Not such a big deal. The menu is in great shape."

She nodded, staring into the distance with one hand on her hip. "I'm in love with Ivan's baklava," she said. As if in memory, she licked her lower lip. "He's amazingly talented."

The unmistakable thrust of jealousy twisted through his gut, and Julian squashed it. "That's why I wanted to keep him."

Portia came back into the room. "What can I do to help?"

Julian was startled—Portia help with a household task?—but wisely retreated. "I have to make a couple of calls. Yell when it's ready."

"Will do, boss," she said, putting him in his place.

Where he needed to stay.

◆　◆　◆

Back at her apartment, Elena took some time to rest and read, only walking over to the restaurant in the very late afternoon. Alvin slumped on the porch, enjoying the sunlight. Roberto washed dishes, singing along to the radio, and Ivan scraped a bowl clean with a spatula. He looked fine, and she realized that she'd been worried that the drinking would make him binge. "You didn't have to come in," she said.

Ivan shrugged. "I know."

"Is Hector here today?" she asked.

"Tomorrow," Roberto said. "He has Sundays off when he can. Likes to go to mass."

"Does he have a sister?" Elena asked.

Roberto raised his head. After a moment, he nodded. He touched his temple. *"Ella es adivina."*

Fortune-teller. "Will you see Hector tonight? Will you tell him for me that I want to see her?"

Roberto nodded. He rinsed the bowl and put it away. From his pocket, he brought out a cell phone and punched in the numbers. Elena left him to it and went to the office. She had paperwork to do.

There was an email from Mia, of course. Ripe anger bloomed in her throat and she was tempted to delete the post unread. Instead, she stabbed the button to open it.

To: Elena.Alvarez@theorangebear.com
From: Mia_grange@askthechef.co.uk
Subject: (no subject)
My darling Elena, I know how angry you are this morning,
but please call me. Please don't see this as a betrayal,
because you'll never forgive betrayal, and it isn't. I swear. I've

been trying to tell you for two months that I wasn't sure, that I might really need to stay with this man, that he's right for me, and you haven't been listening.

Babycakes, my dearest, dearest sister, please call me. I want to tell you the story. It was so romantic—Kevin came to the airport with flowers, begging me to stay. I am so in love! It happens to you all the time, but not to me.

Call me, call me, call me.

I love you.

Mia

Elena glared at the page. "What's that supposed to mean?" she muttered at the email. "I don't fall in love all the time!"

But with shame, she saw a sudden parade of men—serious love affairs. Christopher and Timothy and George and Andrew and Dmitri. Between them, minor connections—a blues singer in San Francisco, a sturdy businessman in New York, a soccer player in Vancouver.

And Edwin, of course, so long ago. The only lover who visited, over and over, the memory of him unsullied, always sweet. She thought of her dream, of his supple, unflawed eighteen-year-old flesh, his unmarked face and furious passion.

Perfect. And of course, no one could ever measure up to a memory.

But Mia, as her note plainly displayed, knew what the price of betrayal was. She had known Elena would not forgive this, and she had chosen a man over a friendship. "Sister!" she said aloud to the screen. "Some sister."

Somewhere at the core of her, Elena wanted to put her

head down on the desk and wail. She had so been looking forward to having Mia here, a woman, a friend, an ally.

But she didn't put her head down—because she already knew this truth: people left you. It was the one true thing she knew. Everyone always left you. She could only count on herself.

And she could count on work. Focus on her job. That was where real reward lay. She deleted Mia's email and pulled up the books and ordering forms. Almost time. She would make a checklist to make sure nothing was missed for this week.

Work.

The first tasting, for the staff on Monday night, went over with wild success, and despite her annoyance at Mia—who called every day to leave apologetic messages on her voice mail, and sent email after email, which Elena deleted unread—Elena felt the first real surge of confidence. Thanks to the long hours of training and establishing the spirit of the kitchen, the evening ran very smoothly.

Elena put Peter on figuring out desserts. He wasn't happy, and it didn't help that the other guys in the kitchen snickered over it—pastry chefs were an entirely different realm. Not really chefs at all, in the opinion of the male world. Peter protested, too, said he was a cook, not a chemist. But she'd seen something in his loving attention to detail that made her think he'd do a good job, that he might be more of a pastry man than he knew.

At any rate, it wouldn't hurt him to do his time at that station. He had a lot of talent and drive and would one day have his own kitchen, she was sure. She told him as much, gave him a raise, and he was mollified.

For the time being.

It turned out, too, that one of the Mexican dishwashers was well versed in tamales. He suggested the upstairs could be a kitchen devoted not only to desserts and tamales, but all manner of prep work, leaving space free downstairs for the actual assembly and cooking.

On Thursday, they would present the tasting menu for the dinner party at Julian's. It happened to be Halloween, which Elena thought hilarious for a horror director, and she developed a theme of El Día de los Muertos for it.

On Friday night, the restaurant would fling open the doors to members of the community invited in to eat for free. It would allow the staff to do a serious trial run of systems—front and back of the house—and uncover any flaws. On Saturday, they would have their "soft" opening, ready for business.

By day, Elena raced around checking details, testing and retesting menu items, refining the systems in the kitchen, rearranging schedules as personalities emerged. By night, she went over the numbers, the figures, the ordering, and woke up in the middle of the night to write notes to herself about things to check in the cooler.

Three days before the soft opening, the dessert menu still had not been refined. Elena wanted to kill Mia on a daily basis, since of course those who might be qualified had already been snapped up. Peter struggled to get something together, but he wasn't there yet.

The printer was waiting for their refinements to the menu after the soft opening, but Elena was beginning to despair. She was taking inventory Wednesday afternoon when one of the Mexican youths came into the kitchen. "*Jefa,*" he said. "Can I speak with you?"

"Sure, Hector." She answered in Spanish. "What's up?"

"I brought my sister here to talk to you—they said you want to see her?"

A thin girl of about nineteen, wearing clunky shoes and a dress that was too big for her, hovered behind him. "Good, thank you."

"Also," Hector said, "there was a fire in Carbondale, at a bakery. The woman who made their pastries was a very fine cook, and she no longer has a job. I thought she might be good. For the desserts, you know?"

"Oh, you fabulous creature!" She squeezed his arm. "When can I talk to her?"

"I can call her. She'll drive over whenever you want."

"Today! The sooner the better. Seriously."

He smiled and nodded. "I'll call her." He turned to his sister and gestured her into the office. "This is Alma."

"Come in, Alma," Elena said in Spanish. The girl slipped into a chair, hands in her lap. Her wrist bones were highly defined. "Don't be afraid."

In Spanish, she said, "I'm not afraid of you, *Jefa.*" There was the faintest emphasis on the "you."

"What then?"

She looked over Elena's shoulder. "There is a car accident. A boy—or man?—I cannot tell. Flying through the air. It will change things."

"That's from a long time ago."

The girl shook her head. "Not a long time ago. Still coming."

Elena scowled. "What good does that do me?"

"It will help you, if you let it." She looked around the room, and Elena had to tamp down hard on her impatience. The girl was fey and odd, but wasn't Elena sitting here with her because a ghost told her to?

Who was strange?

Elena sighed, feeling the ache in her leg, in the base of her neck. "Thank you," she said, and gave the girl two twenties.

She tucked them into her bra. "I'll come work for you, when you need me."

Elena blinked. "Uh. Okay. Thanks."

When the knock came at her door later that afternoon, Elena was peering with grainy eyes at the computer screen in her office, entering the inventory numbers she'd gathered. Not her favorite part of the job, the paperwork and details and numbers, but absolutely essential. More than one brilliant restaurant had failed by neglecting the numbers.

"Come in!" she called, wondering if she needed to get glasses or something. Her eyes were killing her. She raised her head, blinking the sandiness away.

The door opened and a small woman came in. Hard to tell her age—somewhere between fifty and seventy, with the sharp features and leathery skin of a native Westerner and the mouth wrinkles of a lifelong smoker. Her hair was cut short, curling around her head in a style popular in the seventies, and she wore a plain green sweatshirt with the name of a local high school sports team emblazoned over one breast. "I'm looking for Elena Alvarez," she said.

"I'm Elena," she said. "How can I help you?"

"I'm Tansy? Hector said I should come apply for the baker position?"

"Oh!" Elena stood up, trying to cover her surprise. "Sure, come sit down."

"Thanks." She settled gnarled hands on small thighs encased in black polyester pants. On her feet were ordinary tennis shoes, the kind with a cloth upper and rubber lower and nothing fancy in between. Elena didn't even know you could buy them like that anymore.

"Tell me about yourself, Tansy. Hector thinks a lot of you if he would recommend you for this position."

"Well, I did a real good business with those boys." She twirled her rings around her fingers. "They're all so lonely, you know, away from home. It makes them feel loved to get something like they'd have at home—churros and the like, you know."

"Really! Do you do *pan de muerto*?"

"Oh, sure! My late husband—he died of a heart attack nineteen months ago, you know—was a Mexican. I learned to make all of his favorites, and now all the boys who come here to work like to eat my baked goods."

Elena felt a load lightening the slightest bit. "What else do you do? Pies, cakes? What do you think would be a good dessert for a high-end Mexican meal?"

"I can do almost anything you want, Ms. Alvarez. I sold pies and cakes to restaurants for years out of my kitchen, before opening up the bakery. I still bake for the truck stop out on I-70. You know it?"

Elena nodded.

"I haven't seen the menu here, a'course, but I guess I'd

probably come up with something light, something with chocolate. Maybe something caramel." She inclined her head. "Mexican hot chocolate with some fruit might be enough."

"Ah!" Elena was unable to stop the smile on her mouth. "I have an excellent recipe for Mexican chocolate. Take a look at this—" She passed the menu over, with some of Mia's recipes attached. "Can you work with any of this?"

Tansy bent over the page, plucking at her lip with a finger and thumb. "I think so. I can sure give it a shot."

"Good. You're hired. We'll give it a two-week trial, and see how we all work together. What do you say?"

"Okay. Thanks for the chance, Chef."

TWENTY-THREE

TASTING MENU

October 31
Julian Liswood, host
Elena Alvarez, chef
The Orange Bear, Aspen, Colorado

SAVORY CHOICES

Zucchini blossoms stuffed with blue cornmeal dressing and piñon nuts

Assortment of small, savory tamales—elk, duck, traditional pork

Baby corn fritters with chile-spiced honey

Bowls of buttered squashes

Samplings of small enchiladas on fresh corn tortillas—goat cheese with tomatillo, chicken, pork

Posole

Baskets of small, freshly cooked tortillas—red, blue, yellow, white

DESSERT CHOICES

Pomegranate baklava

Mexican hot chocolate
Sopapillas with buckwheat honey

BEVERAGE SELECTIONS
Wines
Tequilas
Beer
Mango spritzer
Iced tea

On Thursday morning, Julian was at his computer before the sun rose, putting the finishing touches on the treatment, a few sample pages of screenplay, and his vision for the piece. It was excellent work, some of the best he'd done in years, and that gave him a sense of mingled challenge, excitement, and fear. Challenge in the test to his skills and talents and knowledge; excitement that it had the potential to be the best work he'd done thus far; fear that Elena would find out and he'd lose her—if not to the restaurant, then to himself.

As dawn angled into the room, slanting in dusty gold through the pines outside the house, he punched the print command and stood up. Swinging open the balcony doors, he stepped outside and took a deep breath of thin, crisp mountain air and stretched his hands hard and high over his head. In a little while, he'd go for a run.

Tonight, his guests would assemble for dinner. Two couples had already arrived in Aspen, and the rest would come in this afternoon—it wasn't a long flight from LA, after all. He'd asked Georgia to prepare several bedrooms, and she'd have a girl make sure everything was covered for this evening in terms of comfort. Someone, he supposed, to provide some of the hospitality details a wife might offer if he had one.

Not that he was particularly interested. His ex, the first wife and the third one, Ricki, would be coming, too. Their love affair had been, in a word, tempestuous, and they wouldn't have married the second time had Ricki not been pregnant with Portia. Julian wanted full paternal rights, and he married Ricki to make sure that happened.

His second wife had been a starlet who dazzled him on the set of his first slasher picture, a beautiful girl who'd gone on to major stardom in television. The divorce had been splashed all over the tabloids, nasty and acrimonious, and in the end, even though she had been the one to leave the marriage, Julian had been forced to pay her a huge settlement, which, it turned out, she didn't even need.

Water under the bridge. He'd been on his own for a while, then he made another movie with Ricki, who was as beautiful as ever. They were older, wiser, thought they might be able to make a go of it. This time, they dated for a year, and Ricki—who was charming and sparkling and devoted when things went her way—had grown up. She got pregnant, they got married, it fell apart in eighteen months.

But for Portia's sake, they were adults. And in that sense, Julian thought they'd done a good job. They both put Portia first, and as a result, the girl had much better grounding than a lot of Hollywood kids; hell, a lot of American kids, period.

His fourth wife—well, they'd meant well, but it was a bad match.

Better to have a maid service and hire help to cook.

So why was he even bothering to worry about what Elena would think when she found out about the movie? It wasn't like either one of them had any faith in the idea of soul mates. It was ridiculous that he was even worried about it—he had kissed her exactly once.

How scary was it that when he thought of a wife, he thought of a woman he'd only known a few months? Had he learned nothing?

Maybe not. But maybe he had. He couldn't help feeling like there was something special here. Something real. Something that shifted the electrons in his body when she was around. She made him feel grounded and quiet and— happy.

With a scowl, he put his hands on his hips. He should tell her about the screenplay. Come clean before she found out some other way.

Tell her, man.

That night—Halloween night—was the tasting party with Julian's cronies. At Julian's house. Elena, Patrick, and Ivan had hammered out a menu and a plan, and at 1 p.m., they headed over to set things up.

Ivan whistled as they stepped out of the van. "Must be nice."

Patrick gave the house a glance and dismissed it. "We'd better hurry."

Ivan gave Elena a shake of the head, cocking his thumb toward Patrick. "Do you believe this guy?" He took a large pan of tamales out of the van. "Oh, I get it. You're a prince yourself. Not like us working-class stiffs."

The back of Patrick's neck was red. "Leave him alone," Elena said, carrying a load of linens brought from the restaurant.

"He knows I'm just giving him a hard time." Ivan leaned over and made a kissing noise near Patrick's neck, almost touching his cheek. "Don't you, Prince Patrick?"

Stiffly, Patrick held the door, his mouth pursed. "It may have escaped your notice that this is your employer's home, Ivan. Perhaps you should pay attention to your job."

Ivan chuckled as he entered the house, the sound as dark as cinnamon. Winking at one of the women hired to help set up and serve, he said, "He's hot for me."

The woman, really not much more than a girl, softened visibly at the sight of the dandy Patrick, hair exquisitely clipped and frozen in a messy style that perfectly offset his fresh-scrubbed face. "Right down the hall," she said, pointing. Julian was not on hand to greet them. Elena heard the sound of vacuuming upstairs.

Once they carried everything inside, she organized the tasks they had yet to do. Ivan took on the last of the cooking while she and Patrick set up the service and the tables. Patrick filled glass bowls with clear marbles dotted with just a few bright ones—turquoise, rose, lime—and put a brightly colored betta fish in each one. At intervals along the table were an eclectic collection of other containers—hammered tin and Oaxaca pottery and wooden vases, each one filled with marigolds and small pink carnations. More marigold heads were scattered loosely the length of the table, along with pink and white and yellow candy skulls. The candleholders were heavy colonial Spanish, each holding a white candle ready to be lit.

Elena admired it all happily, hands on her hips. "Wow, this is fantastic, Patrick!"

"Thank you."

Julian leaned over the mezzanine. "How's it going?"

"Oh, hey! I thought you must be entertaining." Elena waved a hand toward the beautiful table. "Very well, as you see. Is the music ready?"

"It is. Anything else you need?"

"Would you like to come down and take a few nibbles of the food?"

"No, I trust you." He glanced at his watch. "I've got to get showered and get ready. Guests will be arriving within an hour. If you need anything, ask Katya. She's pretty familiar with it all."

"Got it," Elena said. As she returned to the kitchen, she felt stiff and—dismissed. Her temples burned as she realized that she had been creeping up on the possibility that there might be more between them than just the restaurant.

Better to know now. "Let's get this party started," she said. "What's left, Rasputin?"

He flashed a sideways grin. "It's gonna be a show, *Jefa*, trust me. We're gonna knock them right on their asses."

For the first time, Elena was grateful for his endless flirtations. It was impossible not to feel sexy and clever in his company. "Good man."

Ivan's gaze flickered toward Patrick. "You have no idea." He winked, and Patrick bustled out of the room.

Elena put thumbs up. "Let's dazzle them, shall we?"

◆ ◆ ◆

By seven, the guests were mingling in the great room, their understated laughter and elegant natural fabrics filling the room with the unmistakable perfume of Money. The women were exquisite, the men middle-aged and older, some balding. Elena eyed them through the door warily, admiring the Jean Harlow fall of a peach silk halter over the narrow back of an actress who was beautiful on screen. In person, she was so luminous as to be practically unreal. Her husband, the producer, was a tidy man in his fifties, with gray temples and the granite-clean jaw of a brush shave. He wore a nubby jacket and a silk turtleneck and sipped scotch.

Over her shoulder, Ivan said, "They're so rich they're not even Republicans anymore."

She chuckled. "They have their own *foundations*."

"The boss cleans up pretty well, huh?"

Patrick had paused in front of Julian with a tray of stuffed zucchini blossoms and chunks of mango on tooth-picks. "Yes," she said. Julian's long and angular form was cloaked in a lord's finery, his magnificent hair brushed back from the high brow, his beautiful hands gesturing. "Which one are you lusting after?" Elena asked. "Patrick or the boss?"

"Given my druthers, I'd go for the number over there by the windows." Ivan crossed his arms easily, gesturing toward a vision in turquoise. "Excellent cleavage. Not as good as yours, but not bad."

Elena rolled her eyes, but noticed that she didn't mind taking top billing. Over Ricki Alsatian, Portia's beautiful mother. Who might be aging in terms of Hollywood, but barely seemed mortal as she stood in the middle of the party. Her eyes were enormous, the irises twice the usual size, and her skin seemed to leak light. Transcendental. "That's Julian's ex. They were married twice."

"You can see why."

A sharp green tongue of envy lapped at Elena's belly. She gave a curt nod. "It's time to start serving," she said as Patrick gestured toward the table.

"That's a gorgeous table," Ivan said, his bear voice growling. "Your Patrick is a very talented guy."

"Tell him," Elena said, turning toward the stove. She hauled a large steamer from the burner and put it on the counter. Steam billowed out as she took off the lid. Using tongs to gently remove the tamales within, she said, "Start splitting them." When Patrick bustled in, she asked, "Do you want Rasputin to help you serve?"

"Yes, please. We'll carry out the trays and set them down in intervals of three. If you will tell them about the tamales, I'll serve the wine."

"Ivan can describe the tamales," Elena said. "They're mostly his invention."

Across the counter, Ivan paused, eyes narrowing. "It's your kitchen, *Jefa*."

She glanced up from plating the tamales, alternating them by color—they'd dyed corn husks with green, blue, and red food coloring. Ivan wore his chef's whites, with a bandana tied over his head and silver hoops in his lobes. For this occasion, he was cleanly shaved except the small goatee that surrounded the overly sensual mouth. The women would love him, his voice, his sultry eyes and slow smiles. "They'll love you, Rasputin. Just do what you do."

"They'll want the chef," Patrick said. "They'll want you."

Ivan made a sweeping gesture, palm up, toward the door. "Showtime, sweetheart."

Elena felt faintly sick, looking from one to the other. A whirl of images tumbled through her mind, Dmitri and culinary school, the first day in Paris and how intimidated she'd been. There was Maria and Marie and Mia, her knives, and the years and years of nights in kitchens, calling out, learning, plating and creating and working. Always working so hard. She thought of Julian sitting out there, believing in her. She took off her apron, smoothed her smock. "How do I look?"

Ivan brushed back a lock of her hair.

Patrick said, "Lipstick."

Elena couldn't remember where her purse was. Patrick spied it, rushed over and grabbed it. She pulled out the lipstick and applied the translucent berry color carefully, using the end of the tube as a tiny mirror. Blotting her lips together, she looked from one to the other. "Better?"

Ivan dropped heavy lids. "Succulent," he pronounced, licking his own lips.

"Go, *ma chérie*," Patrick said. "Remember, you are a queen. This is your first audience."

She took a breath and headed into the great room, a tumble of images rushing through her mind—hot chocolate at Angelina's; the late, hard nights in Santa Fe trying to prove she wasn't some gangland girl from Espanola, but genuinely *about* something; the heady rush of seeing the skyline of New York City through the windows of an airplane the first time, a thousand images of plates she'd created, menus she'd helped write, all leading—

Right here. Right now.

"Hello, everyone," she said, tangling her fingers together behind her back. She felt small and bosomy in the high-ceilinged room, a robin amidst the pink and leggy pelicans. "My name is Elena Alvarez, and I am the executive chef of the Orange Bear, which is the brilliant Julian Liswood's latest restaurant innovation—" She gestured toward Julian, at the head of the table.

He smiled in that distant, Mount Olympus way. The diners lifted their glasses toward him. He raised a wine globe.

In that gesture, in the inclination of his head, she realized he was a million miles out of her league. It made the whole thing a lot easier, somehow. Of course she had a crush on the emperor—who wouldn't? The only foolishness would be in expecting anything to come of it.

She rocked forward on her toes, smiling. "We hope you'll all make the Orange Bear a new favorite when you visit Aspen, and to that end, we've prepared a tasting menu for you. Patrick and Ivan will begin serving momentarily, and you have a menu beside your plate. If you have any questions, I'd be more than happy to address them after dinner. In the meantime, please enjoy."

Giving a short bow, she left them, her heart pounding. Her cheeks were burning hot as she returned to the kitchen. "Okay, get going," she barked.

Patrick patted her shoulder. "You were great, Elena."

"You were," Ivan agreed, picking up a tray full of exquisitely beautiful plates of tamales, the green, blue, and red husks split open to display the tender masa within. "They all wanted you, sweetheart. Even me."

"Go," she said, shaking her head. "Serve."

They got the tamales out and Elena watched through the door, listening as Ivan charmed them in his bear's voice, and Patrick poured a full-bodied Spanish red into glasses as thin as jellyfish.

Beautiful, she thought, smiling in satisfaction. Spanish guitar tumbled softly from the speakers. Candlelight shone over the hammered tin and with more fierceness over silver cutlery. The pink and orange gave a sense of warmth to the cold autumn night, and the little candy skeletons proved irresistible to the diners, who were arranged like flowers themselves around the long, heavy table. The scent of the food rose, spicy and welcoming, and with great satisfaction, she watched as face after face transformed at the first bite of Ivan's exquisite duck and elk tamales, the surprise and delight of expecting one thing and getting something so much better.

The girl, Katya, stood beside Elena, looking at the diners. "Look at their faces," she said quietly. "They love this food."

Elena flashed her a grin. "Yes, they do." Katya had been very good tonight, showing a rare intuitive gift for knowing what needed to be done, facilitating the work of the others. "Do you work for someone in town here?"

"My mom does housecleaning," she said. "Sometimes I help at parties."

"You like it?"

"Not really the serving." She rubbed her skinny arms. "I'd like to learn to cook. Like you. That would be really cool. But my mom says it's not a great life."

Elena inclined her head, thinking of the challenges, the losses, the fight to be taken seriously. "It's not easy," she said, "but I wouldn't trade it for anything." She gestured back to the diners. "How many of us get a chance to make people feel like that?"

Katya nodded. "I think I'd really like it."

"Keep thinking about it. If you want a job, give me a call."

"Really?"

"You have talent."

The boys came back and they got busy filling platters with the next set of tidbits.

Two hours later, Ivan stood on the deck in the cold night, smoking. He watched the glittering crowd through the windows. What would it be like to have that kind of money? To be so perfect? The babe in the slinky halter was so exquisite she was like fresh truffles, rare and unbelievable—her skin as thin and smooth as milk, covering bones arranged like some precious sculpture, her breasts taut and high. Her face was perfect, her hair, even her long slim hands. Perfect. How could you fuck a creature like that?

A wisp of air moved over his wrist, and Patrick appeared. "We're about finished up," he said with that faint accent, a little British, a little Boston, a lot upper class.

"Did your parents have parties like this, Patrick?"

He gave Ivan a wary glance. "Yes."

"Did you like them?"

"Not then," he said, and swallowed, and in that small, small gesture, Ivan understood that Patrick had been out of place in his parents' world, too. An Irish boy, a macho world, masters of the universe, and there was gay little Patrick, who wanted to go into the restaurant business. How could Ivan not have seen that before now?

Because he was busy with that chip on his shoulder, as usual.

"Are you cold?" Ivan said, opening his jacket, inclining his head in that ironic way so Patrick could refuse. Patrick looked up, hesitating, but Ivan willed himself not to be too ironic, and just stood there, arms open. The air bloomed hot and orange, as Patrick, abruptly, moved in and pressed into the space Ivan made for him.

For one long second, Ivan closed his eyes and stayed perfectly, perfectly still. Patrick was small and sturdy and compact, his shoulders fitting neatly beneath Ivan's arm. Ivan closed his jacket and clasped him close, smelling the waft of soap and aftershave and gel from his hair.

Desire bled between them, sparks in the black night, and Ivan felt the air leave his lungs, felt the airlessness of wanting something so badly it nearly burned, and the fear of retribution for seeking it. Pain and hunger and resignation of loss all wound in a braid as solid as a horsewhip, and he hated himself for the way his hand shook as he lifted it to Patrick's smooth, precisely shaved jaw. "I smell like cigarettes," he said apologetically.

"You smell like you," Patrick said. "I like it."

Ivan bent and kissed him, the plump lips as tender as

pastry, his mouth a hot cavern. It was a tender kiss, and sultry, and full of things that burned the top of Ivan's skull.

"Not here," Patrick said. "We should go. To my place."

"Yeah," Ivan said, his voice barely rumbling in his airless desire. "Good idea."

Once they'd cleaned up the kitchen, Elena let Katya go home, giving her a card. "You want to learn the kitchen from the ground up, give me a call. But I'm hard-core about showing up and being on time. *Sabe?*"

The girl nodded.

Now that the diners were hitting the mellow stretch, lingering in their chairs and drinking coffee and liqueurs, Elena poured a very fine Spanish red into a globe made of thinnest glass and settled on a bar stool. On a heavy ceramic plate were some of the items they'd served, held back for the pleasure of the staff. She took a tiny piece of a zucchini blossom, and slivered off a thin slice of duck tamale. Heady stuff. It made her dizzy it was so delicious.

She sipped her wine and thought of Edwin on that long-ago day in Espanola. What shape would her life have taken if he'd lived? If that night had never happened? Where would she be?

Not here.

She held the glass in her hand and looked around the expansive kitchen with its marble counters and the small squares of window over the sink that looked out to nothing very much but light and probably flowers in the summertime.

Certainly not here.

She took one tiny fragrant sip of wine, imagining Espanola. Or even Albuquerque. Maybe they would have actually made it that far, she studying food, Edwin pursuing business.

But with the perspective of adulthood, she could see what more likely would have transpired. Edwin would have hated the long hours she spent in restaurants. He would have wanted her to have children, and it would have fallen to Elena to do most of the raising. She might have found herself resenting him.

Or not. There would have been other comforts. At worst, they would have stayed stuck in Espanola, where she would have had her sisters to cheer her and he would have come home to eat, then gone out again to his friends and cousins. To play poker. To drink beers at the VFW with his uncles. To tinker with an engine in someone's garage.

The idea of it left her lungs feeling squashed.

At best, they would have created a restaurant together, a life of good cheer and happiness, with children who would now be in high school. And a daughter who would be in college now.

Through her wine, she glimpsed Isobel moving by, just a wisp, her long hair flying through the kitchen. Elena started, realizing that she'd been feeling gratitude toward the fact that the accident had sent her life whirling in an entirely new direction. She'd risen to a height that would have been inconceivable to her seventeen-year-old self.

Guilt blasted her, cold and tasting of blood.

Putting her glass down, she realized it had been a long time since she'd seen Patrick and Ivan. She wandered over to look around the corner.

They were on the deck, looking up at the stars. Ivan angled close and bent in, pressing his mouth to Patrick's neck. Patrick didn't move away. His body was stiff, but swayed the slightest bit toward Ivan's realm.

Elena sighed. "Hmm."

"That sounds like trouble," Julian said, startling her.

"Oh! You."

"Who were you talking to?"

"Myself. Again."

"You did an excellent job tonight, Elena."

"Thank you. It seemed to go very well."

"I think so." He glanced toward the deck. "I guess you guys can head out whenever you like."

She nodded. Coolly. "Understood."

He paused a moment. "Thank you, Elena," he said, and gave her a dismissive nod. "Good night."

As he walked away, she pursed her lips and looked back to Ivan and Patrick. Against the silhouette of a light from below, their heads were close together, Patrick tucked under Ivan's arm for warmth.

Damn. She walked to the doors and pushed them open. Patrick leapt away, glancing at her guiltily. "Let's get things loaded up. We have a lot to do the next two days."

Patrick dashed by her, but Ivan held back a moment. Ivan who was not sneering or coyly seductive, but plainly, painfully gobsmacked. He took in Elena's stare and pulled the pieces of himself from wherever they'd gone. "Right," he said. "We have a lot to do."

She touched his arm. "Are you all right, Rasputin?"

He glanced toward the kitchen, where Patrick had gone. "I'm fine."

Elena nodded. "Get things loaded up, then."

Portia came around the corner, nearly bumping into Elena as she came into the kitchen. "Hey," she said in a bubbly, Betty Boop kind of voice, "whatcha doing? Do you have any more of those little baby tamales? They were *so* good!"

Portia wore a slim blue dress and her long hair was looped into a simple, pretty updo. Her eyes were way too bright. "Whoa," Elena said, putting a hand to the girl's bare arm. "Have you been into the alcohol?"

Her eyes widened. "No!" she breathed, and a gust of tequila washed over Elena's face. "I'm not allowed. I'll get in trouble if they test my urine, I'll be in big fat—ha-ha—trouble!" She swung a hand and her body nearly went with it.

Elena caught her arm. "Okay, sit right here." She settled the girl onto a stool. "I'll be right back. Don't move. Got it?"

"Got it."

Elena dashed out to the van. "I'm going to need to deal with a little situation with the boss's daughter, who is soused. Get this stuff to the restaurant and put it away and then give me a call. One of you can come back for me."

Ivan looked at Patrick, who carefully didn't look at Ivan. Thick, heavy heat swirled around them, fragrant with longing. "Will do, boss."

"I'll bring you my car," Patrick said, "and leave the keys in the ignition. I'm pretty sure no one will steal it."

He gave her The Look. The one they'd all—Patrick and Mia and Elena—used on each other at one time or another, the equivalent of hanging a scarf on the doorknob.

Elena wanted to protest. Warn him. Them. There behind them, behind the dark purple yearning, was an edging of red pain. She wanted to say, *Stop, stop stop! You'll ruin each other!*

But what did she know? And maybe people had a perfect right to ruin each other, even to choose it. She nodded. "Thanks, guys. You did a great job tonight, and I appreciate it."

Ivan neatly climbed behind the wheel. Patrick composed his limbs in the passenger seat. Elena's stomach squeezed and she turned away.

As she went back toward the kitchen, Elena spied a group of men out in the courtyard, smoking cigars. A fire burned in a kiva-style fireplace, providing warmth for the thin-skinned Californians. From the great room spilled the sound of women's voices, talking and laughing in such refined ways that it was almost as if they were instruments layered over the soundtrack of the evening.

Portia was right where Elena had left her, her arms flung in front of her on the counter, her head on one elbow. She opened one delphinium eye. "I didn't move a muscle," she reported. "Well"—she snickered—"maybe my neck."

"Come on, honey. Let's get you to bed, huh?"

"No! I was doing . . . stuff . . . out. There." She shook her head, nearly fell off the stool.

"I'm sure." Elena draped one of the girl's long white arms around her neck, and slipped her own arm around Portia's waist. "You're so tiny!"

"No, I'm so not tiny," she said, allowing herself to be led. "My mom is tiny. Tiny, tiny, tiny." She made a tiny circle with her finger and thumb. "She can't even wear my clothes. How sad is *that*! The mom too tiny for the daughter's clothes!"

At the hallway, Elena peeked around the corner and saw the Masters of the Universe were still wrapped up in their cigars. No one would pay any attention to this dark hallway.

They didn't. Elena navigated Portia down the stairs to her bedroom. Alvin was sleeping there, on Portia's bed. "You traitor!" Elena exclaimed.

He looked apologetic, and flipped the end of his feathery tail the slightest bit, but didn't appreciably move. Portia said, "Aw! Look at him!" She sank to her knees on the edge of the bed and kissed his nose. He groaned softly.

"C'mon, honey," Elena said. "Where're your pajamas?"

"Oh, I'll just sleep like this."

"No." Elena took a guess and found the pajamas on the back of the bathroom door. She held them out. "Can you change?"

Portia rolled her eyes. "Course." She held out her hand and took the flannel pants and skinny T-shirt. At the door, she paused. "Oh, maybe my zipper."

Elena pulled it down for her. "Careful," she said, when Portia swayed.

"Ohhhhh!" she said suddenly, and put her hand to her mouth. She dropped her clothes and ran for the toilet. She threw up impressively, then sank to the floor with a whimper.

"Probably doesn't seem like it, but that's a good thing." Elena took a washcloth from the cupboard and ran cold water over it. Bending down, she handed the cloth to Portia. "If you've had too much to drink, it's never bad to throw up and get rid of the excess alcohol."

Portia put the cloth to her mouth. "That's . . . like . . . bulimia."

"Yeah, well, better throwing up than dying of alcohol poisoning."

With a sick nod, Portia swayed. "I might need help putting on my pajamas."

"Okay." Gently, she helped Portia shed the expensive dress, and into her pants and shirt, helping preserve her modesty as much as possible. Elena pulled the bobby pins out of her hair, and gave her a toothbrush with toothpaste on it, and while it wasn't the brushing job of the century, at least her mouth would feel better in the morning. Finally, she helped Portia into bed and covered her with the duvet. "I'll bring you some water. Do you need anything else?"

Portia shook her head. "Don't tell my dad, okay?"

Elena sat down on the side of the bed. "I can't promise you that, Portia, but let's talk for a second. If you are in trouble if they test your urine, you've been in trouble with drinking before, right?"

"No," she said with a long sigh. "My friend was in trouble. Not me. I was just with her."

"But you still knew you'd get in trouble."

Portia snorted and opened her eyes. "In case you didn't notice, nobody cares what their kids do in this world."

"I think your dad cares what you do."

"Oh, *so* how is it that he didn't even *notice* me drinking when I was sitting righ' at tha' table?" Her words were slurry, but the emotion was earnest.

Elena didn't know what the rules were in talking to a teenager, especially a "troubled" girl. But she knew how to be honest. "He had a lot going on tonight. It seemed to be a business meeting that mattered quite a lot to him, and he wanted to present something and show off his new restaurant food."

"Yeah. So?"

"So, maybe the thing to do would be to support him when he needs you."

"Oh, like they always are there for me?" The purple of her mascara had smeared around her eyelids and made her look like a tired child prostitute. So much anger in those eyes. Too much knowledge.

Elena lifted a shoulder, patted the bed next to Portia to give Alvin permission to come up beside her. If ever a child needed a dog, it was this one. "I don't know what happened before, Portia. Maybe they've never been there for you the way parents are supposed to, but what I see now is that your dad really loves you and he's gone to a lot of trouble to create a safe and stable environment for you here in Aspen."

The girl's eyes closed and tears leaked out, tinged faintly blue with mascara. Alvin leaned in and licked her face, and she laughed.

Elena stood up. "You can keep him overnight," she said, "but I want him home first thing in the morning, understood?"

"Are you sure?"

As if pleading to spend the night, Alvin sighed and put his head down on Portia's belly. "I'm sure. Good night."

"Where is your family, Elena?"

"New Mexico."

"Is your mom there?"

"My grandmother is."

"Is your mom dead?"

"Who knows." Elena leaned on the threshold. "I haven't seen her since I was eight. My mother was a little party girl who dropped me off at my dad's mom's house when I was eight and never came back."

"Wow, that sucks."

"It did, at the time. But *mi abuela* was good to me."

"*Abuela,*" Portia repeated with soft breathlessness. "Tha's a good word."

"It is," Elena agreed, and turned off the light. She waited, but within seconds, dog and child were snoring in unison.

It pained her to leave Alvin, but there it was. It would cause more pain to take him home. He was happy there. Portia needed him. And a dog of her own. She'd talk to Julian about that.

But for now, she went to see if she could find him, or perhaps leave a note somewhere, appraising him of the situation. He should know what was going on.

Ricki Alsatian, Portia's mother, was in the kitchen, pouring a new glass of wine when Elena came into the room. "Oh!" she said, smiling, perhaps in embarrassment, though the wine had been left out just so the guests could help themselves. "I thought you'd gone!"

"I'm on my way. Just a few details to finish up. Is Julian wrapped up in his presentation?"

The woman inclined her head, the blonde hair tumbling down her tiny, toned arm. She was exquisite in the way of the very well tended. "You call him Julian?"

Which, for some reason, reminded her that Julian had once been married to this ethereal being. Twice, as a matter of fact. "I tried to call him Mr. Liswood, but he's not that formal."

She smiled faintly. "I see."

"Have you seen him?"

Ricki sipped her wine. "No."

For a minute, Elena wondered if she knew that her daughter had gone to bed very drunk. She wondered what Ricki was doing here, actually.

None of her business.

"Well, it was nice to meet you," Elena said politely. Her coat was hanging in an anteroom off the kitchen, and she headed there to get it, halting when she heard Julian's voice drifting down from the mezzanine. "That's it, gentlemen. I'm weary of slasher pics, but I'll do another one if you let me do this one first."

She stopped, hands in her pocket. He must be in his office, and the conversation carried into this quiet spot.

Another man said, "Ghosts, Julian? The market for horror is teenagers. How can we get them with ghosts?"

"I'm not sure this *is* a teenager movie. Adults like ghost stories, not kids."

"Kids spend more money at the movies."

As if it were a liquid seeping through the floor, Elena felt Julian's frustration. "And I'll make another slasher picture. After this one."

Obviously, he was busy. Where could she leave him a

message? She went back to the kitchen, found a piece of paper and wrote:

> Julian,
> Alvin asked if he could spend the night and I let him. Give me a call and I'll come get him in the morning.

She hesitated, then added:

> Hope you got what you wanted with the meeting. We were pretty pleased from our end.
> Elena

She carried the note upstairs, past the hallway she had used the night she stayed here, and down another hallway. Wrong way. This led to guest rooms. She headed back the other way, almost landed on the mezzanine to his office, and steered around again. Finally, she found Julian's bedroom and halted, suddenly shy, on the threshold. It was a vast room, well appointed but not terribly personal, as if a decorator had done it all.

But the air smelled intensely of Julian, that particular apple-and-sunlight fragrance she had come to associate with him. It assaulted her, soaked into her body through her skin, through her nose, made her breasts feel heavy. Her neck prickled. She stood there for long, long moments, breathing it in, feeling it calm even as it aroused, as if his flesh would be the ultimate aromatherapy, curing everything, but especially her loneliness.

A sharp trill of laughter shattered the moment.

Blinking, Elena hurried forward and put the note on his bed, hoping suddenly that no other woman would be lying there with him, that his head alone would be on those pillows. Then, shaking her head at the strangeness, she hurried out.

No wonder he was so powerful, she thought, starting Patrick's car. He must have the pheromones of a tiger. A lion, an elephant. Something huge, anyway.

Yet another reason to steer clear of Julian Liswood.

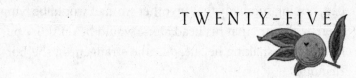

TWENTY-FIVE

PAN DE MUERTO
(BREAD OF THE DEAD)

    1 cup milk
    1 tsp salt
    ½ cup (one stick) butter
    ¼ cup water, just warmer than body temperature
    1 T flour
    1 tsp sugar
    2 packages dry yeast
    5 cups flour
    1 T whole anise seed
    ½ cup sugar
    4 eggs

GLAZE
½ cup sugar
⅓ cup fresh squeezed orange juice
2 T orange zest

Measure the milk and salt into a large glass measuring cup and drop in a stick of butter, cut into chunks. Heat in the microwave until milk is scalded, stir until butter melts, and let stand for about 10 minutes.

Meanwhile, measure warm water into a small bowl and stir 1 tablespoon flour and 1 teaspoon sugar into it. Sprinkle yeast on top and let it dissolve for a few minutes.

While those are resting, measure 1½ cups of flour into a bowl and set the rest aside. Mix in the anise seed and sugar, then add the milk/butter mixture and the yeast mixture, and stir vigorously until well mixed. Beat in the eggs, then stir in the remaining flour 1 cup at a time until the dough is soft and not sticky. Turn out the dough on a counter and knead well for 10 minutes or so, until the texture is as cool and smooth as a young breast or a baby's bottom. Lightly grease a bowl and put the dough in it, turning it so the entire loaf is coated lightly with oil, and then cover with a thin, damp cloth and put it in a warm, draft-free spot to rise until doubled, about 1–2 hours.

Punch the dough down and shape into loaves that look like skulls, skeletons, bones. Let the loaves rise for 1 hour. Bake 40 minutes at 350 degrees. Paint with glaze.

Glaze: mix sugar, orange juice, and zest together, and boil for 2 minutes, then use it as a paint for the loaves. Sprinkle with colored sugar in pink, orange, green, and blue. Serve to the dead.

Or to the living, who tend to eat more of it.

TWENTY-SIX

Julian was in a deep sleep when something blew over his face. He slid one eye open and found himself staring into the face of a very big nose. When Alvin saw he was awake, he woofed softly, putting his paws on the bed.

"Need to get outside, do you?"

Alvin woofed again. Julian put on his robe and padded downstairs to let the dog out. Standing there on the deck, he thought of Elena with a sucking sense of guilt.

The movie was a go. He had not said a word.

He didn't know, now, how he would.

Tell her, man.

But how could he?

On the Day of the Dead, Elena took the morning off from work, as was her annual habit. It was strange not to have Alvin with her, but she'd loaned him out in the service of a good cause. She arose early, smiling at the rustling, the soft whispers in the rooms of her apartment, ghosts gathering in happy anticipation.

It was Isobel's birthday, and Elena cooked all of her favorites—chicken enchiladas and chocolate cake with chocolate frosting. Strawberry soda. She brought in Edwin's favorites, too. Hamburgers from a fast-food joint, and french fries, and Coke in a paper cup. He loved fast food. For Albert, her youngest brother, only fourteen when he died, she cooked chorizo and scrambled eggs and fluffy white tortillas, because he could eat breakfast for days and days.

When the food was ready, she went to the living room to prepare the altar on top of the southwestern-style buffet. First, she spread out a striped serape she used every year, one of the only things she carried with her, place to place to place. It had once covered her bed at the house in Espanola, and now was worn thin and soft, the colors faded. On top of it, she set up the framed photographs—one of Edwin and herself at a wedding dance the year before the accident, one of Isobel at her sixteenth birthday party, wearing a tiara and hamming it up for the camera. There was one of her cousin Penny at seven, which was the only one she could find, and one, always the hardest, of her brother Albert at twelve, grinning with zest into the camera from his prized bicycle, which to Elena's eyes now looked rickety and rusted and old, the tire fat and sturdy. It was painted blue.

When it was all ready, she put out a vase of red roses, and scattered some marigolds around it. The plates of food were there for the taking, the eggs still steaming, the cake neatly sliced, beer poured into a glass for Edwin.

Today, Maria Elena would go down to the crosses she'd

made at the side of the road where the accident had happened. She would take down the worn-out, tattered flowers
from the year before, and repaint the names of her dead
children, and freshen up the items placed there twenty-one
years ago. For a moment, Elena let herself be a ghost with
her mother, dusting away the grime of a year, the tangles of
tumbleweeds speared with dead leaves, the bits of paper
blown in, the odd beer lid or milk bottle cap.

One day, perhaps, she would go to the site again. She
had been there only once, the second year after it happened. By then, she'd been walking well again, and had got
through rehab and worked as a prep girl in a Santa Fe
restaurant. She went home for Easter and her eldest
brother Ricardo took her to the *descansos*.

Elena got out of the car and threw up. It was nothing
she could remember exactly, because really, it was all such a
blur. But she couldn't stay. Not even long enough to put
flowers down. Ricky drove her back home, silently. Mama
clucked over her, washed her face, cried a little. "Oh, *m'ija,
m'ija*," she said, over and over, her hands cold and gnarled
on Elena's forehead. "You shouldn't go there. Never, never.
La Santisima Muerte let you go."

In her Aspen living room, Elena bowed her head as was
her habit, and prayed the rosary on carved ivory beads she'd
owned since her confirmation. Around her, the rustling in-
tensified and the temperature in the room dropped, and still
she prayed quietly, letting them come and taste the offerings, and touch her face and hair and pat her back. She
prayed decade after decade, and there was a little sound of
laughter at her back, and a joke she didn't quite catch, and a
kiss on her cheek and a whispered *thank you* and she let a

few tears fall, but not very many. This altar was not for her, but for them, those who were ahead on the road all would one day walk. A gift to them, a way to honor them.

A knock on the door in her fourth decade startled her, but knowing it was Alvin, she rushed over and opened the door. Julian stood there, looking oddly winded, his hands at his sides. Alvin wiggled happily, and she let him by, patting his head as she put her body squarely in the doorway.

Thinking of his formality with her last night, Elena said, "Thank you for bringing my dog."

"You're welcome." A tangle of sunlight fell through the curls by his temples, edged the line of his dark glasses. The little goatee, artful and self-conscious, surrounded his red lips and drew attention to their lushness. Cherries, she thought. Or plums. She rubbed the inside of her own lip with her tongue.

He simply stood there, and finally Elena said, "Is there something wrong?"

"No," he said, and took off his sunglasses. "May I come in?"

A car drove into the parking lot, taking the turn too fast, tires spitting gravel laid down by snow crews last week. Someone laughed, loudly. Elena swore, shaking her head. "It's a wonder someone doesn't flip a car there every weekend. The kids in this place!"

"It's a dangerous curve," he agreed, looking at the retreating car.

Stepping back to make room, she gestured. "Come in."

With an air of careful reserve, he stepped into her living room, and Elena was, once again, enveloped by his aura. Everything about him stirred her up. The extravagance of his glossy hair, the long, ropy leanness of his arms and legs, the white skin at the opening of his shirt. His deep brown eyes and skillful tongue and the timbre of his voice. She was trying to maintain her aloofness, and yet, there was that scent of apples and sunlight, the echoing vastness of longing she sensed in him.

Isobel was there, solidly, startlingly, because she did not come when other people were around. She said, "His mother is here with us. Tell him."

Elena glanced at the table where her celebration was laid out. He stood in the middle of the room, looking at the candles and flowers and food, the photographs and shimmering air of festivity. She said, "El Día de Los Muertos."

He nodded. "I've seen the altars before."

"You can go closer."

"I . . . uh . . ." He stared at the photos, looking flummoxed. "Is it today? Day of the Dead?"

Elena nodded. The air was the color of tornado clouds around his shoulders, his head, as if he generated a tremendous storm by his presence. She paused for a moment, suddenly afraid.

"My mother was murdered," he said.

She wanted to do as Isobel instructed, tell him that his mother was there, with them, but emotion suddenly welled up in her and made her want to cry. "I'm so sorry."

"I don't think about it very often." He pointed to a photo. "Who is that?"

She picked it up and put it in his hand. "My cousin Penny."

Julian swallowed, looked at the photo with something like dread. "Pretty."

Elena shrugged. "But fat. That was the thing, why she always went with us everywhere. She was fat, so no boys liked her. She hated me." Looking down at the picture, Elena smiled sadly. "I took it personally, you know. Kids do." She touched the face, always young. "In the accident, she was torn in half. They couldn't identify her."

"Elena, don't tell me. I'll use it. Maybe not directly, but in some way or another, it will feed the work." He held up his hand, palm out, revealing the life line and heart line and white pads of flesh to her. "I could pretend I wasn't going to, even mean it, but the story calls me anyway."

She looked at him. Nodded. "It's like cooking for me, right? If I eat something, I can't help trying to figure out how to make it."

A little of the tortured look left the skin around his eyes.

"There are a hundred, two hundred—I don't know how many—car accidents like this every year, Julian. This one belongs to me." Elena picked up the picture of her brother. "Albert was fourteen. He always wanted to tag along everywhere. He was flung out of the car, too, like me, but he landed against a tree." She shook her head. "Died instantly."

He nodded.

She put the photo back and picked up the next one. "This was my boyfriend, Edwin. We met when I was twelve years old, and stayed together all that time. I was thinking last night, in your kitchen, that if he had lived, my life would be very different."

"Jesus!" Julian exclaimed, taking the photo. "Juan looks like him quite a bit, doesn't he?"

She nodded but didn't say that Julian had his eyes.

"Does it bother you?" he asked.

"No." She looked back at the picture. "Edwin was more like Ivan in nature, tortured, not very well treated when he was a boy. Juan is as cheerful as the day is long. A good man."

"How did you meet him?" He still held the photo of Edwin. "What did you love about him?"

"He was smart." A sense of tension eased out of her neck. "He had hair like licorice, very straight and shiny. He was part Indian and very proud of it, and it showed in his cheekbones and his eyes. His eyes were black as coal." She paused. *Like yours.*

"Go on."

"We grew up discovering things about each other. He was going to go into an apprenticeship with an electrician out of Santa Fe, building all these fancy houses. He was supposed to start the week after the accident." Her chest ached faintly. "He and my sister Isobel were on the left side of the car. They were both decapitated." She thought of the ditch, of Isobel's hand in hers. Of Edwin cracking jokes in the dark. "They say it takes twelve seconds for your brain to die when your head is cut off. That's what I can't think about very much. I hate to think of them having any consciousness of that."

He blanched, handing back the photo. "Is that Isobel?" he asked, pointing to the picture of Isobel wearing the tiara.

She nodded. "Yep. When I came to live with the family, she was the one who made room for me. She shared her bed. She shared her mother. She was just happy to have a sister so close in age to her. It was like finding my twin. Like we should have known each other from birth."

"Mischievous," he said.

"Very." Elena took the photo. "I laid in the ditch for almost two hours. I thought Isobel was with me. I thought she was holding my hand. So, when I woke up in the hospital, weeks and weeks later, I didn't believe them that she was dead."

"Elena, I'm so sorry that happened to you."

She nodded. "Me too. But I'm alive. I have to believe there's a reason."

"Do you know what it is?"

"No," she said simply, and put the picture back on the altar. A ghostly hand nipped a piece of cake. She wondered if Julian noticed.

But he was stricken and airless, and Elena thought of his mother. "Now you, Julian." She sat down on the couch and patted the spot beside her. "Tell me about your mother."

He stood in the middle of the room, looking at her. "What should I say?"

"How old were you when she was murdered?"

He looked as if the light bled from his body, leaving him gray. "Twelve."

Elena said, "Come sit down, Julian, and tell me about your mother. Then we'll make something for her and put it on the altar."

He seemed suddenly to lose all supports in his body, and slumped to sit on the couch, his limbs falling forward, his head with the thickness of black glossy hair tumbling forward around his brow. "I was twelve," he said again. "She went to the grocery store and never came back. Two men saw her in a parking lot and grabbed her as she headed for her car. She had groceries in the cart, you know. Eggs, milk, flour, apples. Just stuff. Capt'n Crunch."

Elena folded her hands in her lap. Waited.

"They raped her and killed her, and then dumped her body in a field." He raised a face wiped clean of expression. "Some boys on bikes found her naked and dead. They were close to my age." His voice was hushed as he added, "I hated that, so much, that those boys saw her naked. It bothered me for months."

She thought of his movies, the slasher images. Knives. Broken glass. "How terrible, Julian. I'm so sorry."

He took her hand and clasped it between both of his, pulled her arm across his lap. "My dad never got over it."

"Well, how could you, really?"

"I guess. But how does it help to stop living?" He spread her palm open, touched the heart of it with his fingers, brushing and brushing, touching the pads beneath each finger, the little marks and scars and dried-open wounds at the tips of nearly every finger. "Don't these hurt?" he asked.

"Sometimes."

He lightly stroked the open spot on her index finger then raised her hand without looking at her, and pressed his mouth to her palm. For a moment, Elena hardly knew how to respond. The wet clasp of his tongue, his lips, jolted right up her arm, blistered through her body.

This.

Now.

She let him kiss her fingers, one at a time. Let him press his mouth to her palm, to each small pad beneath each digit, and sweep his tongue over the wounds. It tickled and sizzled and she let him just do what he would, pressing his mouth to her wrist. She spread her fingers on his cheek, feeling the pockmarks from long ago, the little prickles of a missed patch of beard. Beneath the pad of her thumb was the bottom of his goatee, silky soft.

He still didn't look at her as she took off his glasses, his hat, letting his hair fall free in that erotically glossy tangle. She put her hands on his face and leaned in to kiss each eyelid. Lightly. His cheekbones. Finally his mouth, as succulent as cherries, and she sucked on his lower lip until he moved and they tumbled backward on her couch, with the flickers of the candles keeping watch.

"God," he breathed, and they kissed as if that was the only way to stay alive, as if tongues brushing, lips burning like this, could sustain them. Elena buried her hands in his hair and cried out when he pushed up her blouse and struggled with her bra and ended up breaking the clasp in his urgency to put his face to the abundance there, cool and white. Her breath rose high in her throat as she clasped him to her, crying out as he took her breasts in his hands and brushed his face over her, buried his nose, lapped the valley between her breasts, then rose and feasted on nipple and breast and throat. He worked her legs open, pulled their bodies, still clad in jeans, together.

It felt to her that her skin leaked honey from every pore, and Julian, so hungry, starving, so needful, lapped it all away, drinking from the crook of her elbow and the hollow of her throat. He dipped his tongue into her mouth and suckled her tongue until she was whimpering and he was drenched and sticky and they melted out of their clothes. And for a long moment, she wanted only to admire the white column of his chest, and the tensile cords of his thighs, and his organ, ruddy and proud, leaking and leaping, before their limbs and bodies twined and she felt him slide between her legs, into her center, nudging her womb.

And there, he paused and raised his head. "Look at me, Elena," he said raggedly. She opened her eyes, the thudding red pulse of him rising and rising in her, and she made a soft noise as something brushed her face, her hair. He kissed her, slowly, slowly, eyes boring into her, and he began to move again. There was in the room a rustling that scared her, and a pulse of light, and then there was only Julian, and she bit his neck in her hunger, breathing in the wild apple scent of him, the taste of his skin, like golden morning, like wine, like lifeblood. She whimpered and bit him and he hauled her up into him and they shimmered and broke and blazed and Elena had enough sense to think *Oh, shit* before she tumbled over the edge of everything.

Elena hated the part when she had to move. The front of her was in pretty good shape. There was a dent or two on her torso, but they were not terribly evident unless you were looking for them. Her legs were somewhat crooked, she'd been told, but it was her back that was horrific, and as Julian shifted, emerging from the haze, she wondered what next. What next?

He shifted his weight to his elbows. "Am I squishing you?"

"No."

"Don't regret this, Elena," he whispered.

"Don't talk." She put her hands on his mouth. He

opened his lips and sucked her fingers in. With her other hand, she shoved at his shoulder. "I need to get up."

He moved awkwardly. Red crept up his cheeks.

Elena said only, "I just want to get this over with," and stood up, putting her back to him. "It isn't beautiful."

He said nothing. She didn't move. Her shoulders got cold and she turned around.

He was smiling. "Is that a shock technique? I'm supposed to be horrified or something?"

"No. Usually it has quite the opposite effect."

A dark brow rose. "Really. Hmm." He reached out a hand and brushed her pubic hair. "I like this better." When she didn't move away, he slid his fingers lower, between the damp lips.

She found she liked it, standing over him. His body was white and long, with a scattering of dark hair over his chest, and thinly down his belly to the nest of penis, hair, and skin. She'd bitten him and the mark showed on his shoulder. His hair fell around that odd, beautiful face and he looked at her as he stroked her clitoris. Waiting.

Elena smiled and shifted to let him in.

TWENTY-SEVEN

TANSY'S CHURROS

1 cup flour
3 eggs
1 cup water
½ cup butter
¼ tsp salt
Lard or shortening for frying
¼ cup sugar
½ tsp ground cinnamon

It all happens fast, so get it all ready ahead of time—measure out the flour, break the eggs and beat them lightly. In a saucepan, heat water, butter, and salt to boil, then stir in flour. Stir vigorously over low heat until the mix forms a ball, about a minute, then remove from heat and beat the eggs into the dough until everything is smooth.

Heat lard or shortening (about 2 inches) in a heavy frying pan until a bit of dough sizzles.

Spoon the dough into a cake-decorating tube with a fat star tip and squeeze out strips of dough about 4–5 inches long, and fry about three or four at a time, 2 minutes or so on each side. Drain on paper towels and sprinkle generously with sugar and cinnamon while still hot, or try powdered sugar. Makes men and boys your slaves for life.

TWENTY-EIGHT

Elena finally dragged herself to the Orange Bear around three. She'd originally intended to arrive just past noon, but—well. Julian. As she walked through the gilded late-fall day, with wind clattering through the last cottonwood leaves and purple clouds piling up over the mountains, her limbs were liquid, her mind soft. She'd let Julian take Alvin to Portia while she worked, and would send him there again tomorrow for the opening. She was paying Portia for babysitting. Julian promised, bending in to kiss her neck, that he would bring the dog home after her shift.

Elena didn't know if she would survive that long. Flashes of his mouth, his hands, all the things they'd been doing all afternoon, kept slamming into her, as if her memories were gusts of perfumed lust.

Wow. She clutched it all close to herself, smiling. Maybe she *could* fall in love again. Maybe there was one more in her, one more chance—

Stop. She shook her hair out of her face and squared her shoulders as she came up the walk to the restaurant.

Deliberately, she pushed herself into business-mind. This was important stuff—in a little more than twenty-four hours, her first solo menu would debut to the public.

The restaurant looked welcoming and warm in the late day. The outside had been sanded and painted a pale golden orange with white trim, which sounded terrible but looked wonderful against the reddish-brown earth and deep blue and green of the mountains. As winter came, the vivid blue skies and white slopes would provide a spectacular backdrop. She picked up a plastic straw, blown onto the steps from somewhere, and admired the sign, carved by a local artisan. An orange bear with a broad dark nose and the letters in relief. Around the edges of the sign were carved pink and orange stylized flowers, and the lettering—*The Orange Bear*—was a friendly, soft-edged font.

A flutter of mixed emotions moved in her. Excitement. Joy. Anticipation. Terror. Tomorrow night, she'd be a wreck. For tonight, thanks to Julian, she was feeling pretty loose.

The kitchen was in full uproar. The music played and the dishwashers swished and orders rang out in Spanish and English. A prep cook chopped scallions and Ivan was massaging something on a cutting board, his hands and arms covered with meat and spices up to his elbows. He was whistling and lifted his chin in greeting as she came in. Juan stood at the stove, stirring something in a big iron pot. "Hey, *Jefa*," he said, calling her over. "Taste this soup, eh? I'm thinking I found us a new daily special."

She took out a spoon and ladled out a taste. It was a deep, velvety chicken broth with tomatoes and garlic and spices, and floating bits of chicken and tortillas. She closed her eyes, put her hand over her lips to press in the flavor. It seemed she had never tasted chicken broth before, that this was the pinnacle of all. "Good God," she said in English. "That is spectacular."

He smiled, the big gentle eyes lighting up in pleasure. *"Gracias, Jefa."*

"Definitely put it in the rotation." She took out a fresh spoon, ladled out a second taste. "Who taught you to cook?" she asked in Spanish.

"Mi padre. He had a restaurant in Juarez. Good cook," he said. "Not always a wise man, but—" He shrugged. "He meant well. I lit a candle for him today."

"I made a table at home," she said. "My sister would have been thirty-seven years old today."

He looked at her. Nodded in his quiet way.

"Jefa!" Ivan called. "Come taste this."

Elena grinned at Juan. He said, "The boy needs attention."

"Coming!" She headed over to the corner where Ivan was working at a stainless steel table. "Hey, Ivan. What are you up to?"

He grinned at her, lifted a handful of pale meat. "A ground chicken mixture for the beef-adverse. A sausage like chorizo, without all the stuff that makes people squirm."

Elena leaned over the bowl and inhaled the sharpness of cumin, the faint greenness of sage, and the smoky hint of chipotles. "Nice." She narrowed her eyes. "The onions are an odd addition. Wouldn't they come later?"

He shrugged, slapping meat back and forth between his

hands. He inhaled the scent, too, pursed his lips as if to seal it in his nostrils. "I'm experimenting. Maybe a little more garlic, too. And I was thinking about some cilantro."

His eyes were glossy, an almost unreal shade of blue, and a smile played over that sensual mouth.

"Are you high or something?" she asked.

He wiggled his eyebrows. "High on love, sistah, high on love."

"Hoo-kay! Not to offend you, Maestro, but you might want to finish that up. We have a lot of other stuff to do."

"I hear you," he said easily. "This has just been mobbing me for a few days and I suddenly figured out what might be missing."

Elena nodded. "Let me try it when you cook it." She patted him on the back and moved toward the stairs to the second kitchen.

"Hold on there, sis." He grabbed the back of her whites. "You just *patted* me on the back. Let me have a look at you."

Elena composed her face carefully, wiping it clean of any emotion. "What?"

He peered at her through hooded eyes, intently sweeping over details—chin, eyes, neck, mouth. Raising his chin, he smiled with half his mouth. "Aha!"

She tugged away, pretending she had no idea what he saw. "I've got work to do, Rasputin."

He laughed as she ducked into the stairwell and dashed upstairs to the pastry and tamale prep kitchen. The music and mood here were entirely different. North light slanted in through a bank of windows at the top of the wall, giving the room a blue and shadowy cast. Tansy liked the natural light and worked beneath the windows rolling pastry. The music was something Latin and quiet, and the air smelled of cinnamon and frying dough. Elena's stomach growled. "Wow, that smells fantastic."

The scene was as quiet and peaceful as a Vermeer, the woman cooking in denim and a plain white button-up shirt covered by an apron, her wrinkled face softened by the cool light, her arms dusted with flour.

She raised her head. "Hello, sweetie," she said in her smoker's rasp. Then with a grin that showed one missing tooth, "I mean Chef."

"It's all right, Tansy. You alone can call me 'sweetie.' " She ambled over, drawn by the frying dough. "What do we have here?"

"Just churros."

"Which is like Michelangelo saying 'just statues.' " The twists of dough cooled on the butcher-block table in little rows, sprinkled with cinnamon and sugar. Elena grabbed one, still hot, and ate it in a suspended moment of bliss. "This makes me think of feast days when I was a kid."

"Food takes you back, that's for sure."

"Mmm." The churros were crisp outside, hot and airy inside, and the sugar and cinnamon bit into her memories and called forth some unnamed year when she, along with her other siblings, sat in a church hall, dressed in their Sunday clothes, devouring churros from grease-stained paper napkins—explosions of pleasure in every bite.

"Wow," she said, "I think I'm starving. I need a meal."

"Juan said he was going to serve the family meal at four." Tansy glanced at the clock on the wall. "Not long now."

"Good. You have everything—all set for tomorrow?"

"Ready as I can be, I reckon. I think it'll be a fine

blowout, Chef. The crew works well together and the menu is terrific."

"Thanks." Elena opened the reach-in and saw satisfying rows of tamales, mini and regular sized, lined up by color on trays.

"Where is your mama?" Tansy asked.

"Espanola. That's where I grew up."

"Not so far away."

Elena smiled faintly. "Farther than you can even imagine."

A cry rang out downstairs and Elena bolted. She was halfway down the stairs before someone called out in Spanish, *"Jefa!* We need you down here, pronto!"

She scrambled into the kitchen, where the lively chaos had screeched to a halt and centered around Hector, who held his hand wrapped in a bloody towel. It dripped blood to the white floor.

"He cut himself," said Ivan, coming over with ice and a wet towel. "Tell him to bind it, for God's sake! Fuck, this is why I hate bilingual kitchens."

Like there was any other kind. One of the others said something profane in Spanish, and Elena glared at him, too. She bent to examine Hector's hand. She said in Spanish, "Put pressure on it, but first let me see."

She shook her head as she saw the gash, deep and long across the flesh pad beneath his thumb. "You have to go to the ER. Juan, you take him."

The kitchen stilled. Juan just looked at her, then to Ivan. Hector stared balefully at his hand.

"What is it?" Elena asked.

"It's cool, *Jefa,*" Ivan said. "I'll take him. We'll be back in time for dinner." He winked and herded Hector toward the door. "C'mon, man."

Elena narrowed her eyes at Juan. "What gives?"

Juan gave a Latin shrug. "Nobody likes American medicine."

But something was awry. She narrowed her eyes. "C'mon, Juan, what's going on?"

"*De nada*," he said, and put his hand on her shoulder, turning her toward the dining room. "Let's go put the meal out."

For a moment, she stood, testing her intuition. There was something wrong, but she couldn't quite discern what it was. "Go," she said to Ivan.

She caught a wordless exchange of glances between the two men, but for now, she left it alone. "I'm going to check the storerooms. Double-check everything before you go tonight." Then she scowled. "Damn. If Hector's out, who will we get to replace him?"

"I'll ask around." Juan stirred his stockpots. "Hector won't miss, though." He rubbed his thumb and fingers together. "*Dinero.*"

Julian paced around the house, up to his office, down to the kitchen for coffee, for a slice of cheese, for—whatever. Nothing sounded good, no matter how many cupboards he opened. It wasn't food he wanted just now.

Portia, looking weary, brought two water glasses upstairs and put them in the sink. Alvin followed behind her and flopped down on the kitchen floor with a big sigh.

"What's with you?" Portia asked her father.

He shook his head. "Restless."

"Is it the movie?"

A sharp prick of guilt stabbed him. The lie of omission. "Kind of."

She slid onto a stool, crossing her arms on the counter. "Do you have to wait on approval or something? I thought you were past all that with those producers."

He inclined his head. "Well, they want more of the slasher series, but I convinced them to let me do the ghost story. There are some . . . issues with it that I'm trying to work out."

"They should let you do what you want," she said with the innocence of fourteen. "You started with ghost stories."

He gave her a sideways grin. "That's true." The first film had been a remake of *The Importance of Being Earnest*, with a twist: one of the "Ernests" gets killed in a mix-up, and his ghost gives the other one a lot of trouble. He'd been twenty-five years old when he made it, and although it was raw in ways, he sometimes thought it was one of his best efforts. But embarrassment or pride, that was how a life in movies went—you threw yourself into whatever you were doing at the time.

"I like ghost stories," she said.

"So do I, as it happens." He put the kettle on. "Have some hot chocolate with me?"

She nodded. "Is my mom gonna be in the movie?"

Ricki and her newly appointed husband had flown out this afternoon, after a long chat. "I hope so. I wrote the part with her in mind."

Her delft-blue eyes fell on his face, showing nothing. "That's nice. It's been harder for her to get parts lately."

"That's Hollywood," he said with regret. "No matter how beautiful, it's harder for a woman to land a good role after forty."

"Do you think my mom is beautiful?"

Julian chuckled. "Anyone with eyes thinks your mother is beautiful, Portia. She's like a painting."

She nodded, gnawing her bottom lip.

"What's on your mind, kiddo?"

"I don't know," she said. "I guess it hasn't helped her a lot, has it? Being beautiful? She's not all that happy. Five husbands and all those boyfriends and nobody seems to stick. Not that I think *you* ran out on her or anything." She waved a hand. "You know what I mean."

"I do." The kettle began to rumble, and Julian took two mugs from the shelf and opened the cupboard to look for hot chocolate. There, left over from the tasting party, was a stock of Ibarra chocolate in a round yellow package. "Shall we try this kind?"

"Sure. You need the spinner thing, though."

He raised his eyebrows in question. Portia pulled open a drawer and pulled out a whip. "This. And it takes milk, not water."

"Ah." He clicked the kettle off and opened the fridge and took out the milk. "The happiness thing, with your mother?" He found a heavy saucepan and put it on the burner, measured milk into it. "That's why I keep nagging you to find other things to think about than how you look. If you use your body for skiing, and it makes you feel good to be *in* your body, then you're not so miserable when you think somebody else is prettier than you or thinner or whatever."

She swung a foot, her head braced on her hand, a spill of

glittery hair falling on the counter. "That's easy for a man to say. No offense or anything."

"You won't offend me, Portia. Speak your mind."

"Well, men can be ordinary looking and it doesn't hurt them. They can be really smart or talented and they don't have to also be skinny and really handsome and all that stuff. I mean, look at you."

He grinned.

She rolled her eyes. "I mean, you're handsome enough, but you're kind of a geek. You always have been. You're skinny. You have a big nose."

He chuckled. "Don't mince words, kid."

Portia grinned back. "Don't be vain, Dad. You are not Brad Pitt, exactly, and yet you've had really beautiful wives and you have women throwing themselves at you all the time, and your career is going fine."

"I'm not an actor, though. I'm behind the camera."

She made a face. "You know it's different for men."

"It is," he agreed, stirring the milk. "But that seems like all the more reason for you to concentrate on things that are not about how you look."

"That's just the point, though. A woman can be smart and talented and all that stuff, but she *also* has to be good-looking and thin."

"Not always."

She inclined her head. "Name a successful woman who is really fat."

He seriously tried and couldn't come up with a name off the top of his head. Oprah had been pretty round at one time, but she wasn't these days. "But not that many fat men are successful either."

"What about James Gandolfini? Gérard Depardieu?"

"You're right." He could think of a bunch of rap stars, too. Including a few women, but that wasn't the point. He didn't want to convince her to be heavy, but to be healthy and in her body. And ski, for God's sake. "What about women who are not fat but are not thin. What about Elena? She's curvy."

"She's also beautiful and she's a cook, so there's room to negotiate."

"You think she's beautiful?"

"Don't you?" She narrowed her eyes. "Please don't play me, Dad. I notice things, okay? I can see that you have a thing for her."

He pursed his lips, didn't look at her. The milk started to steam. "I just want you to be in your body, kiddo, and love it. Stop worrying so much about what everybody else thinks."

She unwrapped the chocolate and broke it by slamming it on the side of the counter. "Says my dad the director who casts beautiful women in his movies."

Julian glanced at her. "Sometimes you're a little too grown up for your own good."

"I know," she said.

And he realized that he didn't really want to leave her alone, looking so shadowy and wan. He'd been thinking of Elena's lusciousness all afternoon, watching the clock until he could take off and see her after her shift. But he didn't want to leave his daughter tonight. "I'm going to have to take Alvin down to Elena when she gets off work, but in the meantime, you want to watch a movie?"

"What's on?"

"I don't know. We have 147 channels, so there must be something."

"Sure," she said. "You know what else I would like, Dad? Can we get a smaller table so we could eat dinner together? Maybe, like, a pretty tablecloth and stuff like that?"

A memory rose of his family dinner table, a square melamine with vinyl-covered chairs. His mother's pasta in a big bowl, glasses of red Kool-Aid all around. In comparison, the table in the great room looked like something from a medieval banquet hall. "Yeah," he said. "That's a really good idea. We can go shopping this week." He raised his eyebrows. "We do have one problem. Who is going to cook?"

Portia frowned. "Oh, yeah. I forgot." She rubbed a thumbnail over the surface of the counter. "I just liked it when we all ate breakfast together, like a TV family."

"I liked it, too. I grew up like that." He thought for a minute. "Leave it to me, kiddo. I'll figure out a way to get the food in here. You're in charge of figuring out what you want for the table and all that stuff. Deal?"

Her smile was as young and pleased as anything he'd ever seen. "Really?"

"Really." Picking up his cup, he said, "Let's go see what we can find to watch together."

After work, Elena showered the grease and grit of the day from her skin and then padded downstairs for a glass of wine. The candles burned on her altar, and she smiled at the offerings, then spied a sock in front of the couch and bent to scoop it up.

A flash of Julian—over her, touching her, kissing her, driving into her—gave her a sultry shiver, and she straightened, letting the full memory wash back into her mind. His seasoned tongue and thick member and skilled fingers, his surprising earthiness and unselfconsciousness—

Across the room, in soft outline, stood Isobel. She simply gazed at Elena, face impassive. "What?" Elena asked.

"Tell him that his mother is here, too," she said.

"It's a little weird, you know." She tossed the sock on top of the washer as she passed the closet where it was stored, and went to the kitchen for that wine. "And it's weird that you're showing up when he's in the room. What's that about?"

But Isobel never answered questions like that, and she didn't now. She fell on her elbows on the counter, watching as Elena poured white wine into a goblet. "Something's going on," Isobel said. "There's some kind of trouble, but I'm not sure what it is."

"I talked to Hector's sister." The wine was cool and sharp and refreshing. "She said there is an accident coming."

Isobel nodded, peering into the distance. Around her wrists were seven thin bracelets and a big chunk of turquoise. Her eyes, that almost golden brown, shimmered. "Juan. It's about Juan."

Narrowing her eyes, Elena remembered the strangeness about Hector going to the emergency room. Which made her think of Juan and Ivan standing in the kitchen, exchanging that look, and then everything had been all right when Hector returned, stitched but off dish duty. She put him to work in the front of the house for the time being.

She'd forgotten to ask Ivan what was going on because she'd been awash in postcoital blurriness, flashing back to hands and mouth and eyes and—

Shit.

What had she *done*?

The same thing she always did. Let the wrong man get close, let the wrong guy under her skin. And this man was not just one who had power in her life, he was famous and charming, and sexy and—

She realized that Isobel had gone. The kitchen seemed painfully empty, and she sank down on a stool, shaking her head. She wanted to call Mia, talk it out, but even if it wasn't the middle of the night in England, Elena wasn't talking to her friend yet. Maybe Patrick?

No. Patrick had his own relationship stuff going on. He wasn't likely to be particularly reasonable. Or available, honestly.

Her grandmother? No. Maria Elena always just wanted Elena to settle down, get married, stop this foolish chasing-around-the-world stuff. Her relationships with her remaining sisters were too tenuous. There was no one else in her world, no confidante. No best friend to whisper with, or analyze things or solicit advice from. Even her dog wasn't home yet.

Pathetic. How did that happen?

Across the room, the candles on the El Día de Los Muertos altar flickered. "Yeah, I get it," she said to the invisible ghosts. "I have you. Not the same."

In the end, she carried her wine upstairs and flipped on

her laptop. If she *were* speaking to Mia, she would write her an email. So she would just do that without actually sending it.

> Dear Mia,
>
> I'm in a mess again. I had sex with my boss this afternoon, and it was not as light as I expected it would be. It feels like there's weight and substance to it, which makes it even more dangerous. I like him. That's the real trouble. He's the kind of guy you know is going to be too much trouble in real life—too rich, too accomplished, with access to too many really gorgeous women—but I like him more than I want to. He's got issues and he has too much power in my life, but I still like him a lot and I want to see where it goes.
>
> What do I like about him? No, I'm not dazzled by his position. You'd have to meet him to understand that it's just a nonissue.
>
> I like his dark brown eyes, which are kind and intelligent. I like the faint air of the geeky about him, in his wrists and big hands and the cute way he looks in glasses. I like his aura of power. I do like that. I like men who like themselves, who know where they are going and what they're all about.
>
> I like his daughter, and she's part of the problem. I don't want her feelings to be hurt. I don't want her to feel like I've been nice to her just to get to her dad, because it isn't true.
>
> I like

Elena paused, thinking of his tongue, of his hands, of his—it had been so intense. So intense! He was like some thick nectar, dripping down her throat, slow and thick and sweet.

When he knocked at the door, she stayed where she was for a long, long moment. Little hot spots bloomed on her body, chin and inner wrists and the edge of her knees. She thought of his tongue, the golden depth of his mouth.

He knocked again. She stood up. She couldn't leave Alvin out there.

For one more minute, walking down the stairs to open the door, she tried to tell herself that she was going to send him away. Her feet brushed over the carpet, the fibers sweeping her soles electrically, a feeling she'd never noticed before. The air parted, brushing her cheeks and arms and breasts.

She opened the door and Julian was there. Alvin wiggled his way in, brushing her legs, and she bent slightly and touched him, rubbed his ears, even as Julian was tangling her fingers in his hand, drawing her close, and she was pulling him into the room, pushing the door closed behind him. He captured her face in his hands and kissed her, whispering a soft oath as their bodies came together. "I can't stay very long," he said. "Portia is by herself."

Elena nodded, drawing him into the room, up the stairs where it was softer and more comfortable, and she pushed his sweater up, touching his chest, kissing his nipples, and he tugged the blue wool over his head, the black tumble of curls falling around his face. He reached for her T-shirt and pulled the hem over her head, and pushed her back on the bed.

He drew her arms over her head and held them there with one strong hand, touching her with his other hand, his hand roving over her belly and breasts still clad in plain pink cotton, his penis pressed into her thigh, his mouth against her neck. He unfastened the clasp of her bra and her breasts tumbled out, and he halted to look, just look and bend and touch with the edge of his tongue the aroused tips. He licked them and suckled, and lifted her breasts, and she whimpered, "I need to touch you, too."

"In a minute," he said, holding her wrists firmly, kissing one nipple, then the other, then the hollow of her throat. He moved his chest against her naked breasts, erotically brushing hair over her skin. He suckled her lips. "I wish I had all night," he whispered.

"Me too," Elena said, and arched into him. "Please, Julian, I need to touch you as much as you want to touch me."

He raised up a little. "What do you want to touch?" he asked. "I was thinking, before I came here, of your milk-white skin, and the milk chocolate of your nipples." He released her wrists and drew his hand over the places he'd named.

"The licorice of your hair," she said, smiling. She lifted her head and licked his mouth. "The honey of your lips. The . . . pickle of—"

He laughed. "Pickle!" He tugged her hand down. "Don't you mean zucchini, baby?"

"Just give it to me," she said, laughing.

"All yours."

Afterward, they were naked and covered by the sheet and Elena offered him wine from her glass. "I know you have to go soon, but we do need to have a little bit of a conversation."

He refused the wine and propped himself up on one elbow. "Which conversation?"

"The you-are-my-boss-and-that's-a-bit-of-a-problem conversation."

He smoothed a hand over the sheet. Elena just let the pause grow until he finally said, "All I know, Elena, is that I haven't stopped thinking about you for more than five minutes all day."

Quietly, she said, "Me either. Obviously, this part is going to happen. I need to know that I'm still going to have a job when this part is over."

He made a noise, captured her hand and put a kiss on her palm. "That's harsh, killing it before it starts."

She looked at him, smiling. "Neither one of us is that naive, Julian. Things don't last."

"Never?"

"So rarely that it might as well be never," she said, aware of a high sense of emotion lurking at the top of her throat. "And I'm not trying to have some serious conversation at an inappropriate time, but I want this job. I don't want anything to fuck that up."

"Then let's make a pact that we won't let it happen. Whatever it is, whatever we do, the job is yours, Elena."

"Let's just say that no matter what happens with us, the job is about the job, how's that?"

"Deal." He stuck out his hand to shake, and Elena accepted it, and he tumbled her forward. "In the meantime, before it's all over, can we have sex about seven billion times?" His mouth was hot on her throat. "Because that's about how much I'll need to get this out of my system."

"Deal," she said, and this time, she took the lead. In the

back of her mind, she heard the snide voice of Dmitri saying *He just wants to fuck you.*

But it could go both ways, couldn't it? She wanted to fuck him, too, Julian Liswood of the tumbles of curls and throaty laugh and big zucchini. She just had to keep it all in perspective.

After he left, she turned on the television to stop thinking, erase everything. Clicking through the On Demand movies, she saw one of Julian's slasher movies, maybe the first one, starring his ex-wife. Fiercely curious, she punched in the order code.

It was an odd experience, seeing the very young version of Portia's mother. Portia really did look a lot like her, but there was something sturdier in the daughter's face, a legacy from Julian. It was a classic teen serial-killer kind of thing—a young woman trying to outsmart the crazed killer who wanted her dead and killed everyone in his path to get to her. It surprised her with its tongue-in-cheek humor, and also the respect it gave the genre. He never talked down to his audience.

It was also *very* scary. Elena fought the urge to double-check her locks, and told herself that Alvin would go insane if anyone tried to break in.

At the end of the movie, the young woman—bloodied but triumphant—outsmarted her killer, and as she stood there, breathing hard, marks all over her from her struggle, Elena found herself in tears—suddenly knowing more than she wished about Julian, about his losses.

Suddenly curious, she opened her laptop and typed his

name into Google and called up all the movies he'd made. Sixteen in a little over twenty years, starting with *The Importance of Being Earnest,* a ghost story that had been made for next to nothing and was a surprise smash. It had launched his career.

In the body of his work, there were three ghost stories, one historical vampire flick that was a cult classic, a foray into a dark romance, and the rest slasher movies.

He was either killing killers or resurrecting the dead.

Resolutely, she did not look around for her own dead, but turned off the computer, turned off the light, and told herself to get a good night's sleep. As she closed her eyes, she saw his stricken face when he looked at the altar that afternoon. As she drifted toward sleep, finally, she wondered what to cook for him next, how to feed that hungry, hungry heart.

TWENTY-NINE

Vintage postcard of Paris, black-and-white, showing a woman smoking in Montmartre:

Dear Elena,
How long are you going to keep this up? I know you're furious with me and you have a right to be, but will you please just listen for three seconds to me? Haven't I earned that much? I've forgiven you lots of times. Love you (still, even if you don't love me),
Mia

Saturday, the energy in the kitchen was palpable. The restaurant would open at five-thirty, and Elena checked the reservations list when she came in at three. Julian had orchestrated a marketing campaign that would kick in the first of December, but for now, some of the kitchen guys had gone into town with flyers, letting everyone know the restaurant was open. So far, the list showed reservations for six-thirty, seven, and seven-thirty. Not tons, but a satisfying number.

Next, she did a walk-through of the entire restaurant, starting with the front of the house, which had been, thanks to Patrick and Julian and Alan, completely trans-formed. The old tattered, seventies-style furnishings and fixtures had been removed, along with all the kitschy Old West art. The downstairs rooms each had one bright wall— rich terra-cotta rose in one, a warm yellow in another, with intimate corners set up for couples as well as tables for small groups. The light fixtures and hardware had all been replaced with mission-style iron with an Art Deco flair, to complement the early-twentieth-century paintings by

Diego Rivera and Georgia O'Keeffe and other artists from the Taos school. There were small tributes to Elena's New Mexico, in the *milagro* crosses she'd posted in nooks and crannies, and the whimsical El Día de los Muertos skeletons—paintings and little statues—engaging in all the pursuits of life—getting married and dancing and holding little babies and, of course, eating and cooking. Patrick's elegant eye kept everything in exquisite balance—color and ethnic eccentricities together with beautiful art—in both setting and décor.

Upstairs, the open bar area was less formal and just as gorgeous. Here were tables for larger groups, and, by the windows overlooking the valley, a space for those who just wanted drinks and snacks.

Patrick and Alan were in the middle of the room, setting up a long table for the staff meal, at which Juan would serve the special of the evening to servers and cooks and bartenders and hostesses—everyone.

She hugged Patrick quickly. "Great job. It looks so good!"

Alan, who had at first seemed temperamental, nodded. "I can't believe it's the same place."

She went through the kitchens, too, checking stores of prepped items such as guacamole and sliced vegetables and fruits, and the numbers of tamales ready to be steamed and served, and the desserts Tansy had left. She went through the stocks and sauces, tasting, making sure the seasonings were right. "Add a little cracked pepper," she said, "and some lemon juice to the soup."

Juan served the family meal at four, and Ivan narrated the specials of the evening for the wait staff. When he was finished, she delivered a short, sweet pep talk. "We've worked hard for this. Be sure to keep notes of things that work very well or don't work well, so we can talk about them at the staff meeting Monday."

There was, after that, an hour of music in the kitchen, of cooks and servers sharing war stories of openings they'd worked in other restaurants, other times, other places.

It was only then, during the hush before what they all hoped would be a storm, that Elena was suddenly ambushed by memories of the opening of the Blue Turtle in Vancouver. She and Dmitri had worked so hard, the menu there a fusion of southwestern and French cuisine, a blend of such gorgeousness that both chefs had been giddy with the display that first night. And it had been a spectacular opening. From the minute it opened, the Blue Turtle had been beloved by Vancouverites. They loved her dishes in particular, though Dmitri always took credit.

Bastard, she thought again, going through the kitchen one more time. One more time. This time, it was all hers.

Win or lose.

In the end, they did 141 covers, managed to get the diners in and out without much fuss. Elena, sweaty with the hard work of the night, was at her desk, feeding numbers into the computer, when Julian showed up at the door of her office. "Everyone gone?" she asked.

He nodded, came into the office and closed the door. A small smile curved up the edge of his lips. Coming around behind her, he bent as he kissed the back of her neck. "Are you finished?"

"Oooh," she protested, ducking away. "I'm sweaty! You won't want to do that."

"I might," he said, his hands on her shoulders, brushing away the hair from the back of her neck. "I might like you sweaty. I might like—" He bent and touched his tongue to the knobs of bone below her hair. The concentrated nerves there, so unused to attention, leapt up like flowers to the watering lap of that muscle. "Mmm," he said, and did it again, slowly licking from nape to shoulder, "lightly salty."

Elena shivered, closing her eyes. His slid a hand around her throat, fingers lightly brushing into the indentation between clavicles, swirling around her chest, the top of her breasts, that muscular tongue swirling around her neck. He nipped her and a bolt of lightning ran down her nerves to her low belly, making her snap "Ow!" and pull away, a little irritably.

He laughed and caught her around the waist, pulling her into him so she felt the thrust of his cock nuzzling between the cheeks of her bottom, against a thigh. He bit her neck, like a tomcat, and unfastened her shirt with the other hand and then ripped down the cup of a bra so one nipple spilled into his hand, and he deftly rolled it between his fingers, sucking at her neck, holding her in place with one long, strong arm, rubbing his erection into her. Sharp, hot spikes moved from nape to nipple to groin, and she wiggled, trying to free herself or get more, she didn't know which.

"Julian," she protested, pulling at his hands, "I stink."

"No," he said in a raw voice.

"Yes."

He loosened his hold on her and she turned, and then with a low laugh, he pushed her up against the wall, hands on either side of her head, and kissed her. Hard. Then not, pulling back a little to nip the edges of her lips, the side of her mouth, as if to eat them.

"I saw you a long time ago, in San Francisco," he said.

The smell of him, the taste, made her dizzy, off-center. "You did?"

"I saw your mouth and wanted to fuck you on the spot." He was breathing over her, and kissing her, and with skill or perhaps lots of experience, he edged the tip of his cock right against the edge of her clitoris. She found her hips relaxing, her breath coming in hot, open-mouthed gasps.

He bent and kissed her neck, let her arms down to slide the bra off her shoulders. She dug her hands into his thick hair and tried to yank him away, but he was stronger, and only chuckled, and when she looked down, his mouth was closing around her nipple, the sight electrifying—that tongue, that beautiful mouth! She let go of a long breath and found herself falling adrift in the heat, forgetting everything, and then he licked her throat, shoulder, and lifted up an arm and licked her underarm, and it was so electrifying that she slammed against him, pulling his clothes away, and he tumbled her to her desk, papers flying, and thrust into her, hard. She locked her legs around him and felt her body screaming, singing, her breasts bobbling with his violence, her hands finding his shoulder, his hair. They locked together. He pushed his hands between them and touched her, and when she cried out, he covered her mouth with his hand and she bit him and he came, too, and when she opened her eyes, he was looking at her and it was deep, too deep, feeling that pulse between them and seeing so deep, and letting him see *her*, so she closed her eyes.

He fell on her neck, laughing softly. Even in this, he was different from any of the men she'd known, in his pleasure, his laughing. His breath, then his mouth, fell on the place between shoulder and neck and he gathered her with one arm, bracing himself with his other against the desk. "Do you want to go eat somewhere? Have a margarita or something? Portia is staying with a friend. We can play."

"Let's just go to your house."

"Sounds perfect."

She was over her head, she thought, as he helped her up. But she didn't really know what she could do about it now. He was the hungriest man she had ever met.

Elena shredded a pork roast with two forks in the quiet of Monday's kitchen. The sharp spices wafted up to her and she swirled a spoon into the broth, tasted it. Frowned. A little flat. She threw the spoon on the stainless steel counter by the dishwasher and, leaving the forks in the meat, whirled to grab a head of garlic from the shelf over the table, slid cloves from their thin, stiff coats, and crushed them under her knife. Into a small heavy pan, she tossed a dollop of stiff white lard and let it melt, then shook the garlic into the pan, swirling it around to let it go golden, release its flavors into the fat. Some old French folk songs played in her ear from an iPod connected to her shirt, tucked beneath the chef's whites to keep it from getting polluted with dustings of flour and oil and whatever else flew around the kitchen. It was further protected by a thin plastic sleeve; still, she didn't expect it would last long.

"Don't you have prep cooks to do that for you?" Julian came into the kitchen, touched her arm.

Elena grinned and pulled the earphone out. "I'm a chef because I love to cook," she said. "I don't want somebody else doing all the prep without my hand in it, too, at least some of it." She pulled the garlic off the heat and ladled a taste of red chili into a fresh spoon. "Taste this," she said, offering it to him.

He obliged, rolling it over his tongue. "A little flat."

"Garlic," she said, nodding. Scraping the golden bits into the chili, she said, "You're out and about pretty early. What's up?"

Julian raised the newspaper he carried. "We made the paper."

A painful arrow went through her middle. It was impossible to read his expression. "And?"

He handed it to her, folded to the review.

ORANGE BEAR A COLORFUL
AND SPICY DELIGHT
LOCAL FAVORITE TRANSFORMED WITH FLAIR

Patrons of the old Steak and Ale remember the painfully dated décor and crowded grime, but put up with it because the menu, largely written and carried out by former head chef Ivan Santino, was so astonishingly good. There was a collective chatter of worry when Hollywood director Julian Liswood, known for his West Coast eateries, swooped in to take over the failing restaurant. Locals have watched through narrowed eyes as work crews gave the faded, gold-rush-era building a face-lift, and speculated over what surprises might be in store from new executive chef Elena Alvarez, who came to Aspen via Vancouver, San Francisco, Paris, and, more to our purposes here, Santa Fe.

The restaurant opened to little fanfare on Saturday night, and voilà! One of the most delightful transformations in recent memory was revealed. Now called the Orange Bear, in keeping with Liswood's other restaurants, which are all named for animals, the restaurant features a menu that has been completely rewritten to a southwestern theme, upgraded and deliciously freshened by Alvarez's unique eye and flair for combining the best of French and haute cuisine with the ingredients and basic dishes of her roots in New Mexico. In a wise move, chef and owner retained Santino, whose flair for game meats and local produce has been put to extraordinary use here (try the duck tamales with sour cherry mojo, $17).

Happily the Olde West décor has been scraped away and replaced with a sleek and cheerful spirit of Latin America, in both high and folk art. Be sure to notice the crosses hung with milagros and the whimsical plate decorations of pink candy skulls and marigold blossoms.

The Orange Bear, Tuesday–Sunday,
11:30–3 and 5:30–10 p.m.
Southwestern Nouveau.
Call for reservations.

She lifted her head, and grinned. "Yes!"

"Good work, Chef," he said, and offered his hand to shake, formally.

"Thank you, Julian!" She whooped and did a little dance. Her first wish was to call Mia, which she squashed. Her second was to rub it in Dmitri's face. She'd figure out how to do that, for sure.

But mainly, she wanted her staff to know. She posted the review on the kitchen wall for the crew, and as they all came in for tamale duty, they cheered. They gathered in the sunny upstairs kitchen for the assembly line—with such a labor-intensive menu item, it seemed the best idea to spend one afternoon a week in assembly. Tamales froze well. The music played overhead, a mix of Bruce Springsteen and Madonna and Mexican favorites one of the prep cooks had brought in.

The manufacturing line started at one, when a cook spread a dollop of masa in a reconstituted corn husk, then passed it to a cook who filled it with one of the mixtures developed to go inside and then passed it to the last station, where nimble fingers tied them off with thin strips torn from the largest corn husks in each package.

The basic steps for every tamale were the same. The dried husks had to be soaked, and to keep the varieties straight in the storage and serving process, they were dyed in the soaking bath. The masa, made ahead, was flavored slightly according to the filling it would acquire—a little chile mixed into the pork tamales, a little brown sugar into the caramelized pear.

Three assembly lines were formed to create the individual tamales—one for plain husks, slightly reddish masa, and pork filling; one for dark brown husks with duck and cherry; and one for red husks with goat cheese and tomatoes. Elena headed the pork line—her speed and deftness in spreading the masa were better than anyone's.

"Chef," said Alan, appearing at the doorway to the upstairs dining room, "there's somebody here to see you." He gave her a look she couldn't quite interpret.

Elena nodded. "I'll be right there."

Wiping her hands, she gestured for Tansy to take her place, and went out into the sunny, now very appealing bar area. A girl leaned on the bar, long hair falling in silken tumbles down her back.

"Hey, Portia," Elena said, surprised. "What's up?"

"Hi! Um . . ." She shifted, foot to foot, her hands in tiny back pockets. "Can we . . . uh . . . maybe go outside or something?"

"Sure." She pointed toward the broad wooden porch, the smoking area for the restaurant, which overlooked part of the street and a dense stand of dark-limbed pines. Eyeing the woolen scarf Portia wore over her sweater, she said, "Is it cold?"

"A little."

"Let me get a coat." She retrieved it from a hook by the door, and they headed outside, leaning on the banisters of the porch. The air was brisk, warmer where the high-altitude sun crisped the surface, sharper in the shadows, where it carried the promise of snow.

"Might snow tonight," Portia said, looking at the horizon, where dark gray peaks, only just dusted with snow, poked ragged fingers into the sky. A few clouds gathered.

"It's time, isn't it? The slopes open in a month."

Portia nodded, blue eyes narrowing in expertise. "I'm pretty sure those are snow clouds."

Everyone had begun to eye the sky, peering hopefully at every cloud that crossed the sharp peaks and rolled over the valley. *Snow,* they said to each other. *Snow,* they hoped to hear on the newscasts. *Snow, snow, snow.* It sounded like an incantation, a word exhaled on gray and crystal breath. Elena had taken to doing it herself.

"What's up, Portia?"

"Two things, actually. My dad said I can keep my eyes open for a dog—"

"Hooray!"

She grinned. "Yeah. I'm happy. And two—" She took a breath. "We never—um—talked about the party and all that."

Elena met her eyes. "You mean you getting drunk?"

Portia colored faintly. Nodded.

"Well, I haven't said anything to anyone. But I've been thinking about this a little." Mainly when she heard the sound of car tires going too fast around the corner by her apartment—kids laughing, reckless, unaware of all that could happen in the single blink of an eye. "If you knew you could get in trouble, why did you drink that night, much less get drunk?"

"I get stressed out around my mom. Like, she's so hard to be with. I love her and she's kinda going through a bad time right now, but that's what we did sometimes, when I was home. Drink a little bit. It was just our secret."

Working as she had in kitchens for so long, Elena had heard a lot of stories about bad parenting. The industry attracted the abandoned and misfits. Her own mother had abandoned her, she supposed, but it never ceased to shock her how idiotic parents could be.

She didn't want to go off on Portia, however. "You probably don't need me to tell you that your mom needs to get a clue, right?"

It startled her. "Yeah. I mean, no. I think she just does it because she was so young when she had me and it's kind of a high-pressure life and, you know, lots of people are jealous of her? But she doesn't really have it all that good."

Elena lifted an eyebrow.

Portia shook her head. "I know. I do." She met Elena's eyes. "I shouldn't make excuses for her. My counselors said that, too. But sometimes I feel like I was born the grownup and she's the kid."

"Look," Elena said. "Your mom is none of my business. But I need to know that *you'll* be okay. I don't want you drinking like that anymore. If you never have one, you never have too many, right?"

She blinked. "Oh! I never thought of it like that before, but yeah. Okay."

"I'll also keep your secret, and I won't tell your dad under two conditions."

She looked so hopeful it almost broke Elena's heart. "Okay."

"Number one: you don't drink anything. Not anything. When you're in college and you want to revisit the whole thing, that's fine, but between now and then, not one drop."

"That's a long time from now."

Elena shrugged.

"Okay, I agree for now. What's the other thing?"

"You have to ski this winter. Do whatever it is that your dad wants you to do with it."

An exasperated gasp. "Look at my thighs!" she said, and slapped one with the back of her hands. "I bulk up so fast from skiing! It's just not cool. I look like a freak."

"Portia! Athletic is not the same as fat."

"I get that. You just haven't seen my thighs when I'm training. It's gross."

"What if you take your measurements and then if you add more than what—two inches?—you'll quit. How's that?"

For a long minute, Portia stood still as a stone, her exquisite face bathed in the strong Aspen sunlight, her blonde hair tumbling down her shoulders. Youth, health, beauty, wealth—all right there. "Okay," she said at last. "I'll do it. But I want the tape measure thing. You can be my witness. Maybe you guys will see this is not my imagination."

Elena grinned. She wanted to give the girl a hug, but settled for sticking out her hand. "I can't wait to see you on the slopes."

With a wry grin, Portia shook her hand. "It's a deal."

Winter

TRADITIONAL PORK AND RED CHILE TAMALES

Making tamales is traditionally a family activity. It's not impossible for one person to make them, but there's pleasure in the women coming together, grandmothers and aunties and sisters and little girls filling someone's kitchen to cook in a line. The scent of the meat stewing in its spices and lard, the scent of hairspray and soap from the women's hair and skin, the sound of laughter and clucking and the radio playing something in the background. Oldies and dance music and folk songs and Elvis. Green and white linoleum floor. This is my grandmother's recipe. We ate them at Christmas, and sometimes on somebody's birthday.

Pork shoulder, about 2–3 lbs, with plenty of fat
Olive oil or lard
2 onions, chopped roughly
3–4 cloves garlic
6–7 New Mexico red chile pods, dried, seeds and stems
    removed
1 cup fresh chicken broth
1 tsp cumin
1 tsp salt
Corn husks

1¾ cups masa harina mixed with 1 cup plus 2 T hot water,
    cooled to room temperature
⅔ cup fresh pork lard
1 tsp chile powder (use Chimayo chiles if you can find
    them)
⅔ cup fresh chicken broth

PREPARATION OF INGREDIENTS

In a heavy pot, brown the pork roast on all sides in the olive oil or lard, then add the onions and garlic and let them brown a little. Break up the chile pods and put them in a blender with 1 cup of chicken broth and whir it all together. Cook in low oven, 325 degrees, until meat is tender and shreds easily. Taste to correct seasoning. Shred the meat in the sauce and set aside.

While the meat is cooking, put the corn husks in a bowl and pour boiling water over them to cover. Put a heavy plate on top of them, and let stand for at least 1 hour.

Whip ⅔ cup of lard into ½ cup of the chicken broth until blended, then add masa, chile powder, and remaining chicken broth. Whip until fluffy, then cover and put in the fridge until the roast is cooked.

ASSEMBLY

On a counter or table with plenty of space, line up the bowls of husks, masa, and meat. You'll need a stack of paper towels or dishcloths, and a steamer with a removable metal tray and a lid.

Tear two or three soaked husks into thin strips and set

to one side. Spread a towel on the counter and take one husk out of the water. Blot it on both sides and put it down with the pointed end away from you. Scoop out about a solid table-spoon of masa and plop it down in the middle of the husk, then spread it evenly in a rectangle, leaving a quarter inch of space all around. Ladle out a scant tablespoon of the shredded meat and lay it neatly in a line down the middle of the dough, mak-ing sure it reaches all the way to the end of masa on both ends.

Taking both sides of the husk as if you're going to fold it, gently roll the dough around the meat and wrap the husk firmly around itself. Fold the pointed end toward the center and use a strip of torn husk to tie it in place. Leave the other end open, but tie another strip around the top of the tamale to hold the top together.

Repeat until all batter and meat are gone.

Line the steamer with husks and put the tamales on top of the husks with the open end facing up. Cover and steam for about an hour. The husk should come away easily from the dough.

Let stand for a few minutes, then serve.

Tamales freeze beautifully in their husks, and can be indi-vidually reheated in the microwave for 2–3 minutes.

Salud!

THIRTY-ONE

On a snowy November morning, Ivan scrambled himself some eggs in Patrick's fussy, all-white kitchen. A CD played on the sleek stereo in the corner, a combination of bright jazz favorites that lent the air a lilting feel, somehow French. Patrick was taking one of his seven-year showers. Ivan never understood what he did in there for so long—how could it take that long to take a shower?—but Patrick just smiled. He liked showering, he said without apology.

And he did always look very clean, Ivan had to admit, chuckling as he put the eggs on a thin china plate and settled with them at the table. The apartment was over a garage, and someone had taken pains with the conversion. The dining area was bathed with light and opened onto a balcony that overlooked the town.

Life was good. Just now, heavy snow drifted down. Ivan thought of it as feather snow, because it reminded him of the feathers that escaped a down coat. The endless, ongoing sound of chairlifts and traffic was muffled. His eggs were delicious. His body was sated. He hadn't been drinking much, so the slight depression that seemed to follow him around most of the time was lifting. The job was going well. He got along with Elena very well, actually, and although he had resented her at first, the fact that she brought Patrick with her had been one of the luckiest events in his life.

The golden sensation danced around in his chest for long, long moments before Ivan could identify it: happiness. He'd really only known this feeling a few times in his life—when his mother died and he moved in with her sister, his aunt, and he finally had a warm bed every night and food every day. She wasn't the most affectionate human being on the planet and she already had three kids of her own, but she was good to her orphaned six-year-old nephew. The first time she gave him a bath, she cried and cried and cried, washing the crusted dirt from his spine and the scars all over him. She asked him what his favorite food was, and he told her it was French toast, which he'd only ever had one time, but never forgot. She made him some afterward.

He stayed with her through school, until he landed a scholarship to go to culinary school. There he had known this unbound sense of hope, and he'd won the Beard award.

But it usually went to shit sooner or later. How could he hold on to this now? To Patrick? How could he avoid fucking this one up?

In the wintery weeks of late November and into early December, Julian was like a drugged man, waiting all day for the time when Elena's phone call came in and he could go to her, flying through the afternoon to kiss her and tangle his hands in her hair and take her clothes off as quickly as he could. They did so many things naked it became a game. Naked Yahtzee. Naked dancing, which he liked a lot. Lots of naked eating. They did not spend the night together, and they didn't have sex in his house.

To his surprise, his passion for Elena gave him a new tenderness toward his daughter, as well. He was slowly learning how to cook a few things. He and Portia had breakfast together every morning, mostly cereal with strawberries or some yogurt and whole wheat toast. Most evenings, they ate dinner together at the table she'd chosen—a round, solid one made of wood. She nestled it in the breakfast nook with an airy blue and white cloth, and each day, they used different napkins. Julian had found a service that would come in and cook meals in batches, so they could choose home-cooked meals from the freezer, complete with vegetables and breads and everything they needed.

It was surprisingly rewarding and pleasant. They talked about their days, about things they saw on the news. Nothing big. But it gave him a sense of where she was. He learned that she liked English and science and wood shop, of all things. He brought stories about the people in the restaurant, and sly little stories out of Hollywood, insider dish she loved hearing.

A couple of times, Elena joined them, and on those days, she cooked, even though he tried to get her to just sit and enjoy the meal. She waved him away, and brought Portia into the kitchen with her, giving instruction in simple, traditional cooking.

Late at night, or in the mornings after her first stint at the restaurant, he spent time with Elena.

And he was writing, a very dark and very sexy tale of loss and redemption, his screenplay about a thwarted ghost and a woman trying to shake off her losses. It didn't escape him that he was writing a part for his ex-wife, a fragile, midlife creature who needed to learn to stand on her own two feet, but in his mind it was Elena who moved through the scenes.

Casting had begun. Schedules were being aligned. He hoped to start shooting in early summer, get as much of it done as possible before Portia had to start school again in the fall.

He wrote it at night, when Portia was doing her homework or watching movies—they sat together in the great room before a big crackling fire, or in the family room while she did homework. He found he liked sitting in the same room with her, an iPod in his ears to help him focus, his fingers flying over the keyboard in the low light, the rooms feeling more like a home than any place he'd lived in a very long time.

Now and then, he wondered what he would tell Elena. When he would tell her. Not even that marred his floating sense of well-being. He was sure, when the time came, that he could convince her that he was just doing what story-tellers did.

Even the weather was cooperating. Snow started showing up in early November. At first, it would snow one day and melt the next. Then a slow-moving system stuck around for a few days and the slopes were covered with white for the first time. The locals started chortling to each other about old El Niño. It might even, they said to each other, be a season like the winter of 2005–06, when the snow bases had climbed to over a hundred inches in some places.

One night, sitting with a pencil between his teeth, watching his daughter hunch over the coffee table where she did math homework, and savoring the anticipation of seeing Elena in the morning, he realized the strange loose feeling in his chest was happiness.

It scared the hell out of him. And yet, what was life about, except the possibilities of happiness? Maybe happiness, this once, could stick around.

There was really nothing standing in the way this time, was there?

Well, except that one little lie.

To Elena's mind, the next few weeks were a perfectly orchestrated golden time. There were the usual adjustments to staff, the rearrangements and reassignments and a couple of firings, but the main group worked. Elena and Ivan and Juan formed the core of the kitchen; Alan and Patrick and a clever, beautiful bartender named Marta led the front of the house. Beneath them, front and back, was the usual army of servers, bussers, prep cooks, dishwashers, and others. One surprise turned out to be Tansy Gutierrez, the pastry chef who specialized in Mexican pastries. Her homey churros were wildly popular.

One morning, Julian showed up early at her apartment. "I have to go to Vancouver," he said, giving her a newspaper. "There's been a fire at the Blue Turtle."

"What?" She scanned the article. "How bad is it?"

"Dmitri thought they'd have to close for a few weeks, at least. They think it was an electrical fire in the kitchen. Started overnight and caught the grease pits."

She whistled. "It's amazing there's anything to be salvaged."

"Someone saw the smoke and called it in. The fire department came very quickly." He cleared his throat. "I was wondering if you would go stay with Portia while I'm gone."

"Of course. Alvin will be delighted."

After he left, she could not resist one small email.

> To: dmitrinadirov@theblueturtle.com
> From: Elena.Alvarez@theorangebear.com
> Subject: fire!
> Dmitri, I just heard about the fire. You must be so upset. Sorry, sorry, sorry. I hope it's back up and running very soon.
> Elena

Two days later, she awakened alone in Julian's bed, snowed in by a sudden storm that had trapped Elena in the house, and everybody else out of it. Alvin snored at her feet to keep her from feeling too alone. Julian was supposed to return today, and Portia—who had been legitimately stranded at a friend's house—would be home as soon as the snowplows went through.

But for now, in the quiet morning, she was alone in the house. Just her and her dog—no cleaner or other service staff to make her feel self-conscious. She wandered downstairs to make some coffee, and outside, it was still snowing—heavy, thick snow, the flakes like sugar. She let Alvin out and he dived into it joyfully, nose first, then turned over and rolled and rolled, rubbing his back, his nose, his entire, furry self in it, then he leapt up and ran in delirious circles. Standing at the long windows by the kitchen, she laughed. "Silly dog."

By now she knew the layout of the cupboards and supplies. She measured beans into the grinder and buzzed it for a few seconds, counting under her breath, then poured the fresh grounds into the coffeemaker and pressed the button to get it going. The scent, heavy and heady, filled the room with the perfect aroma of coffee. She felt an urge to make churros the way Tansy had shown her, and wished Portia was here.

Instead, she took out some bread and dropped it in the toaster, discreetly hidden most of the time behind a door that rolled down from the cupboard, and took butter out of the fridge. The first fridge, the main one they used all the time, not the backup fridge around the corner. Both stainless steel.

Such serenity in so much wealth! The endless cupboards and conveniences that made life easier on every level. The dual dishwashers and warming drawers for breads and a hole for vacuum tubes in every room so you never had to lug around a heavy machine. The vast counter space, the large bathrooms and closets tucked away here and there. The luxury of the showers—the master bedroom had the greatest shower Elena had ever seen—it poured down from a giant fixture as if it were raining on the showerer, who could admire the forest through a wall of windows while getting clean. At first, it had seemed faintly wicked to be naked in front of those windows, open to view, but Julian teased her, climbed in with her. Their privacy was protected on a gated estate.

Everything. It was all so unbelievable. Taking her coffee and toast into the great room to wait for Alvin to be finished with his romp, she tried to print it all into her memory for the day when she would only be looking back on it. Would this be the moment of remembrance? Sitting alone in Julian's house?

Moments, moments. It was something she'd done through each of the episodes of her life—pressed memories into the folds of her mind for later. It started when she had to part with her grandmother Iris, a funeral on a hot day. Then, not even a month later, her mother told her to go say goodbye to the cooks at the restaurant where her grandmother tended bar all of Elena's eight years of life. She stood in the kitchen, smelling the strong morning scent of bleach and commercial dishwasher detergent and bacon frying on the grill, and hugged Pedro, her buddy, a fat man with a good heart who looked after Elena like she was his own.

So many places, so many people since then. So many men, in particular. She'd tasted them for her sister and her cousin, living lives for three women. No wonder she was so tired! And yet, didn't she love them all, hadn't they all brought gifts to her, one at a time, each one opening his hand to offer her a delight that was his alone to share?

Moments, she thought, pouring coffee on this still and quiet snowy Aspen morning. Gifts.

There was a bluesman named James in San Francisco before she got involved with Dmitri. A tall, lean man with broad shoulders and hands like dinner plates. He was a good deal older than she, and came into a club where she partied sometimes, and ordered fried fish they wrapped up in newspaper. His feet were long and thin, encased in neatly tied, expensive leather shoes, and he wore a pin-striped suit, which Elena had never seen a man wear before. He spied her and made some earthy comment in his low, rich, bluesy voice, and Elena glimpsed something in his eyes, some knowledge she didn't have. He was too old for her, nearly twenty years older, close to fifty at the time, she thought, with his age showing on his neck, and in the thin flesh around his eyes, but not in his hearty body, which he shared generously, and not in his lush, seasoned, and delectable mouth, which offered the best kissing she had ever done. Long kisses, and his long fingers, and his deep and all-encompassing laughter. He had come from somewhere in the South, and lived in a small house in a neighborhood full of trees, and he liked to barbecue on summer Sundays, cooking ribs and chicken in a converted fifty-five-gallon drum. His sauces were made with coffee and vinegar, and he served it in a big messy pile on paper plates with white bread and American beer. James. Yes. She thought of him sometimes when the blues played and when she smelled chicken barbecue and when someone laughed just right. The happiest man she'd ever met—happy in his skin, happy in the world, happy singing or drinking or making love. In the end, too old for her and maybe too simple in his ways. She thought too much, he said, and he hadn't liked her attention to her career, to the restaurant, where she sometimes spent sixty or seventy hours a week. He wanted more of her.

She let him go, but there were moments she liked taking out sometimes—sitting with him in a fish house on a hot summer day in Oakland, with no fans and no breeze and the fryers making it even hotter. The fish was fried perfectly in a crisp, thin batter, salted and rich, whitefish they called it, and sprinkled with hot vinegar. Everyone knew him and liked to sidle up to him, the bluesman who played the clubs downtown, and talk to him about music. He looked over at her and winked, and she grinned back and that was that.

Thinking of James led to thinking of Timothy, her sturdy English lad, and his version of fried whitefish, cod from the fish and chips shop, greasy and hot and salty and sprinkled with vinegar. She met him in Paris, at school, a dark-haired youth of twenty-four with the whitest skin she'd ever seen—it was as thin and pale as milk, delicate skin that was easily irritated by soaps and powders and chemicals, which caused him challenges in the kitchen. He was plumpish and by now was likely quite fat, but then he was still a luminous boy, his beauty in that coloring, that paleness and those vivid blue eyes and the glossy thick darkness of hair. He loved her exotic background—New Mexico!—and the strangeness of her Spanish, a language he spoke quite well, and the warmth of her skin. They traveled together, young lovers sure of the possibilities in front of them, eating octopus on Spanish beaches and drinking ouzo in the Greek islands. Sometimes they found work enough to stay for a few weeks or a few months if they liked it. Sometimes they traveled back to Paris for a respite with Mia and Patrick, who had stayed longer in the city to learn their particular techniques—Mia in an apprenticeship with a patisserie, Patrick as understudy to a sommelier in a three-star restaurant in the Marais district.

Moments with Timothy: in Paris, when they first met at cooking school, cuddled together in a cold loft, a garret, really, so tiny you could barely stand up in it, with a shared toilet down the hall. The long window looked out over the fabled rooftops, medieval and golden in the late afternoon, pale and pink in the mornings like this. Timothy snuggled. He liked holding her all night. She liked waking up to him in the morning, his arms looped around her, his breath on her shoulder.

They were together for three years, and she thought they would be together forever, but they moved back to England and Elena hated the dullness of the gloomy, dark English winter, and she didn't fit in with his old school friends and their girlfriends and wives, and Timothy, doing what Elena had no courage to do, simply, plainly broke it off. Elena had limped back to Paris, devastated.

But thinking of him now, she could smile. It would be fun to track him down and see how he was, if he still cooked and where. She imagined him living in some English village with a busty wife and a tangle of children and a long commute into the city where he cooked for lords. His gift . . . oh, their gift to each other!—had been youth. They had been young together, and free, and full of adventure. She would like to find him and find out if those Greek island adventures, those Spanish beaches, had shaped him as much as they'd shaped her.

But perhaps his biggest gift to her had been what came after. Heartbroken and unwilling to even date anyone else for nearly two years, Elena flung herself into cooking, moved to New York, devoted herself entirely to study, to understanding and incorporating everything she'd been picking up here and there, in this restaurant and that café, from this cuisine and that open fire. In New York, she met Marie, the spice lady, and stumbled into the pleasure of working for a famous and demanding and obnoxious chef who did his best to break her; when she didn't break, he promoted her. For three years, she had allowed men into her bed as required, but none had made it past the walls of her heart.

When she was not quite thirty, she moved to San Francisco and landed a sous-chef position, where she met Andrew, her redheaded Australian, whom she loved for the next two years. That was when her career had taken first place, finally. After Andrew had been her bluesman, and then she met Dmitri at Julian's San Francisco restaurant, the Yellow Dolphin.

Dmitri.

At first, it had been strictly a working relationship. They worked brilliantly together, their work styles and visions of the food complementing and expanding the other's. He'd been promoted to executive after the original chef departed, and when he was offered the development opportunity at the Blue Turtle, he'd leapt at the chance. He and Elena had worked hard.

Funny, she thought now, carrying a second cup of coffee upstairs. Julian must have been around some during the opening of the Blue Turtle, but she'd never met him—and really, that was hardly unusual. Owners were owners. They didn't necessarily get involved in the details, especially to the level that Julian had been involved in the Orange Bear. He was here in Aspen for other reasons. The restaurant gave him something to do.

When she had to give up Julian, what would she recall?

His closet, as big as the room she had shared with three sisters, lined with elegant clothing, a top hat and tails in white and black, and designer suits and linen shirts and cotton shirts and drawers with socks lined up by fabric and color and style. Black silk for fancy dress. Running socks with little numbers on the ankles. Acres of shoes, running shoes and patent leather and boots so old and worn that Elena couldn't begin to guess their age.

Running her fingers along the sleeves hanging down in the closet, she thought she might remember the small vulnerabilities about him. He was older than she by quite a bit. He wouldn't say, and although she could look it up, she didn't. It was a subject too tender—why tease him that way when he was so kind to her? But when he was sleeping, she could see threads of purest silver weaving through the curls. On his head and below, too. Only a few, here and there. When the light was full on his face, she could see that the skin on his throat was going just the barest bit thin. Just the barest bit. He sometimes limped a little upon rising in the morning, his feet sore from being still.

With her arms over her chest, she went to stand by the window—a window in a closet!—and recognized the hollowness in her belly for what it was. Love. And not even a wild, rushing, insane river of it, but something quieter, deeper, finer. Steady, like a flame. If she believed, she would say that here, in this man, she really had found a soul mate.

If she believed.

But that was a foolishness reserved for the young and yet-to-be disillusioned. The facts were sobering. He'd been divorced four times. She'd had six long relationships. They knew these things didn't last, and in this case, with a man so famous, a man who wielded power and faced the end-less, endless temptation of women all day, every day, well . . . what chance did they have?

None, really. Not for the long term.

But maybe that was the secret of happiness—not ex-pecting any one thing to last forever. Maybe, instead of bor-rowing trouble from the future, she could just stay in this world, in this moment, and enjoy what fruits there were here. Love him for now. Let him love her in return and ac-cept that it would not always be this way.

On the next-to-the-worst day of Elena's life, Julian awak-ened abruptly in Elena's bed. It was morning and snowing, the pale blue light cascading through the line of square windows over the loft. Snowflakes piled in little drifts at the corners, like a drawing of a snowy day, as prosaic and peaceful an image as any he'd ever seen. He lay on his back, naked beneath the duvet, his foot against Elena's ankle. Next to him on the floor, Alvin snored.

It was very early. No sounds came from the complex or the street beyond, a slow weekday morning, the skiers al-ready up on the slopes or not yet awake after their party.

He turned over. Next to him, Elena slept, very deeply, utterly still, one arm flung over her head. The duvet cov-ered the other shoulder and most everything else up to her neck. Her face was angled away from him, the flawless line of her jaw catching the light. He lay still on his side and simply looked at her, his member lying heavy on his thigh in exhausted slumber, spent from the night before.

Her hair was too fine to tangle much and simply scattered over the white pillowcase. Her mouth, plump and pink as a baby's, pursed slightly in sleep, faintly open. He could just glimpse the edge of a tooth and thought of the inner flesh of those lips, flashed on the taste of them in his own mouth, against his tongue. His organ thickened against his thigh, and he imagined, remembered, licking the tip of that sleeping tongue. A little buzzing in his ears made him reach for the cover and carefully, carefully ease it downward. The heat had come on, and it rose to fill the little loft almost too much, so her nipples did not pearl in the air as he tugged the quilt away, her naked breasts spilling over her chest, the flesh as white and smooth as boiled eggs. Plump eggs, one resting on her upper arm, the nipple angled toward him, the other pointed at the ceiling, round and high as a girl's.

He did not allow himself to touch the nipple closest to him, but only looked. It was a pinkish brown, and pointed. He imagined licking her there, too, and up over the slope over the white flesh, into the hollow of her throat, and over her shoulders.

She did not stir. Her breath moved softly in and out. He pulled the duvet down her body, an inch at a time. Revealing the belly, soft and white. Her crisp, thin pubic hair. Her thighs, her—

At the edge of his perception was a sound that didn't quite make sense, tugging and nudging him, but he was engrossed in his exploration.

Several things happened at once—the noise grew, a weight suddenly landed on his legs, and there was a screech, and an incomprehensible, explosive sound. Instinctively, he gathered Elena to him, diving under the covers, and he realized that the weight was Alvin, burrowing under the covers with them. Or on top of them.

It all made sense, Julian suddenly thinking, *I didn't know they had earthquakes in Colorado,* and maybe they never did, but the bed and house shook all around them and he kept his arms around Elena, who awakened, rigid and terrified, and she gripped him, and her dog, and cried out, "What is it? What's happening?" and he said, "I don't know, hang on."

The dog whimpered, the most pitiful, terrible noise, and there were crashing noises and something fell from overhead and Julian scooted farther down from the wall, dragging Elena with him, in case pictures fell off the wall. In the bathroom were crashing noises, glass breaking, a *lot* of glass, and he thought, *This is bad, maybe more than a 6.6—* he'd been in the Northridge earthquake of 1994, and that had been a 6.7. This felt worse; he could feel the floor shivering beneath him, and knew a deep, true sense of dread. These buildings were not built for earthquakes—they might as well have been built in Pakistan or some other third-world place—and what if the floor of the loft gave way?

But finally, the shaking stopped, almost abruptly, and there were settling sounds. Quiet. Shouts from far away. In his arms, Elena trembled, or maybe it was Alvin, who cowered in her arms beneath the covers. "It's okay, baby," she said, petting him, rubbing him. "It's all right. You're safe."

Julian pulled his head out from under the covers. The light was wrong, and he couldn't immediately figure out why. Everything was a mess, pictures down, furniture fallen sideways. The glass had shattered out of the bedroom window, and there was a hole in the bathroom he couldn't quite make out.

Close by, someone said, "Fuck. What happened?"

"Julian," Elena said, sitting up. "Look."

He peered over her shoulder.

And Julian saw a kid, a boy about sixteen, who was lying across the bottom of the bed. But that wasn't where Elena was pointing. Where the living room wall had been was a perfect, open-air view of the trees beyond. A car had come through it, a heavy, eighties-model sedan, the kind of car a grandmother might drive. The windshield was shattered. The crumpled nose ticked in the quiet.

"Jesus!" he whispered.

Elena bent over the side of the bed and threw up. The scar on her back seemed almost to writhe as she heaved. He touched her shoulder. "It's okay."

"Call 911," she said, collapsing on the bed.

The boy, shell-shocked but appearing to be fine, blinked at them. "What the fuck? How did I get here?"

Grabbing his cell phone from the night table, Julian shook his head. "You are one *lucky* son of a bitch."

THIRTY-TWO

To: Elena.Alvarez@theorangebear.com

From: dmitrinadirov@theblueturtle.com

Subject: re: fire

Elena, thanks for yr interest. The kitchen is wrecked. Probably take a couple of months to rebuild. I have been talking to a television person I met at a show a couple of months ago, and she has offered me a job, so I am not as upset as I might have been. I will let you know more when it is all final, but I will be moving to Los Angeles in the next month or so.

Dmitri

PS Liswood speaks v. highly of you, like a lover speaks of his woman. Sure you're not fucking him?

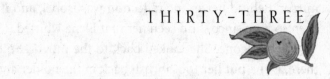

THIRTY-THREE

Elena felt overcome by nausea for several long minutes. Each time she tried to move, she was overwhelmed and threw up again, until there was absolutely nothing left in her stomach. Julian slipped into his jeans after he called the police, and he made the boy stay still—"You have no idea what else might be wrong with you"—while he found some clothes for Elena to put on. Shakily, she managed to shimmy into some heavyweight yoga pants and a sweatshirt. Given the amount of glass on the floor, she asked him to find her shoes, too.

"Was anyone with you?" Julian asked the kid.

"No. Just me." He turned a little green when he looked downstairs. The smell of beer filled the room.

"Thank God."

Elena had to pee. When Alvin trotted downstairs, she gingerly made her way to the bathroom, her body revving with adrenaline. The bathroom was a mess. As in the bedroom, the window had shattered, but the impact had also knocked loose some of the glass brick around the shower, and the door to the steam shower was shattered as well. She peed and brushed her teeth and looked at her face in the mirror. Behind her in the reflection was Isobel, and it had been so long since she'd seen her that Elena whirled.

She was gone. She looked back to the mirror. Still not there. Elena put her toothbrush back in the holder and realized she probably wouldn't be sleeping here tonight.

Another home wrecked.

And today was their grand opening! *Fuck, fuck, fuck.*

Irritably, she stomped back into the bedroom and glared at the boy, who lay on her bed looking sick. "Has it started to sink in yet?" she cried. "That you should be dead right now? You got thrown out of your car and you could have landed on the roof, or in a tree or drowned in the river. And where did you land? On my fucking *bed.* With me in it! On the day that my restaurant has it's grand opening, you stupid little bastard!"

Julian touched her shoulder. "Come on, Elena. Let's go downstairs. The EMTs are here."

And she saw that they were, indeed, right there. A young man and a hard-looking woman with a stretcher, blinking at her. "Sorry," she said, suddenly ashamed. "I'm just mad."

They didn't say anything, just came upstairs and moved by her and knelt next to the kid on the bed.

"Let's get some of your things together, Elena," he said, giving her a small carry-on bag she kept in the closet.

She looked at the dresser, lying on its side, and her underwear scattered out of one drawer and onto the floor, and she couldn't even think of what she might need. Where would she go? Where would she live? "I really liked this place," she said plaintively to Julian. "I hate this."

"I know." He gently took the bag from her and put it on

the floor, then gathered up a handful of panties and bras and tossed them in. "What else? Which drawers have socks?"

Elena knelt and pulled open the drawers methodically, grabbed socks, T-shirts, sports bras for work because they absorbed sweat and let her move freely and also bound her a little more fully in the active environment. From the closet, she took her black jeans, her good boots, a pair of other jeans.

"That's about it for clothes," Julian said, pressing neatly folded jeans into one corner of the suitcase. "Toiletries?"

Robotically, Elena moved into the bathroom. Beneath the sink was a makeup bag and she filled it with her small cache of cosmetics—face lotion and cleansers and heavy-duty hand cream and bag balm for when the splits got worse in winter, and cotton gloves she slept in, and a cache of prescription pain pills of varying strengths and a brush. And her toothbrush.

"Come on," he said. "The police are here, and then we can go get some breakfast."

"Is he going to be okay, that boy?"

He rubbed her back. "Yeah. He's fine, Elena. Scared. But fine."

"That's good," she said, and swallowed back a weird swell of tears. "Let's get this over with."

After a shower at Julian's house, Elena shook her head, wincing at Julian's offer of food. She couldn't even drink a cup of coffee yet, not until her stomach got over this—whatever it was.

In the meantime, she had to get out of here. Out of Julian's house. She'd put her bags in the back of her car, had only brought in a change of clothes and her makeup bag. It might be hard to find a new place to rent at the moment, but she knew Patrick had a spare bedroom.

Carrying her cell phone to the snowy deck, she wrapped her scarf around her neck and blew a soft foggy cloud into the sharp morning.

"Good morning, Chef Alvarez," he answered in a round, orange voice, all juicy happiness. "Are you ready for your big day?"

"Hello, Prince Patrick. I am *so* ready. How about you?"

"Yes, yes, yes." He muffled the receiver and spoke to someone in the room with him. A chuckle. She thought she recognized Ivan's low drum voice, and that made the whole reality of what she was thinking—that she'd just go stay with Patrick in his two-bedroom house—completely un-thinkable. Not with a love affair going on between her sous chef and her best friend.

She shuddered faintly, thinking of the night she'd glimpsed Ivan licking Patrick's face, his long fingers curling up around his skull, as if he were getting ready to devour him, one long lap at a time. No. Not when she had to look at them both at work all day.

"Ivan says hello," Patrick said. "And asks what time you'll be getting in this morning."

"Well," Elena said, improvising madly, "that's why I'm calling, actually. There's been an—uh—incident and I'm running behind. I need Ivan to get over there and make sure the kitchen staff is there and functioning. I called a lit-tle while ago and nobody answered."

Patrick repeated her request, then said, "He said it's still early, really, but he'll head over in just a little while."

"Thanks."

"What incident, Elena? Are you okay?"

She took a breath, feeling a thick, primeval shudder nudge her bowels, the bottom of her stomach again. "Yeah. My condo is gone, though. Some kid drove into it, right through the front window."

"No way!"

"Bizarre, huh?"

"Are you okay?"

"I'm fine, Alvin's fine. Ju—we're all fine," she said. "The kid isn't even hurt badly, because he was thrown over the railing of the loft onto the bed."

"You're kidding."

"No," she said, crossing her arms. A slithering feeling ran down her back, settled into her hip. She shook her shoulders, trying to loosen it all, but the cold was making her hunch. "Look, I'll give you the rest of the details later. I've got to get some more stuff and make sure everything— that I—" She took a breath. "I'm freezing, Patrick, my love. I'll talk to you later, okay?"

"Elena, are you okay, honey?"

"Yeah," she said. "Really. I'm fine. See you in a couple of hours. Call me if there are any problems."

She went back inside, letting go of her breath. Julian was typing on his laptop at the kitchen counter, looking slightly disheveled and ordinary with his black horn-rimmed glasses and a heathery blue long-sleeved T-shirt. He looked both ordinary and not quite—like a record executive maybe, or the publisher of some alternative, hip publication, or maybe a hotshot doctor that all the nurses lusted for secretly. He looked like a husband, with his flat wrists brushed with black hair, and his focus so intently on the screen, and a cup of coffee sitting at his elbow.

Fuck, she thought, emphatically. *I cannot stay here. I cannot start wanting* this.

Tossing her hair out of her eyes, she marched across the room and made a show of sipping her coffee. "I'm going to head over to the apartment and see if they'll let me get some of my kitchen stuff," she said. "I guess I'll see you at the restaurant later, right?"

He looked at her without speaking for a moment, his jaw newly shaved. "Have you eaten?"

She waved a hand. "Too nervous about the grand opening. I'm sure I'll be nibbling all day."

"Are you sure you're all right?"

It was at least the twelfth time he'd asked her. Annoyance snapped at the back of her neck. "Yes," she growled. "I'm pissed off at losing my home and worried about finding a new place on the opening day of ski season and nervous that we're surely going to attract some reviewers tonight, but I'm fine over the fucking accident, okay?"

He didn't wince. "Do you know how many times you've said 'fuck' this morning?"

She rolled her eyes, picked up her keys. "I'll see you later."

He clamped a hand over her wrist. "You can stay here, you know."

Elena bowed her head, suddenly afraid she might cry

and he would see it, and she just couldn't stand that right now. "Thank you, but no." As gently and firmly as she could, she yanked her hand away and headed for the door. Sitting on the top step, pale and thin as smoke, was Isobel, her eyes wide and solemn. Elena ignored her and headed into the cold winter morning. She had work to do, and she'd left her knives at the apartment.

At the condo, there was still a lot of commotion, of course. The car had been hauled out, and a construction crew was stacking and organizing the debris. "I just need to get to my kitchen," she said to a burly man who seemed to be in charge. "I'm a chef, and my knives are in there."

He lifted a finger, signaling her to wait, and listened to a walkie-talkie. "How many?" he barked, his Irish eyes the color of the mountains over cheeks that were red from anger or cold or both. "When did it happen?"

He listened and swore. "Ah, goddamn it. Who do these guys think they're kidding? This whole goddamned county is going to go to hell. It's the first goddamned day of the season!" He acted as if he was going to lob the device toward the ditch, and halted just in time. "Right, Walter. Get back to me when you get the numbers." Shaking his head, he clicked it off and looked at her. "Sorry, sweetheart. What did you say?"

"I live here—lived here. I'm a chef and need to get some things from the kitchen."

"What a deal, huh?" He looked at the yawning hole in the condo. "That was one lucky kid. Let me get somebody to go inside with you." With a burly arm, he gestured at a worker in a hard hat. "Harry!"

Harry loped over. "Take her inside to the kitchen

through the back so she can get her stuff. And who do you know who can come to work tomorrow? We got labor troubles."

"I'll give it some thought."

The back of the condo was fine. Elena pushed open the gate and went in through the patio door. Her knives were in a bundle on the counter, and she picked them up protectively, and quickly filled a small box with a few other things—her stained notebook of recipes, her favorite bowl. Glancing over her shoulder, she didn't see Harry anywhere, and rushed over to the living room to see if she could grab her grandmother's geranium. It had lived through a dozen moves, being neglected by Mia and ignored by others, and being smuggled into three countries. Surely a little car wreck couldn't do any damage. If she had so much as a leaf, she could propagate it.

But it wasn't there. It had sat in front of the picture window, the window that was now completely gone. The car had pulverized the entire area just inside the condo, and whatever had been left had been dragged out when the tow truck hauled the car out. She looked at the floor carefully. One leaf. Just one.

Nothing. The pot was gone, though she saw shards of the red clay. There was a scattering of dirt. And there—she dove for it. But not even she could pretend this leaf would survive. It had been crushed to nothing.

"Oh, grow up," she said aloud. "Go to work."

"Ma'am?" said Harry from the door. "You ought not to be in there. The structure is unsound."

Elena nodded, and stepped over some shattered wood left from her sideboard. "You're right. I'm sorry."

❖ ❖ ❖

As she pulled into the parking lot of the Orange Bear, she took a moment to breathe. She felt hollowed out, as if all of her organs and feelings had been sucked from her body.

But she was absolutely not going to let this freak accident interfere with what was a hugely important day in her life. Pulling on her gloves and twisting a scarf around her throat, she carried the box of kitchen things up to the back door.

Inside the kitchen, things were quiet. Much too quiet. She glanced at the clock, feeling slightly disoriented by a low, constant hum and the lack of music in the kitchen. "Hello?" she called, settling the box on the stainless steel table by the door. Unwinding her scarf, she headed into the dining room, wondering if they were all out there. "Hello?"

Nobody. Frowning, she glanced at the clock. It was only nine, but somebody should be here by now. Where were they all?

With a sense of dread, she headed upstairs. "Hello?"

A knot of people were gathered around a table in the bar. Alan, the daytime bartender, Peter, Tansy, Patrick, and Ivan. They looked at her with long faces. "Hey, *Jefa*," Ivan said, his palms cupped around his elbows.

Elena touched her belly, feeling the scars and empty spots within her fill with liquid dread. "What's wrong? Who died?"

"Nobody died, Chef, but it's bad," Alan said.

"What is it?"

Ivan said, "The INS staged a raid in Carbondale and rounded up a bunch of people. Some kind of government crackdown, to coincide with the first day of ski season."

Elena thought of the man at the condo, swearing into the phone. "Fuck," she said. "How many did we lose?"

A giant well of silence opened into the room. "How many?" she repeated.

"All of them."

"Not *Juan*?" She looked at Ivan. "You told me you checked all of their green cards. You personally vouched for Juan."

"Chef, it's—"

For one long moment, she was stunned. What would they do? "Who staged the raid?"

Ivan shrugged. "The government. They probably timed it this way on purpose."

Elena shook her head, and made a decision. "I don't know why you're sitting there. Get your asses up and let's get to work. Peter, get your buddies in here—tell them we'll pay double for the night. Tansy, call anyone you can think of who might be able to do anything for a weekend."

"You're going to open?" Alan asked.

"We don't have any choice. We've advertised all over town, and passed out coupon books, and the radio ads are probably running right now." Acid burbled in her stomach. She tried not to imagine her entire career going up in flames. Pulling her hair into a thick band, she cocked her thumb in the direction of the kitchen. "Get on it, guys. You've got a lot of prep to get done. Tansy, I need you in the main kitchen—listen to what they tell you."

In her cigarette-ruined voice, Tansy said, "I gotta call home and make sure somebody can watch my grand-daughter, but I'm sure my sister will do it."

Ivan said, "Do you want to simplify the menu a little,

maybe? Cut some things ahead of time that might slow us down too much?"

She nodded. "Do it. Figure out the most time-consuming items and we'll tell the servers to emphasize tamales. We should have enough tamales for anything."

The cooks headed into the kitchen. "Alan," she said, "cut the seating by 20 percent at a time. Marta, you're going to have to prepare for the overload in the bar. Any suggestions on making the wait more appealing? Free drinks, appetizers?"

"Sangria and Mexican coffee? They can have the regular free, and pay one dollar for rum."

"Give the laced away free, too." Elena pursed her lips. "What if we do a bunch of corn fritters in baskets, too? With roasted red pepper jelly and the Pancho Villa honey?"

"Yeah, yeah," Marta said. "Cool. I'll get on it."

Elena took a breath. "Is there anything else that could get in our way before the end of the night?"

"We're short on those little silver bowls. If the dishwasher gets behind, it could be an issue."

"Who can do dishes up here?"

"We'll figure it out." Patrick gestured toward the clock. "You can get to the kitchen."

She met his eyes. "Showtime."

He smiled, very faintly, and bowed. "At your service, madam."

In her office, she sat for a moment at the desk, for one second allowing a sense of disaster to wash over her. She thought of Juan, locked up or in some truck going back to Mexico, and the two dishwashers, and the women and children who would go back with all of the construction workers, and all the money that would go into the pockets of the coyotes who were getting rich on the backs of human dreams and corresponding misery.

It made her furious. The heat of it sucked her throat dry.

Ivan came to the door, knocking with the back of his knuckles, even though the door was open. "You all right, boss?"

She shook her head. "No. But we'll make it work anyway. Do we have any way to get in touch with Juan, once he gets to his hometown? Does anybody know where he's from?"

"I'll find out. He's a good man." Ivan's hooded lids fell over the brilliance of his eyes, and Elena waited. "Chef, I'm sorry. We'll make it work, you know."

"You promised," she said. "You checked every one of them."

"And I did. I swear to God." He held up a hand, palm out. "It's not that hard to fake papers with a social security number, you know? They all had good papers."

Elena sighed. "You're right. It's not your fault." She shook her head. "How the hell are we going to replace Juan?"

He combed his fingers through the neat beard on his chin. Shook his head. "We won't."

"I have to call Julian, then I'll be in the kitchen."

The rush started at six, and by six-thirty the bar was full. They'd prepared as much as they could ahead of time, cutting extra buckets of meat, doubling the prep on soup. Ivan fried twenty-four dozen tiny corn fritters, and Tansy proved herself worth her weight in gold by making dozens of corn and flour tortillas and preparing chiles for the tasting plates; she had fresh churros and giant pans of pomegranate baklava ready to go. Peter and the boys cut extra buckets of everything they could think of—lettuce and tomatoes and onions. Upon hearing about the raid, Portia volunteered to come in and woman the dish machines. Elena was stunned and delighted—another fourteen-year-old couldn't have worked there but dispensation was made for the children of owners. Peter, smitten on sight, proved an able, if sporadic assistant.

At first, it seemed to be working all right. Between Elena, Ivan, and Peter, they ran the line pretty well. Tansy worked prep, soups, and desserts.

Elena had always loved the rush of managing a busy line, the shouts, the clatter of dishes and platters and lids on pots and the sizzle of meat and the swoosh of the dish machine in the background. The music was loud and fast, an eclectic mix of Spanish guitar and Rolling Stones tossed with Devo and a strong helping of pop favs from the eighties—Cyndi Lauper and Madonna. Elena and Ivan danced the line, plating and wiping and tossing in a tango of cooking.

The dishwashing was a critical problem. On a busy night, there were usually at least two boys on dish and one runner, and one inexperienced fourteen-year-old wasn't enough, even though she worked like a demon. Tansy and Peter and the boys all worked on it, and one of the bussers dove in every half hour or so, but the dishes were piling up.

"Running low on saucers!" a server cried, and Portia

dutifully ran a rack of saucers and plates. "Need forks ASAP," said another, bringing in a huge load of dirty dishes. By seven, Portia was flushed and sweaty and frustrated, but to her credit, she never complained.

Everyone else was balls to the wall, too. So to speak.

The first mini-disaster was running out of cherry mojo for the duck tamales, which were proving to be a huge, huge hit with this crowd.

"How did that happen?" Ivan roared, looking around for a victim. Peter ducked away, as if he were going to be hit, and Ivan glared at him. "Dude, what are you doing? I've never fucking *hit* you! Just go get some cherries."

"I looked. We're out."

"Send Julian out for cherries," Elena barked, slamming together an order for seven. "Substitute the roasted red pepper jam and move on."

"We're running low."

"It'll work until the cherries are finished."

As the hours ground on, however, the cooks and the servers and the support staff lost the push of adrenaline and started to wear down. The dish situation grew worse and worse, with servers slamming into the kitchen every ten seconds to call for flatware or glasses or dishes. The cooks ran out of platters at one point and three orders were late going out because of it. Elena pulled Peter and Tansy off the line and asked for Alan to pull a busser to help, too. But that only lasted a little while. They couldn't afford to be without line cooks either.

On a bad shift, disaster accrued drop by drop, like holes in a levee that widened a crack bit by bit by bit until, all at once, the wall gave way and water came rushing through. That night, the lack of dishwashers dripped into lack of dishes dripped into server annoyance and delays on the line; delays on the line made the chefs irritable and start to rush things that shouldn't be rushed, leading to a plate that was unservable, which led to more delay, which led to customers walking out.

Under the force of the tension of the day, Elena's body was tight to begin with, and as the evening wore on, her right hip started screaming, the pain beginning to creep upward, through her spine and ribs to her neck and shoulders, downward to her knee and ankle. She popped six Advils and drank a ton of water.

The servers gritted their teeth and tried to make the front of the house work. They pitched in with dishes and brought Portia virgin piña coladas and cherry Cokes and told her she was doing a great job. Julian pitched in, too, mainly by just being present, talking to customers, signing autographs, trying to smooth the waters. He bought drinks and greeted people and made his rounds. He brought a tray full of beers and sodas back at one point; another time, ice cream from around the corner.

The crew just worked unceasingly, calling out orders, filling plates, arranging food. They ran out of stuffed zucchini blossoms, and then the corn fritters. They made do with other things.

By nine, they were all exhausted. "What's it like out there?" Elena asked a server. "Winding down any?"

He shook his head. "Still stacked up to the ceiling."

"Anybody that you recognized as a reviewer?"

"I wouldn't know," he said. "Lot of celebrities, though. And CEO types with their very young wives. They're all just charmed by Mr. Liswood."

"Good." Elena took a breath and whirled around to plate another order.

Tansy and Ivan started tussling and Elena said, "Tansy, go smoke. Ivan, you next. Make it fast."

Finally, at eleven-thirty, the last of the customers had been served, coddled, and escorted out. Wearily, the kitchen crew mopped up the mess, cleared the counters. A deep silence lay beneath music and the swishing dishwasher and the banging of pots, a silence of exhaustion and review, as they replayed in their minds the running out of dishes and food, the nightmarish backup on the line, the frustration of the servers and the angry complaints of the customers. Through her own exhaustion, Elena saw the gray faces of her staff, and went about filling platters with leftover roasted onion tart and taquitos and the last strips of roasted, shredded beef with Tansy's good handmade tortillas. On another tray, she arranged churros and sopapillas and baklava.

"Come on, gang," she said, only then realizing she was hoarse enough she could barely get the words out, "let's take a break. You've earned it."

"We have a lot to do still," Peter said, gesturing toward the mountain of dishes, the unswept floor.

She nodded. "We have to finish, but first a break."

Ivan shouldered a platter, and Elena carried one, too, despite the thudding tense pain in her back. She was limping enough that even she noticed it, and was too tired to care. "Come on, Portia," she called to the girl, still buried in ungodly piles of dishes and silver and pans and utensils.

Gratefully, Portia came out from behind the machine. "I am so tired," she said.

Elena hugged her with one arm. "I'm so proud of you, girl. You're my hero."

Portia smiled wanly.

"Let's go upstairs," Elena said to the others, and they trooped through the upstairs kitchen and into the bar area. The music played and the servers and bartenders scurried around, stripping tables, cleaning coffeepots. "Marta, bring us some beer, will you?" she called, setting her platter on the table. "And some things to eat with."

They all collapsed around the long table, Tansy and Ivan, Peter next to Portia, the two boys, and the busser who had got stuck in the kitchen. Elena just avoided groaning, but her entire body cried out in relief when she took the weight off her spine. For a moment, the absence of pain was almost like a pain of its own, and she wanted to weep, but didn't dare. Marta brought over a tray full of bottled beer, and a couple of margaritas, one for Tansy, one for Elena. Elena lifted her drink, saying *"Salud!"*

Julian emerged from the front somewhere. "Good work," he said, carrying a piece of paper. "You managed to get out one hundred seventy-three covers tonight."

Peter whistled.

Ivan, arched around his food as protectively as a dog defending his dish, growled, "How many comps?"

"Not that many," Julian said, waving a hand.

Elena's gut dropped. "How many?"

He met her eyes. "Twenty-six."

A bomb of silence dropped on the table. "Fifteen percent," Ivan said, shaking his head grimly. "In-fucking-credible." Violently, he stood up and knocked his chair back and carried his plate into the kitchen.

Elena glared after him, but then looked at the rest of the table. She raised her glass again. "Considering six people did the work of eleven with a full house, that's not too bad, huh?"

Their faces eased as they toasted her.

The phone rang and Marta called Julian. He hurried over to the bar.

"I'm proud of you guys," Elena said. "Cheers to Tansy, who proved herself tonight!"

Tansy gave her torn, ragged chuckle. "Thank you, thank you."

"And cheers to Portia, too! Did she do a great job?"

"I think we should hire her," Peter suggested.

"Thanks but no thanks," Portia said. "I wouldn't mind learning to cook a little, but that dishwashing is for the birds."

"To our missing amigos," Tansy said. "We might have been miserable tonight, but they're all in a world of hurt by now, I can tell you."

Slowly, Elena raised her glass, feeling furiously emotional. "Juan should really have been here tonight. He thought up half the menu."

It was only then that she realized she had no home, either, and her back spasmed. She would have to stay with Julian tonight at least.

As if called, he returned to the table with a glass of

scotch. "Cheers and thanks to all of you," he said. "You'll all have bonuses for your dedication. Now, I think we need to toast your chef. Who lost her house today and still managed to pull off what amounted to a miracle tonight. Good job, Chef."

She nodded, suddenly and completely demolished.

It took another solid hour to get the kitchen cleaned. Breaking her rule, Elena drank two shots of tequila, letting the alcohol do its magic. Once she got back to Julian's, she could take some pain meds, soak in the hot tub, and it would be all right again.

But it bloody burned like fire tonight. A sudden turn could send swirls of bright popping red through her body, making her dizzy. She discovered she couldn't lift much of anything at all. She couldn't find it in herself to care that she limped like Quasimodo.

Ivan worked in sullen silence, as if he blamed her for the comps. She ignored him.

Portia finished the dishes. Peter helped her polish all the stainless steel. They looked like brother and sister, both so blond and fair. She heard them talking about skiing at one point. Obviously, Portia was too young for the nineteen-year-old. She would warn him to mind his manners, but tonight, his crush had served a good purpose.

Finally, finally, the work was done, the night was over, and Elena let Julian drive the three of them home. She didn't have much to say, except, "I'd like to get in the hot tub at your house, if that's all right."

"Of course."

Alvin tapped toward them happily when the door opened, crocodile in teeth, his feathery tail high, his lips curled up in a grin. He flung himself into Elena, who grunted over the starburst of pain it lit in her body, and grabbed for Julian to steady herself. Alvin turned his head down and bumped then into Portia's legs, and she laughed and bent down to hug him. "You are so *cute!*"

Alvin groaned, bumped the crocodile against Portia's hands.

Quietly, Julian said, "Let's get you in that hot tub, huh?"

"I just realized I don't have a bathing suit." This small, terrible thing nearly broke her.

"You can climb in naked," Portia said. "We'll leave you alone."

THIRTY-FOUR

TEQUILA MENU

Tequila is made from the fermented juice of the blue agave plant, and connoisseurs know there are four grades, just as there are grades of scotch or bourbon: *blanco,* bottled immediately; *reposado,* or "rested," aged in oak for two months to less than a year; *añejo,* aged for at least a year; and *extra añejo,* aged for at least three years. We have created a splendid menu of tequila creations for your tasting pleasure.

OUR FAVORITE:

Chinaco Negro Mojito
Extra-añejo tequila mixed with fresh lime juice, crushed mint leaves, a touch of sugar, and Pellegrino.

THIRTY-FIVE

Ivan held up a shot of tequila, looking through the thin gold liquid to the bar beyond, seeing in diamond-shaped blasts of color the outline of martini glasses. He closed one eye to see if that lessened the blur, but it didn't, particularly. He knocked the shot back, feeling it burn all the way down, searing into the damage he'd done to his esophagus over the years of hard, hard drinking.

He poured another.

Patrick sat down beside him, bringing with him a scent of worry and disappointment. "Ivan, it's time to go. You have to stop drinking or you'll feel horrible tomorrow."

"Too late," he said.

Even Patrick looked slightly—only slightly—disheveled after the nightmare service. He'd slipped his tie off and opened the collar of his shirt two buttons. His normally carefully coxcomb hair was damp and flopping. "Why are you doing this?"

"Because I need to get fucked up. Because I totally fucked up."

"It was a bad night, that's all. It just happens."

"No," he said, hearing his own voice rumble from somewhere deep in his chest. "Way before that. Way before." Something told him to stop talking. Not to spill his secrets. That Patrick had loved Chef long before he had met Ivan.

But hadn't he known that this wouldn't last, this sweet little sliver of happiness? "I fucked up a long time ago."

Patrick stood up. He plucked the bottle from Ivan's hand.

"What the fuck?"

"Time to go home," he said in that prissy way, his nose in the air. He carried the bottle across the room to the bar, and put on his coat. "You need to come with me, Ivan. You're going to feel just terrible in the morning, and there's no need to beat yourself up. Come home and let me put you in the bath and wash your back. What do you say?"

"I'm really a bastard," Ivan said, climbing to his feet. "I don't know why you like me."

Patrick half-smiled and helped Ivan into his coat. "Oh, don't go maudlin on me, love. You know it's unflattering."

"It's my fault the INS came," Ivan said.

For one moment, Patrick stilled. "What do you mean?"

"A while back, I tipped 'em off." The memory gave him a vision of his heart as a black, oozing thing. "Like, before I knew she was gonna be good."

For a long moment, Patrick simply stood there, and closed his eyes. He sighed. "We'll talk in the morning. Let's just go home tonight. Get some sleep."

Ivan nodded heavily, suddenly embarrassed to be drunk. Patrick deserved better. He plodded behind him to the car, taking in the bite of the air and a million stars.

Patrick unlocked his BMW with little beeps and Ivan opened the door, but didn't quite get in. With his hands on the roof of the car, he tipped his head back to let the starshine bathe him, cover him with that cold farawayness. "That's so fucking beautiful." His breath came from him in a soft white cloud, blurring the stars. "Do you think there are other planets? You think there's somebody out there on some other planet who got drunk on some local cactus juice who is looking up at the cold, cold sky and our stars and wondering who is out there?"

"Maybe," Patrick said, and he paused, too. "It really is beautiful. We're lucky to live here."

"We are," Ivan said, and dropped into the car, folding his long legs up as he closed the door. He inclined his head, thinking of what a house on another planet might look like, what they cooked. "I wonder what their best delicacy is there, what new things they'll bring to Earth when they come. Maybe it'll be something like a raspberrystrawberrylime. Or the most fantastically chocolate tequila." He laughed softly, and realized Patrick was sitting there quietly next to him. He looked at him, and the same electric zing he always felt blazed through him, lighting up all of his nerves and the back of his throat, and he thought how much he wanted to bend in and kiss him.

Instead, it was Patrick who leaned over, and put his hand on Ivan's face. Touched his hair. "I wish you knew how amazing you are," he said, and shook his head sadly. "I'm not sure I can convince you."

"Try," Ivan rumbled, and bent in to kiss those pretty pouty lips. "Please try."

◆ ◆ ◆

Elena accepted the big goblet of wine Julian offered, and carried it downstairs, where she stripped out of her sweaty, food-drenched clothes and climbed into the hot tub. She sank down to her chin. It was absolutely dark except for the bars of light falling through the patio doors from the great room above. No moon. No sounds except the bubbling of the water. She sipped the cold, crisp Chardonnay and stared upward.

Into the nothingness of her exhaustion flashed a blip of noise—crashing, breaking, crunching metal—and a flash of sky. Like this one.

She sat up, splashing, and the sudden move, even in the heated water, made her cry out softly in pain. She had to stay in the water for a while, let the rock-tight muscles ease a little.

God what a night! The insanity poured through her, the constant Medusa's head of tasks, weaving and waving together endlessly, the chaotic roar of voices and clattering dishes and the rush of her own heartbeat roaring through her ears.

—the cool chuckling of water in the utter silence of cold night and stars overhead and the click of cooling metal in the darkness and the vast, vast loneliness—

She sat up straighter, breathed in, breathed out, a therapist's trick from years ago. Then she took a long swallow of wine. Her own trick.

—a hand wrapping around hers, the starry starry night, and whispered voice, it's okay it's okay it's okay someone's coming—

Elena stood up. Climbed out. Wrapped herself in a thick white robe and went inside. Upstairs. "I need to go to bed," she announced. "Same room as before?"

In the darkness, Julian lay next to Elena. He'd talked her into sleeping with him, assuring her that Portia didn't come to his room for any reason, never even came upstairs. They had not made love. She was too plainly, painfully exhausted, barely able to navigate the stairs when they arrived at the house, and even more haunted looking after the very short stint in the hot tub.

She had fallen asleep finally, but it was not a peaceful retreat—a foot twitched, a hand reached out. She shifted away from him, showing him the ancient scar on her back, cutting through her flesh in a long diagonal from shoulder to hip. When he held her, he found his fingers gravitating toward it, tracing the snake shape on the shoulder blade, the faintness over her ribs. It was just there. Part of her.

And yet in the faint pink light of clouds moving into the night sky, he could see the violence of it, the wrenching loss it represented. She had not spoken at all of the accident this morning, and he worried about that. How could you just absorb so much, over and over? He wanted her to let down her guard, maybe have a good cry, express her fury over losing her home, having a car come through her house, losing all of her best kitchen staff, all in a single day.

Instead, her face showed nothing. But in the darkness now, he heard little moans and expressions of protest. The scar seemed almost to writhe, a snake coming to life, rising out of the bed to reveal secrets to him that he should not know. He stretched out his fingers and very, very lightly touched the swoop of the snake into her hip, where it almost seemed to glow with fierce heat. And it wasn't his imagination—the flesh was hotter here than elsewhere on her body—pain speaking what she could not.

Jesus, how could he help her?

She jolted awake suddenly, sitting up straight with a cry. Julian jerked his hand back, ashamed that he'd disturbed her. She had her hands to her face, covering her eyes, then she smoothed them down her cheekbones, her jaw. She blinked, plainly disoriented, and Julian put a protective arm around her. "You're all right," he said quietly. "You're here with me."

"Don't do that," she said, exhausted. "Don't do that."

"Come, lie down." He tried to nudge her back to the pillows, to the piles of softness and comforters. She pulled against him, and despite himself, he was aroused by the sway and supple plumpness of her breasts in the soft pink light, the curve of flesh beneath her arm, the crease at the bend of her hip, revealed by the comforter falling back. He leaned in and pressed his forehead against her upper arm. "You need to sleep."

She turned her shoulder away from him. "I felt you tracing the scar." She reached a hand backward and scratched the place as if it itched or was irritated by his caress. "I hate that. I hate it!" She stood up, throwing the covers off, and he was pierced by the spectral sight of her, moving away, awkwardly, her body stiff, her back a curve in the darkness, her shoulder, her hip each catching a cupful of light.

He leapt up, touched her. "Elena, come back to bed." He tried to draw her body to him, put his warmth against her stiff cold body.

But she flung him away. "No. You just don't know. You don't understand. I hate that."

She seemed like someone else tonight. Hostile and fierce and sparking with that thick darkness, a lure and sharpness that put him off and drew him in all at once. "I'm sorry. I'm worried about you. It's cold. Come back to bed. I won't touch you, I promise."

"Oh," she sighed, almost a sob, and covered her face, "it's not that, that I don't want you to touch me, but I feel like I'm breaking. I can't break right now, Julian. Not this minute."

He reached for her hand, capturing one finger, so dry and ragged that bits of skin were like cactus. "Climb under the covers," he said, and pulled her under the quilt, tucking it close around her. A choppy spray of fine hair fell inelegantly over her brow. He pushed it away. Vast tenderness welled in him. He traced her eyebrow. Her hand slid from below the covers and clutched his wrist.

"Stop," she said, her eyes closed tight. Tears leaked from beneath her eyelids. "I can't bear it tonight. Kindness, compassion, your sweetness. It will demolish me."

He nodded, pulling back to his own pillow, just one arm over her, over the top of the quilt. "Is that all right?"

She nodded tightly, as if any large movement would cause pain. Tears pooled in the small indentation of her nose. He simply lay there next to her, hoping it was some comfort or warmth. Her foot found his under the cover.

After a long time, she said, "When I woke up in the hospital, it had been three weeks since the accident. My face was so wrecked I didn't even recognize myself. I was in a body cast and couldn't move anything except one arm. There wasn't anybody in the room when I woke up, and I couldn't figure out what had happened to me. I didn't remember the accident right away."

He didn't move anything except his thumb, just a sweep of it to let her know he was listening.

"When I did remember, I wanted to see my sister and Edwin, and when they told me they were dead, I didn't believe them. I remembered Isobel holding my hand after the accident. She sat right there in the ditch and kept me company until they found me."

He pulled out a word. "Umm-hmmm."

Elena ducked her head deeper into the pillows, and he understood that she was crying. "They had been dead for three weeks by then. Three weeks and I didn't even know." She cried very quietly, very intensely. "I don't know why I lived. I don't know why I lived. I don't know why I lived."

He pulled her into him, holding her as gently as he could while she wept. He said nothing, stroking her hair, careful to keep his hands away from her scar, and he thought, *For me.*

When she awakened in Julian's bedroom, her eyes heavy and tired, Elena only lay there for a long moment. The space between her eyebrows, that place of the third eye, felt thick and shrouded. Julian had moved away in the night—neither of them were cuddly sleepers—and she slid out of the bed, not daring to look at him.

She nearly tripped on Alvin, and he groaned as he stretched out his paws, which were growing little winter tufts. "C'mon, honey," she said in less than a whisper, using a hand to nudge him away. The air was cold on her naked body, but everything from her head to her toes screamed in protest at moving quickly, so—hunched over and as crooked as a gnome—she lurched into the bathroom.

Her face in the mirror showed the mottled, swollen remains of her crying fit. Furious, she turned on the taps. Water exploded from the wide, high-pressure showerhead, and she stepped into the hot spray, letting it wash away her foolish emotional storm and her weakness and her indulgence. After a few minutes in the heat, she found she could stand straighter, and breathed in as her physical therapist had taught her, imagining a cord straightening her body, aligning hips and shoulders.

It didn't always work, but it did this morning. She had a lot to do. Not the least of which was getting out from under Julian's roof. Staying here would be a disaster. A thread of bright pink sharpness moved in her chest as she thought of him holding her last night.

No, no, no. She could not want this, want him. She didn't think there were any more broken hearts in her.

And yet, what was she doing with the restaurant? That would break her heart, too. Losing it, failing there.

At least there, she had some control. Before Julian awakened, she was dressed and out the door with Alvin, and letting herself into the kitchen at the Orange Bear. Alvin ate his breakfast in the sunshine of the porch, crunching kibble as a breeze ruffled his fur.

There was no one else about, and she went to the server

station to start a pot of coffee. Across the room, thin as
gauze, was Isobel, sitting on the bar, swinging her legs, her
hands loose in her lap. She said nothing. Elena measured
coffee grounds into the pot and pressed the auto button.
When she headed up the stairs to see if there were any pastries left, Isobel was gone.

But there, in the kitchen, were Hector and Nando, one
of the dishwashers. They looked haggard and a little grimy,
but they were happily eating eggs and tortillas smothered
in chili. The savory scent of pork and chili made her stomach growl.

"*Qué pasa*," Hector said, lifting his chin.

A sense of relief burst in her. "Hey! Where were you
guys?"

In Spanish, Hector said, "There was a lot of confusion,
so we got away. We were afraid to come in last night."

Elena nodded, her legs so rubbery she sank down on the
chair. Nando passed her a tortilla, and she tore it into strips.
"Juan?"

Hector lowered his eyes. Shook his head.

"Damn it."

The walk-in door opened and Hector's sister emerged,
all limbs and big eyes, wearing a flowered dress that was too
thin for the weather. Elena said, "Can you do anything in
the kitchen?"

"Sí," she said, then in English, "I can cook. Wash dishes."
She lifted a shoulder. "I told you I would come work when
you needed me."

Elena measured her. Nodded. "You're hired." Against
her hip, her cell phone buzzed, and distractedly, Elena answered. "Hello?"

"Ha! She lives!" said the voice on the other end of the line. Mia.

A bolt of anger, orange and molten, surged through her, and she turned away from the group at the table. "Look," she said, "I've had a rotten, rotten weekend and I really don't need more bullshit."

"Sweetie!" Mia said in her liquid voice. "I'm never your enemy. Are you ever going to give me a chance to explain?"

"I don't know." Something ached, an empty place, and into the unguarded moment, she spoke a single truth. "It's not like I let a lot of people in."

"I know, Elena. Neither do I. But I fell in love. That's been easy for you, but not for me."

She stood in the blue north light of the upstairs kitchen and felt the cell phone get hot against her ear. She couldn't think of what to say. "This is not a good day to have this conversation, Mia. It was a terrible weekend, all right?"

"Okay. But promise you'll give me some time. Soon, okay?"

After a moment, Elena said, "I'll try."

Mia was quiet. "Fair enough, I guess. Listen, though, I called with something you might not hear about in time—a friend of mine is a secretary at the Travel Channel and they've just slated a special on Aspen restaurants. You might want to see what you can do."

The first breath of hope she'd had in twenty-four hours lightened Elena's heart. "Oh, that's great news. Do you know when?"

"It's supposed to run on Valentine's Day, so they have to start choosing restaurants soon."

"Thank you, Mia. Seriously."

"Try to forgive me, will you?"

"I'm working on it."

Julian was disappointed, but not surprised to find Elena gone when he awakened. His habit was to run long on Sunday mornings, and it had taken some adjustments to figure out how to work in six miles on snowy roads, but he had the gear and had learned which roads would likely be plowed first and regularly. Most days, he was on straight pavement or mud. This morning, there was a fresh layer of snow, but he had found some netting to fit over his shoes to give a better grip, and in all but the worst conditions it provided the traction he needed. The day was sharp and bright, very still under the blanket of snow. There were footprints ahead of his—one of the things he most liked about Colorado was the way people surged outside, hungry for the snow and sun and fresh air in a way he rarely saw elsewhere. Southern Californians loved plenty of exercise, too, but the weather quality couldn't hope to compete.

The run shook a lot of darkness out of his pores, and he headed back feeling clearer. He showered and went down to the kitchen, finding that Elena had put a covered plate of churros and tortillas, leftovers from service last night, on the counter. He skipped them, knowing Portia would gobble them up, and made himself some peanut butter toast, his usual post-run breakfast, along with a pot of coffee.

As the coffee brewed, he fired up the laptop he'd left on the counter, and settled in, pushing up his sleeves to run his daily rounds. He started with email, of course, which had little of interest on a Sunday morning, and then waded out into the industry sites—*Variety* and the *Los Angeles Times*—for anything of notice. Nothing much. The coffee finished, and he poured himself a big mugful and then tried to see what he could find out about last night's grand opening. Somebody somewhere would have written about it, he was sure.

Julian loved the Internet for instant feedback. He had not expected any reviews to show up in the major Colorado papers after last night—it was too soon—but he could find information and reaction in several other ways. First he simply Googled *Orange Bear* and found mention of the restaurant—the announcement of the opening and the good review from the *Aspen Daily*. Next, he moved to a few restaurant review sites he knew and checked to see if anyone had posted yet—these were often nasty rather than nice, because it was more fun to be witty and evil than to write about great service and great food.

Not that the Orange Bear had delivered that last night. He didn't blame anyone except bureaucracy, and he assumed theirs was not the only restaurant in town that had been hit last night, but the other restaurants were already established, with whatever reputations they'd earned to this point. The Orange Bear was not, and he wanted to get a handle on what might have been said.

Not even anything there, though he did see a positive mention on one site, just a couple of lines praising the food and décor. "Great remodel!"

Then he searched blogs from several places. Still not much, but one chilled him: a *Food and Wine* reviewer had been there last night, and savaged the food, the long wait, the "inept" vision of chef Elena Alvarez. It was a blog piece now, but Julian feared it would show up elsewhere, and the weight of the reviewer was substantial enough that the review could cause real damage.

Damn. What were the alternatives? Invite the man back? Ignore it? Explain? No, never that.

Something, though. Something.

THIRTY-SIX

THE ULTIMATE RESTORATIVE CHICKEN SOUP

Because there are those poor souls who will never like chiles

> *Olive oil*
> *1 high-quality, whole stewing chicken, cut into pieces*
> *1 large onion, diced*
> *2 cloves garlic, minced*
> *2 stalks celery, sliced*
> *2 big carrots, sliced*
> *Salt and pepper*
> *Water*
> *If desired, noodles or rice*

Wash and dry the chicken, and tuck gizzards, liver, and neck into cheesecloth tied with string or a cooking bag. Cover the bottom of a big heavy pot with olive oil and let the onions and garlic warm. Add the chicken pieces, vegetables, salt and pepper, and water to cover. Add the bag with gizzards, etc., and bring soup to a boil, then turn down the heat and let it simmer for several hours, adding water if it gets too low. When the broth is a deep, velvety yellow, remove the pan from the burner and discard the bag of gizzards, etc. With a slotted spoon, fish out chicken pieces to a plate, and let cool until they can be easily handled. Remove the skins and bones and discard, then shred or chop chicken into small pieces. Put them back in the broth and correct seasonings. Add 1–2 cups of rice or pasta if desired, cook until done and very hot. Serve with milk and saltines.

THIRTY-SEVEN

Excited by the possibility of making up for last night's debacle, Elena went downstairs to her office and dialed Julian's number while she opened the computer to the Internet. "Hey, Elena," he said smoothly when he answered. "How are things over there this morning?"

"Not bad. Couple of our guys showed up again, and I've got Ivan working on getting their papers straight." She typed in a search with the words *Aspen, restaurants, Travel Channel,* and *Valentine's Day.* "I told everybody here that we need bodies desperately, and we'll pay more to get them. We may eat the profits until we're up and moving, but that raid hit every restaurant in town. They're all hurting this morning."

"I'm sure. Do what you have to do."

He sounded a little standoffish, and Elena thought about apologizing for last night, for this morning, for her aloofness. But if she didn't reestablish some distance between them, she was going to be lost. "The reason I'm calling is to let you know that my friend Mia called to let me know there's going to be a Travel Network special on Aspen for Valentine's Day." As she talked, she clicked links on the search page. "Might be a good chance to—" She started reading a blog from Jenna Bok, a notoriously difficult critic. "—revenge this fucking review! Have you seen the Jenna Bok?"

"Not that one," Julian said, and she could hear him typing in the background.

"There's more?"

"Elena, don't go around looking for bad press. It's just going to make you crazy."

Taking a breath, she clicked the icon to close the Internet. "You're right. Focus on the positive."

"Exactly. Prepare and execute."

"I've got everybody out there combing the restaurant underworld for bodies, and if we can get some good press from this special, it would really help mitigate last night's disaster." Her neck felt tight and she squeezed the muscles. "I'm sorry, Julian. I let you down."

"It was one bad night. It's gonna be okay." He cleared his throat. "Will you be coming here tonight?"

A hard pinch on her esophagus made it hard to breathe for a minute. "I hate imposing, Julian. It feels so awkward. But there's absolutely nothing available. I thought about crashing with Patrick but—"

"Now *that* would be awkward."

"Exactly."

"I'm sorry you feel uncomfortable at my house," Julian said in a slightly formal tone. "What if I make the tower room yours for now? Would that make it easier?"

Elena closed her eyes. *No,* she wanted to say. *I need to sleep with you. I want to breathe in your skin and dream with you and curl a toe around your ankle in the middle of the night.* "Don't you think we should be kind of careful, Julian? Just keep a little distance? That way nobody gets hurt."

"Very smart," he said briskly. "I'll make sure you have what you need when you arrive. I can take Portia out for dinner and you'll have the house to yourself for a while this evening."

"Julian, I don't mean to—"

"Never apologize, never explain," he said. "I'll see you later."

By midafternoon, Elena could not do one more thing. Lifting her arms took such effort it left her sweating. Putting one foot in front of the other required extreme concentration.

Ivan found her in the walk-in, where she was standing on her toes as if to lift herself up and away from the claws in her hip and lower back. "Go home, Chef. I can handle it from here."

"I'm fine."

"I can see that," he said, and abruptly grabbed her arm, put a fist against the knot in her back, and rolled his big knuckles over the spot.

She groaned at the burst of both relief and pain. "Oh, ow, good!"

"Yeah. Go home, call Mindy or Candy or whatever her name is, and get some rest. We start over tomorrow."

In the frosty cubicle, she let Rasputin knead the agonizing place in her lower back, letting go enough that she leaned in and rested her forehead against her hands. "Okay," she said. "You're right. But we need to—"

"Nothin' we need that bad today, *Jefa*. We've cut the reservations to a manageable level, and with Hector and Peter, I'll handle this shift." He raised his brows. "You're not going to be any help anyway. You need some rest. Eat some chicken soup."

She took a breath. "Okay. I'll see you tomorrow."

"Monday is your day off. You need to take it."

Elena straightened, and headed out of the walk-in. "No. I have too much to do."

"You keep up like this, you'll hit the wall."

She scowled at him. "You know the rules, Rasputin. A chef is never sick."

He made a face. "I know a lot of burned-out, drunken cooks, too."

"Right."

"I mean it," he said. "Go sleep and I'm going to send somebody over with my auntie's chicken soup."

She nodded. "I'm going."

Outside in the bright, sparkling day, Elena felt better. Everything hurt still, but just being outdoors eased some of the tight places, and when she thought of the Valentine's Day special, it gave her a sense of possibility. As she headed toward the car, Alvin tagging behind her, people swished by in nylon ski gear and laughed with vacation fever and tossed brightly colored scarves around their necks. Weekend lunches would be a boon.

But not this minute.

Then, as she climbed into the car, her back screamed and she remembered she didn't have a home to go to, and she put her head down on the steering wheel in despair. What was this about? Why had the heavens bothered to spare her if she was just going to fail, over and over? If, just as she started to make her dream come true, her broken body betrayed her?

A knock on the window startled her, and she looked up to see Hector's sister shivering beside the car. In Spanish she said, "I am supposed to tell you to call your mother."

Alarmed, Elena started to open the door. "What? Did my family call? Is she sick?"

Alma shrugged. "Nobody called," she said, and patted the hood of Elena's car, then drifted away, putting her arms into the sleeves of a dark blue sweater. For a long moment, Elena watched her, wearing those odd clothes and the too-tall shoes and swinging her skinny arms, and wondered if she was a ghost, another vision of something Elena had conjured up.

But apparently, everyone else could see her, too. A man slid sideways as she passed, and turned to admire the swish of her tiny bottom beneath the skirts. A girl shook her head at the strange clothes. No, Hector's sister wasn't a ghost. She was just an eccentric.

Elena started the car. She would call her mother later. First, she had to get somewhere warm, call the massage person, get some sleep. She thought she would keel over from exhaustion if she didn't sleep.

She had no choice but to return to Julian's, but there was no one there when she rang the bell, so she punched in the security code he'd given her and went in through a side door. Alvin found his crocodile and carried it downstairs, looking for Portia, and he didn't come back up. Elena climbed the stairs, one excruciating stair at a time, focusing not on the pain but on the sound of the water falling from the upper level, on the silver-ribbon beauty of it, and the tremendous effort it took to raise one foot, then the other.

In one part of her brain or heart or soul, she recognized that these issues were getting worse. She'd always had days when cold or overwork or a bout of the flu made everything hurt. Or rather, hurt more, since she pretty much had some pain nearly every day. The walking helped keep her in motion, and she'd had plenty of that here. Aspen proper was not a large place, and both her condo and the restaurant were centrally located, so she walked several miles every day. In the past, that would have been enough.

It wasn't now.

One step. One more. One more. She leaned on the railing and focused, just as she had long ago when she'd first tried to move around again, nearly eight months after the accident. They had not been entirely sure she *would* walk. Then they hadn't thought she would walk without limping. She'd proved them wrong.

At the top of the stairs, she had to make a decision—her tower room with the loft, where she would be alone? Or Julian's bed, which was closer, bigger, and didn't require climbing any more? It was an easy choice.

There was also a television in there. Elena clicked it on, stripped off her clothes, and staggered into the shower, where she let the heat and steam ease away some of the trouble. Afterward, she realized it was impossible for her to bend far enough to pick up her bag, stuffed with clean underwear and other things, and simply found a pair of Julian's running pants and a T-shirt to put on.

Then she climbed into his big, comfortable bed, pulled the quilt around her neck, and collapsed.

Julian and Portia went to Elena's house to gather her clothes, but the police wouldn't let them in, citing the instability of the structure. "Do you think you could figure out her sizes?" Julian asked his daughter.

She shrugged. "Pretty close."

"Let's go shopping, then."

Portia brightened. "How fun! I love to shop for people! Don't you think she would look good in pink?"

Julian inclined his head. "I haven't seen her in many clothes except the chef's whites. Pink might be nice. Do you think she'd like it, though?"

"Yeah," Portia said. "Trust me, Dad. If there's one thing I get, it's women's clothes."

So, as much to give his daughter the obvious pleasure of shopping as to bring Elena something to give her comfort, they headed to the main drag to buy overpriced silk T-shirts from the boutiques. In one such shop, Portia rummaged through the shirts on hangers, fast, and said, "You like her, don't you?"

"Of course."

"I mean, *like* her like her, as in kissy kissy."

He chuckled. "Kissy kissy?"

"You know what I mean!" She pulled out a diaphanous pink and green paisley print with long sleeves. "Ooh, this is good." She put it in his hands.

For a moment, Julian didn't know how to answer her.

And then he fell back on his vow to be real and honest with her as much as he could. "I do like her. She's real."

Portia nodded. "Yeah, that's why I like her, too."

She tugged him over to a new area, and flipped through blouses and shirts and skirts. Pulled out a blue T-shirt, silky and simple, and Julian imagined how gorgeous Elena's breasts would look beneath it. He took it from her. "I choose this one."

She laughed. "You do like her!"

The airlessness in his chest, his sadness, swirled up. "Yeah."

"Do you think you'll ever get married again?"

He quirked his lips mockingly. "Five times the charm?"

"Why doesn't anyone stay married? I'm scarred for life, being a Hollywood child, you know." Her voice was unconcerned and she held a shimmery gold top against her chest. "I think you should buy me this to make up for it."

Julian snorted. "I'll buy you something, cupcake, but not that. It's way too old for you."

She grinned, looking suddenly like her eight-year-old self. "I'd really like some new jeans. And maybe you could buy me sushi?"

"Will you see the ski instructor on Tuesday?"

Portia smiled faintly, and pulled out a red shirt with a square neckline and floaty sleeves. "I already called him," she said, and put the blouse in his hands. "That one for Elena. She'll look hot, trust me."

"You called the ski instructor?"

"Yep."

Standing there in the boutique with the smell of expensive fabrics and signature perfumes in the air, with natural light pouring over his daughter's faintly freckled nose, Julian was overcome with love. On some level, he knew this was a minute he would remember, this very one, standing with her, and took the time to press all the golden pleasure of it into his pores, his heart, the gray folds of his memory.

"I'm glad" was all he said.

After dinner, they returned to the house. On the stoop was a big bag with a big plastic container inside. A note in a mannered hand said, *Chicken Soup, for Elena. From Ivan.* Julian carried it inside. It was still warm.

Alvin greeted them cheerfully, but without the crocodile. "Hey, honey," Portia said, bending down to kiss him, her packages forgotten in her rush to hug the dog, "whatcha doing? Where's your toy?"

Alvin backed up, still smiling, his tail still wagging, and wuffed softly.

"Go get it," Portia said.

Alvin didn't move, just inclined his head, turned away, turned back.

"What's wrong, honey? Where's Elena? Where's your mom?"

The first soft ripple of worry moved through Julian's throat. "What's up, Alvin? What do you need? Show me."

The dog turned around and trotted down the hall, looking over his shoulder to make sure they were following. Not to the kitchen, but up the stairs. "I'll go, Portia. You can take your stuff to your room."

"Can I get on the Internet?"

"In the great room, yeah."

Julian followed Alvin upstairs and into his bedroom, where Elena was buried beneath the covers in his bed. She looked about six, with her mussed hair and the covers up to her chin. The television was on, the sound muted, and the blue light touched her cheekbone.

She was very much asleep, her mouth open, a faint snore coming from between her lips. Alvin went to the edge of the bed and nudged her back, and when she didn't open her eyes, he jumped up on the edge of the bed and put his paws on her shoulder. "Alvin, no," she said in a pitiful voice.

He patted her shoulder, tugging with his claws at the duvet, pulling it off her shoulder. She made a soft noise, but it took a lot of effort to turn over. "Alvin—" She saw Julian. "Hi, sorry to be in here. The loft was just—" She sighed.

"You look terrible. What can I get you?"

"I just need to rest. I'll be all right in the morning."

"Did you need to get into the hot tub?"

She shook her head.

"Let's get you down there. That will help."

"I just don't think—is Portia here? I don't want to freak her out."

Julian sat down next to her. "What can I do, Elena? Let me help you."

"It's just stress. It will be better in a day or two."

"Will a massage help?"

"Maybe." She tangled her hand in his. "Will you be giving it?"

He bent to kiss her. "I can. Purely nonsexual, of course."

She hesitated, then reached for his hand. "Help me sit up."

He did and she reached for the hem of her shirt, and pulled it off over her head, and with great effort turned over. "I actually do know a little about this," he said, pushing the quilt away. "My fourth wife was a massage therapist."

"I thought she was a yoga teacher."

"Both." He went to the bathroom and came back with some unscented oil. "Lucky for you, I have some oil left over from those days."

It drew a small chuckle. "Really. You've been moving it from house to house all this time."

Alvin seemed satisfied and slumped nearby the bed on the floor. Julian said, "Brace yourself," and turned on a lamp on the nightstand. Elena didn't move. The light put the scar over her shoulder into relief, a thick cord of dark pink. He started there, at her shoulder blades, moving his hands lightly at first, from shoulder to shoulder, up into her neck, down the channel of her spine. The main scar submerged about halfway down, turning into a very thin white line. There were faint dots on either side of the spinal column, as if there were stitches or pins there once. Below her ribs on the left side, the scar reemerged in two rivers—one neat and clean, a surgical incision that healed well, the other a ragged gash where something must have pierced her.

He thought of the boy yesterday, flung onto the bed, and it made him think of a seventeen-year-old Elena lying in a ditch in the dark, thinking that her sister was there, holding her hand. "I hate it that this happened to you," he said, and his voice was thick. "That you're still in so much pain."

"Better this than dead."

"Absolutely." He kneaded the lower back with the heels of his hands, moved into the buttock. "Jesus, Elena, these muscles are like rocks."

She groaned, half in pain, half in pleasure. "Oh, that hurts so good."

For a while, he worked in silence. "What were your injuries, exactly, Elena? That you had to spend so much time in the hospital?"

"Broke my back in four places," she said, eyes closed. "Shattered left hip—that's what that scar is. Broken clavicle and right shoulder blade and many ribs. Lost my left kidney. The back is the big problem."

He dug into her left buttock, feeling the glutes like iron cords. "Not your hip?"

"Maybe." She shifted a little to look at him. "It's not like this all the time. I just got stressed out, and I didn't want to take any muscle relaxants and—"

"How long has it been since anyone looked at all of this? A medical professional?"

"A while, probably five years. There's not much they can do. This is the legacy of catastrophic car accidents. That's what one guy told me—that if you survived a big wreck, this was what you had to look forward to."

His hands stilled. "How do you know they haven't come up with a thousand ways to make you feel better? It's been twenty years."

"Julian, can we not have this conversation right this minute?"

"Sorry."

"Talk to me about you, instead. How's the screenplay going?"

A frisson of worry lit up the nerves in his body, all at once, then subsided. "Very well, honestly. I'd like to start filming this summer, while Portia is out of school."

"Ah, very good. I wondered how you'd manage that."

"It won't be easy, but she's my priority for the next four years. I should have done it sooner. But . . . well, that's water under the bridge. I can do it now." He worked deeper, feeling some looseness starting to emerge. Good. "I think I'm going to have to get her a dog."

"Yes!" In her enthusiasm, Elena turned over. "She is such a dog person! And I think there might be any number of possibilities."

Her breasts, white and plump, drew his eye, and without heat, he touched them. "Okay. We can talk about it. I'd love your thoughts."

She covered his hands. "Thank you, Julian. I think I might be able to make it to the hot tub now without freaking out your daughter."

He smiled down at her, aware of a vast tenderness. She was pale and there were shadows below her eyes and in this light he could see the fine lines. Her hair was a tangled mess on the pillows. And he felt more at home, sitting in this quiet pool of light, than he had in his entire life.

She pulled his hands up and kissed the palms. "What put that pensive look on your face?"

"It's so easy to be around you," he said. Touched her hair. Thought the words but didn't say them, *I love you.*

She kissed his thumb. "I know," she said. "Me too." Struggling to a sitting position, she said, "Can you get in the hot tub with me? We'll wear bathing suits."

"Sure. Sounds good. Ivan brought you some soup. And Portia and I brought you some things, too."

"What things?"

"Portia will like showing you." For one more moment, he let the softness rush through him, that sense of home, and bent to kiss her bare shoulder. "C'mon."

As she struggled into a standing position, he knew he would have to tell her, soon, that the movie was about her life, her losses. But it needed to be at just the right moment. The right circumstances.

THIRTY-EIGHT

POLVORONES
(MEXICAN CHRISTMAS COOKIES)

½ cup butter
½ cup lard
½ cup granulated sugar
2 large egg yolks
1 large orange; entire peel grated to zest, plus juice
2 cups all purpose flour
2 cups finely ground almonds

Preheat oven to 400 degrees. Grease a baking sheet or use parchment. In bowl, beat the butter, lard, and sugar until creamy. Add egg yolks one at a time, beating them into the sugar mixture well. Add the orange zest and the juice of the orange, then fold in flour and almonds in small batches, blending well. The dough will be crumbly. Roll it out on a floured surface to ¾ inch, and cut out small circles, an inch or so. Bake about 15 minutes, until lightly golden, no more. Sprinkle with powdered sugar if desired.

THIRTY-NINE

Things normalized in their new pattern over the next week. Elena put herself on waiting lists around town for various apartments and condos and even one tiny house. In the meantime, she stayed at Julian's. Which wasn't all bad. It gave her access to the hot tub, which would buy her some time on her feet. Alvin had a place to stay every day when she was at work.

But the biggest pleasure was in her connection to Portia. It was as if she had suddenly inherited a smart, pretty niece who wanted to do everything with her. They made Christmas cookies—a ritual the girl had never had the pleasure of performing—and decorated a tree and put garlands around the windows. They shopped for Christmas presents. Elena visited the dog kennel with her, and cleverly extracted information about rescue dogs and why Portia felt so passionately that anyone who wanted a dog should go to the rescue services to get one. Portia herself had been eyeing a mixed-breed pup that nobody seemed to want for fear he would turn out to be savage— pit bull mixed with husky. The pup was very smart, fluffy, and funny looking. Elena carefully reported the news to Julian.

Things in the kitchen began to normalize as well. The bad reviews did hurt business, and one—painfully—would run in *Condé Nast Traveler* magazine in January. They had seen an advance. But Julian had gone to work trying to find out who was in charge of the Travel Channel show, pulling his considerable strings. If they could get the Orange Bear into that Valentine's Day special, it would help.

They were still wretchedly shorthanded, as was every kitchen in town, and they were all in fierce competition for any available body they could find. Julian put ads in Denver and Grand Junction newspapers, but it ended up being both Peter and Ivan who were the biggest help in recruiting. Ivan knew everyone and worked the nepotism angle, bringing in a dishwasher and commis, and Peter put the word out among the ski bums.

Despite the challenges over housing, scrambling to find replacements for the decimated kitchen staff, and her ongoing—and very private—body pain, Elena's spirits lifted as Christmas edged closer. She enjoyed the bustle in the shops, the Christmas music playing. She and Patrick went out shopping one afternoon between shifts, and had a beer in an upscale pub.

"Have you talked to Mia?" he asked, picking delicately through the nuts on the table and choosing the almonds.

"A week or so ago, I talked to her."

"We've all three fallen in love," he said.

"I'm not in love," Elena said with a frown. But she looked at him more closely. "But—wow! You so are."

A tinge of color rosied his cheekbones. "I feel like I came to Aspen to meet Ivan. Seriously."

"I would never in a million years have chosen him out of a crowd for you."

"No?" Patrick inclined his head, his gaze direct. "Why?"

"He's very sexy, no question." Didn't he see how different they were? "But there's a lot of darkness in him. You're so sane and levelheaded."

"I had a good childhood," he said. "Ivan didn't."

"I think he could be pretty volatile, that's all. And he's very, very much in love with you. Be careful."

"He won't hurt me, Elena. I'm absolutely certain of that."

Elena was not, but she said, "I'm more worried about what you could do to him."

"It's sweet that you're worried, but don't, okay? We're good. Very good." He sipped his Pellegrino through a straw. "Back to you, girl. And Julian. Our boss, oh my God. What were you thinking?"

"I know." She shook her head, and a vision of Julian rose in her imagination, playing with Alvin and his crocodile, or sucking on her lower lip, or massaging her back with such care. "I'm keeping my distance, don't worry. And we agreed that my job is safe, no matter what."

"That's not what I meant, exactly. He's not the type to backstab you. You've gone through a lot of lovers, *ma chérie*. Maybe it's time to let one of them in?"

"What are you talking about? I fall in love all the time. Just ask Mia."

"All with men who are not your equal in some way or another."

"That's not true! What about Timothy?"

"Oh, the spoiled little English lad who didn't have the IQ of a chipmunk?"

She chuckled. "Okay, so he wasn't that bright. We had a good time traveling."

"Nothing wrong with that, but he was never going to be your soul mate and you knew it."

"That's not true. My heart was broken big-time when he broke up with me."

"Nobody has ever broken your heart, Elena, because you don't give it to them. You just like to put on a good show, and wallow around feeling bad for a few months."

His words stung. "I loved some of them. Maybe Timothy was a little convenient and situational—you know, falling in love on holiday—but I really did love Dmitri. And he really did break my heart."

"No, he pissed you off," Patrick said. "You didn't like it that he took up with somebody else, but that man was seriously in love with you and no matter what he did, he couldn't get through to you."

Elena leaned back in the booth, looking at him, feeling a hollow sense of recognition she found difficult to brush off. "Do you think that's really what I do? Keep myself aloof from them?"

"Yes." He plucked another almond out of the bowl. "But I think you might want to let this one in. And it would be good for you."

She made an exasperated noise. "Patrick, has it escaped your notice that he's way, way, way out of my league? He's wealthy and good-looking and could have a dozen women at the snap of his fingers. He works with beautiful actresses all the time."

"So?"

"So, who could resist that, over and over?"

"I was working in the San Diego restaurant when he broke up with one of his wives," Patrick said. "He took it hard. Went on the wagon, both from women and alcohol. He didn't date for almost three years. Not at all. That shows a lot of strength of character."

A wave of something rose in her, closing her throat, making her feel vaguely ill. She even felt as if she might cry. "I can't want that," she whispered, waving a hand. "It's too much."

"He's the first one who has ever deserved you," Patrick said, reaching across the table. "Just think about it, Elena. You deserve some happiness. We all do."

"I am happy," she said.

He smiled. "You know what I mean."

She breathed against the terror. "I know."

"You need to call Mia. That's all that happened to her, too. She fell in love, really really really in love, and as much as she wanted to be here, she couldn't leave him. Is that so terrible?"

"No. It's not." She bowed her head. "I'll call her by Christmas," she said. "Promise."

Danger arrived on the Tuesday morning just before Christmas.

Ivan understood happiness didn't last. He wasn't some

seven-year-old who needed to believe in happily ever after, forever and ever, amen. Not like that.

What he hated was that happiness ran away so fast every time, and there he was, flung back out to suffer before he'd had a chance to really enjoy the peaceful time. He was tired of it, so tired that when the man arrived at the service door, Ivan almost lied and said they had filled all the positions they needed. Unfortunately, Elena was close by and called out a cheery, "Come in, talk to me! I've got to finish this mole, but I can listen while I cook."

The man was six feet or a little better, glistening gold all over—sun-bleached streaks in gold hair, shaggy the way a lot of skiers wore it, eyebrows and arm hairs bleached by constant exposure to the sun. Cheekbones chiseled like swords angling down to the mouth of a comic-book hero—firm, sharply cut. The guy should be a model. Everyone turned around to look as he crossed the room, his tight ass and tiny waist impossibly fit. As if he felt Ivan's gaze, he looked over his shoulder and winked, all self-assured elegance.

Fuck. Ivan wanted to slam things, bang and storm, but he did not. He carefully moved around the room, wondering where Patrick was, if he'd seen this Adonis come in.

Naturally, Elena hired him. A ski bum. Dag, who not only looked like that but turned out to have a Danish accent, which gave him that little soupçon of extra pizzazz, as if he needed it. When Patrick met him, Ivan was in the room, and Patrick just coolly shook his hand and said, "Welcome," before he rushed off to find Elena.

Dag turned around, watching Patrick, and he smiled,

with a smooth, slow perfection that made the top of Ivan's head whirl off. Stepping close, Ivan growled, "Back off."

"Ah," he said, grinning, and lifted his hands, as if under arrest. "No problem. No problem."

On Christmas Eve, the restaurant closed at eight, and by ten, Ivan and Patrick were settled in front of the Christmas tree at Patrick's place, drinking eggnog and listening to rock-and-roll Christmas carols, which Ivan insisted upon. Springsteen sang "Santa Claus Is Comin' to Town," in that raw, ragged voice, and Ivan leaned back happily, drink in hand, to watch the lights sparkle. Patrick was cutting out paper snowflakes that he was going to use for table decorations tomorrow, when a few people would come over for a Christmas goose with all the trimmings. Patrick had made a special request for it, tickled by the idea of a Dickens sort of Christmas, and Ivan tracked down one of his suppliers to get a honking big bird—he laughed every time he said this—and it was marinating now. Ivan would get up at dawn to put it in the oven so it would be ready for dinner. He'd also secretly rented a Victorian-era costume, complete with a top hat, in which he thought he looked pretty hot.

The restaurant was closed. All of Liswood's restaurants were closed for Christmas and again on New Year's Day. He felt everyone deserved a couple of days off every year, no matter what, something Ivan found remarkable.

"This is great," Ivan said.

Patrick smiled up at him. "It is. I'm so looking forward to our dinner tomorrow! Thank you for cooking goose."

"One big honking bird," Ivan said, laughing.

"The joke might be a little overdone," Patrick said, but he was grinning. He unfolded thin white paper to reveal a beautifully intricate snowflake. "Sure you don't want to try one?"

"I'm sure."

"What was happening in your life last Christmas?" Patrick asked.

Ivan had to think about it. "Nothing very good. The restaurant had problems because the owner was putting all the profits up his nose. I was living in a trailer out by Carbondale and it sucked. But I got a good review in the *Denver Post* for my steak pie. I haven't made that for you, have I?"

"No. I'd love to try it."

"You're easy, man. It's great to cook for you."

Patrick inclined his head crisply. "Thank you." He took another piece of paper from the pile. "Were you seeing anyone?"

"Not really. I hadn't been back here long." Sipping the creamy, rummy eggnog, he pursed his lips. "How about you, lover? What were you doing last Christmas?"

"I was living in New York. I went home to Boston for Christmas, but it wasn't particularly pleasant. My boyfriend wouldn't come with me—he said my parents were stuck up—so I went alone and we were on the outs, so I wasn't happy."

"Was that the bartender, the one who almost came here with you?"

Patrick nodded. "He wasn't very nice, honestly. It was way past time to break up with him. You just get used to things being a certain way."

"Are your parents stuck up?"

"Yes. But they are still my parents."

"Do they like your boyfriends as a rule?"

"They've only met one or two." Patrick placed another snowflake neatly on the pile. "They'd rather I wasn't gay, but they're big on dignity, so they're polite enough."

"They'd hate me, wouldn't they?"

"Why do you say that?"

"Not exactly in their world, am I? All rough edges and crooked teeth."

"You're a James Beard–winning chef. That will impress them." Patrick touched his ankle. "And seriously, they love me, so when someone is important to me, they do their best to like them, too."

"But they don't always."

"Of course not."

Ivan thought of Dag, the polished Dane, with a twist of worry. "Have they ever met Elena?"

"Several times, when she lived in New York. My mother isn't crazy about her, but my father thinks she's hot." A smile quirked his lips. "One is connected to the other, I'm quite sure."

"Wouldn't they like it if you were with someone like old Dag?"

Patrick looked perplexed. "Dag?"

"The new guy in the kitchen. The Scandinavian."

"The ski bum? You must be kidding. He's a player. I don't like players."

"I'm a player."

"No," Patrick said, putting down his scissors. "You pretend to be, but you have a very passionate heart." He inclined his head. "You just haven't had anyone love you through thick and thin, that's all."

Stung by those blue eyes, Ivan looked away. "Wow."

Then Patrick came to sit beside him. Touched his hand. "I think I fell in love with you at first sight, Ivan. And I'm pretty sure you felt the same way. Let's try to just enjoy it, shall we? We got lucky."

Ivan pulled him close, his hand spreading open over the tumbled blond hair, feeling the preciousness of his skull. "Yeah," he growled. "Yeah, I did. Thank you."

"I really don't like jealousy. It will ruin things."

"I'll do my best." He thought of breakfast. "Tomorrow morning, I'm going to cook you my very best French toast. You will so love it."

"Ivan, I'm going to get fat!"

"No, you won't," he said. "We'll work it off."

Elena finally remembered to call Maria Elena on the evening of Christmas Eve, when she was setting up the kitchen in Julian's house to make tamales with Portia. They had dozens at the restaurant, but when Elena told the girl about making them with the women on Christmas Eve, Portia really, really wanted to try it. And Elena didn't mind it.

Mama answered with a slightly irritated "Hello?"

"Hi, Mama," she said. "How are you?"

"Elena, *h'ita*! It's so nice to hear your voice. What are you doing? We got your package yesterday—so many presents for all the little ones, you must be getting rich!"

Elena laughed. "It's just little things, Mom. Be sure and put out all the chocolate on Christmas Day."

"I guess since you sent it, you're not going to be here on Christmas this year, huh?"

One year, Elena had flown into Albuquerque and rented a car and arrived at Mama's house in time for mass on Christmas Eve. Maria Elena had never forgotten it, and every year, Elena could hear the hope that Elena would repeat the surprise. For one minute, Elena imagined how that would be, crowded into the little house with too many people, and lots of children, and the happy sound of laughing, and the smell of coffee and pine, chill and chocolate, in the air. "I'm afraid I can't this year, Mama. We're still getting the restaurant up and going. Maybe I can pop down in January sometime."

"I'd like to see you, *m'ija*. What are you doing for Christmas?"

"I'm working mostly. I'll spend some time with my friends—you remember Patrick? I brought him with me when I lived in New York. We came for something—maybe your birthday, huh?"

"Sure, sure. Nice boy. Not married, though."

Elena's lips twitched. "Not yet. He's here in Aspen, too. I hired him to be my sommelier."

"That's nice." In the background was music on a radio, tinny and thin, and the sound of clattering pans. "We're having Christmas at Darla's this year. She's got more room and all the kids can play easier in her basement."

"That's a good idea." She tucked her phone between her ear and shoulder and ripped open the corn husks she'd bought at the store. "Hey, I'll tell you, I am making tamales with a young girl here. She's fourteen and dying to learn. We've already made six kinds of Christmas cookies."

"Very nice."

"You okay, Mom? You sound tired."

"Oh, it's just that time of year. Too much to do. Not enough time to do it all."

"Well, don't wear yourself out."

"I won't, baby. You enjoy yourself, okay?"

"I will. I love you, Mama."

"I love you, too. Be good." And then, defiantly and laughing at once, she added, "Find a husband!"

Elena groaned. "Bye, Mama!"

On Christmas morning, Elena felt shy, waking up next to Julian. They'd stayed up late together the night before, drinking hot chocolate by the fire in his bedroom and listening to his vast collection of CDs. Then they'd made love for a long time in the fire-lit dark, and fallen asleep naked and spent, well after midnight.

Julian was still asleep when she wakened, and for a few long moments, she simply looked at his dark curls, the blunt nose. His mouth was open a little, and he made a soft whistling sound as he breathed, somehow endearing. Tiny threads of silver showed in his chest hairs, and the texture of the skin there revealed his age. He would be fifty next year, she'd finally found out, not that he looked it most of the time. The running and yoga kept him supple and younger than his years.

Still. If she let him in, that would be something to contend with, that he was more than a decade her senior and she would likely outlive him. It scared her to even think in those terms, long terms, as they had only been together a couple of months. But, looking at him, lying here, she knew there was something real in this bond, in whatever it was that was blooming between them.

It made her stomach hurt. There was always that other shoe, wasn't there? Death, disease, other women, boredom and contempt, all those things people did to each other.

It had been hell trying to figure out what to give him for Christmas—they were at that awkward stage of not dating a terribly long time, but they were also *very* intensely involved. He was also quite wealthy, so he bought whatever he liked. She needed to find something that would show him she'd been paying attention. It took ages, but she finally realized what it should be, and wrapped up her gift and put it under the tree, but now she was nervous. What if he didn't get it? What if it was too personal?

Portia, on the other hand, was a breeze. Elena had found plenty of cute dog toys and accoutrements for the puppy Julian had arranged to have delivered this morning. Elena squinted at the clock. They would be here with the puppy in twenty minutes. She slipped out of bed and shimmied into jeans and a T-shirt. In the kitchen, she started a pot of coffee and let Alvin outside, then brushed her teeth and peed in the powder room off the kitchen. It was one of her favorite bathrooms, this one, with a brown glass bowl sitting on a counter for a sink, and the faucets coming out of the wall, imitating garden art.

Don't get used to it, she told herself. Ease, comfort, luxury. It wouldn't last.

But for today, this was the most fun she'd had at Christmas in a long time, and she couldn't wait for Portia to get up and meet her dog. She skimmed a brush through her hair, let Alvin back in, and there was a knock at the door.

Her heart leapt and she rushed into the foyer to answer it, punching the numbers on the alarm to let the woman in. She carried a dog kennel, and Alvin, who'd been eager to see what was going on, lowered his head with an apprehensive expression. "It's okay, baby," Elena told him.

The woman said, "He's been groomed and fed. I wish I could be here to see Portia's face when she sees him."

"I'm excited."

"Thank you again, and please thank Mr. Liswood for the extraordinarily generous contribution."

"I will."

After the woman left, Elena knelt and opened the kennel to take out the young dog. He wasn't much more than four or five months, still a puppy with his broad head and big paws. He wiggled and trembled in her arms, looking at Alvin, who was just perplexed. Elena knelt and let them smell each other. "Be nice, you guys."

The pup shivered against her knees as Alvin sniffed him thoroughly, head to toe, stopping every so often—the joint of the left back leg, the edge of his ear, a spot midway down his back—to sneeze or snuffle or take another deep sniff. His tail wagged slowly as he inspected this creature, and then he stepped back and bent down and barked. Sharply.

The puppy jerked, then wiggled to get free, and dopily walked over, head down, to play. He was so adorable—big nose and soft fur and that wide bulldog head and the curly tail of a husky.

After she ascertained they'd be okay, Elena captured the

pup and called Alvin and they headed upstairs to haul
Julian out of bed so they could wake Portia up.

Portia's reaction was squealing and absolute astonishment.
"Oh, how did you know?" she cried, hugging the puppy,
who obviously recognized her and wiggled in a far more ef-
fusive way when she hugged him than he had when the
others greeted him. "He's the best little pup and nobody
wanted to adopt him, and oh, look at him!" She blinked
back tears, and gazed at her dad with adoration. "Thank
you, Daddy. He's the best dog and I promise I will take very
good care of him."

Next to the bed, Alvin whined, his crocodile in his
mouth.

"Oh, I still love you, too," Portia said. "Do you have a
toy? Come on!" She patted the bed. "Come on up!"

Alvin looked at Elena, who rolled her eyes. "Oh, go
ahead, you traitor."

Julian pulled her forward. "Elena helped."

Portia grinned, rubbing both dogs with one hand each.
"I figured. Thank you, Elena."

"You are so welcome."

"C'mon. Let's go upstairs and open presents. I have stuff
for you guys, too!"

They all tramped upstairs—two dogs, a girl, and two
adults—and Elena realized this was the first Christmas
morning that felt like Christmas morning in years and
years. What if—

Don't borrow trouble, said a voice. Her own. *Live now.*

So she shyly gave Julian his dual gift, and Portia her pile of dog things, and they each gave her boxes, too, and they all tore into them. Portia had a pile of things from her father, who insisted she needed to be spoiled at Christmas because she'd been doing so well in school and in her job. All she had required, it seemed, was a stable environment. She got new skis and ski pants and books and—

"A laptop? My own laptop?"

Julian nodded. "I'll still be checking on you, you know, and you can keep it upstairs, but it's yours. You don't have to ask for permission to use it."

For the second time that morning, Portia's eyes welled. She leapt up and hugged him around the neck, her checkered pink and purple pajamas riding low on her strong hips. Elena ducked her head, feeling like an interloper.

And not. Because Portia had showered her with presents—beautiful cut-glass earrings and a silver bracelet and a blouse with airy sleeves, all exactly to her taste.

And Julian gave her a small package, not so small it was jewelry, but small enough to intrigue. "You first," she said, nervous now. Ready to get it over with.

The first was obviously a book and he opened it. "*The Best Book of Potato Latkes,*" he said, and stared at it for a long moment. Elena's nervousness grew. Did he remember their early conversation about special food?

He raised his eyes, and smiled. "Perfect. Thank you."

"They go together."

The other box held a small, antique menorah she'd found online. It had come from a New Jersey estate. He took it out. His voice was raw when he said, "Thank you,

Elena." He reached for her hand, squeezed it, and she real-ized he was hiding enormous emotion.

"Your real gift is not here yet," he said. "I ordered it and there was a small delay. This is just a little something I thought you'd like in the meantime."

She grinned and opened the package, which was a Day of the Dead skeleton in a small kitchen, wearing roses in her hair. Elena laughed and kissed him. "It's perfect," she said. "Thank you."

FORTY

IVAN'S FRENCH TOAST

Perfect for that New Year's Day celebration

*6–8 slices thick-sliced cinnamon raisin bread or rich bread like
    brioche*
5 eggs
½ cup milk
1 tsp each grated lemon and orange zest
½ tsp vanilla
Powdered sugar and raspberries

Whip eggs, milk, zests, and vanilla together in a glass bowl.
Get the skillet ready by heating till drops of water dance and disappear. Dip the bread and let the mixture soak in, then grill till
golden. Garnish with fresh butter, raspberries, and powdered
sugar.

FORTY-ONE

The turn of the year brought a serious cold snap, with temperatures dropping below zero at night, making the entire mountain region an ice rink no matter how hard the sand trucks and snowplows worked. Enough snow fell that the slopes stayed prime, and Aspen partied. The hotel rooms were packed, the restaurants filled to capacity, everyone was happy, making pots of money on the tourists and skiers who wanted to mingle with the beautiful people.

The Orange Bear was full every night and word of mouth was excellent, but the bad reviews still rankled. The day the Condé Nast magazine hit the stands, Elena and Julian bought every issue in town and threw them in the Dumpster at the back of the restaurant. Slapping her hands together crisply afterward, Elena grinned. "That felt better!"

The kitchen staff worked itself into its new alignment. There were a few struggles for dominance among the line cooks, and there was never going to be the ease between Ivan and Dag that there had been between him and Juan, but the Danish skier had a lot of talent and he showed up reliably, so they had to keep him. Twice, Elena clamped down on them when a struggle broke out; the rest of the time, she looked the other way. Dag deferred to Ivan in the kitchen—this was a personal struggle.

She missed Juan. Terribly. He was an excellent chef, with a personality to calm the roiling waters, but it was Juan himself she missed. The twinkle in his eye, his old-world mannerliness, his easy chatting with her in Spanish. Having him around had been like having a piece of her home with her every day. She'd come to rely on him and his soothing influence, and she really wanted to get him back. Through Hector and Tansy, she found out the name of his hometown in Mexico, and asked Julian to help her find him. Maybe if they requested this particular cook, they could make a case to the authorities. It was worth a try.

In the meantime, she cracked down on the legality of the papers in her kitchen. Hector produced a legitimate green card somehow, and his sister married a local— probably for *her* green card, but Elena didn't care, and a loophole in the law allowed the restaurant to request a certain number of work permits, which they sucked up as fast as they could.

Elena also wrote letters. Lots of letters—to her congressmen, to the INS, to the local state and city officials. She even wrote a letter to the President. The laws, in her opinion, were idiotic and benefited no one—not the employers, nor the illegal immigrants flooding in to take the jobs, nor the American citizens who supposedly wanted the jobs the illegals were taking. Nobody won.

Entire projects were shut down throughout the city because there was no one to work them. Potholes on side streets grew to the size of small lakes with no one to man the trucks to fill them up. Restaurants could seat only 70 or 80 percent of their former numbers. And construction projects sat silent, heavy plastic flapping beneath the brilliant skies.

One thing that had come out of the decimation of the kitchen staff was that Elena found herself leading a kitchen with a much higher than average percentage of women. She and Tansy; Hector's sister Alma on dishes; the line-cook-in-training—i.e., kitchen slave—Katya, who had come to them through the party at Julian's; and another slave Ivan had unearthed somewhere, a squat girl with mean eyes who didn't talk much but could wield a knife like nobody's business.

The only real challenge was her body. Which was falling apart, slowly but surely. The hot tub helped, and she had found a second massage therapist to work on her twice a week in addition to Candy. She walked on a treadmill for an hour every day, since long walks around town were impossible with the banks of snow, some up to ten or twelve feet deep.

Nothing really worked. She was in almost constant pain, in her back, in her hip, taking more and more drugs, which made her irritable and sometimes a little confused. Mostly, she'd learned to cover it, but the strain was showing in her face, draining her strength.

Secretly, she found a doctor who did X-rays and confirmed what Elena had dreaded—she needed more surgery. There wasn't a lot they could do for the hip, which was riddled with arthritis, but the surgery on her back would, he was sure, be an almost complete fix. It would require her to wear a brace for four to six months, and for the first two, she couldn't be on her feet, not for any length of time.

And she would need help. Lots of it. She couldn't be on her own.

That day, she went back to the tower room at Julian's house, closed the door, and wept bitterly. To relieve the pain, she would have to give up her kitchen. How could she make that choice? To relieve the pain, she would have to depend on others to help her, and show her weakness.

Maybe, she thought, it was the extreme cold making it so bad. When the weather got better, she'd feel better. So she took some more drugs and scheduled massages for nearly every day of the week and hid from everyone the pain she was feeling. It wasn't as easy to hide the stiffness, a fact that embarrassed her.

Maybe, she thought, more and more mornings, she should go ahead and have the surgery. Ivan was stable. He could run the kitchen—especially if she let him get rid of Dag—and he wouldn't undermine her. Maybe Patrick would let her stay with him, or she could hire a nurse. But where would she live after this mythical surgery? She could not bear to let Julian see her that vulnerable!

It was taken out of her hands, anyway. On the fifteenth, she had an email from Dmitri, out of the blue.

To: Elena.Alvarez@theorangebear.com
From: dmitrinadirov@traveltvcommunications.net
Subject: ouch!
Saw the slam from Bok. Condolences. Heard you had trouble with INS, which no one can predict. Bad luck.

Here is some good news for you, however—would you consent to be interviewed for my television show? We'll be in Aspen end of January to shoot a feature that will run on Valentine's Day: "Aspen for Lovers." Julian Liswood has always been good to me, and I'd like to feature the Orange Bear, and you, with your gorgeous lips.

Ciao,

dmitri

PS you were right about Jennifer. She was too young for me.

Of course, she thought. Of course. Because the universe couldn't let her have one *freaking* minute of peace. She wanted to punch her fist through the monitor. Instead, she opened a reply and wrote:

To: dmitrinadirov@traveltvcommunications.net

From: Elena.Alvarez@theorangebear.com

Subject: re: ouch!

Dmitri! What a great surprise—you must be absolutely thrilled to be hosting the show. It's just your cup of tea (remember the reporter in Vancouver said you were from the Mick Jagger school of beauty?) and I can't wait to say I knew you when.

Of course I'd be delighted to be interviewed. Name the time! If you want to call me the numbers are: 970-555-4398 (restaurant) and 970-555-0936 (cell). If there is anything we can do to make your stay more enjoyable, please don't hesitate to let me know. I look forward to seeing you again.

Warmly,

Elena

Before she could add anything snarky, she hit the Send button.

His reply was instant:

> To: Elena.Alvarez@theorangebear.com
> From: dmitrinadirov@traveltvcommunications.net
> Subject: re:ouch!
> Very good. We will be arriving 28 January and will stay through 1 February. Will call before then to arrange details.
>   ciao,
>   dmitri

Ivan felt as if an anvil were hanging over his head. Dag was a constant, needling presence, continuously flirting with Patrick, who ignored him for the most part, but every so often, Dag got through, like when the skier made a plate of blintzes for somebody's birthday on Sunday afternoon, always a more relaxed day, the end of the workweek, since the restaurant was closed on Mondays. He served them with cherries, red and plump and sinful, and ricotta cheese whipped with lemon curd.

Patrick's eyes widened at the first taste and he blinked at Dag. "Marvelous!" he said. "Yes, please. I'd like some more."

Chuckling in his loose way, Dag served the blintzes. He winked at Ivan. "Would you like some, Rasputin?" The nickname had stuck, and Ivan rather liked it, but he didn't want to touch anything Dag made. Burning inside, he nearly flipped the entire pan of cherries on the floor. Instead, he rolled his eyes in disdain and stalked outside to smoke.

He simmered through the shift, steam coming from his pores like a volcano about to blow. He felt the unrest and turbulence in him and tried to calm it down, going out to smoke regularly, staying away from Dag as much as he could. He drank some herbal tea Elena kept around, and forced himself to pay attention to his own work.

A therapist he'd been sent to after one or another of his drinking violations—driving and fighting, mostly—told him to notice how a thought wasn't always a directive, it wasn't even real sometimes. The woman showed him how to break it down—event, reaction, thought. He tried to practice it this afternoon. The event was Dag's fucking annoying behavior. He needled Ivan deliberately, trying to find his weaknesses and make him crazy.

No, that wasn't the way this worked. Ivan spun in his station, broiling lamb chops, acknowledging orders with a volley of commands, giving orders, spraying vinegar water over a flame leaping too high, and reviewed.

The event had no emotion. Dag made blintzes. Offered them to Patrick, who ate them and liked them.

Marvelous.

After that, Ivan's reaction was to feel annoyed. Jealous. His thought was that Patrick didn't love him and would leave him for Dag. Or someone else more beautiful or more polished or more whatever.

The dark knots of fury eased away from the back of his neck. Patrick did love him. Ivan honestly didn't know why—Ivan was difficult and high-strung and given to wild mood swings—but it seemed to be true. Dag was trying to get to him, trying to get Ivan to react and do something stupid to mess up either his job or his relationship—while

Patrick was faithful, it was impossible to miss that Dag wanted him. If Ivan allowed himself to fall for Dag's game, Dag would win.

More tension faded. Whew. Maybe he was getting the hang of this sanity thing. Damn. He grinned to himself.

And it all would have worked out just fine, Ivan thought later, if they hadn't stopped to have a drink at their favorite nightclub after work. The crowd was thin on a Sunday night. Patrick and Ivan found a booth in the agreeable dark and ordered an ale for Ivan, a pinot grigio for Patrick, who never, ever had more than one. "I'm hungry," Patrick said, and glanced over the very small menu. "Maybe some mushroom caps?"

"And some wings." Ivan wiggled an eyebrow across the table. "I'm in the mood for something sloppy."

"It was busy tonight," Patrick commented, leaning back with a sigh. "Good to see it."

Ivan nodded. Music from a very good jukebox played quietly. Weariness pooled in his elbows and lower back, tingled through his knees, calves, feet. Sometimes lately, he could really feel his age. Not like Elena, though. "What's with Chef, anyway?"

The quick shuttering fell over Patrick's face, making it a blank mask. It irritated Ivan a little, that Chef was more important, or higher in Patrick's loyalties, but he remembered his mantra: event, reaction, thought. Patrick had known Elena a long time, and in fact, wasn't loyalty one of the things Ivan found so appealing about him?

"What do you mean?" Patrick asked.

"Here lately there've been times she can't even stand up

straight. She's in serious pain a serious amount of the time."

Patrick lowered his eyes. Nodded. "I've noticed, too."

"What's the deal? How does she get better?"

"I don't know. She hasn't ever been this bad. I mean, sometimes at the end of a long week or a long trip, she might limp around a little, but . . ." He took a breath. "Not like this."

Something in Ivan broke a little, thinking of the way her mouth pinched by the end of a shift. He thought of her scar, that thick cord of violence that ripped her back apart. "Sucks. That she should get the kitchen and then—"

"Do not say a word, Ivan, not to her and not to anyone else, do you hear me?"

"Jesus, man." He scowled. "I like her. I feel bad for her. Why do you always think the worst of me?"

"I don't," Patrick said, and straightened. "But you're competitive and she took the kitchen that used to be yours. You called the INS. I'm over it, but you wanted revenge, right?"

Ivan found this didn't set off his temper. Huh. "I hate that I did that," he said. "I did want revenge, before I met her. Before I knew her. I don't anymore." With an ironic little twist of his lips, he lifted his bottle of beer. "If not for her, you wouldn't be here, now would you?"

Patrick's mouth pursed into that pleased little smile Ivan liked so much. "That's true."

"Why don't you get a backgammon board and I'll go play some music?"

"Back in a flash."

Ivan ambled over to the jukebox and leaned over it, his long arms folded on the top so that the light flashed over his face and chest, purple neon, his favorite color. He fed a few bills into the slot and started punching in his favorites—some Springsteen and Prince and Mellencamp for himself, some Melissa Etheridge and Toni Braxton for Patrick.

"How sweet," said a voice nearby. Dag, as clean and tucked as a new shirt, leaned on the jukebox. "Choosing songs for your sweetheart?"

A ripple of irritation crawled up the back of Ivan's neck, but he twitched his nose, blew it off. He was here with Patrick to relax and have a good time after a long night at work. He didn't look up again. "Get lost, Dag. I have to put up with your shit at work, but not on my own time." He pressed a set of numbers gently with great control, and flipped the cards inside the jukebox, looking for something lively. Cheerful, like Cyndi Lauper. Hard to get too pissed off when she was singing. He spied the Bangles and put in "Walks Like an Egyptian," too, for good measure.

Dag leaned in close. "He's too young for you."

A sizzle, like too much electricity, buzzed over his ear, but Ivan ignored him. There was the Lauper. He punched it in.

"Look at that ass," Dag said. "I keep thinking of those sweet cheeks, that pretty mouth. It's ti—"

Before he knew he was swinging, Ivan had connected with that foul mouth. He saw it almost in slow motion, the arc of his fist, large and knotty and strong, fueled by the anger of nearly forty years of assholes like this, starting with his mother's boyfriends, hurting him and teasing him, then kids at school because he was too thin, later because he was gay, always taunting him, for one thing and another and another, always putting him down, making him feel like he didn't measure up; he saw it flying and Dag noting too slowly that it was coming, and then the flesh of his left knuckle and Dag's mouth collided. Ivan felt something give, in his hand and in Dag's mouth, a tooth, and then there was blood, and he had time enough to think, *Fuck, I never even had a chance to get drunk,* before Dag roared and tackled him, a bull. He slammed his fist into Ivan's face, and he felt the crunch against his cheekbone—Jesus, it was like getting hit by an anvil. Then Ivan's street sense kicked in and he managed to get a few punches in, and then people were hauling them apart, and the bouncer was dragging Ivan outside, while the patrons—all fucking punkass skiers—were crowding around Dag, who spit on the floor.

"Stay the fuck out of my bar, Santino!" said the bouncer, and Ivan was flung to the sidewalk outside, stumbling in this sudden rejection, shivering in the cold. He sat there for one long minute, humiliated and stinging as tourists in expensive boots and thick coats steered around him, looking down in disdain at his sweat-stained shirt and his bloody mouth.

He was expecting Patrick to come out, waiting for him to step outside and help him to his feet and gingerly tend his wounds. But he didn't come. Ivan stood up, feeling the punch to his eye more than he wanted to. Through the window, he saw the commotion had already died down, and the music Ivan had chosen was already starting to play. "When Doves Cry" came through the windows faintly.

He didn't have his coat. His lip was bleeding pretty

fucking bad. Patrick was sitting in the booth, drinking his wine. Didn't he know what happened? Dag sauntered over to the booth and Ivan saw him pointing toward the door. Patrick nodded.

And didn't move.

Ivan stood there, blinking. How was that fa—

Fair.

Pierced to the bone, he headed back to the Orange Bear, where his car was parked. What the fuck. He'd get drunk somewhere else.

Because what had toeing the line got him? Same fucking life he had all along. What was the point?

What was even the fucking point?

Julian watched Elena moving around the bedroom and took her arm. "I'm worried about you."

As she always did, she made a conscious effort to straighten her spine. "I'm just tired." She sank to the ottoman and took off her shoes. Her skin was pale.

"You're not fine, Elena. You need to see a doctor."

"So they can tell me how bad it is, Julian? So they can show me the intolerable choices left to me?"

Alvin jumped up and came over, his tail swinging nervously.

"You're worrying him," Julian said.

She bowed her head. "I'm sorry. I did see a doctor. Last week." She swallowed. "They want to do more surgery."

He sank down beside her, took her hands, even though she was trying to pull them away. "Elena. Stop resisting me."

She smiled a little, let her hands still. Took in a breath. "So much for your chef, huh?" she said, and couldn't quite cover the despair she felt. The blue of her irises seemed to bleed right down her face.

He cupped her face, touched her hair. "What kind of surgery?"

"A lot. Pins and cages and braces and things."

"And what's the prognosis?"

"I didn't get that far. It would mean being in a brace for maybe six months. I can't run the kitchen that way."

"Do you think we—"

Her cell phone rang. In the quiet, the late hour, the sound seemed ominous. She shot him a glance and grabbed it from the table. "Hello?" Through the line, she heard a voice, rushing and urgent. "Slow down, Patrick. I can't understand you." She put a finger against her opposing ear. "What happened? Who is—"

The color bled from her face. "When? How did that happen? I thought he'd been on the wagon." She listened a little longer, made soothing noises. "I'll be there soon. Don't freak out. It's not your fault."

She clapped the phone closed. "Ivan got into a fight with Dag at the bar, then got in his car and drove it into a tree." She stood up. A white line edged her mouth, and she swung her hair over her shoulder. "I've gotta go to the hospital. Patrick's losing it."

"How's Ivan?"

Her shoulders twitched. "He's in surgery. They don't know."

"I'll drive."

She shook her head. "That's not necessary. Why should

both of us be sleep deprived?" As she spoke, she moved stiffly around the room, picking up bits and pieces, a blouse, her socks, a bracelet she wore on her left wrist where most people wore a watch. Her defenses were so thin and tattered they were like an ancient negligee. He could see right through them.

He went to her, pulled her into his arms, and held her against his chest. "Elena, let go for once in your life, let go before you shatter."

She only allowed his comfort for the blink of an eye before she pushed him away. "I can't."

"Be hugged or let go?"

"One leads to the other, and I can't afford them. Not right now, Julian, okay?"

And suddenly he realized that she might *never* let him in, that this might be an entirely one-sided relationship, with Elena offering tidbits here and there, while Julian poured himself, all of his heart and soul and longings and dreams, into it. He thought of her friend Mia, whom she'd cut out of her life so coldly, after how many years of friendship?

As he stood there, he felt the distance between them widen, or perhaps it was that he was only now seeing the truth of it, the truth of the dynamic, that Elena stood aloofly at the top of an icy mountain, and he—her swain, her supplicant—tried to scale the slippery summit to no avail. He saw that the events of her life had stranded her there, alone, that she had not gone willingly. And yet . . .

"I'll drive you to the hospital and drop you off. If you need to get back, Patrick can bring you."

She looked at him, and he could tell she sensed the distance, too. "Thank you. Don't wait up. I'll probably stay with Patrick. He's a mess."

Julian nodded.

Alvin whined softly.

Ivan awakened slowly to a sensation of gagging and a headache that was like bombs going off. In his body were aches and pains and one dead zone around his ankle, which felt muffled or smothered.

A voice said, "He's coming around," and Ivan coughed as something slid out of his throat. There was rawness in his throat, a blast of pain in his face, his mouth. He opened his eyes a crack, gathering details, trying to piece together what he remembered, but there was a buzz in his brain and he couldn't really think, and this room was lit with a cold bluish fluorescent light. He could hear the buzz of it. Someone took his hand.

Patrick said, "Ivan?"

He opened his eyes. There was Patrick, peering at him, his face ravaged with tears. "What happened?" Ivan rasped, and the words barely came out around the rawness.

"You wrecked your car. Ran into a tree three blocks from the Orange Bear." Patrick glared at him. "You must have been going sixty to wreck the car that badly, they think."

Ivan slowly shook his head. "I can't remember anything." There was a wisp of something, some faint unpleasant memory, and his bruised head skittered away.

"It's all right, don't worry. It will come back." Patrick took a breath. "I thought you died, Ivan." Tears spilled down his face. "I thought you died." He kissed him, and Ivan tasted the salt and tears and there was something wrong, but he couldn't remember what it was. As Patrick kissed him, he just let the light of that fill him up, and he fell asleep.

Around 3 a.m., Elena sent Patrick home for a nap and a change of clothes. He was upset in ways she'd never seen, pacing and weeping. "I should have gone outside, made sure he was all right. It was humiliating for me, but how much more for Ivan? That wasn't fair. I'm not usually so mean. But I was tired of him fighting and being jealous and I wanted to teach him a lesson."

Elena nodded, rubbed his back, listened and listened and listened as he covered the same ground, over and over. "I'll sit with him," she said. "Then I'll go home when you get back."

Alone in the room with Ivan sound asleep, Elena dozed. When she awakened, Isobel was there, sitting on the end of the bed, her legs teenager skinny, her neck looped with a dozen cheap necklaces. Her trademark. "He almost killed himself," she said, putting her hand on Ivan's knee. He didn't stir. "He's got so much love in him, poor guy."

Elena nodded, feeling hollow as she listened to the blips and bleeps and gurgles, the faraway sound of pages—why did hospitals still use such noisy technology anyway, when every nurse and doctor could wear a cell and be paged via text? Then patients could sleep.

"Is there anything more depressing in the world than a hospital room in the middle of the night?" Elena said.

"You were there a long time," Isobel said. She was still looking at Ivan with a slight frown.

Elena nodded. It made her feel hollow to sit there, looking at Ivan's ravaged face. His lower lip, always so sensual anyway, was swollen twice the normal size and had a split through the middle of it, angry and moist. One eye was swollen shut, and there was an odd mark on his cheek, a fabric imprint. He'd broken a few ribs, and his left ankle, but it was cleanly broken and after a week he'd be able to stand on the cast. They thought he had a concussion, and he was covered with assorted cuts and bruises and stitches, but considering the impact, he'd been very lucky.

The chef computer in her was running scenarios of how to make the kitchen work without him for a few days. At least he hadn't broken anything critical, like a wrist or a shoulder or—

Isobel touched his brow, his hair. "He doesn't say how bad it was," she whispered. "When he was a child."

"How bad?"

"Bad," Isobel said. She kissed his forehead. "Now he has you. You have him."

He made a sound and moved restlessly. "Hey, *Jefa*," he said. His voice was ragged.

A swell of emotion burst in Elena, and she jumped up, feeling tangled and hot and relieved and furious and grateful. So many emotions charged through her throat that she couldn't find words. "Don't you ever do something like that again, Ivan, do you hear me?"

He looked stricken, and that wasn't her goal. She didn't know what her goal was. She picked up his scarred, tattooed hand, feeling tears well up in her eyes and cascade over her face and pour out in such waves that she couldn't speak. She put her hand on his face, lightly, gently, and shook her head. "I need you, Ivan. I need you to live, okay?"

He raised a hand and pulled her head down to his chest and she wept and so did he. "Thank you," he growled.

Isobel put her hand on Elena's head. Then she was gone.

When Patrick returned, Elena called Julian. "I need a favor," she said. "I need to do something today. I need to go to the airport."

When he picked her up, he was aloof and quiet. Which she deserved. "When will you be back?" he asked finally, when they stopped at the curb at the airport.

"This afternoon. I'm just going to see my mama."

He reached out and turned off the ignition. "I need to get something off my chest before you go, Elena."

"I don't really have a lot of time, Julian," she said, putting her hand on the door, ready to bolt.

"You have enough time." He pulled off his sunglasses. "We're at a crossroads, Elena. I'm not the kind of man who can settle for a little bit of you, here and there, whenever you feel like letting me in."

Enormously uncomfortable, she looked away, watched a woman in an expensive parka cross the street. "Julian, this is not the time for—"

"There's never a good time." He reached into the back seat and pulled out a notebook. "Before I give you this, I want to tell you that I am in love with you." He took a breath. "Not a little bit. I love you like you were made for me. I think you love me, too, but you have to get over your fears and let me in, or it will never work."

"Julian, don't do this right now! It's been a really long night and I'm feeling very emotional and I just want to go see my mom, okay? I'll be back this afternoon."

"There's one more thing." He held the notebook in his hands. "I have a confession to make. The movie we're going to start filming in June is a ghost story. About a woman who lost her soul mate in a car accident and is haunted by him."

Elena stared at him.

He took her hand and put the notebook into it. "This is the script," he said, his rich dark eyes direct. "Take it and read it. If you hate it and you don't want me to make the movie, I'll pull it."

She started to shove it back at him. He pushed back, patiently, quietly, that same stillness that had so captured her the first time they sat together over a meal in Vancouver rippling from him and touching her.

"Just read it," he said. "Give me a chance."

Afraid she'd fall apart right there, Elena yanked open the door. "I'll call you when I get back."

He leapt out of the car and came around. In the bright cold, in front of God and everyone, he said, "I love you, Elena."

She nodded, and ducked away, tucking the script under her arm. She knew she was being cold. She heard Patrick and Mia and everyone else telling her to let her guard down. But it was her guard that had held her together.

This one time, though, she turned around and made

her lurching way back to him. "I'll read it," she said. "But I am who I am, too."

"I get that."

It was a wildly expensive but fairly short commuter flight to Santa Fe, bumpy and probably dangerous. Elena recognized a famous actress behind giant sunglasses, and in the front of the plane was an Arab businessman in a five-thousand-dollar suit. He wore heady cologne.

Elena wore her sunglasses as well, to cover the ravaged swollenness of her eyes. She was exhausted, emotionally, physically, and mentally, but this was her one and only day off, and she didn't have any time to waste. She didn't read the script, not yet. It sat in her lap, burning hot, but she didn't let herself think, a trick that had worked for her for twenty years, the only way she'd found to cope with her losses. *Look forward, never back.*

The propellers were very loud, and she leaned against the window and watched the mountains zigzagging away beneath the plane, thickly coated in white. Here was a land where you could still find isolation if you wanted it—there was a single house, with a plume of smoke drifting into the sky, so still it looked as if it had been painted there. There were tiny ribbons of road in places, and sudden, open vastness of valleys that stretched for miles and miles and miles between ridges of mountains. It was rugged, dramatically beautiful country, the blues and whites so calming. The beauty gave her rest. She dozed.

The plane landed at the tiny Santa Fe airport, and Elena went to the ladies' room to wash her face. She looked a little better than she had this morning, the mottled marks of heavy weeping faded, but she still looked tired and wan. She washed her face in cold, cold water, feeling it wake her up a lot, and then, from her purse, she fished out a makeup bag and repaired the damage as well as she could. A little cover to hide the dark circles, some mascara to make her look like she cared about herself, a touch of blush to cover the sallowness.

Every bone in her body hurt, and that pain showed. It was turning her into an old woman. Taking a breath, she squared her shoulders, then combed her hair and marched out to rent a car and drove into Santa Fe proper for breakfast. She was starving.

It had been a long time since she'd been in the sophisticated little town where she had spent so much of her time as a kitchen slave, learning the basics of a kitchen, the arrangements and the hierarchy and the toughness she'd need. It came easily to her. She worked hard, harder than anyone, because she had no other life, and only this chance. She never complained. She spoke Spanish. She knew food and understood it. When the male quadrant tried to intimidate her, she donned an icy aplomb and gave back as good as she got, winning their respect.

To stretch out her spine and hip, she walked around the still-quiet plaza and surrounding side streets, ambling by the places she'd worked. Some were still there. Some were gone, replaced by some other up-to-the minute hot spot.

The wintertime sun was warm, and the walking eased her body, and she circled the shops around the plaza peacefully, stopping happily in a drugstore she'd frequented to buy a postcard, and ducking beneath the roofed and ancient porches. Indians set up their wares along the Palace of the Governors. A woman in her sixties with dreadlocks and sandals walked by, bracelets by the thousands weighing down her skinny wrists. A pair of homeless people, young, unidentifiably male or female, smoked on a bench in the center. Not many others on a January Monday.

She ducked into the Plaza Café for a breakfast to fortify herself, and was slammed, hard, by the heady scent of chile and pork and eggs, all made the New Mexico way. She heard the sound of her accents, her home, the sound of Spanish and Indian layered over English, and stared, stunned and hungry, at the shapes of faces she had missed, the broad cheekbones and particular grins. Dark-skinned men with long hair falling down their backs, clad in worn jeans and boots and checkered shirts, sat next to a knot of locals in their sixties, speaking ancient, colonial Spanish, next to a well-tended Anglo couple in their sixties dressed in golf casual. The wife wore a huge yellow diamond on her finger.

Elena felt dizzy and pulled the sunglasses off her face, breathing in. "You okay, honey?" the hostess said, coming over. She had black hair worn in a style not worn by anyone but old Mexican or Italian women of a certain age, curled tight to the head, neatly done by the beauty parlor every week.

"I will be," she said in Spanish, "when I've had a good breakfast of my own kind of food."

The woman grinned and replied in kind. "You been away, then, huh?"

"*Long* time," Elena said, settling into a seat by the wall, with a view of the restaurant all around her. She ate carnitas and blue corn tortillas and drank two big mugs of coffee with sugar and cream, letting the sound of home wash over her like Chinook winds, restorative and warm. The Spanish, the Indians, the Anglos. The smell of onions, the bustle of glasses and silverware clanking.

She sat a long time, feeling lost pieces of herself thawing, flowing back into place. She watched a trio of Indian men with thin long legs and barrel chests rib each other and the waitress and the busboy. The table of Mexican couples, exceedingly well tended, as clean and pressed as fresh laundry, who had obviously been meeting every Monday for a long, long time, maybe decades, talked about somebody's funeral in a cheerful way. The CEO and his I-don't-do-casual wife paid with an American Express card. One of the Indian guys pulled a wad of crumpled bills from his pocket and counted out the ones, smoothing each one as he laughed over something one of the guys said to him.

In her stunned and exhausted state, she could make no sense of the well-being that flooded her, the feeling of alignment that fortified her for what lay ahead. But she didn't have to make sense of anything. She just had to take one step and then another. She felt oddly disconnected, as if some fake front person had taken over, or maybe her ghosts, and she was just along for the ride.

The next step was climbing into her car and driving north. She took it.

FORTY-TWO

CARNITAS

MARINADE
Juice from two fresh limes
1 T lime zest
1 tsp fresh ground pepper
1–2 garlic cloves, peeled and whole
1 cup water

MEAT
2 lbs. pork butt
2½ lbs. lard
½ cup water
1 large onion, cut into quarters
2 garlic cloves, slivered
1 T ground cumin
1 tsp salt
1 tsp black pepper
3 long strips lime peel

2–3 New Mexico green chiles, roasted, peeled, and cut into strips
Water

MARINADE: Mix all the ingredients except the water in a glass bowl. Put the meat in the bowl and add water to cover meat lightly. Marinate for 2 hours or overnight.

MEAT: When ready to cook, pour off the marinade. Place the lard and water in a deep heavy pan like a cast–iron Dutch oven and add the onions, garlic, and spices. Warm over medium heat until the lard is melted, then add lime peel and the meat. Reduce heat to medium low and let the meat simmer until it is stewed through, but not browned. Take out the meat and skim the onion and garlic from the fat, then replace the meat, turn up the heat to medium high and let the outside get nicely browned and crispy, about 15 minutes.

Serve with fresh cilantro, pico de gallo, lime wedges, avocados, grilled onions, and, of course, fresh tortillas.

FORTY-THREE

It was a blustery day, with wind scudding in blasts over the road. A tumbleweed the size of a tractor tire danced and bounced along the length of a fence. A plastic grocery bag swooped and sailed on a current, then fell abruptly to the ground. Elena felt the gusts against the side of the car, bumping her first to the left, then to the right. Correcting for the wind, she would have to correct again when it stopped.

"I hate wind!" she cried aloud. Then more quietly, "Hate it."

Espanola had grown a little since the last time she was there, but not very much. A Wal-Mart had sprouted in what used to be a field, and the main drag now boasted a couple of fast-food chains, but mostly it was the same weary-looking gas stations and liquor stores and farm stands now closed for the season, everything all the more bleak in January, when the color was leached from the grass, and the sky wore a thick sweater of eggplant clouds.

Once she could have named nearly everyone in town, Spanish, Indian, or Anglo. She would have known the cousins of cousins and who loved who and what they did on Saturday nights and whose grandma was sick. At any given function, from county fair to church potluck, she would be related to at least a half-dozen people, often many more.

After the accident and her long, long hospital stay, she'd come home for a short period, but by then, the town, her family, everyone related to the accident victims, had moved on. Elena, hobbled and vividly scarred, was a painful reminder of what they had lost. Conversations died when she entered a shop. Everyone was excruciatingly polite. Even her family seemed like strangers, so solicitous and focused; they didn't seem to know what to do with their eyes when she sat with them. It was as if she were a giant, life-sucking shadow, and no one could be happy while she was in the room.

Her mother wept when she left for a job in Santa Fe after only a few weeks home. "There's work here," she said. "Stay and Uncle Glen will help you find work in a restaurant if that's what you want."

But you couldn't go back in time. Elena had to move forward.

Each time she returned, never for more than two days, usually only one, she felt as if she were driving under a heavy rock of emotion that squeezed all the life out of her. It was hard to get a full breath in Espanola, and today was no different. She felt as if there was some curse hanging over her, a spell with a ticking clock—if she stayed longer than forty-eight hours, the clock would run out and something terrible would happen.

Her mother's house was down a dirt road, a frame

house painted white, with faded green trim. An elm stood sentry over the small, neat square of lawn, carefully enclosed by a chain-link fence covered all summer by sweet peas. Elena parked. A black and white dog, fluffy and friendly, rushed to the fence to bark a welcome. For a moment, Elena was startled—her mother had raised enough children, she always said, what would she want with a dog?

And yet, that was undeniably Maria Elena's '88 Buick parked precisely under a fiberglass carport. It probably had all of thirty thousand miles on it. Mama drove it to mass and the grocery store.

As Elena got out of the rental, the dog sat down expectantly, black button eyes and soft curly fur, as adorable as a toddler in mittens.

"Hey, you. What's your name?" she said, chuckling. "Is it okay if I come in?"

The dog barked politely in return. Shifted foot to foot and waited as Elena came up the walk, reached over the gate, and petted its head. "You are adorable!" She opened the gate and squatted down to scratch the wiggly, ecstatic creature.

"Who's there?" said a voice, and Elena straightened. A figure came out onto the porch, a very, very old woman in a flowered blouse and neat blue slacks. Elena's heart caught. Her grandmother's hair was completely white, wispily pulled into a long braid that hung over one frail shoulder. Her hands were misshapen, twisted with arthritis. She wore giant, very dark sunglasses—she had macular degeneration and couldn't see very well.

"It's me, Mama," she said, coming closer. "Elena."

"My daughter?" the old woman said, peering, and Elena

realized she couldn't see her. With a pang, she rushed forward and put her hands out, taking her grandmother's cool, veiny hands into her own to kiss them, then raised them to her face. "Yes," she said, "your daughter Elena."

The elder Elena made a tiny noise and began to cry. "Oh, *m'ija*! Oh, I am so glad to see you!"

"Let's go inside, Mama. I brought doughnuts. You want some?"

"Sure I do! Let's go have some coffee, too! Did you meet my little dog? That's Henry. He's such a good boy. He sleeps with me and everything, can you believe it? Come on, Henry."

"I have a dog, too," Elena said. "Alvin. He sleeps with me. Or, well, he did. He sleeps with a young woman I know. She lives with me."

Mama settled Elena into a chair. "Tell me everything."

Sitting in the kitchen of her childhood, still painted a cheerful yellow, the table covered with an oilcloth that was probably as old as she was, Elena took the dog on her lap, feeling the terror and sorrow fly away from her. Here in her mama's kitchen, she was safe. This was where she had learned to cook. In this tiny room with its tiny stove and deep sinks, with this tiny woman.

Safe.

When they'd eaten and gossiped and laughed over the shenanigans of the dog, Maria Elena finally said, "Tell me why you came today, *m'ija*."

"Mom, I need to go to the place where we were in the accident. I don't think I can go by myself. Will you come with me?"

Mama didn't even hesitate. She nodded. "Sure. We can

take Henry, too. He'll like it." For a minute, Maria Elena sat in the chair with her hands folded in her lap, peering at her daughter. "You sure? You got sick last time."

"I'm sure. I need to—" She paused. "Say goodbye."

Maria Elena nodded, patted her hand. "It's about time."

The night they wrecked, Elena, Isobel, Edwin, Penny, and Albert had gone to see a movie. Isobel smuggled in a bottle of rum she stole from somewhere, and Elena drank some of it, but not very much because she was pregnant and didn't want to hurt the baby. Edwin promised to drive them home and left it alone. Penny and Albert poured some into their Cokes.

After the movie, Elena was very sick to her stomach and curled up in the back seat. Albert, who worshipped Edwin, sat in the front passenger seat, scorning his seat belt. Isobel and Penny got in the back with Elena.

Twenty years later, on a bright January day, Elena and her mother drove down the narrow road toward the site. It wasn't hard to find. It was on a narrow strip of road leading east from Espanola into the mountains, curving and dangerous and utterly ordinary. She drove beneath the long stands of cottonwoods that grew along the road, bare now, but in the summer, this was a deep tunnel of shade. The trees were nourished by the water in the acequia that ran along the road, carrying irrigation water to the farmers who grew melons and chiles and tomatoes in the sunny fields.

There was a small café at a junction, and Elena parked the rental car there. A dog trotted along on an errand, skinny and cheerful, and overhead, a magpie squawked, then lifted off, showing off his black and white splendor.

Elena turned off the car. Mama, holding Henry on her lap, said, "You go. I'll stay right here and wait."

Elena nodded. Zipping up her jacket, she got out. The quiet stunned her. The only sound was a thin finger of wind rattling leaves from last season that clung to the bare branches of cottonwood trees.

She headed up the road a little way. It wasn't far. Four crosses marked it, two very well tended, one less so, one nearly completely faded now. Clusters of pink plastic carnations were twisted around the base of one wooden cross, painted white. Names had been varnished into each one, with dates and other little markers. Elena stepped between the prongs of the barbed-wire fence alongside the acequia, then gathered her aching parts and jumped over the ditch to an enormous, old cottonwood tree.

At shoulder height, a deep gouge in the shape of an uneven star showed in the creasing of bark, and she put her fingers to it. Her palm fit it exactly. Here the car had hit and come apart, exploding like a rocket into a dozen pieces. Her brother had told Elena it took days to find all the pieces.

So many years, so many many many years, she had blocked this moment. Now she reached back trying to bring it forth. Beneath her hand the tree was a living being, pulsing with sap drawn from the earth. It had memories. Surely it could give forth the violence of that single, horrific moment so many years ago.

But the air remained undisturbed. Elena's memory offered nothing but the same things she'd thought of a thousand times, that single, clear moment when they went airborne, when they sailed as if in an airplane, high into the night sky. She saw stars and held on to the edge of the seat. There wasn't time to be horrified, only curious, and slightly protective. She clung to the door handle, watching the sky and branches entwine, and then there was a huge explosion of noise.

There was the gap. She was flung from the car and landed in the ditch. The next thing she could remember was the depth of silence, the only sound the tick-tick-tick of cooling metal. Her body and mind were strangely separate, as if her head was in some entirely different location than her arms and legs. She could feel, far away, the cold on her feet, and across her belly was the sinuous movement of water, but she couldn't seem to communicate with any part of her body to change the circumstances. She drifted. She thought perhaps she might be dead.

And yet, there was a woman singing to her, brushing her hair from her face—La Llorona, the weeping woman, tending Elena until someone could come.

And after a time, there was Isobel, sitting next to her. "I couldn't find you at first," she said, and took Elena's hand. "There's a man coming. Hang on. He had to go back and call an ambulance."

Elena tried to speak and could not. La Llorona stroked her forehead and hummed. She patted cool mud into the bleeding cuts on her back and Elena did not mind. Her sister sang an old song that one of their brothers liked to play on his guitar, about a man who chased his wife into heaven to kill her and her lover a second time.

"Where's Edwin?" Elena asked, or thought she did, but no one answered. There was no sound at all except that soft, gleefully mournful tune. High, high in the darkness, four stars shot across the sky, and the next thing Elena knew there was a man bending over her, swearing in Spanish.

So long ago, Elena thought. Her spine felt watery and she bent to press her forehead against the tree.

After a time, she sensed the presence of her sister.

Isobel stood nearby. "It looks different in the day," she said, looking around. In the bright noon light, her braided hair had a sheen like a waxed floor. "None of us knew a single thing. It was so fast. It made it hard for us to know what happened."

In the middle distance, where the acequia bent toward the fields to the south, there were four other figures. Waiting, Elena knew. There was Edwin with his fall of shoe-black hair, and Albert and Penny, as chubby as always. A little girl, watery, holding Edwin's hand. Elena found herself sinking to her knees, in the cool mud that saved her life.

There in the dark, she'd held on to her sister's hand with all her might. "Don't leave me alone, Isobel!" she had cried.

"I won't leave you," Isobel had promised.

And she had not.

"Why did all of you die and I didn't?" Elena asked now.

"It wasn't your day," Isobel said simply.

"It shouldn't have been yours."

Isobel smiled softly. She bent and kissed Elena's head, right at the part, and tears like a volcano gushed up through Elena's esophagus. "I have to go now, Elena."

"Please," she said, and held out a hand. "I don't want to be alone!"

"You aren't alone anymore." She moved away on strong

sturdy legs, wearing the striped shirt she'd borrowed from Elena's closet that night. Elena watched them through a wavery glaze of tears, the family that had stayed with her until she found her own—brothers in Patrick and in Ivan, a sister in Mia, a daughter in Portia. And her mother, waiting there in the car.

And Julian.

Julian.

Elena bent her head to the earth and let her grief pour out, her sacred tears watering the ground. She wept and wept and wept, all the tears she'd been holding for a lifetime. Then, when she was finished, she lay on the ground and released it all to the earth. To the heavens.

When she could breathe again, she stood and brushed herself off. At the line of crosses, she paused and tidied it up, plucked away a stray weed, and straightened the flowers, then went back to the car.

Maria Elena had fallen asleep with her head against the glass, her dog curled in her lap. With a vast tenderness, Elena bent and kissed her cheek. "I love you, Mama," she said. "I'm sorry I have stayed away so long."

Maria Elena opened her eyes, and for a long moment, she blinked in confusion. "Elena? I wasn't dreaming?"

"No, Mama," she said. "You weren't dreaming."

Mama kissed her hand. "Good. I been saying a lot a prayers for you, you know."

"Thank you."

On the way home, she read the script. It didn't take long. It was a tale of a woman tortured by the loss of her family, long ago, and how she made her way to a whole life again. When Elena finished, she closed the folder and lightly pressed her fingers against it, and looked out the window, letting it fill her up.

It was a mature ghost story, scary, but also tender and wise. And it wasn't really about Elena and her losses at all, but like everything else he wrote, it was Julian's attempt to make sense or make peace with his mother's murder.

So much love, she thought, gazing down at the craggy tops of mountains. So much love he had in him.

FORTY-FOUR

Julian was writing in his office when he heard Elena come in. He put his pencil down and walked to the mezzanine, where he could see the entryway. She hobbled into the hallway and bent to give hugs to Alvin and the pup, who came racing out to see her. Portia, too, came leaping down the hallway, an elfin creature who said something chirpy to Elena and took her coat. Elena said, quite clearly, "Please don't mind when I do this, okay?" And hugged the girl.

Portia hugged her back, fiercely. "I don't mind at all. Not at all."

He took a breath against the arrow of emotion that went through him. Elena said, "Where's your dad?"

"In his office, I think. Are you ready to eat? I made macaroni and cheese. From scratch."

"You did?" Elena squeezed her arm. "You are becoming quite a cook, aren't you? Let me talk to your dad for a minute, then I'll be right back down."

"I'll set the table," Portia said, and this, too, pierced her father, standing overhead. He'd never known till now that such a little thing like that could make such a difference. A simple meal, eaten together. She loved to set the table. "And should I maybe make that spinach salad? Would that be good?"

"Perfect. You have good instincts."

"Thanks!" Portia bounced off to the kitchen, followed by hopeful dogs.

Though he was tempted to spare Elena the climb, Julian stayed where he was. Behind him, in the study, played the soundtrack he'd created for the restaurant, which had somehow become the soundtrack in his head for the script. Below him was the great room, and beyond that, the brightly lit kitchen where his daughter sang along to her iPod and made supper for them all. He was standing almost exactly where he'd kissed Elena the first time, and now he waited as broken Elena made her way up the stairs in her determined and laborious way.

A softness of air moved over his face. Julian thought he smelled Tabu, the strong and exotic perfume his mother had loved. For years after she died, things she'd owned still smelled of it. He wished that he really did believe in ghosts, that he might one day really see his mother again.

Elena came down the mezzanine, one hand on the banister, and she stopped a few feet away from him. She looked absolutely exhausted, her face bare of makeup, her eyes swollen. She held up the script. "I read it," she said.

He nodded.

"I went to Espanola today," she said, and he could see she was struggling with great emotion. "To . . . um . . . see the place where we wrecked. I haven't been able to stand it before this."

He waited.

"That night," she said, her voice breaking slightly, "we went to see a movie. It was a ghost story. I thought it was the saddest movie I ever saw in my life, and not a single person in that theater seemed to understand that it was a movie about losing somebody you love and not ever wanting to say goodbye." Tears were pouring down her face now, a remarkable thing all in itself, but Julian felt so poised for her next words that he couldn't take that in yet.

She took a breath and steadied herself. "The movie was *The Importance of Being Earnest,* by this hotshot young director, who didn't know he was writing my life, because he was writing his own."

He moved as she did, and he gathered her into his arms and she fell hard against him, and both of them were crying, and it was so strange and so weirdly beautiful. "Maybe there are soul mates, huh?" he managed to say.

And his broken love, his sad and lonely lost soul mate, nodded against his chest and clung to him. He pressed his mouth to her hair, and touched the scars on her back, and said, "Please let me take care of you."

"Yes, please." She raised her head and breathed in. "What is that perfume? Something you wear, sort of dusky. It feels like I should recognize it."

A sweet waft of air brushed his face, smelling of Tabu, and Julian was too overcome to speak. He let his own tears fall into her hair and they stood like that, rocking back and forth.

The doorbell rang.

Julian raised his head, smiling. Perfect timing. "Remember that I ordered a Christmas present for you that didn't quite get here?"

"It's here?" Elena asked. "Cool."

"I've got it!" Portia cried.

The sound of voices reached them, and Elena's face went absolutely still. She looked up at Julian, eyes filling with tears. "Is it Juan?"

"Merry Christmas," he said. "It took a little bit of doing, but he's here to stay."

"Oh, Julian," she whispered. "You are the real thing, aren't you?"

"I guess you'll just have to stick around and find out."

From downstairs, Portia called, "Come and get it, every-body!"

Elena took Julian's hand.

"Let's eat," she said.

MEXICAN WEDDING COOKIES

1 cup butter
½ cup white sugar
2 tsp vanilla
2 tsp milk
2 cups all-purpose flour
1 cup chopped almonds
½ cup confectioner's sugar

In a medium bowl, cream the butter and sugar. Stir in vanilla and milk. Add the flour and almonds and mix until well blended. Cover and chill for at least 2 hours.

Preheat oven to 325 degrees. Shape dough into small balls and bake for 15–20 minutes. Let cool slightly, and roll in confectioner's sugar while still warm. Cool completely, and roll one more time through the sugar.

ABOUT THE AUTHOR

Barbara O'Neal fell in love with restaurants and the secret language of spoons when she was sixteen. She spent more than a decade in various restaurants, dives to cafes to high cuisine, before selling her first novel. O'Neal teaches workshops nationally and internationally, and lives with her partner, a British endurance athlete, in Colorado Springs.